T0285277

# ELEANOR
## — and —
## THE COLD WAR

AN **ELEANOR ROOSEVELT** MYSTERY

# ELEANOR

*—and—*

## THE COLD WAR

## ELLEN YARDLEY

**KENSINGTON**
PUBLISHING CORP.

kensingtonbooks.com

KENSINGTON BOOKS are published by

Kensington Publishing Corp.
900 Third Ave.
New York, NY 10022

All Kensington titles, imprints, and distributed lines are available at special quantity discounts for bulk purchases for sales promotion, premiums, fund-raising, educational, or institutional use. Special book excerpts or customized printings can also be created to fit specific needs. For details, write or phone the office of the Kensington Special Sales Manager: Attn. Special Sales Department. Kensington Publishing Corp., 900 Third Ave., New York, NY 10022. Phone: 1-800-221-2647.

KENSINGTON and the K with book logo Reg. US Pat. & TM Off.

Library of Congress Control Number: 2024943945

ISBN: 978-1-4967-5007-5
First Kensington Hardcover Edition: February 2025

ISBN: 978-1-4967-5009-9 (ebook)

10 9 8 7 6 5 4 3 2 1

Printed in the United States of America

# ACKNOWLEDGMENTS

Many thanks to the team at Kensington Publishing, especially my editor, John Scognamiglio. Also, heartfelt thanks to my agent, Evan Marshall, for suggesting I write historical mysteries and for being a champion of this book from the early stages. As always, I must acknowledge and thank my amazing critique group for their comments and support, as well as friends whose expertise and advice made this book richer.

Finally, thank you to my readers. You make this all possible.

# ELEANOR
## — and —
## THE COLD WAR

# CHAPTER 1

*Once a weapon is discovered, it will always be used by those who are in desperate straits.*
    —Eleanor Roosevelt, My Day, September 25, 1945

*Aboard the* Royal Blue *train*
*Union Station, Washington, DC*
*September 1951*

When Kay Thompson landed a job as secretary for Eleanor Roosevelt, the former First Lady, she never dreamed her work would include discovering a body.

The *Royal Blue*, the streamlined train that had glided in at 1:30 p.m., stood at the platform, completely stationary.

But Kay could have sworn it swayed under her feet as Mrs. Roosevelt opened the washroom door at the end of the lounge car, revealing a compact space of chrome and Formica . . . and a young woman's body lying in a ghastly pool of dark red blood.

Roaring filled Kay's ears. Putting her hand up to her face, she shielded herself from the sight. Spots of color exploded in the corners of her vision. Her legs wobbled, behaving like her aunt Tommy's picnic aspic jelly, which Kay had notoriously dropped on the lawn when she was eight years old.

Since she was perched on three-inch stiletto shoes, wobbling wasn't a good idea. That jelly had hit the ground with a formless splat.

Dizziness swept over her . . . until she saw that Mrs. Roosevelt, standing at her side, did not look ready to pass out.

The porter who had led them onto the train gave a gasp of horror as he peered into the tiny compartment, even though he had been the one to tell them a body had been found on the train.

Kay thought working with Mrs. Roosevelt would involve behind-the-scenes politics, fabulous social events, and the chance to meet the kind of single, attractive men who moved and shook Washington. Heads of state like movie-star handsome, bachelor Prince Rainier of Monaco.

Instead, just after she began her temporary post, she had helped Mrs. Roosevelt hunt for the missing daughter of a foreign atomic scientist. Now, at Mrs. Roosevelt's side, she was staring into a cramped washroom at that young woman—who had been stabbed horribly in the chest and stomach, ruining her lovely pearl-gray suit.

The poor woman had long platinum-blond hair that looked impossibly natural. That pure white blond wasn't the kind that came out of a bottle. Kay knew—she'd tried to match Veronica Lake's blond color once and after the awful yellow grew out, she never touched her red hair again.

But with the expression of terror transfixed on the victim's face, Kay couldn't be sure this was the woman they had been searching for.

"Is it her?" she managed to choke out. "She doesn't look like—like the photograph Mrs. Meyer sent."

"I think so, Kay," Mrs. Roosevelt said, her voice heavy with sorrow. "I believe this is Susan."

Susan Meyer. Daughter of Elsa Meyer, the famous atomic scientist who had escaped Nazi Germany for Sweden. The daughter who Mrs. Meyer feared had been recruited as a Soviet spy. In the black and white photograph Mrs. Meyer mailed by airmail from Sweden, her daughter had a heart-shaped face, high cheekbones, luminous eyes. Susan could have been a stand-in for Ingrid Bergman. This poor young woman's face, frozen in a mask of terror, barely resembled that picture.

Kay felt she had fallen into an Alfred Hitchcock movie. Like *Notorious*. Except gorgeous Cary Grant was nowhere to be seen.

Mrs. Roosevelt gingerly stepped over the pool of blood in her sensible, low-heeled shoes. She wore a gray tweed jacket over a navy blouse and skirt, with a fox fur around her neck. Her gray hair was arranged in curls and parted down the middle, secured under a dark blue felt hat. Despite being sixty-six years old, she knelt beside the poor murdered woman.

"Mrs. Roosevelt! What are you doing?" Kay cried.

As a former First Lady, Mrs. Roosevelt lived in the kind of social stratosphere where Kay assumed she should never have to get her hands dirty. But Mrs. Roosevelt was gently touching the woman's wrist. There was barely room in the tiny space for Mrs. Roosevelt to move, yet she dealt with the situation without revulsion.

"No pulse, of course. But I had to make sure. She is dead, but she has not been for long. Her hand is still warm."

Kay's stomach wanted to rebel and give up the piece of toast that had been breakfast. But Mrs. Roosevelt looked sad but also calm and resolute.

"Her hands are slightly damp. She must have been washing them, the poor thing—" Mrs. Roosevelt rose astonishingly swiftly to her feet. "Kay, you are as white as a sheet. You should sit down. You look as if you are about to faint."

Kay's aunt Tommy, Mrs. Roosevelt's regular secretary, had told Kay many things about "ER" to prepare her for the temporary job while Tommy recuperated from illness. ER was

Mrs. Roosevelt's nickname, to go along with her husband's, FDR. She had also been known as "Mrs. R" at the White House. Aunt Tommy explained that inner calm was Mrs. Roosevelt's first personal requirement, and she expected her staff to display it also. ER's remarkable inner calm was one part training and breeding and schooling, Aunt Tommy said. The second part? Living through loss and pain and finding strength.

"I'm fine, ma'am," Kay lied. She wanted to be the perfect secretary and show Mrs. Roosevelt she could be equally as unflappable.

Then she caught sight of her reflection in the washroom mirror. Her blush stood out like pink circles on her pale cheeks, her Revlon Love That Red lipstick looked like a garish smear, and one of her false eyelashes was sticking to her eyebrow—she must have brushed it off when she covered her eyes. She hastily pressed the lash down into place.

She always managed to make eye contact with her reflection. It wasn't just vanity, it was important. She used to eat salads for her waistline until she once discovered she had been smiling flirtatiously at an unmarried vice president with a glob of lettuce between her teeth.

Mrs. Roosevelt stepped out of the washroom. She nodded at Kay, then looked to the porter. The distinguished-looking man, who had cropped, grizzled gray hair, had sagged against the wall and was passing a pressed handkerchief over his forehead. "Mr. Jeffers," Mrs. Roosevelt said, "we will have to call the police."

He straightened hurriedly and Kay moved back to let him speak to Mrs. Roosevelt. When she moved back, she didn't have to look at poor Susan's body anymore. That helped to keep her head from swimming.

Mr. Jeffers's uniform was immaculate, but sweat had leaked once more onto his forehead from below his white cap. "I shouldn't have brought you here, Mrs. Roosevelt. I didn't realize it would be such a horrible sight. But you were asking about a blond woman, and Jackson, the young porter, was shouting about how he had found a woman's body on the train, and I thought you should see if it was the woman you knew."

"It is poor Susan Meyer. And I would not have been spared the sight. I would have made myself available to the police anyway, Mr. Jeffers. But the police must be contacted. At once."

Kay realized she had sunk her teeth into her lip—a nervous habit she hadn't done for years. "Mrs. Roosevelt, you can't be involved with the police."

Her boss, who she barely knew and who barely knew her yet, frowned. "I don't understand, Kay. What are you talking about?"

Kay swallowed hard. When Mrs. Roosevelt smiled, she was warm and friendly and kind. But her brows were drawn in a way that showed she was not pleased.

"Mr. Sandiston won't approve," Kay said. "He told me what working for a former First Lady should entail."

When she began her job two weeks ago, Mr. Sandiston of the State Department had invited her out for drinks to talk about her new job. Over too many martinis, Sandiston told her to keep him apprised of Mrs. Roosevelt's "activities," especially her search for missing Susan Meyer, because Susan was suspected of being involved with Communists.

Mrs. Roosevelt's tone was frosty as she pointed out, "Kay, you work for me. Not Mr. Sandiston."

Kay knew disapproval when she heard it. Dratted Sandiston—she'd recognized at once he was trying to get her to act like a spy. She'd told him no.

He had bought her another drink, then leaned over and told her she was an attractive woman. With his wide shoulders, muscular build, blue eyes, and sandy-blond hair, he was a good-looking man. Kay's gaze had flicked down to the ring finger of his left hand—no band of gold, but she knew men. She sensed he was one of those husbands who didn't wear his ring.

Then he told her why Mrs. Roosevelt's name could not be

associated with a Communist sympathizer at this particular moment and why the entire country needed her to be on board with assisting him.

"I'm sorry, Mrs. Roosevelt, but he warned me that you could lose your seat as a United Nations delegate if the Senate does not vote to ratify you. He told me you shouldn't be involved in this at all." She didn't add the rest of what Mr. Sandiston had said. *I can't stop her. But with your help, Kay, I can mitigate the damage.*

"Sandy will have to lump it," Mrs. Roosevelt said calmly. "I am involved in this. And I certainly intend to answer questions for the police."

Kay bit back a groan. She had annoyed Mrs. Roosevelt, and Sandiston would be angry with her too. This was why she wanted to make a good marriage, give up working, and move to a big house in the country with a successful husband, where her only job was shopping. What did she know about police investigations? What she knew was how to make great excuses for a boss who came back to the office tipsy after lunch.

"I'm worried about Jackson, Mrs. Roosevelt," Mr. Jeffers said in his baritone voice. "I know he is innocent. He found the body and he ran out shouting about a dead woman, but I am certain he didn't do it. But Jackson is a young Black man and if the police assume he did it, they don't have to continue investigating."

"We will not let that happen, Mr. Jeffers," Mrs. Roosevelt declared. "I will not allow an innocent man to be condemned and a murderer to go free. There were times . . . well, I wish I could have done more, but sometimes being the wife of the president proved more restricting than empowering. Now there is no one who can tell me I can't have an opinion or that I cannot fight for an innocent man."

Kay flinched a little. She had definitely put her stiletto in it thanks to Mr. Sandiston. But this was a situation where she could display some brains.

"The porter is innocent," Kay declared. "I can give the police proof of that. I think."

Both Mrs. Roosevelt and Mr. Jeffers swiveled around to stare at her.

"There was a man in that washroom who was wearing Caswell-Massey Number Six. The scent is very strong, it hasn't faded away, so I think the murderer was wearing that cologne."

"Cologne? None of my porters wear cologne to work," Mr. Jeffers said.

"Caswell-Massey is an expensive brand favored by men in Washington," Kay said. "George Washington wore it. John F. Kennedy, that attractive congressman, wears it."

Mrs. Roosevelt looked at her in appreciative surprise. "Are you certain?"

Kay felt a surge of relief. "I know men's colognes very well," she said. Especially in close quarters.

"That is very perceptive, Kay. It will be helpful in directing the police toward the real culprit and prevent them from immediately suspecting the porter."

Kay sucked in a sharp breath.

"What is it?" Mrs. Roosevelt asked.

"It could mean the killer is a Washington politician. An important man."

The sort of man who was the villain in a Hitchcock thriller. Also the kind of man she had been hoping to meet while working closely with Mrs. Roosevelt.

Kay shivered. She forced herself to look around the tiny cubicle, away from Susan, and around Mrs. Roosevelt, at the tiny sink and the built-in toilet. She had found one useful clue. Maybe she could find more. . . .

"She doesn't have a handbag with her," Kay said.

Mrs. Roosevelt nodded. "No, she doesn't." She added briskly, "Someone must stay to watch over the body. Then we can inform the police that nothing was tampered with. I will stay. I think you should remain here, as a representative of the B&O

Railroad Company, Mr. Jeffers, if that is acceptable to you. Kay, do you feel up to going into the station and calling the police? I am sure Mr. Jeffers can arrange for a porter to escort you. For your safety."

"I can do so, Mrs. Roosevelt," Mr. Jeffers said.

But Kay echoed blankly, "My safety?"

"I expect the person who committed this awful act disappeared into the crowd and left the station, but it is possible that the murderer remained and is pretending to be an innocent traveler awaiting another train."

"He might still be here?"

"I will go into the station if you prefer to stay on the train, Kay."

Kay looked out of the lounge car window. Masses of people crowded the platform, pushing to get a closer look at the train. Men in business suits and fedoras, briefcases in hand. Tired-looking women in dresses and cardigans, loaded with bags. Squirming children.

Jackson's panicked shouting had caught the attention of many people in the station. Maybe most of them.

"No, Mrs. Roosevelt. I can do it." Kay needed to prove she was loyal, helpful, and good at her job. She couldn't get fired. Not again.

She pushed open the door. The crowd immediately pushed forward. She saw a line of porters trying to hold the mass of people back.

"There's been a murder on the train!" someone shouted.

"It was Mrs. Roosevelt!" another voice cried.

"Mrs. Roosevelt was murdered?"

A flashbulb went off in Kay's face.

Kay sagged. A reporter was already here. Mrs. Roosevelt's search for Susan Meyer wasn't going to be a secret anymore.

If Mrs. Roosevelt lost her position as a U.N. delegate, Kay was sure Sandiston would see that she was fired. Possibly arrested. If he could. He had been exceedingly grumpy when she'd told him she wouldn't dream of spying on Eleanor Roosevelt.

Of course, the former First Lady had been seen and recognized. Dozens of newspapers had printed the photograph of Mrs. Roosevelt holding the Universal Declaration of Human Rights. Thousands of people listened to her radio program and read her daily My Day column. Mrs. Roosevelt had traveled all over the country as First Lady, meeting people face-to-face. It would be difficult to find an American who didn't recognize Eleanor Roosevelt.

Alfred Jeffers leaned out and shouted for one of the porters to come over. "James, you take care of this lady. Take her to the stationmaster's office so she can call the police."

The tallest young man Kay had ever seen nodded and held out a gloved hand to help her down the steps. Kay followed him down carefully on her spike heels.

Aunt Tommy had insisted she dress modestly while working for Mrs. Roosevelt. She had to give up her figure-flattering dresses and wear full skirts, cardigans, and sensible shoes. She agreed to the cardigan but refused to give up her heels. Now she appreciated having the extra height.

The crowd jostled one another, getting a better view of her—the first person to emerge from the train car where there had been a murder. Tall men pushed past small women. Children threaded between adult legs to see the excitement. After the war, it wasn't unusual for people to become unruly. A sale on women's stockings could provoke a riot. Soon there were so many people, it appeared some might fall off the other side of the platform, under another train.

Kay had spent most of her adult life in New York City. She could elbow her way across the platform, but when James stepped in front of her, she let him take over. He used his height to carve her a path through the crowd. Another shiver raced down Kay's back. Like Mrs. Roosevelt had said, somewhere in the mass of onlookers, a killer might be watching. Pretending to be a rubbernecker. Pretending to be innocent.

She was in the middle of the crowd, halfway to the stairs that led up to the concourse, when she caught a whiff of citrus, bergamot, and musk. For a moment, she flashed back to the image of Susan's blood-soaked body lying in the washroom.

It was *that* cologne. Caswell-Massey Number Six.

She knew it because the scent was almost wrapping around her.

Kay looked around desperately. Her eyes locked with those of a man in front of her.

Ice-blue eyes. Fair hair under his hat. Sculpted cheekbones. The coldest, most ruthless-looking face she had ever seen. His cheek was even *scarred*.

And he walked toward her.

# CHAPTER 2

*I have often wanted to be more effective as a woman, but I
have never felt that trousers would do the trick.*
—Eleanor Roosevelt, If You Ask Me, *Ladies' Home
Journal*, October 1941

"Mrs. Eleanor *Roosevelt* found a body? That's a good one. It
would have been funnier when she was the First Lady. *That*
would have been a hoot. Stop wasting our time, young lady."

The telephone disconnected with a sharp click.

Kay glared at the telephone receiver she clutched in her
hand. The desk sergeant, who had barked his name, Willis, into
the phone, cut her off before she could tell him about the poor
dead woman. Or about the man on the platform who smelled
of Caswell-Massey Number Six.

The man with the gray fedora and ice-cold blue eyes had
pushed past her, jostling her shoulder, and almost sent her tum-
bling into the crowd. James had caught her as the man headed
toward the stairs. She shouted, "Stop him!" But she only confused people. Some grabbed at the man, but he broke free and
took off running.

Until he was deep into the crowd, then he stopped. Once he
wasn't sprinting, her cries meant nothing. No one could tell
who she was talking about. If she had shouted, "Grab the man

in the gray fedora!" about half the men on the platform would have been gripped by the other half.

She had acted without thinking. If he was the murderer, he knew she suspected him. And he knew what she looked like.

But just because he saw her, he didn't know who she was. Except the press would know Mrs. Roosevelt was here and if Kay was hustling Mrs. Roosevelt away from reporters, her photograph would get snapped.

Had her impulsive cry of "Stop him!" put Mrs. Roosevelt in danger?

She was making everything worse.

Mrs. Roosevelt had faced down obstructive Soviet delegates to achieve the adoption of the Universal Declaration of Human Rights by the United Nations. Kay could not return to Mrs. Roosevelt and tell her that she'd failed to contact the police.

She needed this job.

The buzzing sound of the disconnected telephone startled her, and she placed the receiver back on the cradle.

Kay was seated in the stationmaster's office. The wooden chair that predated the Great War pressed painfully against her spine. Blinds were pulled down over the windows. Timetables covered the walls. Stale smoke slightly overpowered the lingering sweaty odor of a male occupant who obviously never bothered with cologne, expensive or from the five-and-dime.

The chair on which she sat suddenly tilted backward. Old springs squeaked so loud her heart almost stopped. Kay grabbed the edge of the oak desk in a panic before she toppled over.

She couldn't give up. A Hitchcock heroine—or hero—was never believed. Perseverance was the key.

She picked up the receiver and dialed the number of the Washington police once more.

The now-familiar voice bellowed, "Sergeant Willis. First Station."

Kay barked in equally commanding tones, "This is Miss Thompson, secretary to Mrs. Eleanor Roosevelt. Mrs. Roosevelt is waiting for the police with a murder victim on the *Royal Blue* train at Union Station. This is not a prank. The murderer—I mean a *suspect*—escaped in the enormous crowd on the platform. He is *at large*."

Willis was able to sift through a conversation and find the one kernel that was important to him—because it could make his life difficult. "*What* crowd?"

Now she knew the way to keep Willis attentive.

"There are *hundreds* of people on the platform at the station who heard a murder occurred. They are all squeezing to the edge of the platform. Someone is going to get trampled. *You* may think this is amusing, but *Mrs. Roosevelt* does not. Not when there is a murderer on the loose."

"And you know who this murderer is?"

"I don't know *who* he is. But I know what he smelled like."

A long pause.

Oh no. She was losing Sergeant Willis.

"A reporter is already here," Kay added quickly. "It will be a great story for the newspapers if the police do nothing. The man at the top of your police force"—she had no idea what he was called—"will be embarrassed in the press. I would suggest you send officers to the train station. Right *now*."

"Hold your horses, young woman."

"Miss Thompson," she said, as imperiously as possible.

"Union Station, you said?"

"Yes, the *Royal Blue* train."

"We will be right there, Miss Thompson. There's no need for the press."

"The press is already here, Sergeant Willis."

"Damn it," Willis muttered.

She agreed.

Willis disconnected and Kay returned the receiver to the cradle. Minutes later, sirens wailed outside. Sergeant Willis had done something after all.

Kay pulled her compact out of her small handbag. She ensured her false eyelashes were in place and touched up her lipstick. She couldn't go out in public looking like a disaster.

She would meet the police and take them to the train. Mrs. Roosevelt wanted to speak to the police, but she had to get Mrs. Roosevelt out of the station without being hounded by the press.

The question was how.

It would have been easier to ensure she was at the platform before the police if she hadn't been wearing stilettos. But Kay hurried across the huge, vaulted concourse as fast as she could without skidding and ending up on the terrazzo floor on her rear end.

At the top of the stairs, she almost collided with a woman coming up, carrying a young girl in her arms.

The girl looked old to be carried—about six, with long, slender legs and dark hair in braids—and the woman was sagging as she tried to support the girl's weight. The girl banged her fists against the woman's shoulder and struggled to break free. The woman looked disheveled and exhausted and ready to cry, then Kay saw she was younger than she appeared. Married when she finished high school, Kay bet. She winced. It made marriage and motherhood look horrifying.

The woman was passing Kay just as her daughter delivered a kick to the shin.

Her arms opened and the girl almost fell.

Kay caught the child, managing to stay balanced on her shoes as she set the girl's small feet on the ground at the top of the steps. "Don't kick your mother," she said.

The girl kicked her, but Kay's full skirts absorbed the blow. "Don't! Please behave," the woman cried. But she didn't thank Kay.

"You're welcome," Kay said. "It was no trouble."

"S-sorry. We were trapped in that mob!" the woman said breathlessly. She wore a belted blue coat that showed off her tiny waist, and her face was clean scrubbed and pretty, but her hat was askew, her brown hair was sticking out in all directions as her struggling daughter had pulled at it.

"My baby was almost trampled!"

Kay thought the girl was hardly a baby and appeared to fight like a demon, but she could sympathize with how terrifying it was to have your small, fragile daughter caught in that crowd with all those huge bodies looming over her. The child was almost drowned by a cardigan over her dress, probably bought large so she could grow into it.

"I'm looking for my husband. I can't find him anywhere." The woman looked ready to burst into tears.

"What does he look like? Maybe he is still in the crowd, looking for you?"

"I—oh, I'll find him. I don't need any help!" The woman gripped her daughter's slim shoulders and began to pull her away.

"Wait," Kay cried. "You were on the train. The police are coming. I think they will want to talk to passengers."

"The police!" The woman shrank back. "I can't! I . . . I need to take her home."

"But the police will want to find possible witnesses. There was a murder."

"I didn't see anything!"

The little girl cried, "Momma, you're hurting me." She wriggled her shoulders, trying to break free of her mother's grip.

The woman hurried away, almost dragging the crying

child. Her low-heeled shoes made a frantic patter in the large space.

Once the police entered, would the whole crowd of people run away before they became involved? Maybe that was the way Kay could whisk ER out of the station and away from the press.

The wail of sirens ceased. Kay heard thundering footsteps. The main doors had opened, and constables in uniform streamed across the concourse.

A man strode with determination behind the constables. He was tall, over six feet, in a dark suit and black fedora. His pinstripe suit was off the rack, but the way he filled it out was mesmerizing. Broad, broad shoulders. You didn't encounter a man in a desk job with a lean build and wide shoulders like that every day. That build said he was the man in charge.

He had to be the detective—they wore plainclothes. And there was something about him that promised he'd follow a case to the ground.

Kay ran her tongue over her teeth so they weren't stained with lipstick. She waited for him on the steps.

Perhaps he wasn't quite the good detective she thought because he was so busy instructing his constables to keep people on the platform that he didn't notice her until she reached up and tapped him on the shoulder.

He swung around.

She saw his face. Up close.

*Montgomery Clift*, she thought. Thick, raven-black hair slicked back with Brylcreem. The sensitive, brooding face with high cheekbones, straight black brows that were a little too thick, and big green eyes. Not brown with a bit of something that could be green. Clear-as-glass green.

At that moment she felt like Elizabeth Taylor, until she remembered this man was a police detective, not a movie star, a murderer was on the loose, and poor Susan Meyer lay dead in the lounge car washroom.

"You should get back, miss."

"No, I shouldn't. I am secretary to Mrs. Eleanor Roosevelt, and she is on the train with the body. I also saw the murderer." Then she amended, "I think."

"You did."

The weary way he said it annoyed her. She'd expected him to be pleased. Deferential. Impressed with her accomplishment— she had picked a man out of a crowd by his cologne. Yet the detective acted as if she was a kook making up a story.

Hitchcock's heroines were also never respected.

"Why don't I take you to the body?" Kay asked, annoyed. "I was the one who had to call your desk sergeant repeatedly until he believed me. Maybe after you see the victim, you'll be more interested in what I can tell you, Detective."

"O'Malley!"

A booming voice barked from behind them. A tank of a man bore down on them. His cheap brown suit looked ready to give up and explode at the seams.

Kay assumed the large, loud detective was in charge, until the one called O'Malley quietly directed the big man to oversee the crowd. "I'm going to see if Mrs. Roosevelt is really on this train," he said.

"She is," Kay said.

Hitching up his belt, the large man looked Kay up and down. "Who are you?"

"Mrs. Roosevelt's secretary. Why don't you follow me, Detectives, and I will bring you to my boss?"

"Let's follow the pretty lady, boyo," the loud man said. Kay gritted her teeth and saw the detective flinch at the same time. The older detective was as dismissive of Detective O'Malley as both men were of her. Nice to see Detective O'Malley didn't like it either.

"I am Miss Thompson. Please use my name."

"Yes, ma'am. Don't get your—"

"Stop right there, Detective." Kay suspected the next word would be "panties." "Follow me."

Kay saw Detective O'Malley smother a grin. He followed right behind her, but she wasn't sure if she was leading him or he was indulging her by letting her go first. After she tried to push through the crowd, and got elbowed in the ribs, he took over and shoved his way through. Kay walked between the two men.

Constables were moving the crowd back, trying to corral them. Including the reporter—Kay spotted a camera with a big, silver flash attachment. A slender, young, brunette woman held the camera, not the cigar-smoking, grizzled reporter Kay expected.

But at least, with the constables pushing people back, the girl reporter couldn't get snaps of Mrs. Roosevelt.

"It's the lounge car," Kay said.

She followed Detective O'Malley's broad-shouldered back to the train. At the steps, he held out his hand to help her up. She ignored it, grabbed the shiny metal bar, and pulled herself up, careful not to embarrass herself with a slip of her heels.

Mrs. Roosevelt was seated in an armchair, legs crossed, her hand at her chin as if she were deeply pondering. Alfred Jeffers stood at attention with his back to the washroom door, almost acting as a guard.

Mrs. Roosevelt rose. "Kay, did you not wish to stay in the station?"

Thinking of her job, Kay said, "I want to be useful. These are the police detectives."

Mrs. Roosevelt extended her hand. Detective O'Malley came forward and accepted it.

"Detective Timothy O'Malley. First Station. Homicide. I

recognized you right away, Mrs. Roosevelt. From your pictures."

"Good detection," Kay said softly.

He glanced in her direction, and she feigned an innocent look.

He pointed at the large man. "This is my partner, Detective Barlow. Sergeant Willis told me there's a murdered woman on the train. It sounds like the plot of a Hitchcock movie."

"Clever," Kay murmured.

The detective ignored her. "But since you're here, Mrs. Roosevelt, I assume this isn't a joke."

"I assure you it is not," Mrs. Roosevelt said grimly. "I almost wish this were a terrible prank and not the very real murder of a young woman of twenty-one."

Kay caught her breath, sinking her teeth into her lower lip. She was twenty-five, though she wouldn't admit to anything older than twenty-three. Susan Meyer had been so very young.

"You found the body, ma'am?" Detective O'Malley asked.

"That was the young porter. I do not have his full name, but I am sure Mr. Jeffers can help you with that. I instructed another porter to give him a strong coffee. He had a terrible shock. But do you not wish to see the body first?"

"You're supposed to be asking the questions, boyo, not Mrs. Roosevelt," Detective Barlow muttered. "But she's got you standing to attention. Remember that no one is above the law, boy."

Kay saw the grimace again. Detective O'Malley did not like to be called "boy." Maybe that was the reason for the weary expression.

The detective produced a notebook from the pocket of his suit. He asked Mr. Jeffers for the name of the young porter.

Mr. Jeffers stood tall, and he was no longer sweating, but his voice came out as rasp as he said, "The porter who found the body is Winston. Winston, like the English prime minister. Jackson is his surname."

"Are you his superior?"

"Yes, Detective."

"How long has he been working on this train?"

"He's new. This is his second day."

"Hell of an initiation," Detective O'Malley muttered. "Where is the body?"

"In the washroom," Kay said.

"The washroom?"

He looked surprised by this. As if it were an everyday occurrence to find a murdered woman in her seat. But in the washroom? That was strange.

"Yes," Mrs. Roosevelt said. "Come this way." She led the detectives to the washroom. The lounge car was thoroughly modern, with shiny silver metal panels lining the walls. A vinyl-clad semicircular bar stood in the middle of the car. The polished wood of the bar gleamed like a mirror. Dozens of bottles sat on shelves behind the bar—every type of liquor Kay had ever seen. Arranged in groups through the car were comfortable leather and chrome armchairs and padded bench seats in wine-red leather.

Walking behind the two men, Kay heard the older detective muttering to Detective O'Malley as they passed up the aisle between the seats.

"What's that thing on her shoulders?" He didn't keep his voice down. "On Mrs. Roosevelt. It looks like she's got a dead fox draped around her neck. It's got eyes and paws."

"It is a dead fox draped around her neck," Tim O'Malley muttered. "It's fashion."

Kay had to smile. She had thought Mrs. Roosevelt could look so much smarter. Up to date. But Mrs. Roosevelt preferred loose clothes, heavy sensible shoes, and the most unbecoming hats.

"You know, in her pictures she looks like she's all teeth," Detective Barlow added. "Not so much in real life."

"Keep it down," Tim O'Malley ground out.

But Kay couldn't resist. "I was told a lot of people judge Mrs. Roosevelt's looks. Until they meet her in person and see her smile."

She was pleased to see Detective O'Malley blush. Nothing could make Barlow blush, she suspected.

"Let me ask you a few questions, Mrs. Roosevelt. You didn't find the body, but you're here, in the lounge car. Why is that?"

Detective Barlow, looking inside the washroom, interrupted with another whistle. "Pretty girl. Looks like that movie star. The one with the peekaboo blond hair falling over her eye. Who is that?"

"Veronica Lake," Kay supplied. "But I feel she looks more like Ingrid Bergman."

"And perhaps a whistle is not the most appropriate sound," Mrs. Roosevelt said.

"Well, that's not a sight you see every day. Not even in this job," Barlow said, looking like a large and sulky boy.

"Do you know the victim, ma'am?" Detective O'Malley asked.

"I don't know her, but I know who she is," Mrs. Roosevelt said.

Barlow snorted. "What does that mean?"

"Her mother asked me not to involve the police, but her daughter has been murdered. You must be given all the information I have." Mrs. Roosevelt hesitated, and Kay saw her look uncertain for the first time. "Elsa will simply have to understand," she said.

"I'm sure she will," Kay murmured, trying to be helpful.

"Thank you. To begin, Detective, the name that girl goes by is Susie Taylor."

"Goes by? That's an interesting way of giving me her name. What do you mean by that, ma'am, and what's her real name?"

"She was born Susan Meyer. Her mother is Elsa Meyer. An atomic scientist who lives in Sweden."

"She's Swedish?"

"Oh no. German by birth. But her daughter changed her name to one she felt sounded more American. She hoped to become an actress on Broadway," Mrs. Roosevelt explained.

"She lives in New York?" Detective O'Malley asked.

"No, here. In Washington."

"Not that good on geography in Sweden?"

"Susie was a waitress at Martin's Tavern in Georgetown," Mrs. Roosevelt explained, with a calm that Kay admired—she doubted she would be so cool and collected. "She missed her shifts for the last three weeks. Nor was she at her apartment—her roommate has not seen her. A week after that, Susan's mother contacted me, concerned about her daughter, who had not returned her telephone calls or letters for several weeks. Elsa Meyer is a dear friend. We have been close since I interviewed her for my radio show. She asked me to find Susan."

"If her daughter was missing, why didn't her mother want to bring in the police?" O'Malley asked.

"I will explain, Detective, when we speak in the train station. I think it is best to be methodical. I know I must gather my thoughts in order. I do not want to confuse you."

"I don't get easily confused," the detective said, frowning.

"I'm sure you would if I spoke hurriedly and without organization to you now."

The detective did look confused, Kay thought, and she almost smiled. Until she thought of poor Susan.

"You ladies should go into the station," O'Malley said. "We'll take your statements after I examine the victim."

"I would rather stay, Detective," Mrs. Roosevelt said.

"There are certain things I noticed that I wish to point out to you."

"You might have been First Lady, but you aren't a detective, ma'am," Barlow said, his tone close to snide, but Kay saw that his rudeness didn't trouble Mrs. Roosevelt at all. Kay wished she could possess such inner calm. She wanted to stomp her heel onto Detective Barlow's foot.

Barlow leaned toward his partner and muttered, "The porter— he was sweating like a garden hose before. Bet he was involved. He's acting like he has something to hide."

"He's acting like a man who just saw a dead body on his train."

"He is nervous," Kay said, "because he is afraid the porter who found the body may be considered the prime suspect, even though he is innocent."

"I bet he is," Barlow said, sarcasm heightening every word.

"We'll question him in due time," O'Malley said, flashing a look at Barlow that warned him to be quiet. "I'll take a look at the body." Detective O'Malley paused at the washroom door. "Who touched the door handle?"

"The young man who found her," Mrs. Roosevelt explained. "And I did. To open the door. I was wearing gloves. But if there were fingerprints, I presume they are smeared and destroyed."

Kay saw Detective O'Malley blink in surprise that Mrs. Roosevelt had thought of that.

Kay kept thinking of how she could possibly get Mrs. Roosevelt off the train without people noticing her. It wasn't just Mr. Sandiston who wanted Mrs. Roosevelt's search for Susan kept quiet. Aunt Tommy had said the same thing. And Aunt Tommy was the only family Kay had left.

But other than throwing a towel over Mrs. Roosevelt's head, she was sorely out of ideas.

Detective O'Malley stepped carefully inside the washroom. "There's no sign of the weapon. Did either of you ladies take it?"

"I wouldn't pick up a bloody knife," Kay gasped.

Mrs. Roosevelt patted her arm. "No, Detective. I did touch Susan's neck to feel for a pulse, but other than that we did not touch a thing."

O'Malley looked at Jeffers. "Did you take it? Or the other porter, Jackson?"

"Neither of us would touch a crime scene, Detective," Mr. Jeffers said, almost affronted his behavior would be questioned.

As the young detective studied the wounds, Detective Barlow leaned into the washroom and said, casually, "You think that someone wanted to have his way with her and when she wouldn't play ball, he got mad?"

Kay let out a gasp of shock. She was sure Mrs. Roosevelt would be horrified at that. But despite being born in the late eighteen hundreds, she wasn't. She looked calm and intrigued and was listening.

"I'm not thinking anything yet," the younger detective said.

"What's that smell?" Barlow asked, grimacing. "Smells like lemons and pine tree."

O'Malley took a sniff. "Her perfume?"

Kay was going to interject, but the older detective hitched his pants up and said, "She's a nice-looking dame. Great legs. Notice you're looking at her stockings. Seams are straight on them."

Kay's eyes almost bugged out, and Mrs. Roosevelt said, "Really, Detective," in a frosty voice.

Then Kay noticed Detective O'Malley was sketching a picture of Susan's leg in his notebook. "There's a tear in her stocking," he said, as he studied his sketch, then drew a copy of the small, circular tear in the correct location on his picture, Susan's lower right thigh, about two inches above her knee.

"That makes sense," Detective Barlow said, nodding. "She arranges to meet a man in here for some hanky-panky and changes her mind. A woman that gorgeous only had to crook her finger to get a guy to follow her in. When she won't put out, he tries to force it. She starts screaming and he shuts her up."

"And her stocking seams stay straight?" Kay muttered.

She noticed Mrs. Roosevelt's brows go up. Perhaps she should stay quiet, but she couldn't help it.

"Did anyone hear a scream?" Detective O'Malley asked.

"No, Detective," Alfred Jeffers put in. "No one heard anything. No one knew what had happened until Winston found her."

"If a strange man followed a woman into the washroom, I think that woman would yell. These walls aren't thick. Someone would have heard her." Crouching down, Detective O'Malley stared at the pool of blood. Then he rose and looked at the sink. "Water was sprayed over the counter as if the taps had been turned on hard. Did one of you ladies turn them off?"

"They weren't on," Kay said.

"Could the splashing sound of water running hard cover a scream?" Detective O'Malley posed the question. Then shook his head. "Maybe the killer got blood on him and washed it off. I can't touch the body until the police surgeon has a look at her. He should be able to give an approximate time of death. But from the way the blood has pooled and not spread, I figure she was killed when the train had stopped."

"There are things my secretary noticed, Detective O'Malley."

Mrs. Roosevelt had moved behind him and he almost jumped when she spoke.

"The scent is a man's cologne. Caswell-Massey Number Six. And her handbag is missing."

"Maybe it was at her seat."

Kay looked at him as if he had lost his mind. "Look at her

lips—" She pointed and tried not to look lower, at the blood-stains on Susan's beautiful pale-gray suit. "That's Stormy Pink. And her brows are beautifully penciled in. No woman wearing such perfect makeup would go to the washroom without taking her bag."

"It could mean the guy who killed her took it."

"I betcha that young porter took the bag when he found her," Barlow interjected.

"My porters are good men," Mr. Jeffers protested. "None of them are killers. Or thieves."

Detective Barlow snorted as if that was the funniest thing he'd heard.

Kay saw Detective O'Malley narrow his eyes.

Mrs. Roosevelt said, "You see the small gold links on her collar, Detective?"

Kay blinked. She hadn't. She hadn't let herself go that close to poor Susan's body.

"I believe they are from a necklace," Mrs. Roosevelt said. "It may have been wrenched from around her neck."

Detective O'Malley got down on his haunches again to take a closer look at the collar. Kay noticed how his expression softened as he looked at the young woman's face.

His gaze went down to the wound, and his face hardened again, his jaw ticked.

"A missing handbag and necklace. And a man's cologne."

"It's looking like a robbery gone bad, boyo. My money would be on those porters."

"They don't wear cologne," Kay said, but both men ignored her.

"I was thinking more about identification. Personal things were removed. But then, you knew who she was," Detective O'Malley said. He then looked at Mr. Jeffers. "The passengers shouldn't have been allowed to leave."

"The passengers had disembarked by the time she was found," Jeffers said.

"So the killer gets off the train with the other passengers and disappears," Barlow said. "It took guts. Someone could have walked into the washroom right after the guy—some lush needing a last-minute piss."

"That's enough, Barlow. There are ladies present." Still crouched by Susan, Detective O'Malley looked over to Mrs. Roosevelt. "While I wait for the doctor, there's no reason for you to be here. Jeffers, please escort Mrs. Roosevelt and Miss Thompson into the station. Then you can give me the information you felt would be better discussed in the train station, ma'am."

"Of course, Detective O'Malley," Mrs. Roosevelt said.

"What we need to do is to question the porters," Barlow interjected. "And search them for that necklace. I'm going to get on that. Already given the guy too much time to hide his loot."

"I was afraid of this," Alfred Jeffers said, looking with despair to Mrs. Roosevelt. "The police won't look beyond my porters for a culprit."

"I promise you that I will," Detective O'Malley said. "Barlow, get statements from the porters. But don't start arresting them."

"I'll arrest 'em if they're guilty," Barlow snapped. He strode away. The car shook with his heavy steps.

Detective O'Malley let his gaze travel over Susie's prone body once more. "There's no ring on her finger," he observed. "She wasn't married. Or engaged. Is that right?"

"As far as I know, that is correct," said Mrs. Roosevelt.

"The number of wounds look like she was attacked by an angry killer. Could she have had a jealous boyfriend?"

The detective straightened to his full height.

Mrs. Roosevelt looked him in the eye. At almost six feet tall, she looked most men in the eye. Or they had to look up to her. "I warn you this may not be as straightforward as I am sure you believe, Detective."

"Her lipstick is absolutely perfect," Kay said, suddenly. "If she was fighting off a man, her lipstick would be a mess." But the blond, ruthless-looking man in the crowd had to be the killer. Why else would he take off like a shot?

As if he had read her mind, the detective said, "You told me you saw the murderer, Miss Thompson. Who was he?"

"I may have seen him," she corrected. "I smelled the cologne in the crowd."

"You have a good nose."

"He was standing right beside me. I shouted for him to stop, but he took off running. I only got a quick look at him."

"You shouted at him?" Mrs. Roosevelt regarded her with concern. "You took a great risk, Kay."

"I recognized the cologne and I wanted to stop him." She'd wanted to act. She wanted to prove herself. "But he got away."

"If you saw him, then he saw you," the detective said.

"I know." Her voice came out as a croak. This was the first time she had been near danger—real danger, not the kind of danger of a man in the office putting his hand on her behind.

Mrs. Roosevelt looked troubled, but she took Kay's hand. "You will be quite safe. He could not know who you are, and we are very secure at the Mayflower Hotel."

Kay wanted to believe that. Mrs. Roosevelt's hand patting hers in a motherly way gave her a feeling of reassurance—Mrs. Roosevelt could do that with most people.

But Kay remembered the flashbulb going off as she opened the door of the lounge car. Someone had snapped her photograph.

Mrs. Roosevelt felt Susan's murder was more important than protecting her position. But Kay may have endangered a lot more than that.

Kay looked over to Susie, lying with her eyes blank and wide open.

In a Hitchcock movie, ice-blue eyes would hunt her down.

Detective O'Malley stroked his chin. "I need to get this down from the beginning. You were both on the train, a woman is murdered, and somehow you became involved, Mrs. Roosevelt. Have I got that right?"

"No, Detective O'Malley. We were not on the train. I came here to meet Susan."

# CHAPTER 3

*Without doubt human beings are the most interesting
study in the world.*
      —Eleanor Roosevelt, My Day, January 5, 1939

Kay leaned back on the hard, wooden desk chair in the station-master's office. It still dug into her low back, but she had mastered the balance point. She stretched out her legs and smoothed her knee-length black lambswool coat. As she did, she downed her second cup of black coffee. Coffee was safe if you avoided the cream. A moment on the lips, a lifetime on the hips, after all.

The door to the office flew open and Kay jerked in the chair, so quickly the springs squeaked, and she had to gasp as she flew upright.

Montgomery Clift strode in.

It was Detective O'Malley, but his pensive, troubled look gave him a more brooding allure than the actor.

The detective stood by the desk. She realized she had taken the stationmaster's chair and Detective O'Malley had expected to sit there, in charge, while she sat in one of the visitor's chairs. She looked at him innocently under her false lashes.

He pulled a chair over with a quick jerk. But he didn't sit on it. He put his foot up on it, so he towered over her.

"I'd like to ask you a few questions, Miss Thompson. For the record. Can I have your full name?"

"Honoria Kay Thompson." She winced. She had used her middle name since high school.

"Your age."

Kay straightened her shoulders. "I hardly see why you need to know that."

"For the record."

"Twenty-five," she sighed, unwilling to lie to the police.

"And you're Mrs. Roosevelt's secretary?"

"Temporary."

"Pardon?"

"I am her *temporary* secretary. My aunt Tommy is Mrs. Roosevelt's regular secretary."

"Aunt Tommy?"

"It's a nickname. Her name is Malvina Thompson. Mrs. Roosevelt's daughter, Anna began calling her Tommy and it stuck. My aunt lives at Mrs. Roosevelt's cottage at Val-Kill, and her health is not good. Mrs. Roosevelt needed a replacement in New York. I was out of work and my aunt . . . put in a good word for me."

Kay felt heat creep into her cheeks.

"Lucky for you."

"It was," she said in all honesty. "I am lucky to have the job. It's my fourth since secretarial school. I haven't had much luck keeping jobs."

"Why, Miss Thompson?" Detective O'Malley cocked his head. It was a gesture that made him appear friendlier. Kay knew it was calculated, but she saw no reason he should not know of her checkered past employment. He was the police. She should be truthful.

"No deep, dark secret. I just tend to get myself into trouble." She held up her hands. "Nothing illegal. On my first job, my boss turned out to be . . . handsy, if you know what I mean. He wouldn't take no for an answer. Until I dropped hot coffee in his lap. Then he fired me."

"Uh-huh."

He scratched down some notes. Kay wondered if they were sympathetic to her or to her scalded boss.

He was waiting, so she went on. "At my second job, one of the women in the typing pool was let go over a small error. But she was expecting a child, and I knew the supervisor wanted to replace her instead of letting her work until the baby came. I wanted everyone to stop typing for an afternoon in protest. I was told to stop typing there permanently. But, Detective, I don't see how this helps."

"It may throw a light on things," he said.

"While I was working at my last job this spring, where I was a secretary for a financial firm, I went to Capitol Hill to march in support of the Moton Student strike," she said. "I was in a picture that ran in the newspaper. My boss called me personally to tell me not to come back to work, though what I did had nothing to do with my job."

The detective's gaze truly bored into her now. "I had just been promoted to detective. You were in the mob that was pushing at the cops."

"To be accurate, they were pushing at us. I was standing with a sign, not causing any trouble."

"You were blocking a street," the detective said sourly.

"That is the nature of a protest," Kay returned. "Otherwise, why would anyone pay attention to the message?"

She could see he was not impressed.

"Are you from New York?"

"Does that matter?" It wasn't her story that was important—it was Susan Meyer's.

But the detective waited for her to answer. "I was born there. When Aunt Tommy went with Mrs. Roosevelt to the White House, my mother brought me to Washington. She worked at Garfinckel's. We lived here until 1946, when we went back to New York. My mother passed away a year later." She shrugged.

"So, yes, I've lived in New York for five years. On a clear day you can hear the sirens."

She doubted she was impressing him, but she hated explaining things about herself. She waited for the obvious question—all this talk about her and her mother, what had happened to her father?

"What does your work for Mrs. Roosevelt entail?" he asked.

Kay arched her carefully penciled eyebrow, filled in to look just like Elizabeth Taylor's dramatic, dark brows. "I don't see how that is important to what happened today."

His green eyes held her gaze. Long enough for her heart to make a small skip. She ignored it. He waited for her answer.

"I respond to her correspondence."

"What does that mean?"

"Letters. Requests. She receives mountains of letters. Hundreds in a week. On top of that, dozens of telephone calls. When Mrs. Roosevelt is in New York City or Washington, she attends four to five events a day—political meetings, ribbon cuttings, speaking engagements, charitable dinners. She even goes to the occasional movie or Broadway show. She also dictates her daily My Day column, which I type. At the end of the day, she reads and signs all the letters I prepare. Most nights she will be up until almost one in the morning just signing."

She saw the detective had stopped trying to keep up with her flow of words.

"How did Mrs. Roosevelt just happen to find the body of the woman she was supposed to meet on the train?"

He had changed direction. Perhaps to catch her off guard. Or because, as a woman, she had never been able to understand the strange directions that characterized the male train of thought.

But what did she say? Hadn't he talked to Mrs. Roosevelt? Her job was to keep Mrs. Roosevelt from being publicly involved in this.

Mrs. Roosevelt was the head of Committee Three at the

United Nations, the committee that wrote the Universal Declaration of Human Rights. Mrs. Roosevelt decried segregation at home. She supported India under Gandhi's leadership as it won independence from Britain; threatened to resign if Truman failed to recognize Israel as a sovereign Jewish homeland; met with Chilean protestors and rebels, victims of the atomic bomb, and displaced Palestinians.

Aunt Tommy bluntly said Mrs. Roosevelt had more power, more clout than some men wanted her to have. They wanted to see her stopped. They wanted to see her removed from the U.S. delegation and see the United States out of the United Nations altogether. They wanted to scuttle the achievements Mrs. Roosevelt had made. Some male politicians wanted Eleanor Roosevelt discredited. Hoover wanted her imprisoned.

"Miss Thompson?" the detective prompted.

She leaned forward. She wished she had removed her coat. She had a figure to rival Jane Russell. In the right dress, she could maybe get what she wanted. "Detective, can't we keep Mrs. Roosevelt out of it? She is an important person. She was searching for Susan Meyer to help a friend. She doesn't need to be involved in a murder."

"She is involved in a murder," the detective said dryly.

"Have you spoken to Mrs. Roosevelt?"

"I'm speaking to you first."

"I really don't know very much—" Then the wildest thought came to her. "You don't suspect *Mrs. Roosevelt*, do you? She didn't do it."

She saw the flicker in his green eyes—with those dark lashes of his, she couldn't look away.

"I was with her all day. If you are going to be ridiculous and suspect her, I'm her alibi. Mrs. Roosevelt shouldn't be involved in this, but she is willing to speak to the police because she is worried that young porter could be wrongfully accused by the Washington police department." Kay lifted her chin. "I've heard about the corruption in the police. Since Mrs. Roosevelt spent so much time in the White House, I'm sure she has too."

She expected him to get angry. He just looked more troubled, more brooding, and more annoyingly like Montgomery Clift.

"I don't wrongfully arrest people, Miss Thompson. The porter, Winston Jackson, found the body, but he jumped off the train shouting about it. I'm inclined to think he would have quietly left her in the washroom if he was guilty. He's a young man who looks afraid of his own shadow. But if you and Mrs. Roosevelt want to ensure justice is done right, you need to answer my questions."

He was right. And since Mrs. Roosevelt was determined to do her part, Kay was going to do it too. "I will. As best as I can."

"Tell me what you know about the victim. And why Mrs. Roosevelt was looking for her."

"I know just what Mrs. Roosevelt told you in the train car. Her name is Susan Meyer, and she used the stage name Susie Taylor. She disappeared from her work and apartment three weeks ago. Susan's mother, Elsa Meyer, thought she might be . . . in New York looking for acting jobs. She asked Mrs. Roosevelt to look for her."

"But Mrs. Meyer didn't want the police involved."

Kay leaned forward, just a little. "Mrs. Roosevelt told me how Elsa Meyer fled Nazi Germany in 1938, just before the war. In her My Day column from then, Mrs. Roosevelt wrote that Hitler had tried to force Mrs. Meyer to divulge her knowledge. When Mrs. Meyer escaped to Sweden, she gave her information to a scientist over here, in America. She doesn't know how much she contributed to the development of the atomic bomb, but it might have been something."

Kay had read the column—Aunt Tommy had all the original copies filed. About Elsa Meyer, Mrs. Roosevelt wrote, "At the foot of the pyramid there was a woman who had the courage to face new knowledge."

Ruefully, Kay had realized no one would ever write that about Elsa Meyer's secretary, if she had one. Secretaries didn't change the world.

"Do you think Susie Meyer's death is related to her mother being a scientist?"

"I don't know."

"When did Mrs. Meyer call?"

"Two weeks ago. Susan had been missing for a week then. I had just started my job."

"Did you overhear their phone call?"

"Oh yes," Kay said mischievously. "I pick up another extension and listen in on Mrs. Roosevelt's private conversations all the time."

The detective had the grace to blush.

"What about the cologne you say you can recognize?"

Kay sniffed. "I can recognize it. I know the scents men wear. And I know the difference between a good scent and"—she looked innocently at O'Malley—"something from the five-and-dime store. Would you like a description of the man I saw on the platform? It seems like important information to me."

The detective picked up his pen. "Shoot," he said.

"The cologne I smelled was Caswell-Massey Number Six. Caswell-Massey has been around since the seventeen hundreds. George Washington wore it. As for the man, he was under six feet, but he carried himself well. He walked like a soldier. I would guess his weight at one hundred and eighty pounds, and he had a trim build. His trench coat must have set him back a couple of hundred dollars. He was clean shaven, which revealed two scars on his cheeks. War wounds, perhaps, but he had the look of a man who wasn't unaccustomed to rough living. His hair was fair—pale blond. But it was his eyes—they were pale blue. Ice-cold eyes without a speck of warmth in them. He looked like an evil Tab Hunter. Though a few years younger."

Detective O'Malley was gripping his pen, looking at her in shock. "I thought you saw him briefly before he ran."

"A woman learns to size a man up quickly."

He scribbled hastily, then looked up, meeting her eyes. "You seem to be good at it. Did the man have any blood on him?"

"No, but he had his trench coat done up to his neck. If there was blood on his suit, the overcoat would have hidden it."

Kay hesitated. She didn't know what Mrs. Roosevelt wanted her to reveal. She couldn't tell him that Elsa Meyer feared her daughter had become sympathetic to Communists, that her daughter might be a spy. And she couldn't tell him that a week ago, Mrs. Roosevelt had asked her to look up an address.

It was a house in Glen Cove. On Long Island. The house was called Killenworth. Mrs. Roosevelt insisted on driving there on her own. Kay went out and did a little research at the New York Library. It was a mansion built just before the First World War. But in 1946, the Soviet Union had purchased it to use as the country retreat for its delegation to the United Nations.

"Is there anything else, Miss Thompson?"

If she said no, she suspected he would guess she was lying. "There isn't anything more I can tell you. You will have to talk to Mrs. Roosevelt."

"Then I thank you for your cooperation."

He took his foot off the chair, walked to the door and opened it, clearly indicating she was dismissed.

She walked past him in her heels.

"There is one more thing," he said.

Kay paused at the door.

"If Susan Meyer was missing, how did Mrs. Roosevelt know she was on that train?"

"I believe Susan called her," Kay said. "She was missing for three weeks, then, out of the blue, she telephoned Mrs. Roosevelt and asked her to meet the train. But Mrs. Roosevelt talked to Susan—she can tell you more."

She was about to leave, then stopped. "It's my turn to ask you one more thing, Detective."

He was tapping his pen on his book, frowning. "What, Miss Thompson?"

"Are you going to take me seriously and look for the man with the ice-blue eyes? If he is a Soviet agent and he knows Mrs. Roosevelt is involved, she is in *danger*."

"It's my job to keep people safe."

She studied him. "I hope so."

Then she turned on her heel and walked away. She noticed James was waiting for her. "I'll take you to Mrs. Roosevelt, miss," he said.

Following James, Kay thought of what Mrs. Roosevelt had also said about Elsa Meyer. They did a radio interview in 1945, just after Hiroshima.

Fervently, Elsa Meyer had insisted no government should have sole access to a nuclear arsenal that could destroy humanity. Peace could only be ensured by creating a stalemate amongst world powers.

# CHAPTER 4

*I found it was better to be fooled occasionally than always
to be suspicious of other people's motives.*
 —Eleanor Roosevelt, My Day, September 28, 1945

Mrs. Roosevelt waited for Detective O'Malley in the former
Presidential Suite of Union Station.

Eleanor settled back against the turquoise-colored vinyl-
covered sofa. This room had been built after the assassination
of President Garfield as a place for presidents to safely await
their trains. Her husband had often sat here before boarding
the *Royal Blue* and returning home to Hyde Park.

She had been here in August for the ribbon cutting when the
suite was reopened as a U.S.O. lounge. President Truman dedicated it as a home away from home for U.S. Armed Services
members. World War Two might be long over, but the work of
servicemen and servicewomen was not. Though the president
called the conflict in Korea a "police action," and the troops
serving were U.N. forces, people were worried.

Alfred Jeffers had brought her here while Detective Tim
O'Malley waited for the police doctor to arrive, then Mr. Jef-
fers had excused himself to answer the questions of Detective
Barlow.

She had noted Detective O'Malley did not look comfortable

about his partner's immediate assumption that the porters were involved—in either the murder or theft. She approved of the fact he had asked Jeffers to sit in on the interviews. She would have offered, to protect those men, but she was certain she would have been refused.

Eleanor had once told the *Washington Times-Herald* that she would list herself as a housewife—with some experience in writing a column and speaking—and that's all. Her work as First Lady and at the U.N. had opened her eyes to the need for human rights. But she had never truly thought of herself as a crusader or a proponent of justice.

She had also never dreamed she would be involved in any way in a murder.

Poor Elsa! The loss of a child. Eleanor had lost Franklin Junior when he was not quite eight months old. Her heart had never quite recovered. How would Elsa's?

"Mrs. Roosevelt? I brought you more coffee."

Kay came into the lounge, moving gracefully on her high heels, carrying two steaming cups. She wore a demure, high-necked, full-skirted dress of dark blue and a pale-gray cardigan buttoned over top, under her open black coat. Tommy had warned her that Kay's dresses might be rather flashy—bright colors and form-fitting—but her dresses had been sedate so far. Even in a plain shirtwaist, Kay could not hide her marvelous figure, Eleanor thought.

With her auburn hair piled in a chignon and her perfect movie-star makeup, Kay was quite stunning to look at. She had dark eyes, a deep brown that made an attractive contrast with her creamy pale complexion. Dark red lipstick colored her lips, and she wore dramatic eyeliner.

Eleanor had never had a secretary who was so feminine and attractive. Not even Lucy Mercer, her first secretary, was so beautiful.

Tommy worried about Kay. "My niece is man mad," she had told Eleanor. "She thinks her life must be dedicated to a man.

She has brains, but she refuses to use them—at least when she is around men. But she is a superb secretary. Organized. Conscientious. Clever. Loyal. The best replacement for me I can suggest. To be blunt, I hope that when she works for you, Mrs. Roosevelt, her eyes will be opened to the possibility of having a career and paying work and the self-worth that comes with those things."

"I am not certain I can change her mind," Eleanor had said. "But when I went away to Allenswood for school, my mind was opened, expanded, enriched. Marie Souvestre took me to Paris and let me walk about the city by myself. This, at a time when most girls like me were not allowed to go out alone. Mme. Souvestre shocked me into thinking. I gained confidence in the value of my ideas. That, I think, is most important to a young woman."

"Kay is not that young," Tommy said drily. "She is twenty-five. She fears she will never marry. I'm afraid that will lead her to do something rash and foolish. But I've told her that if she works for you, she can't leave to get married until I am well enough to return to work. I'm hoping that will keep her from making a silly mistake."

Talking with Tommy, Eleanor had thought of her own past, where a woman's opinions were those of her husband. Men in the White House had not liked the fact she had her husband's ear before they did. While they were engaged, she took Franklin to the poorer boroughs of New York and showed him how people lived in crumbling, overcrowded tenements. When she was his wife and the First Lady, the New Deal gave her the chance to help Americans. She had been quiet as a child—but when people's lives mattered, she ceased to be silent.

But she would not have been so courageous without her time at school with Mme. Souvestre, who taught her to be confident in her abilities and express her personality. Mme. Souvestre even encouraged her to stand tall and be proud of her height.

When Eleanor learned that Kay had lost previous jobs by

speaking up about injustices, she knew Kay was interesting. She agreed to take Kay on as a secretary and hoped to open Kay's eyes as hers had been opened.

Today, Kay's knowledge of the cologne had been a crucial clue. Her pursuit of a suspect was foolhardy but very brave.

"Thank you, Kay," Eleanor said as Kay crossed to the chair at her side and set the cups down on the low table in front of them.

Eleanor took hers, and Kay sat beside her, perched on the very edge of the seat. Kay didn't pick up her coffee. She stared straight ahead.

"How was your interview with Detective O'Malley?" Eleanor asked. "You look troubled."

"I'm worried the man I saw might learn that I am your secretary. I don't want to put you in danger, Mrs. Roosevelt."

"Any danger I encounter is entirely of my own choice."

Eleanor sipped her coffee—it was deliciously strong, and Eleanor suspected Alfred Jeffers had brewed it himself to ensure he gave her a good cup.

She worried that she had made a mistake by involving Kay in her search for Susan Meyer. Had she put Kay in danger? Tommy would never forgive her.

"Mrs. Roosevelt?"

Detective O'Malley entered the lounge and walked toward her. Eleanor admired his confident air, his broad shoulders, his easy stride. His hair also appeared more rumpled, despite the Brylcreem that was intended to keep it neatly styled. He had run his fingers through it. He looked worried, as if his confidence was for show and he was unsure how he would find a killer in Washington with so few clues to go on.

Eleanor wondered about that too.

"Here, boyo." Detective Barlow leaned in the doorway of the lounge. "I can talk to Mrs. Roosevelt."

With a groan, Detective O'Malley went back to his partner. He leaned in and said something quietly.

Barlow was not quiet. He boomed, "I'm a Republican. Never believed in the New Deal. I'm not likely to be kowtowing to anyone."

Detective O'Malley's voice rose. "Have you finished questioning the porters?"

"Yeah."

"Did you find Susie's purse and necklace?"

The large man shrugged. "No. But I told ya. They've got rid of those already."

"Then go and question people in the crowd. Find witnesses."

While the two detectives argued, Eleanor leaned over to Kay. "With his black hair and those green eyes, Detective O'Malley is rather good-looking, isn't he?"

"He's a police officer. They face danger every day, and they don't make particularly good salaries," Kay said.

"Money is not the key to a good marriage," Eleanor pointed out.

"Having no money certainly isn't," Kay said.

Eleanor marveled at how cynical and knowing Kay seemed to be for someone so young. She also supposed Tommy would not approve of her pointing out a handsome man to Kay.

"Here he comes," Kay said. She got to her feet as Detective O'Malley came up to them. Detective Barlow had disappeared.

Though Barlow was the older of the two, and the biggest, it was clear Detective O'Malley's personable manner and obvious brains made him the leader.

"I would like to ask you a few questions, Mrs. Roosevelt."

"Of course." Eleanor touched Kay's hand gently. "Why don't you sit over by the reading lamp and look through the magazines? And do drink your coffee. You will feel better. And you do not need to worry about me."

"I do, Mrs. Roosevelt. Aunt Tommy told me that was my job."

Eleanor was rather taken aback.

Tommy meant well. After Franklin's death, when she began as a U.N. delegate, Eleanor had verbally sparred with men from the Soviet Union and managed to forge agreement for the Universal Declaration of Human Rights, yet everyone still worried about her and treated her as if she were more delicate than she was.

Eleanor was surprised to see that the detective's gaze did not follow Kay as she walked across the room. There were soldiers in the other armchairs and they certainly looked.

The detective lowered into the chair across from her. He set his notebook on his knee.

"I noted that you spoke with Kay first," Eleanor said. "I presume you wished to hear her evidence before she had a chance to clear her statement with me."

He cocked his head. He looked most endearing when he did that. "Both of you saw through that. Is there more you can tell me about Susan Meyer, Mrs. Roosevelt?"

"Before we speak of that, there are some points on the scene of the crime I wish to discuss with you."

"I was about to say the same thing," the detective said, his tone easy and gentle. "I would like to know what you observed."

Eleanor looked on Detective O'Malley with respect. The young man had approached this questioning in a unique way. Inviting her to give her thoughts, not grilling her. "All right. Please ask your questions."

"First off, when did you enter the train car?"

"It was about ten minutes after the train arrived. Miss Thompson and I were waiting on the platform."

"Miss Thompson told me that Susan Meyer called you."

"Yes, she telephoned my New York apartment. I had told Elsa to give Susan my telephone number when Susan first came to New York. I felt it would be good for her to have a friend she could contact if she was ever in need."

"Was she in need, when she called?"

"I don't know." Eleanor explained that Susan would not tell her where she had been for the last three weeks, but she agreed to meet in Washington. "I told her how worried her mother is. She said she would see me so I could put her mother's mind at ease."

Eleanor paused. "Susan said she wanted her mother to leave her alone. When I asked if she was all right, she said, bitterly, that she had been a fool. She wouldn't explain any more. I was worried about her.

"I suggested we meet in New York, but Susan wanted to meet today, and I had to be in Washington yesterday to attend a dinner and to call on President Truman this morning."

"To call on the president?"

"Yes. The president and I had a productive meeting about the upcoming work of the United Nations, and President Truman's hope that the Senate would soon confirm the nine United Nations delegates."

Eleanor paused as he scratched notes, then continued. "Since Susan was planning to return to Washington, she asked me to meet her train. Then she ended our telephone call."

"Jeffers said that you were asking him if a blonde had disembarked from the train. At that moment, Jackson jumped down, shouting about a murdered woman. You asked to see her. How did you know it was Susan Meyer?"

"I didn't. I feared the worst."

"Why did Mr. Jeffers take you to the body?"

Eleanor gave a sad smile. "I am a former First Lady. I believe he felt I was a person of importance, not that I truly am."

"I'd say you are," the detective said, surprising her.

He looked at his notebook, then up at her. "Why were you searching for Susan, Mrs. Roosevelt? Why didn't you tell Mrs. Meyer to call the police?"

"I did, but Elsa did not want to involve the police."

"Miss Thompson said it was because she escaped from Nazi Germany in 1938. Did she equate the Washington police with the Nazi regime?"

"It was not your police department that frightened her. She feared Susan has—had Communist leanings. Elsa has seen the work of Senator McCarthy and the House Un-American Activities Committee. She was frightened that Susan would be arrested and detained as a suspected Communist."

Eleanor lived through two world wars, the Great Depression, and her husband's death, but she said solemnly to Detective O'Malley, "I cannot imagine anything worse than fearing your child is in danger. I did advise her to contact the police, but Elsa begged me to conduct a discreet investigation. I could not turn down the request of a distraught mother. Now I fear I made the wrong decision.

"I had reason to fear Elsa was correct about Susan's involvement with Communists, most specifically the Soviet Union. I was advised by a friend in the State Department to leave the matter alone, but I could not abandon Elsa in her time of need. Unfortunately, due to the connection with the Soviet Union, I think you will not be on the case for very long. Which is unfortunate. I want justice for Susan. And I like you, Detective."

The detective plowed his fingers through his thick dark hair. The hair cream could no longer contain it. A lock fell across his brow. "I don't understand."

"I fear this case will be taken from your jurisdiction."

# CHAPTER 5

*No man is defeated without until he has first been
defeated within.*
    —Eleanor Roosevelt, You Learn by Living: Eleven Keys
    to a More Fulfilling Life

Seated at the cherrywood desk in Mrs. Roosevelt's suite at
the Mayflower Hotel, Kay typed out the handwritten draft
Mrs. Roosevelt had provided for her My Day column.

Despite the shock of finding Susan in the afternoon,
Mrs. Roosevelt had returned to the hotel and wrote up her column. Mrs. Roosevelt wrote of her day in Washington without
mentioning Susan's murder. She spoke of meeting with President Truman and of an idea she had read that impressed her: *We
know we have an enemy. Many are not quite sure who or what
it is.*

When Kay saw she had typed "Resident Fruman," she groaned
and yanked the piece of paper out of the typewriter.

Even when she knew she was about to be fired at her other
jobs, after she had spoken out, her typing had always been
flawless.

Tonight, she couldn't think about work.

She'd loved the thriller movies *Notorious* and *Saboteur* and
*Cloak and Dagger*. There had been bodies on the screen, the

plots filled with spine-tingling suspense, but that hadn't been real.

This was real. The man she saw, the man she described to Detective O'Malley might be a murderer. Kay had tried to steer Mrs. Roosevelt out of a back entrance of Union Station, but Mrs. Roosevelt did not feel "such subterfuge" was necessary. As they left the train station, the brunette female reporter had jumped out. The flashbulb of the camera blinded Kay. She had turned her face away, but she couldn't hide Mrs. Roosevelt and she couldn't hide her red hair. At least the paper would print her in black and white.

But by this coming morning, when the papers printed the story of the murdered woman and the fact Mrs. Roosevelt had been at the station, the ice-blue-eyed man would know who she was.

The image of Susan in the washroom flashed through her mind. Her mind played it out in black and white, like in *Spellbound.*

*Susan's eyes go wide with terror. The blond man with the ice-cold blue eyes invades the cramped washroom. He slaps his hand over Susan's mouth. She struggles to fight him off, clawing at him. Tries in vain to scream—*

No, that wasn't right. His hand would have rubbed off her lipstick.

"I thought I heard the typewriter! You should be in bed, Kay."

Kay jumped, her hands struck downward, and all the typewriter keys jammed together against the platen.

Mrs. Roosevelt had come out of her bedroom, having changed into her nightgown and robe.

"I am afraid I startled you, Kay. You've had a very painful and shocking day. Your aunt Tommy wouldn't approve of me keeping you up to these hours."

"I . . . I wanted to finish your column."

"I could have typed it."

"No, ma'am. I'll finish it. It won't take me long."

Kay untangled the typebars, managing to pry them apart without breaking a nail, then typed so slowly it was excruciating, but this time she didn't make a mistake. Once done, she pulled out the page. Mrs. R offered to take it down to the reception desk, but Kay said, "It's part of my job, Mrs. Roosevelt." She hurried out, running as fast as she could in heels.

It was only when she reached the elevator that Kay thought: What if ice-blue eyes had waited and followed them to the Mayflower? He wouldn't even need to look at the morning papers if he'd done that.

The elevator door slid open, revealing a tall, broad-shouldered figure in a dark suit. Kay let out a cry. But it was Edward, the elderly elevator operator. He greeted her with a polite "Good evening, Miss Thompson. Did I startle you?"

"Sorry. I was distracted," Kay mumbled. "Good evening, Edward. I need to go down to reception."

He pressed the button, the door closed. Kay's heart pounded the entire way down. When they reached the lobby, she peeped out before she stepped out. Guests streamed out of the other elevators, and groups of people crossed the lobby, coming and going. Sofas and chairs gathered around tables to make conversation nooks, and sky-high potted palms in huge ceramic vases were placed all over. The ice-blue-eyed man could easily hide anywhere. Behind a column, behind a palm tree.

But she must be safe—the lobby was so crowded, so public. She hurried to the desk and instructed the concierge to wire the page to the United Features Syndicate. Mrs. Roosevelt diligently completed her column even while traveling, so the staff of the Mayflower were familiar with the request. My Day was published in ninety newspapers across the United States, six days a week, and was read by over four million people.

It was only when she was back in the elevator, sighing with relief to know she was safe and sound with Edward operating the buttons, that she realized the lobby had been filled with men dressed in tuxedos and fine suits, leaving for nightclubs and Washington social events. All kinds of well-to-do men, visiting Washington. And she raced past them all without even a glance.

Letting herself back into the room with the ornate key, Kay found Mrs. Roosevelt sitting by the telephone, gazing down at the receiver solemnly.

"What's wrong, Mrs. Roosevelt?"

"It will be morning in Sweden in a few hours. I must telephone Elsa. I asked the detective if I could tell her, but of course it is the duty of the police to contact her. I . . . I feel such guilt, to tell her I failed. She trusted me to keep her daughter safe. I am afraid to telephone her. I thought I had become used to facing fear. As my late husband famously said: 'There is nothing to fear but fear itself.' But I am dreading this moment."

"Mrs. Roosevelt, it wasn't your fault."

Mrs. Roosevelt brushed at a tear. Kay had never seen her cry—Aunt Tommy never had. If Mrs. Roosevelt ever cried, she didn't do it in front of anyone.

But her eyes watered now.

Kay grabbed her handbag and drew out a handkerchief that was almost all lace, pink, with a *K* monogrammed on it. A frivolous thing a serious secretary should never have, but Kay loved it.

"Here you are, Mrs. Roosevelt. You don't have to call Mrs. Meyer. I can call and give your condolences. I've always done that sort of thing for my male bosses. Give condolences, buy cards and gifts—usually anniversary gifts for a wife."

"No. This is something I must do. But there is something I must tell you, Kay. About the man you saw on the platform. Do you remember when we received the picture of Susan that Elsa sent to us by mail?

Kay nodded.

"I recognized Susan. Two months ago, I was dining at Oscar's Delmonico's with David in New York."

Kay knew of David Gurewitsch, a handsome doctor who was almost twenty years younger than Mrs. Roosevelt. Aunt Tommy did not approve of him—she thought he played up to Mrs. Roosevelt because he enjoyed the "star power" she provided.

But Kay knew not to comment on Aunt Tommy's dislike of the man.

ER continued. "Across the room I recognized a tall man with leonine white hair. He was Lev Valentsky, the Soviet Union's lead delegate to the United Nations. With him was a beautiful blond woman. She looked young enough to be his daughter, but he was obviously infatuated with her. I saw the way he touched her back as he led her to her seat. It had a reverent intimacy—the touch of a man in love. The blue-eyed man you saw on the platform is Lev Valentsky's aide, Dmitri Petrov."

"Then it was the Soviets," Kay breathed.

ER looked thoughtful. "I met Mr. Petrov in Geneva," she said. "He slid across the polished marble floor of the entry hall of the Palais des Nations in Paris."

"He slid? By accident?"

Mrs. Roosevelt gave a smile. "No, we both did it deliberately. For fun, after the Human Rights declaration was ratified. Our reward for many hours of work."

Kay couldn't picture *Mrs. Roosevelt* sliding across the marble floor like a surfer on a wave. "You and a Soviet?" she asked. She couldn't quite believe it.

She thought of the man she had seen on the platform. Her heart skipped a small beat as she remembered his sculpted features and icy-blue eyes. He looked as if he had never smiled in his life. "Fun" seemed an incomprehensible word to attach to him.

"I went first," Mrs. Roosevelt said. "Mr. Petrov saw me, so he tried it too. I could tell he very much enjoyed himself. Underneath his cold demeanor, he seemed to be a very likable young man."

"Likable young men can be dangerous."

The words had come from her heart so quickly they hadn't paused for an instant on her lips. It was something she shouldn't have said.

For a heartbeat or two, Mrs. Roosevelt studied her face. Then asked, "It is very interesting that you say that. Why do you feel that way?"

"It's something my mother told me," Kay said evasively. That wasn't true. But also wasn't not true.

Mrs. Roosevelt had a way of looking at you and you believed she saw everything that troubled you. It must come from years of being First Lady: meeting people, hearing their troubles, and thinking of a way to help.

Kay did not want Mrs. Roosevelt to see that deeply inside her heart.

"The curious thing is: Why was a Soviet aide wearing Caswell-Massey?" Mrs. Roosevelt mused.

"I suppose even Soviets want to smell good," Kay ventured.

"Mr. Valentsky condemned all things American. But he was dining at a very nice restaurant. Perhaps you are right. Perhaps Mr. Petrov has discovered American things."

"Susie must have been a spy," Kay said. "If she was meeting Lev Val-Valet—"

"Valentsky. It does appear that way. But that is not definite proof." Mrs. Roosevelt sighed. "I told Detective O'Malley that I saw Susan with Mr. Valentsky as he wished to know why I believed she was involved with the Soviets. It is now a matter for the authorities. My part in the investigation is done. Except that I must telephone Elsa Meyer. I believe she will be awake now."

"I will put the call through."

Kay dialed the overseas number, then the telephone number for Elsa Meyer in Sweden. Elsa had given the laboratory number first. Her home telephone number had been added as an afterthought. "Do not telephone that one," Elsa had said. "I am never there."

But Kay thought Mrs. Meyer would be at home since the police must have called her.

It rang with a distant clicking sound. The ringing abruptly stopped. The crackling began. A woman's voice barked unintelligible words down the line.

"Wait!" Kay cried, for she had the sense that the sudden cessation of the shouted words meant the woman was about to disconnect. "This is Mrs. Roosevelt's secretary—Elsa Meyer! Meyer! Is she there? Don't hang up!"

"I speak English," the woman said.

"I would like to put Mrs. Roosevelt on for Elsa Meyer," Kay said.

"I am Mrs. Meyer's housekeeper. She is at the laboratory. You must call there."

With a click, the line disconnected. "She hung up!" Kay looked up at ER. "Mrs. Meyer has gone to her laboratory. I'll call her there. But I don't understand—I would have thought she would be at home, grieving. Is it possible she doesn't yet know?"

"Very astute, Kay. I will be careful in what I say. But it is also possible that she was told and went into work."

"Why?"

"Her work is important to her. She may have felt it necessary to return to her work at once. One must carry on."

In her heart, Kay could not believe it was possible to put work ahead of a daughter. Then remembered Mrs. Roosevelt had been First Lady with four sons enlisted and serving in World War Two.

If it had been Kay's body on the floor of the *Royal Blue*'s washroom, she had no mother to grieve over her. Her father had vanished, her mother had died four years ago. Though she supposed Aunt Tommy would care.

Kay dialed the number for Mrs. Meyer's laboratory. This time a male voice answered. He spoke English with an accent that made the words sound terse and abrupt. Kay managed to make out that Mrs. Meyer would speak to no one.

"It is Mrs. Eleanor Roosevelt on the line for Mrs. Meyer. I'm sure she will want to speak to Mrs. Roosevelt."

"She is in a critical stage of her work," he insisted.

"Ask her!" Kay cried. She worried that not having the chance to speak to Mrs. Meyer would break Mrs. Roosevelt's heart.

He continued to refuse, Kay continued to plead, in her sweetest voice. He threatened to hang up. Kay threatened to call over and over. The man finally relented. He went to fetch Mrs. Meyer.

Kay handed Mrs. Roosevelt the receiver. Kay left for her bedroom to give Mrs. Roosevelt privacy.

Her bedroom was small but pretty, decorated with Federalist furnishings and painted beige and light blue. Her bed was made up, waiting enticingly. The flowered chintz curtains were drawn to block out the lights of Washington, DC, which glowed on Capitol Hill, on the White House, on the Washington Monument.

From the doorway, she heard Mrs. Roosevelt's voice. It was hoarse and heavy with sorrow.

"Elsa, is that you? It is I, Eleanor . . . Oh, Elsa, you know. You've been told. I am so very, very sorry. . . . You are going to come to Washington? Yes, I think that is the best thing for you to do."

Kay closed the door.

She doubted she would be able to sleep.

But after tossing and turning for hours, she dozed off. In the morning, she woke to find Mrs. Roosevelt in the sitting room. It was seven a.m. Despite often working until after midnight, Mrs. Roosevelt rose early. Kay was accustomed to that—she usually got out of bed at five a.m. to take the requisite two hours to do her hair, makeup, and get dressed in bra, corset, stockings, dress, and heels.

The Mayflower's room service had sent up an urn of coffee and two orders of scrambled eggs, toast, and jam for breakfast. The *Washington Times-Herald* had also been delivered.

The largest headline read: SOVIET'S SECOND ATOM BLAST IN 2 YEARS REVEALED BY U.S.

To the right was a slightly smaller headline: BODY ON TRAIN FOUND BY FORMER FIRST LADY.

Kay's heart sank.

# CHAPTER 6

*Probably the best thing that can happen to anyone at a*
*time of personal loss is to be drawn back to work by a job*
*that has to be done. If something must be done that*
*requires concentration, that takes the individual out of*
*himself, it is the best antidote for grief that I know.*
　　—Eleanor Roosevelt, My Day, September 11, 1941

Cab drivers whizzed by on Connecticut Avenue. Kay let out a
shrill whistle and stepped to the edge of the curb, waving her
arm. The wind sent her full blue skirt fluttering around her
legs.

She was still looking around, keeping a watch for ice-blue
eyes.

A Yellow Cab abruptly applied its brakes and screeched to a
stop at the curb.

The driver, a squat man with thick black hair and an even
thicker black mustache, hopped out. He pointed behind Kay.
"Excuse me, but is that Mrs. Roosevelt, the former First Lady?"

"It is," Kay said. "And she needs a cab."

Mrs. Roosevelt patted her arm before getting into the cab.
"You have a skill at procuring taxis."

Kay shook her head. "He stopped for you, ma'am. I don't
think I had a lot to do with it."

The cab driver opened the door for Mrs. Roosevelt. "Are you certain you don't need me with you, ma'am?" Kay asked.

"No, I will be fine. And you have important work to do," Mrs. Roosevelt replied as she slid into the back seat.

Kay closed her door, but the taxi didn't start off right away. Through the window, Kay saw the driver give Mrs. Roosevelt a stub of a pencil and the back of a receipt, and she gave him an autograph.

As they pulled away from the curb, Kay whistled down her own taxi. When it stopped, she said, "First District police station, please."

As the cab glided into traffic, the driver glanced at her in the rearview mirror. Probably wondering why she was going to a police station.

Kay stifled a yawn. ER had retired to bed very late, after speaking to Mrs. Meyer. Then ER awoke just after dawn to begin her day. ER probably had three hours of sleep, but she was as efficient and alert as ever.

Despite the shock of yesterday, Mrs. Roosevelt was carrying on with her schedule. First, she had a meeting with President Truman and Mr. Acheson, the Secretary of State. Then she would meet Mr. Sandiston of the State Department for lunch.

Three telephone calls had come that morning. The first was Mr. Sandiston. Aunt Tommy called almost immediately after.

"Kay, have you seen the newspaper?" Aunt Tommy said, her voice controlled, but Kay heard her fear and bewilderment. "How could Susan Meyer have been murdered? Why did you let Mrs. Roosevelt find the body?"

"I don't think I can prevent Mrs. Roosevelt from doing what she believes is right," Kay said.

"Elsa Meyer should never have asked Mrs. Roosevelt to look for her missing daughter," Tommy fretted. "It put Mrs. Roosevelt in a terrible position. I know that Mrs. R believes in jus-

tice. But as a delegate to the United Nations, she is doing good
for the world. We don't want her voice silenced."

"But—" Kay broke off. Mrs. Roosevelt held her hand out
for the receiver. "Your aunt? I will speak with her."

Once she took the telephone, she said, "I know you are worried, Tommy. But my involvement in the story will soon die
down."

Mrs. Roosevelt listened, then said, "After I speak with Sandy
at lunchtime, I am quite certain I will be told that this matter is
in the hands of the authorities. But I will bring Elsa to Washington . . . there is a weekly flight from Oslo in three days. She
will arrive at Idlewild Airport. I shall meet her, drive her to
Hyde Park, then bring her to Washington to arrange for the in-
terment of her daughter."

Kay could hear Aunt Tommy's voice over the line but
couldn't hear what she said.

"Have the maid prepare a bedroom at the cottage. Oh dear, I
only wish I hadn't failed Elsa. I know she will have questions,
and I have no answers . . . yes, I promise I will now leave this
matter to the police," Mrs. Roosevelt said before ending the
connection.

The next telephone call was from Detective O'Malley. "Miss
Thompson?" he asked.

"Yes." Over the phone, his voice was deep, intoxicating, and
had the most mesmerizing Irish lilt.

But then, Kay did not doubt Prince Rainier had a delicious
accent.

"I'd like you to come down to the police station and answer
a few more questions about the murder of Susan Meyer," the
detective said.

She paused. "Me? Not Mrs. Roosevelt?"

"You, Miss Thompson."

"But why me?"

"Are you not willing to come in, Miss Thompson?"

Despite the alluring lilt in his tenor voice, he sounded deadly serious. Kay couldn't help but say, "Am I a suspect, Detective O'Malley?"

Instantly she regretted her words. This *was* serious.

Her answer didn't make her feel safe. "Why don't you come in and we'll talk about it."

For her second visit to a Washington police station (her first had been after the Moton strike), Kay wore a full-skirted navy-blue and white polka-dotted dress with a blue bolero jacket. In New York, Kay discovered the garment district sold their samples at a huge discount. The beautiful clothes at rock-bottom prices made it so much easier to justify saying no to desserts. When she began her work for Mrs. Roosevelt, she had hastened there and bought three full-skirted, demure dresses. It had pinched her pocketbook and depressed her spirit, but she desperately wanted to keep this job.

Kay waited for Detective O'Malley at the desk at the entrance, her handbag dangling from her hands.

From his perch behind the desk, Sergeant Willis, the man who hung up on her, was quizzing her about the murder.

*Was the victim wearing clothes? What was the first thing Mrs. Roosevelt said? Does she know who did it?*

"No comment," Kay said.

She was thankful when Detective O'Malley approached with long, fast strides. His broad shoulders made the most out of his inexpensive blue suit. He wore a thunderous expression on his face, and she wondered what had made him mad.

His gaze met hers and his angry expression softened.

Her heart gave a quick patter.

Could it be that the detective liked her? At least, liked the look of her? She felt a flare of warmth at being appreciated by Detective Tim O'Malley.

Then remembered exactly what she had said to Mrs. Roosevelt. He was a police detective, taking terrible risks for very little money. Her father had made very little money, she knew, forcing her mother to work to support them. And when her father left, he took her mother's savings from her lingerie drawer. He left her mother with unpaid bills, literally leaving his family with less than nothing.

Detective O'Malley held the wooden gate open for her so she could cross the area she knew was called the "bullpen."

In the bullpen, telephones jangled, typewriters clacked. The most interesting people filed in and out. Witnesses, victims, and perpetrators, she assumed. A woman in a ratty fur coat, with teased hair and thick makeup, wobbled on her heels past Kay. "Dragged through a hedge" was how her mother would have described her appearance. Kay could have made her over into a head-turner.

A man in an expensive suit, his trousers stained and his tie askew, sagged over the corner of a desk, but he whistled as Kay walked by. She ignored him. He clearly had money, but she didn't like where it was going.

A blind was drawn over a windowed door marked SUPERIN-TENDENT.

Would she encounter any politicians here because they had been up to no good? Then she thought of Susie and sobered. It was very possible one Washington politician had done the most heinous crime of all.

"Please take a seat, Miss Thompson."

Kay did, crossing her legs, coolly letting her gaze meet Detective O'Malley's green eyes. They were seated at his desk, a wooden affair equipped with two uncomfortable chairs. His rolled and reclined like the one at Union Station. Hers did not.

When he didn't open with a threat of arrest, Kay asked, trying to muster Mrs. Roosevelt's calm, "Did you ask me here because you arrested someone? Am I to identify him?"

"Not yet. Whoever did it walked out of Union Station cool as a cucumber and got away with it. So far. Canvassing witnesses at the station gave us very little. An elderly couple insisted they saw a tall man in a trench coat who acted suspiciously."

"Was it the man I saw?"

"The description they gave was a dead ringer for Humphrey Bogart, so I'm not taking that seriously. I want to know more about what you and Mrs. Roosevelt did to find Susan Meyer."

Kay listed what they had done. "Mrs. Roosevelt spoke to Susan's roommate in her apartment in Georgetown, and to the other waitresses at Martin's Tavern. They had no idea where Susie went. Her roommate was worried and annoyed. She had no idea if Susan would pay her rent. The other waitresses got stuck covering her shifts. I looked for her in New York. I walked all over Broadway with Susan's photographs, checking all the auditions to see if anyone had seen Susan. I checked hotels around Broadway, then went to seedier and seedier places, but no luck."

"Seedier places?"

"I assumed Susan didn't have a lot of money for hotel rooms. No one recognized the photograph, even when I offered cash for information. She hadn't gone to an audition in weeks. It was really like she had disappeared into thin air."

Detective O'Malley nodded. "I followed up the Washington end myself, yesterday evening. Her waitress friends thought Susie had a boyfriend, but they didn't know his name."

"You know, from what Mrs. Roosevelt said, I don't think the other waitresses were her friends. It sounded like there was jealousy and Susan kept to herself."

"Even if they weren't friends, I'm surprised Susie kept the boyfriend a deep, dark secret. No one saw him. Isn't that strange behavior for a woman?" he asked.

"It is. Unless he was a Soviet delegate to the United Nations. Mrs. Roosevelt told me that she told you about seeing Susan with Mr. Valentsky."

"Yeah, Mrs. Roosevelt described him as a man in his early sixties. I can't see him as Susie's boyfriend. Miss Thompson, why does a woman keep a boyfriend a secret?"

"Because he wants her to. Because," she added slowly, "he was married."

"If you knew there was a boyfriend in her life, I'd like to think you, or Mrs. Roosevelt, would have told me. But this is Washington. A town of loyalties. There are scandals here that never make the newspapers. Because people hush things up."

Kay gaped at him. "You think Mrs. Roosevelt kept information from you and you're hoping I'll be dumb enough to spill it."

The detective did not even look abashed.

"Detective, if I knew the name of a man who Susan was seeing, I'd give it to you right away."

He appeared to accept she was telling the truth because he took a different tack. "I'd like to question Valentsky. And his aide, Dmitri Petrov. It sounds like he was the man you saw, the one who ran from the platform. But I don't know how to contact them. I'm hitting a brick wall. I wondered if you knew how to do it."

"I have no idea, Detective. Have you tried the embassy?"

"Yeah, and I got nowhere."

"I don't believe Mrs. Roosevelt just calls up the Soviet delegates on the telephone." She squirmed a little, because as Mrs. R's secretary, she probably should know.

"I suppose not."

He watched her. Kay had a sense he was hoping to learn something from her, but she had no idea what it was. His next question startled her.

"What do you know about Alfred Jeffers?"

"Mr. Jeffers?"

"He was on the train. He works the *Royal Blue* five days a week—a promotion after spending years on the sleeping cars."

"Detective, you can't think Mr. Jeffers murdered Susan. Why? Because of his skin color?" She felt color prickle in her own cheeks and knew they were red because she was angry.

"No, Miss Thompson. I would never condemn a man based on the color of his skin. And I don't think he did it. But I can tell he knows something that he's not telling me. I wondered if he revealed something to you and Mrs. Roosevelt when you were with the body."

"He was very upset. But I think that is natural, don't you?"

Detective O'Malley was about to speak when the blind-covered door flew open and a voice boomed, "O'Malley!"

A corpulent man filled the doorway, complete with ill-fitting suit and fedora. Following him out the door was the bulk of Detective Barlow.

The first man glowered at Detective O'Malley and approached, jowls shaking. "Who's this? Nothing to do with that Eleanor Roosevelt case, right? You're off that one, boyo. It's being turned over to the FBI. I don't need trouble with the State Department. I don't need you setting Sandiston on my as—I mean, my rear end."

"Boyo" seemed to be the detective's general nickname. O'Malley jumped to his feet. "I don't like the idea of a guy involved in Washington politics investigating a case that could involve a Washington politician."

"Doesn't matter what you like. Now send this young lady on her way, or I'll bust you down to beat cop."

With that, the large man turned and smacked into Barlow. "You, get out," he barked. Then he stormed out and yanked the door shut behind him.

Detective O'Malley looked annoyed. And he was blushing.

He obviously hadn't liked getting chewed out in front of her.

"Let me escort you back to the door, Miss Thompson," he said stiffly. "The interview's over."

# CHAPTER 7

*We are only just beginning to realize that the obligations of democracy outweigh the privileges.*
—Eleanor Roosevelt, *Western Mail* (Perth, Australia), October 21, 1943

On the way to her lunch appointment with William "Sandy" Sandiston, her taxi took Eleanor past the White House.

Yesterday morning, before Susan died, she had met with Harry Truman at Blair House, where he had lived since 1948 while the White House was gutted and extensively renovated. For the twelve years she lived in the White House as the wife of the president, Eleanor changed very little. For example, the many drapes were riddled with mended tears. Acerbic comments were made about this. Why did Mrs. Roosevelt not replace them?

The answer was simple. She entered the White House in the Depression, which gave way to the Second World War. Leaving the draperies untouched was a cost-saving measure in straitened times.

Now the interior had been stripped out so the structure could be reinforced. Only the exterior walls were untouched, so from the window of her taxi, the house looked the same. She glimpsed the familiar columns and portico through the fence.

Memories burst into her thoughts like the bright colors of fireworks. . . .

The first inaugural ball. Posing for photographs in her floor-length gown, wondering how she would manage to be a First Lady. Her first interview with reporter Lorena Hickok, who she came to call "Hick." Their travels together as Eleanor toured the country in the 1930s as FDR's eyes and legs to see firsthand the living conditions of her fellow Americans. Christmases with the children and grandchildren . . .

The day she met Harry Truman as he arrived at the White House and told him that FDR had died. Harry asked what he could do for her. She had answered, "Is there anything we can do for you? For you are the one in trouble now."

Continuing, her taxi passed by her hotel, the majestic Mayflower, which filled almost a city block. Sandy had invited her to The Colony, a fine dining restaurant just north of the Mayflower Hotel.

Traffic was light. The car pulled up alongside the curb, and within minutes she was escorted by the maître d' through The Colony. They passed the bas-relief mythological figures. The many mirrors positioned on the dusky pink walls reflected her face back to her—her black-rimmed glasses, her small hat and veil perched up on her thick, wavy gray hair. Fortunately, she never traveled without a black suit, and she had put it on this morning with a heavy heart. Kay had pinned a black-jet brooch to the lapel.

Last night Kay had stayed up late to type a perfect copy of her column. She was a very useful secretary. Efficient, clever, and Eleanor wondered how many other secretaries would quit when plunged into a terrible murder. She remembered Kay lifting her penciled eyebrow and stating that likable young men could be dangerous.

Eleanor had liked Dmitri Petrov. Most of the Soviet delegates did not engage in debate—they repeated what they had been told to say by their government. Mr. Petrov, when out of sight of Lev Valentsky, was far more open-minded. She could not think he was dangerous. . . .

But if he had committed murder, he obviously was.

She wondered what Detective O'Malley had wanted to ask Kay. She was surprised, in truth, that the detective was still on the case.

Probably not for long, she thought, as Sandy spotted her. He rose from his chair, his large hand outstretched, but he wore no smile. He looked gravely serious.

It was rumored William Sandiston had boxed his way through Harvard, and Eleanor saw no reason to doubt the tale. His hands were enormous, his fingers long, his wrists thick and strong. His suit bunched over his arm muscles. His close-cropped sandy-blond hair was receding at the temples. He must be well over forty now, and he was beginning to spread with age, but the ruddy face was familiar—she'd worked with Sandy since 1938, when FDR was in the White House, and afterward, in 1946, when she started as a delegate to the United Nations.

Sandy must be displeased with her. She had been on the front page of the newspaper, associated with a murder. But, of course, the reporters knew nothing of Susan's involvement with Soviet delegate Valentsky, so Communism had not been mentioned.

During the years of FDR's presidency, many men in government had been annoyed with her. Many still were. But she said, "Do what you feel in your heart to be right—for you'll be criticized anyway."

Sandy took her hand. Not in a handshake but a gentle, reassuring squeeze. "Mrs. Roosevelt, so good to see you again. But I am sorry for the circumstances."

The maître d' held Eleanor's chair, then quietly disappeared.

When she met with Sandy, she always asked about his wife, Letitia, and his twin daughters, Margaret and Maisie, but today she was prepared to go directly to the point.

"I expected a reproach," Eleanor said bluntly. "I did exactly what you warned me not to do—I have become involved in something scandalous right before the Senate ratifies the delegates."

"Mrs. Roosevelt, it is not my place to reprimand you."

"No, but you tried to use my own secretary to keep tabs on me."

"I tried it. She refused," he said.

Eleanor knew he was not abashed at all. Men in his position never were. She almost admired him for that blasé belief that he was right, that the ends justified the means.

"You warned me to stay out of it," she said. "You must have known I would not refuse to help a friend worried about her daughter. But I now suspect your warning came not because I am a delegate, but because the State Department was already keeping tabs on Susan. Is this true?"

There was a pause. Then Sandy answered her question with one of his own. "Is Elsa Meyer traveling to the United States?"

"Yes, she is flying from Oslo through to New York. She will be arriving in about four days if travel goes well. The flight takes almost twenty-four hours with refueling stops. I have offered to host her at Hyde Park for a night, as she adjusts to the time change. Then we will travel here so she can make the arrangements for her daughter's funeral."

Sandy looked down. "I'm damn sorry. I am working hard to get your name out of this. It isn't just the ratification or any involvement of the State Department with Susan. I don't think FDR would have liked his wife's name in the paper, associated with a murder."

Eleanor bristled. "I think I am the best judge of what my late husband expected of my behavior. My husband is gone, and I am no longer in the White House. I've done nothing wrong, and now that I've been interviewed by the police, my part in this is over."

Sandy relaxed back against his seat.

"I did tell the police detective what I had told you: that I saw Susan dining with Lev Valentsky in New York. It was at Oscar's Delmonico. You said nothing at the time, but did you already know? Was she seen there by your men?"

"Yes."

"That means you were following Susan before you knew of her involvement with Mr. Valentsky. Why, Sandy?"

"We keep an eye on the Soviet delegates. Discreetly. Susan Meyer was not on the radar until she was spotted leaving the Commodore Hotel in New York in the company of Comrade Valentsky."

"You could have been up front with me," Eleanor said.

"The affairs of the State Department are never that simple, even when you are involved, Mrs. Roosevelt."

"But why didn't you tell me that you knew where Susan was?"

"Because," he said grimly, "we didn't. She went to the Commodore Hotel one afternoon and never came out. Must have taken a back exit or slipped out in disguise. We lost her. And she disappeared."

"So you told me to stop looking for her, but you also hoped I would find her, didn't you?"

Sandy looked embarrassed. "I guess so. Didn't expect you would find her dead on the train."

Their conversation had to pause. At The Colony, three waiters took care of your comfort from the moment you entered. The wine steward, wearing a traditional black apron, with a huge key to the wine cellar hanging, presented the list. Eleanor demurred. Sandy ordered a glass of burgundy.

When the wine steward left, Sandy said, "Susie was a fool. You know how brutal Valentsky is. He was one of the legal masterminds of Stalin's Great Purge. When we learned he was in contact with Elsa Meyer's daughter, frankly, we were worried."

Their menus arrived, giving Eleanor time to consider Sandy's statement as she perused the pages.

She had debated Lev Valentsky over the Declaration of Human Rights. To prepare, she read transcripts from the Zinoviev–Kamenev trial in which Valentsky was a prosecuting attorney.

He had attacked with such statements as: "These enemies cannot hide their slathering jaws, their dripping fangs, their grasping talons from the people! . . . We must bring an end to these miserable, stinking mongrels once and for all!"

Eleanor had been prepared for vitriol and hyperbole. Valentsky made speeches lasting for hours, filled with criticism of the United States. He denounced capitalism and segregation (that she could not defend) and the immorality of America. He made it sound as if the Soviet Union was a victim.

In return, she kept her speeches to under fifteen minutes. In her speech given at the Sorbonne, Paris in September of 1948, she clarified, "We here in the United Nations are trying to develop ideals which will be broader in outlook, which will consider first the rights of man, which will consider what makes man more *free*. Not governments but *man*."

Valentsky, on hearing her words, had reputedly turned bright red. But for once he had no comeback.

"Are you ready, Mrs. Roosevelt? Mr. Sandiston?" the waiter asked, drawing Eleanor's thoughts to the present.

The wine steward filled Sandy's glass while she and Sandy gave their orders.

When they were once again alone, she expressed her thoughts to Sandy. "Lev Valentsky arranged for the prosecution of people and saw them sentenced to execution. But carrying out violence with his own hands is quite different."

"Probably just waiting for the opportunity," Sandy said. "You know Elsa Meyer's rhetoric. I think Susan was feeding scientific information to Valentsky."

Eleanor frowned. "If Elsa wished to hand over atomic research to the Soviet Union, there were simpler ways. Ways that did not endanger her own daughter."

"My bet is that Elsa Meyer didn't know. Elsa Meyer had tapped out an academic career for Susie, but that was too dull for such a hot little piece. A gorgeous blonde like Susie didn't want to be toiling away in a dingy lab, draped in a big white coat. Inspired by her mother's crazy idea of handing over the power of nuclear weapons to other countries—including Communist ones—she saw the opportunity to make some cold hard cash."

Eleanor frowned at his description of Susan. "You believe she sold information?"

Sandy took a long swallow of his wine. It was a fine vintage, but it was disappearing like a glass of Coca-Cola.

"Susie was hard up for money. Elsa Meyer didn't approve of her daughter being here as an actress. Considered them little more than prostitutes."

Eleanor made a small sound of pain. She remembered Elsa's words after begging her to look for Susan—as the only person Elsa felt she could trust. *I don't know where she is; I don't know what she has been forced to* do.

She thought Elsa meant what she had been forced to do to pay her bills or get acting roles. But perhaps Elsa's use of the word *forced* was literal.

"I think she was getting information from someone else," Sandy said. "She was seen around Glen Cove." He paused. "I know you visited Glen Cove."

"I did. But while she was seen in the small village—her likeness to Ingrid Bergman made many people notice her—there was no evidence she visited Killenworth."

"Why else would a woman like Susie go there?" Sandy asked. "She didn't look like the quaint, small-town type."

Eleanor could not dispute that. The woman she saw out with Valentsky had looked as glamorous as a movie star.

"She was also seen around the old Camp Upton armed forces

base, now used as a nuclear laboratory," Sandy said. "Brookhaven Laboratory. I think she was meeting someone who worked there."

"She may have been, but for innocent reasons." Eleanor considered. "There were scientists who feared the rise of Nazism in the 1930s and immigrated here. Isn't it possible that Susan was meeting someone who was a friend of her mother's?"

"She traveled to the base but was never seen in the company of anyone there. We think her visits were a signal for a meeting to take place, but not at the base. She met this person somewhere else."

"You know who it is," Eleanor observed.

"We might," Sandy said.

The waiter arrived to mix their salads at the table. The Colony was famed for its table service. Naturally their conversation must wait again.

Once the waiter placed their salads before them, Sandy launched into his food. He always enjoyed his meals. Yet he ran, lifted barbells, and had the physique of a prize fighter, albeit one who was growing older.

Between bites, he punctuated his words by waving his fork. "Susie was a platinum-blond Mata Hari for the Cold War. We think she was meeting the scientist from Brookhaven, two Soviets, and I believe she was indulging in pillow talk with the Washington elite. She met them at Martin's Tavern, seduced them to get information out of them, and sold it to Valentsky."

"Do you have proof?" Eleanor asked.

Sandy paused to finish his wine and signal that he wanted his glass refilled. "Not concrete proof, but what else would Susie be doing with Lev Valentsky?"

Eleanor remembered that night at Oscar's Delmonico. Her treat for David's birthday. People thought her foolish, thought she was an old widow who had fallen for a young, handsome man. David was a friend. There were many kinds of love—the love Eleanor had for her friends was a deep, loyal, and generous love.

At the restaurant, she spotted that leonine head of white hair, recognizing Valentsky. Eleanor had thought, with a smile, that even Communism did not deter a man from having his head turned by a blonde. At the U.N., Valentsky strongly disapproved of America. But he was savoring American freedoms at the restaurant that night.

"I saw the way Valentsky touched Susie's back as he led her away from the table. It was a gentle caress. An intimate touch," Eleanor said.

Sandy grimaced. "Valentsky supports an ideology that sticks their women in gunny sacks, working their fingers to the bone in factories that look like prison blocks," he said. "But he wanted to get his hands on a beautiful blonde in a figure-hugging dress. He used her work as a spy to put the moves on her. But I think Susie was a sexpot who knew what she was about."

He paused. "My apologies for my bluntness."

Eleanor waved it away. She had been involved in politics for a long time. "But is it true?" she mused.

Sandy might be trying to shock her, but she was not going to stop asking questions. "If Susan was intimate with Valentsky and with Washington politicians, do you believe she was a double agent? That is a terribly dangerous game that could end tragically."

Sandy shook his head. "Susie wasn't coaxing intelligence out of Valentsky and bringing it back for us. She wasn't working for us."

"I wonder if Susan was in love with Lev Valentsky," Eleanor mused.

Sandy's fork clattered to the floor.

A waiter glided over with a clean one. After the waiter left, Sandy growled, "With that old man? Never."

"He is close to my age," Eleanor said. "Yet with his head of white hair, his broad shoulders, his autocratic features, he is still very handsome."

Sandy was clearly shocked at the suggestion. "There was no way Susan Meyer did it for love."

"It is possible, Sandy."

"It's not," he said shortly. "Susie was the kind of girl who would play fast and loose. But it's not the thing I want to talk about with a lady."

"You say this about Susan, and I would like to know how you came to this conclusion. I assure you that I will not swoon."

He hesitated. Finished his glass of wine. Then said, "She went frequently to the Commodore Hotel in Manhattan. Usually in the afternoons."

"Who did she meet?"

"John Smith, of course. But John Smith was multiple men. One was Valentsky. One was our mystery scientist from Brookhaven."

"What was his name?" Eleanor asked.

Sandy hesitated. Then he said, "You might as well know, since you're involved in this. If I can't trust you, Mrs. Roosevelt, who can I trust? The man Susie was meeting was a twenty-nine-year-old fusion scientist named Josef Jakuba. Used to work with Klaus Fuchs. He was corresponding with Fuchs up until Fuchs's arrest in Britain as a Soviet spy."

Sandy twirled his empty glass. "A third man started to meet with her about three weeks ago, just before she disappeared. Dmitri Petrov, Valentsky's aide. The man your secretary saw on the platform matches Petrov's description."

Of course Sandy knew about that—he would have acquired information from the police.

"Valentsky may not have got his hands dirty," Sandy said. "Sounds like he sent his aide to do the job."

Eleanor considered thoughtfully as Sandy had more wine poured.

Dmitri Petrov was tall, blond, with classically handsome features, but as Kay had observed, his face bore damage from the war. He wore an expression of cold arrogance, but in the corridors of the various United Nations buildings, he had proved surprisingly friendly.

The first time Eleanor had entered the Palais des Nations chambers as a United Nations delegate, she had whispered to Stephen, a State Department aide, "I would love to slide on these polished marble floors."

After the Declaration of Human Rights was adopted on December 10, 1948, Stephen had whispered to her, "You can now take your slide, Mrs. Roosevelt."

Eleanor launched herself across the marble.

She hadn't realized she had been observed until Valentsky's handsome young aide, Dmitri Petrov, ran, jumped, and slid across the shiny floor behind her.

As he came to a stop at her side, he said, "Mrs. Roosevelt, I would not have been able to do it so gracefully if I were wearing your heels."

She had laughed and he gave a charming, boyish smile.

Were either of these men—Valentsky the orator or boyish Petrov—capable of murder?

Their main dishes arrived and were presented with a flourish. Eleanor waited until Sandy had tucked into a few bites before asking a question that seemed logical to her.

"If Susan was supplying information to the Soviets and was not acting as a double agent, why would they harm her?"

"Maybe she demanded more money. Maybe she wanted out. Maybe the Soviets thought she was spying on them. Maybe they came to the wrong conclusion and feared she was a double agent."

But Eleanor frowned. "I am not convinced it was the Soviets."

"It had to be."

"But why the train? So conspicuous. It would have been very easy for them to eliminate Susie and . . . dispose of her where she would never have been found."

"True. But so far, they've gotten away with it. It was bold, but that is the Soviets' way to thumb their noses at us."

Sandy had ordered steak. Asparagus and green beans were on the side, along with whipped potatoes, all glistening richly with butter. He was making fast headway through the meal. The food at The Colony was a far cry from her early White House years, during the Depression, when she had given instructions and demonstrations on how to prepare inexpensive, nourishing meals. Eleanor did not have much appetite for her coq au vin, as delicious as she knew it would be.

"It seems more like, if Susie was spying for the Soviets, that it was our side who was worried about her activities."

"She would be arrested, not murdered," Sandy said.

Eleanor wondered.

"This could be a crime of passion," Sandy said. "Susie is sleeping with both Valentsky and Petrov. Maybe Valentsky learned she was meeting his underling in the Commodore Hotel. He might have followed her on the train, goes into the washroom to find out what is up between her and Petrov. He sees red when he learns she prefers a young, handsome Soviet like Petrov, and he kills her. The same works for Petrov. He doesn't want to share. Or he was going to lose her to the old man."

Eleanor shook her head. "I simply can't believe Susan was that type of girl. The fact that she was beautiful does not immediately mean she was immoral."

Sandy set his cutlery on his empty plate. "The thing is—if it was one of the Soviets, I won't be able to get near him. He'll vanish back behind the iron curtain."

Eleanor nodded. Yet she was not convinced Sandy's suppositions were correct.

"Mrs. Roosevelt, there are a couple of men who want to talk to you. Rising stars in Washington political circles. They want this crime solved and they want the murderer to pay. I respect how busy you are. I've heard that to get a chance to meet with you, politicians have had to jump into your taxi and ride with you to your next destination."

That had indeed happened. "I would be happy to speak with them," she said. "I want justice for Susan Meyer, and I will make as much time available as they need."

"They suggested dinner tomorrow in the Mayflower's dining room, so you are not inconvenienced."

"That is very thoughtful."

She was curious. Who were these two rising stars? And what could she help them with?

The waiter came with a dessert menu.

"I'm having the apple pie," Sandy said. "Bring your best dessert for Mrs. Roosevelt."

After the waiter left, he winked. "Expense account."

In moments, a cake that appeared to be a mountain of chocolate was placed in front of her. Sandy faced his large slice of apple pie and spherical scoop of ice cream with a gleam in his eye.

Mrs. Roosevelt surrendered after a few bites. Sandy mowed through his pie until his plate was clean. With a soft groan of satisfaction, he leaned back in his chair.

"You want to hear a strange coincidence, Mrs. Roosevelt?" he asked. "I was on that train when Susan Meyer's body was found. Traveling in a first-class compartment. Letitia was with me. The two men you are going to meet were also there with their wives. One is Jimmy Price—you two worked together at the U.N."

Mrs. Roosevelt nodded.

"Jimmy had his daughter along. Letitia and I brought the twins. We were returning from a series of Democratic party meetings in New York and decided to take the wives along to catch some Broadway shows and let them shop. I had no idea Susie was on that train."

It was an astounding coincidence, Eleanor thought.

Or was it not a coincidence at all?

"You are aware that my secretary recognized the scent of a man's cologne in the washroom. Caswell-Massey Number Six."

"I guess it's lucky for me that I don't wear Caswell-Massey," Sandy said jovially. "I'm an Old Spice man. Letitia likes it on me."

# CHAPTER 8

*The most important thing in any relationship is not what you get, but what you give.*
      —Eleanor Roosevelt, *This Is My Story*, 1937

K ay tapped her heels on the parquet floor as she waited for the elevator.

"Miss Thompson—wait."

Kay paused. Detective O'Malley jerked open the bullpen gate and strode toward her. "You can't ask me more questions, Detective. You're off the case."

He looked so disgruntled, so much like a bear that had been woken from its hibernation early and poked in the ribs, that she almost laughed.

"You really wanted to remain on the case," she said.

His green eyes gazed steadily at her. "I want to make sure this murder is solved."

Mrs. Roosevelt said it was up to the authorities now. But to do what? Hide the truth? Pervert justice? "You're afraid the truth will be covered up," Kay whispered.

"If a politician is involved," he said softly, "that is exactly what I am afraid of. I met Mr. Sandiston of the State Department yesterday. Big guy wearing a fawn-colored mackintosh raincoat. He was built better than the walls of the precinct. I was thinking that if a car ran into the station, I bet it would go through the walls but come to a stop at that guy."

"I've met him. He has a powerful build." She didn't say more—about how he knew he was well built and handsome, and he had bought her drinks, flirted with her, and tried to coax her to spy on Mrs. Roosevelt.

The detective glowered. "I don't trust him."

"He is a longtime friend of Mrs. Roosevelt's."

"When he was relieving me of my case files, he let slip that he has been following Susan Meyer for months. I wondered if the guy had gotten obsessed with her. Following a woman that beautiful, keeping tabs on her day and night . . . it could get to a man."

"Would it get to you? Following such an attractive woman?"

"Maybe. But I'm not partial to blondes."

Her brows rose. "Then you must be the only man in America."

"I doubt it."

"What is your taste?" she asked.

"Elizabeth Taylor. She's my type."

Raven hair. Violet eyes. Dewy skin. Astounding figure. "Get in line, Detective," Kay said. "She's *everyone's* type." The line came out with more sarcasm than she wanted.

"If this were a Hitchcock movie, like you said on the train, Detective, Mr. Sandiston would obviously be the villain." Kay warmed up to the theory. "Just like in *Spellbound*, when Gregory Peck, who has lost his memory, thinks he is the murderer, but he has been manipulated by the real killer. Mr. Sandiston becomes obsessed with the target of his surveillance, falls in love, and murders her because he can't have her. Or because she is involved with the Soviets, and he feels betrayed. Or maybe he murders her because he puts his patriotism above his desire for Susan. . . ."

Kay saw the detective staring at her. "Let me guess," he said. "You're a secretary who wants to be an actress?"

*I'm a secretary who would rather be a pampered wife.*
"That's how I think Hitchcock would write it," she said defensively. "But I don't know if murders work that way in real life."

"In real life, murderers try to get away with the crime."

"I just don't understand how someone killed her and she didn't scream. If she'd screamed, the porter on the lounge car would have heard."

The detective nodded. "That's what puzzled me."

"That's why you asked me about Mr. Jeffers. But Jackson was the porter on the lounge car."

"No, he wasn't," the detective said. "Jackson told me that Alfred Jeffers worked on that car."

Kay stared. "He never said anything about that. What did he tell you when you questioned him?"

"I can't tell you that. Ongoing investigation."

"No, it's not. You aren't involved anymore."

He flinched and she saw again how much he had disliked the dressing down in front of her. And how angry he was to be off the case.

Instead of telling her more, he said, "You saw a man who might be the murderer, Miss Thompson. I think the Washington PD needs to be involved. To look out for this man."

"Mrs. Roosevelt believes he is Dmitri Petrov," Kay said. "She describes him as a likable young man."

The detective's thick dark brows drew together. "A Soviet?"

"They are people too, Detective."

"Mrs. Roosevelt told me about Petrov," he said. "He's an aide to a United Nations delegate. He has diplomatic immunity."

He paused as another officer walked by. As soon as the man passed, he said, "I didn't run after you to ask you more questions."

To speak quietly, Detective O'Malley bent down to her. She smelled his aftershave—not as elegant as Caswell-Massey but it smelled nice on him.

His deep voice was dancing, his Irish lilt on full display. "I realized I was watching you walk out of my life, Miss Thompson. I don't want that to happen. I hope this isn't too forward, or inappropriate considering the circumstances, but I would like to take you out for dinner before you go back to New York."

Kay thought suddenly of Susan, a beautiful young woman who would never go on a dinner date again.

The elevator door slid open.

"I'm sorry, Detective O'Malley. I'm afraid I'm too busy with my work for Mrs. Roosevelt. Try Elizabeth Taylor. I hear she's single now."

She turned after she got in, and pressed the button for the ground floor.

Detective O'Malley leaned against the wall, trying to look cool. She imagined gazing at him over a restaurant table and she wondered if she'd made a mistake.

But she didn't want her mother's life, scrimping and saving. And worrying that her husband might not come home from his dangerous job. Or what if he just left, like her father had done? A world leader could divorce her, but he couldn't abandon her, she thought sagely. She would know where he lived.

As the door slid closed, she murmured, "If you're on the arm of Mr. Wrong, you'll never meet Mr. Right."

"The cocktail lounge?"

"I have a proposal to put to you, Kay," Mrs. Roosevelt said, as she removed her outdoor coat and her small, veiled hat.

"Can I . . . get changed? Won't take a minute. . . ." Kay hurried into her bedroom with both hands behind her back to start pulling at the zipper.

"I should change as well. I have a dinner engagement afterward," Mrs. Roosevelt called out.

Kay was already muffled in her dress. She tossed it on the bed. Flinging open the wardrobe, she thought: did she dare put on one of the dresses that Aunt Tommy had told her not to wear on the job? Poppy red? Scarlet? This was a lounge, after all. But Susan had died. Pushing the others along the rail on their hangers, she came to her black dress.

A half an hour later, Kay was sipping her Manhattan at the table in the Mayflower's cocktail lounge, wearing a black cocktail dress that hugged her figure and skimmed her knees. The color was demure, the fit wasn't. Kay had wondered if Mrs. Roosevelt would look shocked, but she hadn't said anything. Still, Kay felt nervous—as if she had done something wrong.

The Mayflower's lounge was packed. Chairs were grouped around dozens of round tables. Tall columns framed the bar, detailed with Art Deco tile and large statues. Large ferns provided exotic greenery. But what was most fascinating? Given the before-dinner hour, it was *filled* with men.

Too many cologne and cigarette-smoke scents mingled for Kay to identify the cologne from the train. Highball glasses, tumblers, beer glasses rose. Slick-haired men in tailored suits relaxed back in their seats. Raucous laughter filled the room.

Kay crossed her legs and sipped her Manhattan. Mrs. Roosevelt had a cup of steaming-hot tea. Aunt Tommy said Mrs. Roosevelt disliked alcohol—her father had died of the disease of alcoholism, and it took her brother's life as well. FDR had enjoyed his cocktails and mixed them happily during his daily cocktail hour, but while Mrs. Roosevelt attended the occasions, she took a cocktail with reluctance.

It must be raining outside. People entering shook off their coats and umbrellas. Now that it was autumn, it was already dark.

"Mr. Sandiston believes the Soviets are responsible for Susan's murder," Mrs. Roosevelt said. "He gave me two theories. The first: Susan was murdered because she was a spy, using her feminine wiles to gain information from men in Washington and sell it to Mr. Valentsky, and she either wanted more or wanted out, so she was killed. The second theory is that Susan was the lover of two Russian men, Valentsky and his aide, Dmitri Petrov. The motive was jealousy."

"Mr. Sandiston has a lurid brain," Kay said. It didn't surprise her. While he had been telling her to keep Mrs. Roosevelt out of the press, he had let his hand rest on her knee. Why men groped the knee, she was never sure.

Then she realized she had insulted Mrs. Roosevelt's longtime friend. Detective O'Malley didn't trust Sandiston as far as he could throw him. But surely Mrs. R wouldn't count you a friend unless you had some integrity?

"I'm sorry," she said.

"Oh no, you are quite right," Mrs. Roosevelt said. "Sandy described Susan as a platinum-blond Mati Hari who indulged in pillow talk with politicians."

Kay thought that sounded exactly like Sandiston.

"Sandy admitted he did not have proof," Mrs. Roosevelt said. She added thoughtfully, "I postulated that Susan might have been in love with Lev Valentsky."

"Do you think she was?"

"Lev Valentsky was obviously attracted to her. She smiled at him and gazed into his eyes that whole night at the restaurant, but whether that was love—or something else—I don't know."

"But isn't he an old man?"

"He has an intellect. He has power. Old-world charm. And aging in men is considered more acceptable than aging in women."

"True," Kay said ruefully. She and Mrs. Roosevelt were on the same page in that regard.

"When I suggested it, Sandy got quite upset," Mrs. Roosevelt said.

"Hmmm." Kay sipped her cocktail.

"He was so flustered he dropped his fork. He also described Susan as 'a sexpot who knew what she was about.'"

Kay sputtered her cocktail. She couldn't imagine Mrs. Roosevelt saying "sexpot," yet she'd just heard it. Embarrassed, she knew she needed to add something thoughtful. "That sounds like a man who was turned down."

"I agree. But it does not necessarily mean that he murdered her."

"But if he admitted to Susie that he was attracted to her, and she is a Soviet spy—" Kay stopped. She was getting close to putting her foot in her mouth, stiletto and all. This is what got her fired. "He is your friend, Mrs. Roosevelt," she added quickly. "You know him well and I assumed that must mean he is a good man."

"We can never know someone completely," Mrs. Roosevelt said. A pensive look flashed across her face.

Sandiston was Mrs. Roosevelt's friend, but Kay was pleased to see Mrs. Roosevelt didn't blindly trust him. Mrs. Roosevelt's worldliness amazed her. She thought a First Lady lived in an ivory tower. Safe from all that was sordid.

Apparently not.

"Detective O'Malley suspects Mr. Sandiston," Kay said. She summarized their brief meeting. "He has been pulled off the case like you predicted. He suspects Sandiston of covering up . . . or of being involved. He isn't happy."

"No. I can see that Detective O'Malley has a great deal of integrity."

The word struck a chord with Kay. She had applied it to Sandy Sandiston. She had been correct. Mrs. Roosevelt recognized the quality. And admired it.

"I am sure there are policemen who would shrug and be relieved the work was taken from their shoulders," Mrs. R continued.

"Detective O'Malley isn't that type," Kay said with conviction.

Mrs. Roosevelt smiled.

Kay realized she hadn't seen Mrs. Roosevelt smile very much since Susan's death. Kay had another sip of her Manhattan.

"Sandy told me he was on the train."

Kay almost sputtered her drink. Again. "He was on the same *train* as Susan Meyer?"

"Yes. He was traveling with two other men—men whom Sandy described as rising stars in Washington political circles. I know Mr. Price, one of them."

"Isn't it an enormous coincidence that Mr. Sandiston was on the same train as Susan Meyer and Dmitri Petrov?"

"Perhaps it was no coincidence at all," Mrs. Roosevelt said.

"What do you mean?" Kay asked. "They set it up?"

Instead of answering, Mrs. Roosevelt said, "We do not know that Mr. Petrov was on the train. Only that he was on the platform."

Mrs. Roosevelt wanted to believe he was innocent, Kay thought.

She thought of her aunt Tommy, disapproving of David Gurewitsch because he was young, handsome, and because Mrs. Roosevelt cared about him. Aunt Tommy was worried that Mrs. Roosevelt was being taken advantage of. But Kay thought Mrs. Roosevelt was too savvy for that.

Still, she wasn't as trusting of evil Tab Hunter as Mrs. Roosevelt.

Even now, when she had been glancing around at the men filling the lounge, she had been looking for fair hair and ice-blue eyes.

She hadn't seen him.

"Mr. Sandiston and the two men were traveling from New

York with their wives. Both Mr. Sandiston and Mr. Price had their daughters with them," Mrs. Roosevelt said.

Kay nodded. "I guess that gives Mr. Sandiston an alibi. If he was with his wife and daughter."

"Daughters. Sandy has twin girls. But I wonder . . ." Mrs. Roosevelt mused. "It would be simple to slip away alone, with the excuse of visiting the lounge car. A man could suggest he would return with a drink for his wife."

Kay was amazed. Mrs. Roosevelt really did not wear rose-colored glasses.

It was easy to picture it like a movie. The train hurtling through the night . . . well . . . it was the afternoon, but it had been a cloudy, gray autumn day. Sandiston is on the train with his wife and two young daughters. He runs into Susie Taylor there by chance. Or maybe Susie was on the *Royal Blue* because she knew Sandy was on it. Susie threatens to go to his wife and reveal their affair. He agrees to meet her. He promises he will tell his wife, tell her that he is going to leave her. Susie thinks she has won. Then he shoves her into the washroom and kills her. . . .

"What are you thinking, Kay?"

Kay flushed. "Nothing."

"Tell me. Your thoughts are always perceptive."

Mrs. Roosevelt appeared to be telling the truth. No boss had ever said that to her. Feeling the heat in her cheeks, Kay outlined her thoughts.

"That is a very vivid scenario," Mrs. Roosevelt said. "It would explain why this happened on the train. I felt it was strange to plan such a thing for a public space. So much easier to lure Susan to an isolated location. It makes more sense that the murder occurred on the spur of the moment."

Kay swallowed hard. "Susan might have thought she was perfectly safe. Because of the people on the train. Even when people were disembarking, there was the porter in the lounge . . ."

"Yes. And there is the issue of the knife. If the knife was taken on the train by the murderer, then it was premeditated. But there is another solution. The bar counter. The knife could have been there, used to cut up fruit for drinks. I wonder what Winston Jackson told the police."

"Detective O'Malley told me that Mr. Jackson wasn't the porter on the lounger car. Alfred Jeffers was."

Mrs. Roosevelt looked truly taken aback. "Mr. Jeffers? I wonder why he didn't say."

"You don't think . . . he did it?" Kay asked. "Why wouldn't he have heard Susan scream? Why didn't he say anything about a man going into the washroom with Susan?"

Mrs. Roosevelt shook her head solemnly. "I don't want to believe that of Mr. Jeffers. He has always been an honest man. I knew that from the days he was building the Brotherhood of Sleeping Car Porters. He endured a great deal to create the union which has helped so many families."

"What if he was paid to do it? Or it was like *Strangers on a Train*?" Kay had loved that movie this summer.

Kay stopped. "No. He wasn't wearing that cologne. I certainly would have smelled it. He can't be the one."

Mrs. Roosevelt looked relieved.

"But it doesn't explain why he took you to the body but didn't tell you that he was working in the lounge car," Kay said.

"It is possible he was offered a large tip to leave the car and he thought it was an assignation. If that was the case, I am sure he feels guilt and does not want to admit he accepted a bribe to leave his post."

"But wouldn't he say who bribed him? When he realized that man killed Susan?" Kay asked.

"Yes, I would have thought so. I felt Mr. Jeffers was struggling with something. I first believed his state of nervousness was due to fear for young Jackson and concern that the young porter might be blamed. I could talk to Mr. Jeffers. . . ." Mrs.

Roosevelt sighed. "Sandy insists I am to stay out of this now—at least, after I have met with these two gentlemen to tell them what I know about Susan. The FBI has taken over, and Sandy knows Mr. Hoover would want to try to paint me as a Communist sympathizer. Apparently, Mr. Hoover has a very thick file on me and refers to me as Public Enemy Number One."

"That's ridiculous!" Kay exclaimed, loud enough that the heads of Washington men turned to look. "How can these men say such things? You've done so many good things."

"Your sense of fairness and your vehemence are important qualities, Kay."

"Ones I usually have to hide in my jobs as a secretary."

"You do not with me," Mrs. Roosevelt promised. "But to protect my position as a delegate to the United Nations, Sandy told me, as we were leaving, that I must ensure my photograph does not appear in any more newspapers. All I am allowed to say is 'no comment.'"

"Mrs. Roosevelt, you are the one woman who never says 'no comment.'"

Kay knew her job was to encourage Mrs. R to do just that, but she didn't want to. Unless that was the Manhattan talking.

ER gave a surprisingly impish smile. "When I was First Lady, everyone had an opinion on what I should do and should not do. I knew I must do and say what I believe in. Everyone must live their life in their own way."

It was good to see Mrs. Roosevelt smile. And as Kay had told Detectives O'Malley and Barlow, Mrs. Roosevelt was beautiful when she smiled. Kay tried to smile in ways to not induce wrinkles. Mrs. Roosevelt's came from her soul.

Mrs. Roosevelt glanced up at the large clock near the bar. "The young men should have arrived at the restaurant by now."

"The young men?" Kay echoed.

"Mr. Price and Mr. Kennedy. The rising stars in Washington."

"Mr. *Kennedy*?" Kay's thoughts went to Congressman John

F. Kennedy. Young, wealthy, attractive. The most eligible man in Washington.

"I will introduce you," Mrs. R said. "I would like you to meet them."

Kay was stunned. She gazed down at her dress—the black velvet followed the curve of her hips and definitely showed she had a bust. If one of the men was Congressman Kennedy, she wanted to look beautiful.

Mrs. Roosevelt looked very elegant in a becoming black satin sheath with an embroidered black jacket over the top. Kay had picked out the ensemble.

Kay was astonished. Secretaries were usually invisible. No matter how much work she did for a client, she was always in the background. The only time she spoke was to ask if he wanted cream in his coffee. Or get herself in trouble. "Are you certain you want them to meet me?"

"Yes. I am afraid I cannot ask you to stay for the meal as the young men will want to speak freely," Mrs. Roosevelt said. "Take the rest of the night off, Kay. But I would like you to meet these two men. They were on the train, after all."

Kay nodded.

"From what I gathered from Detective O'Malley," Mrs. Roosevelt said, "you are skilled at sizing up men quickly. That is a skill I must call upon right now."

# CHAPTER 9

*It is the sum total of what we do as individuals that makes the world.*
    —Eleanor Roosevelt, My Day, August 9, 1943

As they were led to a table in the Mayflower's restaurant, Kay noticed all eyes turning to them.

They were looking to see Mrs. Roosevelt. She raised her hand in greeting to those she knew—and had to stop to speak to those she did not but who recognized her and jumped up from their seats to introduce themselves.

Watching the clout Mrs. Roosevelt had in Washington impressed Kay. She had thought ER was an important person because of her marriage to the president. Now she saw ER was an important person due to her own accomplishments.

A waiter passed adroitly, his silver platter bearing a half-dozen dishes. Kay saw the orange-pink hues of a lobster and smelled the aroma of grilled steak.

Kay remembered her mother diligently following Mrs. Roosevelt's tips for preparing inexpensive meals in the Depression. "The main cause of malnutrition was not lack of food but a lack of knowledge of menus that were both inexpensive and used simple but nourishing ingredients," Mrs. Roosevelt had said. Then she famously served a "seven-and-a-half cent" luncheon at the White House of hot stuffed eggs with tomato sauce, mashed potatoes, prune pudding, bread, and coffee.

There weren't any inexpensive ingredients in the dishes here, except maybe J. Edgar Hoover's well-known lunch of lettuce leaves and cottage cheese. Kay wondered if he was there and wanted to spit out his lettuce as he watched Mrs. Roosevelt walk in. Then she remembered he took his lunch in the men-only bar known as the Rib Room so that eventuality would never happen.

Two gentlemen rose as they were led to the table toward the back of the restaurant — a quiet table in a private spot.

Kay caught her breath. One of the young Kennedys stood at the table. But not Congressman John F. Kennedy. She knew Robert Kennedy from photographs taken with his brother — photos printed in the serious newspapers and in the tattler rags.

"Mrs. Roosevelt. It is a pleasure to see you again," he said, warmly shaking her hand.

"Kay, this is Robert Kennedy. This is Kay Thompson, my secretary. She must leave us, but I wanted to take the chance to introduce her to you."

"Miss Thompson. Call me Bobby," Mr. Kennedy said. He held out his hand to Kay, giving her a firm handshake. He had a broad, boyish smile with gleaming white teeth with a slight overbite. His heavy-lidded, attractive eyes made Kay instinctively pat her chignon into place.

Kay glanced down to his left hand. A gold band encircled his ring finger. She remembered seeing pictures in a gossip magazine that he had married last year.

His brother John, known as Jack, was still single. And eligible.

"Mr. Kennedy lives in Georgetown, I believe," Mrs. Roosevelt said.

"I do. With Ethel. I've started working with the Internal Security Division of the Department of Justice."

"Prosecuting espionage and subversive-activity cases," the second man said, as he shook Mrs. Roosevelt's hand with a grin of pure admiration. "Mrs. Roosevelt, it is an honor to see you again."

"So good to see you," Mrs. Roosevelt said warmly. She clasped her hand over his, intimating she knew this young man well. His accent was Midwestern, his looks what were called "all-American."

If Bobby Kennedy was a handsome man with an alluring smile, Jimmy Price was even more so. Movie-idol handsome with sculpted cheekbones, vivid blue eyes, and surprisingly dark long lashes for a man possessing thick golden-blond hair. He had slicked it down.

The only flaw was a large scratch that ran across his cheek. A fresh scratch, dotted with red scabs.

Kay exchanged a glance with Mrs. Roosevelt. She had seen it too.

Mrs. Roosevelt looked worried as she introduced the blond man to Kay. "This is James Price."

"Jimmy," he said, extending his hand. His gaze went over her from her red hair to her black dress in a way that said: *I like what I see.*

But Kay couldn't take her eyes off the scratch. A woman's fingernail could have made it.

"Jimmy is with HUAC now," Kennedy said.

Kay bit her lip. She knew the acronym, as did every American. The House Un-American Activities Committee. Headed up by Senator Joseph McCarthy. The organization that carried out Communist witch hunts. The one Elsa Meyer had feared.

"So, you did join Senator McCarthy, after all," Mrs. Roosevelt said. Disappointment flashed across her face.

"It was my duty, Mrs. Roosevelt. When I was at the United Nations, hearing the Commies condemn American freedoms and democracy made me mad. I know there are Communists here, at home, hoping to cause trouble, hoping to bring down our democracy. Watching men like Valentsky made me see that I must protect America."

"You are protecting our ideals. I cannot find fault for that, Jimmy, but I don't admire that man's methods."

Kay saw that Mrs. Roosevelt was not afraid to say what she believed.

"Maybe not, and maybe I can be helpful there," Jimmy said. "But I'm afraid the Communists will get a foothold unless we root them out. You said yourself that you will always be opposed to the communist form of government."

"Yes. But I am sure the more we study communism or socialism, the more tolerant we will feel. The very best thing would be to travel to such countries and see for yourself. We are not afraid of a known situation. It is the unknown we fear." Mrs. Roosevelt gazed at Jimmy seriously. "I merely hope that you do not become prejudiced, and you do not adopt vindictiveness. Never forget that we all must adhere to human rights. With no exception."

"I always think of your principles, ma'am. I vowed to do you proud. And my country proud."

Kay saw that Mrs. Roosevelt believed his words—but she did not believe that working for Senator McCarthy was the way to do democracy proud.

"I suppose being here, in Washington, has given you much more time to spend with your lovely young bride, Jimmy. What was her name? Debra?"

"That's right, Mrs. Roosevelt. Though she isn't such a young bride anymore. Our daughter is six years old." He looked at Kay. Appealingly. "Can you stay for a drink, Miss Thompson?" He pulled out a chair for her while Mr. Kennedy drew out a chair for Mrs. Roosevelt.

She'd watched Jimmy Price's eyes drop as he asked about the drink, until he'd been carrying out the conversation with her bosom.

Mr. Kennedy cleared his throat. He looked awkward and Kay

took the hint. "I must go, but thank you for the offer, Mr. Price."
She began to push her chair back, but Jimmy Price launched up
and drew it back for her.

"It was a pleasure to meet you," Bobby Kennedy said.

"My pleasure as well," Kay answered, looking from him to
Mr. Price.

"Shame you have to go," Jimmy Price said.

Kay lifted her carefully penciled-in eyebrow.

As she was leaving the restaurant, she reviewed her impres-
sions of both men. Attractive. Polite. Smart. Accustomed to
being considered important. Mr. Kennedy hadn't looked at her
bosom or her legs, but Jimmy Price had drunk her in.

A lot of men looked, made comments, even flirted, though
they didn't intend to pursue it. Their egos liked to think that
every attractive woman was interested. And all men postured in
front of one another—they liked showing the other men that
they appreciated a woman, and they wanted to be the man who
got the most attention in return.

Jimmy's appraising gaze didn't necessarily mean he was
cheating on his wife.

But there was the scar on his cheek.

A woman's fingernail could have made that scar. While she
was fighting for her life.

Kay looked back at the table from the doorway, hesitating.
Was she doing the right thing, leaving Mrs. Roosevelt alone?

But she had to. Mrs. Roosevelt had asked her to. And the
restaurant was crowded. Mrs. Roosevelt was perfectly safe.

Whiskey arrived for the gentlemen, more tea for Eleanor.

Small talk was briefly exchanged as they looked over the
menus. Eleanor asked politely after Robert Kennedy's father,
Joe Kennedy, even though it was well known that though Joe
Kennedy Senior had supported FDR's nomination for president, Eleanor did not approve of his public support of Ameri-

can neutrality during the war. He had wanted to limit the numbers of refugees and Eleanor had not approved of that.

She had hoped Jimmy would change his mind when he announced he was leaving the State Department to hunt out Communists with HUAC. But he clearly had not.

Jimmy had been a sweet, disarming young man. Now, watching his handsome face, Eleanor wondered if Senator McCarthy's inquisitions and witch hunts had changed him. He looked older, wiser, and more cynical.

She decided to get on with things. "I presume you both wanted to meet with me about Susan Meyer?"

Bobby Kennedy nodded. He looked sorrowful. "That was a great tragedy. We want to find her killer as quickly as we can."

"I assume there are things about Susan you don't want to come to light."

"We know you told the police detective about seeing Susan with Valentsky, ma'am."

"Did either of you meet Susan?" Eleanor asked. "She worked as a waitress at Martin's Tavern in Georgetown."

"I've been to Martin's. My brother Jack frequents it often when he is in town for Congress."

Eleanor noted he hadn't said whether he had met Susan.

"There was a pretty blonde waitress at Martin's," Jimmy said. "She looked like Veronica Lake. Sandy said that was Susie Meyer."

"Yes. She was a very beautiful young woman," Eleanor said. "Sandy told me that the three of you were traveling on the *Royal Blue* train the day she was killed."

Jimmy nodded. "I guess we must have disembarked before she was found."

"Did you hear the commotion? When the porter ran out of the train?"

"I was up at the taxi stand with Ethel," Bobby said. "Sandy

had already left with Letitia and the girls—he had a car waiting for them. Jimmy, where were you?"

Jimmy took another swig of whiskey. "Out of the action. My daughter was feeling poorly, and we got off the train as soon as it reached the station. I heard shouting on the platform, but we were up in the concourse. We got a taxi to the house."

He set down his glass. "Sandy said he filled you in on what Miss Meyer was involved in."

Bobby Kennedy smiled. "Sandy had no concerns about taking you into his confidence." He took a sip of his strong coffee.

"With good reason," Jimmy said loyally. "This is Mrs. Roosevelt. The president's eyes, ears, and legs, they said."

Eleanor said, "From my meeting with Sandy, I understand there is no direct proof that Susan was spying. Only the fact that she met with Lev Valentsky and with his aide, Dmitri Petrov."

Jimmy was about to speak, but Bobby Kennedy said, "I agree, Mrs. Roosevelt, that it is a theory right now without definitive proof. Except Susan's body on the train, the poor kid."

"I asked Sandy, and I will ask the same question of you both: If Susan was feeding the Soviets information, why would they remove her?"

Jimmy ran his finger around the rim of his half-empty glass. He gave her the same response as Sandy. The idea of a love triangle where Susie was involved with both Valentsky and Petrov. "Sandy said she was meeting them at the Commodore Hotel in New York. An expensive hotel for a struggling actress who had to wait tables. We figure the bill was being paid by the Soviets. Sandy tried to talk to Valentsky and Petrov. Both are holed up at Killenworth. They won't talk to us. Whatever their motive, this has to be their handiwork."

"You visited Glen Cove," Bobby Kennedy said.

Of course they knew about that because Sandy did. "I was looking for Susan. She had gone missing. Elsa had told me she was concerned that Susan was involved with Communism, and I realized, when Elsa mailed me her photograph, that I saw her in New York with Lev Valentsky. I took her photograph around the village of Glen Cove."

"Do you think that's where she went when she disappeared?" Jimmy asked. "That she went to Killenworth?"

"I do not know what to think," Eleanor admitted. "She was seen in Glen Cove."

"She had to be holed up in Killenworth," Jimmy said. "Maybe that's where the two Soviets began to realize she was playing both of them."

"That is a theory," Eleanor said. "But we don't have proof."

"True," Bobby agreed. "No one knows where she was when she disappeared."

He broke off while the waiter delivered second drinks for the men and a fresh pot of tea for Eleanor.

"Is it possible Mrs. Meyer was involved in Susie's espionage activities? Didn't she specifically ask you not to talk to the police?" Bobby Kennedy asked.

"Sandy postulated the same theory. But I do not think Elsa Meyer would have involved her daughter in something so dangerous. Her explanation for not going to the police was the harsh and unreasonable tactics of Senator McCarthy. She said she feared Susan would be arrested for being a Communist agent."

"We don't convict innocent people," Jimmy said.

"I fear there have been occasions where Senator McCarthy did try," Eleanor said.

Jimmy's dark eyebrows went up—that combination of dark brows and long, dark lashes with fair hair made him very handsome.

"It doesn't sound like Susie was all that innocent," Jimmy said.

Eleanor maintained her calm. There was no proof of what

Susie had done with Valentsky. But she added, innocently, "Jimmy, there is a scratch on your cheek."

She had seen Kay's eyes rivet to the long mark, scabbed over. His hand jerked upward. He touched it. "My daughter," he said. A light blush came to his cheeks. "I was tickling her. She bites her nails, and they get ragged and scratchy. I'd hoped it would heal up by now. We've tried everything to get her to stop biting her nails. No punishment seems to work."

"I don't think punishments ever do," Eleanor said.

It was a perfectly reasonable explanation.

It was also, possibly, a lie.

The waiter returned with three plates heaped with food, balanced on a large platter. Conversation halted while they were served.

Eleanor had worked with Jimmy for three years. Devotion to his country was his hallmark. He adored his pretty, young wife and his daughter.

But could the scratch have been made by a woman trying to fight him off? Could it have been made by Susan?

Eleanor hated to even think it.

# CHAPTER 10

*We know nothing about each other and each one thinks
that the other is trying to hoodwink us, to put up a show
for our benefit, to make us believe something which isn't
true.*
— Eleanor Roosevelt, My Day, May 17, 1948

Kay had the night to herself. She was worried about Mrs. Roosevelt, but she rationalized that Mrs. Roosevelt was in a public place, and she was so famous and recognizable that nothing could happen to her.

She hailed a taxi on Connecticut Avenue. "Martin's Tavern in Georgetown," she said.

Rain began as the cab traveled down M Street, lined with classic buildings. They turned onto Wisconsin. Martin's Tavern was at the corner of Wisconsin and N Street.

Kay handed the driver a bill, told him to keep the change. As she got out onto the sidewalk, a blustery autumn wind hit her. Rain pelted her coat. She threw a scarf over her hair to protect it.

Maybe this was a crazy idea. When Mrs. Roosevelt came here before, when they were searching for Susan Meyer, Mrs. R had asked if Susan had a boyfriend. None of Susan's fellow waitresses knew anything about any men Susan was seeing.

But if Susan was seeing a married man, the other women

might have kept it quiet. That married man might have been spotted around Martin's Tavern. He might have obviously flirted with beautiful Susie Taylor. There might be a clue as to who that married Washington man was.

Three married Washington men had been on the train, after all: Sandy, Bobby Kennedy, and Jimmy Price.

The cab peeled away from the curb. As it moved, another gust of wind hit her. Her stiletto pumps skidded on the wet sidewalk, and the wind pushed her toward the edge of the curb. She lost her balance—

A dark shape whizzed toward her.

Someone grabbed her before she fell to the street, and jerked her back up, pulling her to safety as a shiny teal-blue sedan with a bright chrome grill roared past her. The driver leaned on the horn—it screamed in Kay's ears.

Off balance, with her heels sliding, she fell in the other direction, away from the road.

"*Blin,*" a deep voice growled, and Kay was pulled against a tall, masculine body.

"Your umbrella!" someone shouted.

"Umbrellas are replaceable. Ladies are not," the accented voice rumbled, using *s*'s that were not soft, but harder, longer, like drawn-out *z*'s.

Kay's cheek was pressed against a damp gray raincoat. Her breathing came at a hundred miles an hour. She smelled rain and . . . the same scent as she'd smelled in the *Royal Blue* washroom.

She jerked back from the man who had pulled her back from the car hurtling toward her. Who had saved her life. Who was wearing Caswell-Massey Number Six.

Piercing pale-blue eyes met her gaze evenly. His hands had hold of her arms, steadying her. The gusty, cool wind tousled blond hair, tossing it free and across his broad forehead. She gazed up at the sharp lines of his cheekbones and the etched lines of two deep scars.

"You're Dmitri Petrov," Kay breathed. Then wished she had kept her mouth shut. She tried to pull free, but his grip was too strong.

"You are secretary to Mrs. Roosevelt. You saw me. On the platform of the train."

"Let me go! Did you follow me here? If you don't let go of me right now, I'll scream."

At once he released her. "I did not follow you. I come here because this is famous tavern in Washington."

"And Susan Meyer just happened to work here."

"I do not know woman."

Kay lifted a brow. For a man with such a hard, arrogant expression, he did not lie well. When he denied knowing Susan, his cold eyes had softened. "I can see you do. Your eyes give you away. You know she was murdered on the *Royal Blue* train when it arrived in Union Station. I saw you on the platform. Did you get off that train?"

"Yes, I came from New York. But I know nothing about Susan's murder. I saw it in newspaper. The young woman murdered. Beautiful woman. But I do not know her."

Kay felt a tug of . . . not jealousy. It did get tiresome to keep hearing about how gorgeous Susie had been, as though she were nothing more than a mannequin. But those lovely looks didn't do Susie very much good in the end. "You're lying. You call her Susan as if you knew her well."

"It is idiosyncrasy of your language."

"It was emotion," Kay insisted. "And why did you run away on the platform, Mr. Petrov, if you didn't even know Susan was murdered?"

"You started shouting. I am Soviet. I thought I would be arrested, even though I was innocent man doing nothing wrong."

"You had to know Susan. She was dating your boss, Mr. Valentsky."

She had scored a hit. His eyes flared, filled for a moment

with passion. And anger. Then he controlled himself, giving a careless—and unconvincing—shrug.

"Comrade Valentsky enjoyed squiring pretty American woman on town, as you say. Miss Meyer's mother is famous. Revered scientist."

He certainly did know Susan. Kay stepped toward the door of Martin's Tavern. People hurried by, driven by the rain and the cold to race home. No one was paying any attention. She hoped that would change if she had to scream. "I am going into the tavern. And you are going to let me go."

"Are you going to call police?"

"Actually, Mr. Petrov, if you want, you can come inside and join me for a drink."

His brows shot up. "Do you not think I am criminal because I am Russian?"

Kay moved to the door, put her hand on the handle. She felt safe enough to turn back to him and ask, "Did you murder Susan?"

He stood in the middle of the sidewalk, glowering in the light spilling out of the windows of the tavern. "No, I did not harm her. I would not."

"Because you were in love with her too?"

He looked startled. "No, because I do not harm women."

"You were meeting Susan in a hotel room. While she was having dinner dates with Mr. Valentsky. You had to be lovers."

Petrov looked stunned. "How do you know this? I was not lovers with Susan. That was not why I met her."

"Then why?" Kay's heart beat fast. She was taking a huge risk.

"You think I am the villain. Like in a movie by Albert Hitch-cock."

"Alfred. And how do you know of Alfred Hitchcock?"

"I watch in theater in New York." He walked past her, to the varnished oak door of the tavern and opened it. "I will escort you inside, miss secretary. Buy you a drink. I will explain."

Kay wondered if she was going to end up at the wrong side of a gun. She had been terrified to encounter ice-blue eyes and now she was agreeing to a drink with him. But she had never done anything so thrilling in her life.

This beat dictation.

Also, if Dmitri Petrov had wanted her dead, he could have stood idly by and watched the car do it for him. A witness eliminated.

"All right. I'll have a martini," she said, as she walked past him, past the bow window with leaded panes that made her think of *A Christmas Carol*, and into Martin's Tavern. Every seat at the bar was occupied by a suit-clad man, with either a pint of beer or an old-fashioned glass with ice and scotch at the tips of his fingers.

Wood paneling gave an old-time tavern feel. Tiffany lamps hung over the long bar, the warm, tinted light glinting on the array of glasses and bottles. Intimate booths ran along the wall, with dark wood bench seats upholstered in green. A masculine-looking place, Kay thought. The sort of place men took refuge on a blustery Washington day like today.

Raucous cheers came from a room that bore a brass plaque reading THE DUGOUT ROOM. Susan Meyer/Susie Taylor must have made a lot of tips from Washington men.

Dmitri Petrov escorted her to a booth. He sat across from her.

The warm light of the swag lamp above them turned his hair to gold and enhanced the sharp planes of his cheekbones.

A waitress came over, a heavy-set, young, dark-haired woman. She took their order and in almost no time, two martinis came. Kay plucked her olive off the toothpick with her lips.

Petrov ignored his drink, gazing directly at her. "What is

your name? I called you secretary. Would you tell me your name?"

Being in a public place gave her confidence. Mrs. Roosevelt would question him—and do it courageously, she was sure. "My name is Kay."

"I was not in love with Susan, Kay. I knew her from many years ago when we were young. Before war. My father worked with her mother in Germany. My father had to leave when the Nazis began to round up the Jewish people. My father was not Jewish, but he was afraid. He feared that a Russian who possessed intelligence would be targeted and imprisoned. A year after he left, Mrs. Meyer also escaped."

His father escaped from Nazi Germany to end up in Communist Russia? He had leaped from frying pan to fire, in Kay's opinion.

"I encountered Susan by chance in New York. She was leaving an audition. A beautiful girl, but when she sang . . ."

"She was good?"

"Her high notes made my back teeth ache," Petrov said solemnly.

"But Susan wanted to be on Broadway."

"I told her that she should go to Hollywood. It is glamorous there and they discover blond women at counters in diners."

"I think most of those stories are made up, Mr. Petrov."

Boyish enthusiasm had lit up his face. Impulsively, Kay said, "I didn't think you would approve of America, Mr. Petrov. Your boss, Valentsky, doesn't."

"Hyperbole. He must serve his masters. We cannot be seen to accept what Americans say."

"Ah. Is that why Mr. Valentsky condemns us but likes to go out to American restaurants?"

"Maybe that is so." He downed his martini in one gulp. She stared in astonishment. As he set his glass down, she saw he was left-handed. She saw he was missing his pinkie finger.

He glanced down. "Bullet wound. I was sniping Germans and forgot the movement of the cloud—it passed across the moon, allowing the silver light to reflect off my weapon and I became target. I did not know about shooting in war. Paper targets and deer never shot back. But there was no sympathy. I was seventeen—old enough to have many more wits. I had to keep firing."

"You were in battle? At seventeen?"

"When the Nazis invaded, we went and signed up. We just shrugged and said we had lost our birth certificates. We thought we might be caught. Until we learned they did not care who they sent out in front of machine gunfire."

"You survived. You were fortunate."

"Most days we thought those who froze to death at night were fortunate. Those who woke up were the cursed ones."

Kay signaled the waitress. Another drink arrived for Mr. Petrov. She thought getting him inebriated might get her the truth.

Halfway through his second martini, he was talking expansively about the war.

"Mostly we walked. They had no way to take us anywhere. No mechanized vehicles. We walked through the soles of our flimsy boots as our feet blistered. They said we did not walk fast enough to honor Stalin. One man argued and they shot him in front of us. It worked. The rest of us walked faster.

"I was taken prisoner in the mountains in early December, late in the afternoon, as the light was dying. As we marched, we came upon a village. There was one little boy, his face wet from crying. There was nobody to take care of him. He called for his mother. We were so sad for this little boy.

"I thought of that boy often. I do not know what happened to him. If he lived or died. He was alone, his family killed. My heart hurt for him. What good was the war? What good if we orphaned the German children or they orphaned ours? What use if all children starved and froze and died in the mud and the snow?"

Kay blinked tears, swallowed hard. But part of her wondered if he was telling her stories to play on her emotions.

"I should not talk of these things. You do not have your drink."

"No, no, please do talk to me. You survived the war, despite being captured."

"Many died. Millions. There was no food. We were always cold. I grew thinner, but I was too strong to die. I thought that I might be dead, and I was in a hell where I was paying for the lives I took."

"You had no choice," Kay said.

"After the war, I went to the United Nations, working for Comrade Valentsky. He knew my father—in truth, he was the one to ensure my father was shot."

"Your father was shot?" she gasped.

"He was accused of sabotage and tried by Valentsky."

"And you *worked* for him? The man who had your father *shot*?"

"It allowed me to get on train, leave the Soviet Union, and get out of automobile in Geneva. It allowed me to come here. Would my father say—stand on your pride, stand up to that butcher, die like me? Or would he say—bide your time and one day you will be in a place where if you want a new job, you can change it. If you want to talk, you can speak. You can shout if you want, without fear."

"You can't quite shout everywhere, Mr. Petrov, but I understand what you mean."

"My father would have said, hold your tongue, Dmitri, swallow your anger, and you will get to that place where you can have your own thoughts and you can have knowledge and people do not fear you for that. He would say that he will lie happier in his grave knowing his sacrifice was not made only to get me shot. I was last of us. What use if I die too?"

He threw back the rest of his drink as if it was water. "I have worked hard. I have been dutiful to the Party. But one day, I was out in New York City. I was where there are theaters and a woman almost collided with me. I was struck dumb. I knew her face. I remembered her from past. She took me to diner. I had a cherry soda. And a hot dog with yellow on top."

"Mustard," Kay said.

"If life is to end in hell, why not eat hot dogs with this stuff you call mustard and drink cherry soda?"

Petrov waved the waitress over and asked her what soda flavors they had. He deliberated for minutes before deciding on orange.

In that moment, Kay could picture him sliding on the floor with Mrs. Roosevelt.

And she knew.

It was not Susan Meyer with whom he had fallen in love.

"Mr. Petrov," she said, keeping her voice to a husky whisper, "you fell in love with America."

He said nothing. Kay stayed quiet as his orange soda was served. Once they were alone, she pressed her point. "You want to stay in America," she said. "Is that why you are wearing an American cologne?"

"Susan bought some for me. She said she liked the scent. She joked that if I wished to live in America, I should embrace this very good cologne. Then she said she could help me."

The hotel room meetings. "Were you meeting with her at the hotel to plan a defection?" she asked. "Was Sandiston involved?"

"No."

"Jimmy Price?" she asked.

"I do not know this man."

"Was it Mr. Robert Kennedy?" It could be any government man, but she knew she had scored a hit when he said, "I cannot say."

It also meant Robert Kennedy did know Susan Meyer.

Petrov laid his hands on the table. "I am an innocent man, Kay. And you must call me Dmitri. I did not hurt Susan. But I would break neck of man who did."

"Do you have any idea who it was?" She hesitated, then plunged on. "Could it have been Valentsky?"

"No, he cared about Susan. He loved her, old fool."

"But he might have been jealous. Jealous of you."

Petrov reared back in surprise at her words. "He would not think me as rival for Susan. I have lowly position."

"Did Susie tell you about any men in her life? Boyfriends. If you weren't a boyfriend, I mean."

"She told me she was in love. The last time I saw her, she told me she was going to be with man. She said he loved her deeply. He would give up everything for her."

"What did she mean?" Kay's heart pattered. Had he meant he would give up his marriage for her?

"I do not know," Dmitri said. "But I think bas—villain killed her."

"You came here for the same reason as me," Kay said. "You want to find Susan's killer. You want him to pay."

"I came here yesterday to ask waitresses, but they won't talk to me."

"They are probably suspicious of you. Why don't I try?"

Kay waved their waitress over.

She was ready to try to get at the truth.

Or was the truth sitting across from her, smiling wistfully as he took the last slurps of his orange soda?

Like Mrs. Roosevelt, she *liked* Dmitri Petrov. He wasn't the cold, hard Communist she expected. She felt sorry for the teenager whose heart had ached for a boy even younger than himself. Whose scars came from a horrible war in which it was a mercy to freeze to death. She liked this man who had lost so much and who loved the simple pleasures of America, its freedoms and democracy.

She sensed everything he told her was true. But was it because she *wanted* to believe it?

Susan had bought the cologne for Dmitri Petrov. Had she also bought it for someone else? The man who loved her deeply?

Dmitri Petrov reached out across the table, but he didn't touch her hand.

She gazed at the elegance of his long fingers and the one that was half missing. She had to remember: those fingers had brought death in battle.

But because he had to do it.

She let her fingers slide forward a little more, so her red-polished fingernails (matching her lipstick) almost grazed his fingertips.

His pale-blue eyes gazed at her earnestly. "The Kremlin demands I return to Moscow. Valentsky is at Glen Cove, holed up, claiming diplomatic immunity. My plan is to turn myself in to police, offering to answer their questions. The State Department will remove me, put me in their custody, and while Kremlin fights with your State Department to extract me, I disappear. With the help of your government, I get new name. New home."

Kay wanted to believe him.

*Don't be a fool*, she thought. But she couldn't help it. She wanted him to be innocent.

He stood suddenly, giving her a small formal bow. He was tall, taller than Detective O'Malley. She no longer saw him as evil Tab Hunter. He was as handsome as any Hitchcock hero.

He placed several bills on the table—far more than their few drinks had cost. "I must go. I left Killenworth to stay at Hotel Harrington in Washington. But the Kremlin will find me."

"Then go and talk to the police. Let them know you are innocent and that you want to stay here," she said, breathlessly.

He nodded.

Was she mad? Could she trust him?

She had even told Mrs. Roosevelt not to trust likable young

men. Yet looking into Dmitri's blue eyes and handsome face, she more than liked him. And she wanted to trust.

He left then, walking out into the dark, rainy afternoon. Kay had picked up the money he had left and had it folded in her hand as the curvy dark-haired waitress returned. "Left you with the check, huh?"

Kay was going to protest Dmitri's innocence in that regard, then she saw the look of sympathy. It was a way to win the woman's trust.

Ruefully, she nodded.

"The good-looking ones always do that," the waitress said, her voice heavy with cynicism. "Maybe they're generous at first, but then they start forgetting their wallets. They promise to pay you back, but they forget that too. They *know* how handsome they are."

"It's so true," Kay sympathized.

She had her way in.

# CHAPTER 11

The Un-American Activities Committee seems to me to
be better for a police state than for the USA.
—Eleanor Roosevelt, My Day, October 29, 1947

Bobby Kennedy and Jimmy Price wolfed down their two-
inch-thick steaks as only young men could, while Eleanor related her telephone conversation with Elsa Meyer in detail. She
described her search for Susan.

She explained that Susan telephoned her and asked to meet
her at the station.

"Why at the station?" Jimmy asked.

"I don't know. Susan said she wanted to meet me and tell me
to put her mother's mind at ease. She did say that she had been
a fool," Eleanor said.

"A fool? Maybe Susan believed she was in danger," Bobby
Kennedy theorized. "She felt you were the only person she
could turn to, Mrs. Roosevelt. The only person she could trust."

"Possibly," Eleanor said.

"Guess we'll never know," Jimmy said.

"No, I suppose not."

Had Susan been killed to prevent their meeting? But who
would know of it? What had Susan wanted to tell her? Eleanor
sensed it was more than simply reassuring Elsa. The phone call

from Susan, telling Eleanor she was safe and sound, would have been enough.

And why had Susan bitterly recriminated herself for being a fool?

"I can't figure why no one caught this guy," Jimmy said. "Susan must have screamed in that washroom when the guy pulled out a knife. Why didn't the porter break the door down and rescue her?"

"That is the most curious thing," Eleanor said. "The police detective surmised that Susan was killed after the train had reached the station and the passengers left the lounge. That makes sense. There was a small window of opportunity between the passengers leaving to return to their own seats and the arrival of the train in the station. A window of opportunity to be unobserved by other passengers."

"What about the porter? Didn't he see or hear anything?"

"That is also a curious thing. Mr. Alfred Jeffers was the lounge car porter, but when he took me to Susan's body, he did not tell me that."

"Maybe he did it," Jimmy said.

"I don't think so," Eleanor replied, frowning slightly at Jimmy. "You knew Sandy was keeping tabs on Susan before she was murdered?"

Jimmy nodded. "Sandy put HUAC in the loop."

"We were hoping to learn if Susie Meyer was spying and who her American contacts were," Bobby Kennedy said.

Their dinner plates were cleared away. The gentlemen's plates were almost licked clean. Eleanor had barely touched her meal. The waiter gave his suggestion for dessert, and within minutes, thick slices of the Mayflower's signature banana nut bread dessert came out, along with port for the two gentlemen and coffee for all three.

Jimmy and Bobby tucked enthusiastically into the banana bread.

Eleanor stirred her spoon in her coffee.

She was not supposed to be involved. But Kay was correct. What if Sandy was covering for someone? What if Sandy was covering for himself?

She could not ignore that possibility.

All the men *claimed* to have left the platform before the porter ran out, shouting about finding a murdered woman.

If she could ascertain that Sandy, Jimmy, and Bobby Kennedy had been with their wives, they had alibis. Even if the men were covering for one another, would the women lie? To cover up for a husband who murdered his mistress? Eleanor didn't think so. There was a limit to what a woman would tolerate.

"It is so remarkable that you were both on the train with Susan. But neither of you knew that she was there?" Eleanor asked.

"No, ma'am," Jimmy said, ingenuously. His slice of banana bread was already gone.

Was that a flicker in Robert Kennedy's heavy-lidded eyes? "Did you, Mr. Kennedy?"

"Sandy was keeping me informed. He told me Susan Meyer usually traveled on the *Royal Blue* back to Washington on Thursday after she'd spent a few days in New York, supposedly at auditions. I knew she might be on the train."

"Did you look for her?"

"No, ma'am. I was 'off duty,' traveling with my wife and child."

"It is so unfortunate that one of you gentlemen didn't see anything suspicious. One of the Soviet men on board, for example."

Jimmy held up his hands. "I wish I had. But like Bobby, I had my family with me and was not focused on the job. I took Debra and little Belinda up to New York so I could show them the city in between meetings. The wives went shopping together when we men had engagements."

"Were you all together on the train?"

Jimmy looked to Bobby Kennedy. "We had seats close together. I was going over papers, and Debbie was keeping our girl amused, taking her for walks up and down the carriages. You know what kids are like."

"I do." Eleanor smiled. Jimmy spoke like a world-weary father, when he had been a parent for only a half-dozen years. Eleanor had raised five children after losing one.

"Then Belinda started to feel sick. I surrendered my seat so she could lie down. I found an empty one in the next first-class carriage. When we were close to the station, I went back to my carriage to get the bags. Debbie and Belinda had come back from being out on the observation platform. They went out to get some air."

"You were together when the train reached the station?"

"Yes, ma'am," Jimmy said.

"Ethel had the baby with us," Bobby said.

After Eleanor congratulated him on the birth of their daughter he continued. "When she was in the washroom with wee Kathleen, I decided to walk through the carriages and stretch my legs. I passed by Mrs. Price and went out on the observation deck."

"That meant you passed through the lounge car."

"I did. I got some ginger ale for Ethel on my way back."

"And you didn't notice Susan?"

"No, ma'am," Bobby said. "I didn't. If I passed her, I think I would recognize her. I admit Susan was hard to miss. Sandy got up a few times too. I assumed he went to the lounge himself. He went out onto the observation deck to have a cigarette."

"When was that?" Eleanor asked.

Bobby frowned. "I can't remember. He smoked a few cigarettes on the journey. He looked worried."

"What of Mrs. Sandiston?"

"Letitia stayed in her seat, reading *Modern Screen*. I remember she was annoyed when we got off the train because she had to look for Sandy."

Sandy was not with Letitia when the train arrived, Eleanor noted.

"I wish I had gone to the lounge," Jimmy put in. His words slurred a little after the whiskeys and the glass of port. "I might have run into one of those Soviets. Either Valentsky or Petrov. But we'll get them, Mrs. Roosevelt. Don't you worry."

"I have every confidence in you, gentlemen," Eleanor said.

She looked at them both appealingly, with the air of a confused grandmother. "I have a question for you both, as young gentlemen."

They shared a look of surprise, and she went on. "I want to buy some cologne for my friend David Gurewitsch. Something distinctive to Washington. What would you young men recommend?"

Jimmy grinned. "I use Aqua Velva myself. My father used it when it was first introduced and sold as a mouthwash."

"I'd recommend Caswell-Massey," Bobby Kennedy said.

Eleanor nodded. "Which would you recommend? Is there one that you wear?"

"My brother likes their Jockey Club," Bobby Kennedy said.

"And yourself?"

But Mr. Kennedy summoned the check. Eleanor asked again, but he smiled disarmingly and said he thought his brother's cologne would make a better choice for a gift. After that, he stood, shook her hand, apologized for rushing off, then he was gone.

Jimmy walked her out of the restaurant.

"It was really nice to see you again, Mrs. Roosevelt."

"Jimmy," she said impetuously. "I will be coming back in a few days. With Susan Meyer's mother. May I invite you and Debra to dinner here at the Mayflower before I leave for New York?"

Jimmy hesitated. "Sorry, Mrs. Roosevelt, I know Debra would be awestruck to meet you, but my schedule is completely full. I'm working day and night for HUAC."

"Perhaps another time then," Eleanor said.

Jimmy shook her hand and left, turning back to wave.

As she waved in return, Eleanor knew she should not be involving herself in any investigation. But she thought of the scratch. Of the fact that Sandy had not been with his wife or the other men as the train entered the station.

# CHAPTER 12

*I found him a brilliant man with a quick mind, anxious to learn, hospitable to new ideas, hardheaded in his approach . . . he wanted, I felt convinced, to be a truly great president.*

—Eleanor Roosevelt, circa 1961

Kay pushed over Petrov's stack of bills. "Keep the change."

The waitress's eyes widened as she estimated the size of the tip that would come from that pile. She had thick, jet-black hair arranged on top of her head in big curls, held with hairspray. Her dark brows needed to be plucked into a more defined line, but she possessed the longest eyelashes Kay had seen on a woman. The kind of lashes that usually maddeningly adorned a man's eyes.

Like Detective O'Malley.

"Why don't you sit for a moment?" Kay asked the waitress. "What's your name? Let me buy you a drink. I'm sure you need one. I tried waitressing once."

"I'm Lucia," the waitress said. She was clearing the empty glasses, placing them on her tray. She then gestured toward the bar. "I'm not allowed to sit until the end of my shift."

"I can wait," Kay said. "You know, I only lasted one night as a waitress. A man grabbed a handful of my rear end, and as I swung around to tell him off, all my dishes went sliding off my tray. I was fired at the end of the shift. But at least the guy who grabbed me watched his dinner end up on the floor.

Lucia grinned. "Serves him right. And you know, the grabby ones are bad tippers."

"I'd like to talk to you about Susan Meyer."

"Who?"

"Susie Taylor," Kay corrected, using Susan's stage name.

"Oh. Susie."

"Can I buy you a drink at the end of your shift and we can talk?"

The waitress looked at her warily. "I go home right after work. My mother gets suspicious if I'm late."

"I won't keep you long. I'm Kay Thompson, secretary to Mrs. Roosevelt—the former First Lady."

Lucia nodded. "I met her. When she came before, asking about Susie. I didn't know what had happened to Susie. She just upped and left. I was stuck covering for her."

"You must have read that her body was found on a train," Kay said. "She was murdered."

"I don't know anything about that," Lucia said sharply.

"I'm not accusing you of anything. But I think you can help. Help get justice for Susie. I think you didn't tell Mrs. Roosevelt everything you knew."

It was a bluff, but it worked. Lucia looked down at the table, blushing. She looked ashamed. "I couldn't. Mrs. Roosevelt had been sent by Susie's mother. I thought Susie had gone away with a man. And with those kinds of men, a girl usually has to come back. I didn't want to snitch on Susie to her mother."

"And now you're worried. Because you knew she was seeing someone—and that man might have killed her."

"I already talked to a police detective about this."

"Mrs. Roosevelt isn't the police. But she is trying to help Susan's mother. If you can help, you must. You can't let a murderer go free."

"I don't know who the man was," Lucia said. "That's what I told the police detective. I don't know anything about him."

"You must have seen him."

"He never met Susie in here. She always went out to his car." Lucia's eyes slid away again.

"You saw him, didn't you? I bet you followed Susie once, to see what he looked like. You wanted to know which of the men who came here was dating her."

Lucia stared at her like she could read minds. "I did," she admitted. "He never got out of the car. I never saw his face. He obviously didn't want anyone to know he and Susie were an item. I figured he was married."

"That's why you didn't tell Mrs. Roosevelt?"

"I didn't want Susie's mother finding out. Susie told me that her mother didn't want her to date. She would get angry about it. I understand. My mother wants me to marry the boy next door. The chubby one who is tied to his mother's apron strings. Susie was always telling me I could do better." Lucia rolled her big brown eyes. "I keep hoping I will find Prince Charming here. Susie was the only one who got close with her tall, blond, handsome man. So far, I've served a lot of beer to many frogs."

"I kept thinking I'd find a handsome, charming executive with a big house in the country. So far, it hasn't worked." Kay rolled her eyes too. "But when Susan was murdered . . ."

"I talked to the detective and told him what I knew. My mother was angry I involved myself with the police. She wants me to quit. She thinks I'm going to get murdered next." Lucia shivered. "I keep wondering if it was one of the men who come in here—"

"Lucia!"

Lucia swiveled toward the terse shout. Kay looked too. A big man in a suit pointed to the other booths.

Lucia lifted the tray. "That's all I know. I have to go." She started to move away.

"Wait," Kay called. "If you didn't see him, how do you know he was tall and blond?" The words flew out, almost as fast as Kay's heart pounded.

"I didn't see him, but Susie had caught me spying. The next day she said she couldn't tell me who her boyfriend was, but he was tall, blond, and handsome. They had to keep the relationship a secret. But whoever killed her was a coward. A pig."

Lucia began to move away.

"Would she have told any of the other waitresses about him?" Kay asked swiftly. "Did she have a close friend?"

"Susie wasn't close with anyone. She didn't really make friends," Lucia said. She hurried away, stopping by a booth filled with rowdy men in suits.

Leaving Kay deep in thought.

Tall. Blond. And he needed to keep the relationship a secret. Sandiston? Jimmy Price? Or Dmitri?

She was attracted to a man who could be a killer. And instead of running as fast as she could, Kay wanted to dig further.

She supposed it wasn't worthwhile talking to the other waitresses. She supposed if Susie had been a spy, Susie didn't want to make other friends.

"Penny for your thoughts," a male voice said. "You look troubled."

The strong Boston accent startled Kay. She looked up and found herself face-to-face with Congressman John Kennedy, who was standing by her table.

"I . . . I'm fine, thank you," she began. Then she stopped, her tongue tripping helplessly in her mouth. She took in the head of thick, slightly unruly hair. The suit that looked a bit too large. The charming smile and brilliant eyes.

"I'm Jack Kennedy."

"I know."

He turned toward the tall, powerfully built man who stood by the bar, to introduce him. "My friend, Hal Green." His-friend was giving their order to the bartender. Hal gave her a friendly wave and got back to business.

"I'm K-Kay Thompson," she stuttered. She never stuttered around men. "I work for Mrs. Roosevelt."

"Which Mrs. Roosevelt?"

"Eleanor Roosevelt," Kay said.

"I'm impressed. Miss Thompson, can I buy you a drink?" Jack Kennedy asked.

Hal, who had joined them, laughed. "You never have your wallet on you. You'll end up borrowing the cash from me." He looked at Kay. "His father pays all his bills. He never carries money, and he doesn't care what things cost consequently. I usually end up footing the bill for drinks. Why don't I get drinks and we'll go back to the Dugout?"

Jack Kennedy offered her his arm. Kay accepted with a beguiling smile.

At least, she hoped it was beguiling.

She had been thrown in the path of Washington's most eligible bachelor.

But all she could think of was Dmitri Petrov and whether he had lied to her all along.

# CHAPTER 13

*Perhaps it isn't a bad thing when your emotions are stirred in the right direction, to have them become a wellspring of action.*
—Eleanor Roosevelt, My Day, February 23, 1943

Room service delivered breakfast. While they ate eggs and toast, Kay quickly related to ER what she had discovered the day before.

"You took a great risk meeting with Mr. Petrov, but you were very clever to stay in a public place with him," Mrs. Roosevelt said. "It is very interesting to discover that Mr. Petrov wishes to leave the Soviet Union and remain in America."

"When he spoke of his past, of his worries for that small child, I couldn't imagine him killing Susan. But he *is* tall, blond, and handsome."

"Handsome even with the scars?"

"Now that I know how he came by the scars, they do make him seem more heroic. He is missing part of his finger." She told Mrs. Roosevelt the story.

"And he is left-handed?" Mrs. Roosevelt asked.

"Yes. The wound is on his left hand." Kay finished her coffee. "I talked to the other waitresses who were there, but they couldn't give me any more information about Susan's mystery boyfriend. No one saw him. His car was a black sedan. How more unidentifiable and ordinary could it be?"

"How did you size up Mr. Petrov?"

"Innocent," Kay breathed. "I think he is innocent."

"What of Mr. Kennedy and Mr. Price?".

Kay blushed. She knew Eleanor liked Mr. Price. "Mr. Kennedy seems like the kind of man who grew from a boy with an overbearing father. He is obviously clever. For all his family has the reputation of being Casanovas with women, I think he is a different sort of man. I saw the loving smile he gave whenever he spoke of his new wife."

Kay nibbled on her toast thoughtfully. "I don't think he would murder someone for himself. But he might . . . to protect someone he loved."

"What of Jimmy Price?"

"I could see Susan falling for him. And I think his ego would have enjoyed her attention. And he has that scar."

"He explained that his daughter scratched him."

"It's plausible. I guess."

"I would like him to be innocent," Mrs. Roosevelt admitted. "I know it is not so simple. I know we are not supposed to be investigating, but talking to people we know is not really investigating."

Kay had thought Mrs. Roosevelt would scrupulously follow the rules. She was also astonished that Mrs. Roosevelt said "we."

"When I am at the U.N., there is much that happens in informal meetings I hold at night—more gets done there than in the formal sessions."

Mrs. Roosevelt poured Kay more coffee, ignoring Kay's protests that she should do that.

"I met someone else last night. A man who frequents Martin's Tavern. Congressman Jack Kennedy," Kay said. Her cheeks felt hot.

"What did you think of Jack Kennedy?"

"Charming. Relaxed around women. Very intelligent. He's a war hero. We had drinks in the Dugout room with his friend, Hal Green. Jack—I mean, Mr. Kennedy," Kay corrected with a blush, "told me that he once took Susan out to the Shore Club. He insisted it was only one date. In fact, he said he would like to take me out with him before I return to New York, if his schedule allowed. He is planning a six-week tour of Asia with his brother Bobby. He said he would call."

Kay knew her blush had deepened. Too often men said they would call a woman . . . and didn't.

"He is a very eligible bachelor," Mrs. Roosevelt said. Kay was certain there was a twinkle in her eye. She wondered if that was encouragement . . . or a warning.

"Do you think he is a possible suspect?" Kay asked. "His hair could not be described as blond. It is medium brown with a definite reddish tinge."

Mrs. Roosevelt nodded. "I believe we must be careful. But it is true that Mr. Kennedy is not blond." She finished her coffee and added, "My schedule is packed with events all day. I had hoped to go to Union Station when the *Royal Blue* arrives, but I fear it will be impossible. I wanted to tackle Mr. Jeffers with the truth that he was working in the lounge car."

"I'll go."

"I don't like the idea of you confronting him alone."

"Mrs. Roosevelt, you would have gone alone. I promise I can take care of myself."

"Be very careful."

"Do you think—?"

"I don't think Mr. Jeffers is guilty of committing the crime, Kay. But he lied, and he must have had a reason to do so. Confronting him may make him feel threatened. That is why you must be careful. You should have someone else with you."

Kay shook her head. "I don't think he will open up unless I'm alone."

A knock at the door surprised Kay. She answered it and a bell boy handed her a bouquet of red roses wrapped in paper. He handed the card, looking hopeful. Kay put the flowers down on the small table that sat by the door, and fetched a quarter. She handed it to the young man, then she closed the door. The card surprised her.

*Nice to meet you. Will call. Jack.*

When she told Mrs. Roosevelt the flowers were from Jack Kennedy, who she'd met the night before, Mrs. Roosevelt said, "It's said his ambition is to run for president one day." Kay saw her eyes twinkle again. Jack Kennedy said he took Susie dancing only once and likely that was the truth.

"I will call room service and ask them to bring a vase," Kay said. Her heart gave an excited thump. If she played her cards right, could *she* end up as a president's wife?

As Kay helped Mrs. Roosevelt prepare to go out, Mrs. Roosevelt spoke of the days when the porters set up their union, the Brotherhood of Sleeping Car Porters.

Helping Mrs. Roosevelt on with her coat, Kay realized Mrs. R was telling her about this to explain the strength and uprightness that Alfred Jeffers possessed.

Before they unionized, the porters' jobs required them to leave their families for weeks at a time, receiving no more than three hours of sleep a night. It made for a horrifying twenty-one-hour workday. They were subjected to discrimination within their jobs and from the people they served. Porters could be fired without reason or recourse. Most porters were nicknamed "George" by their customers, who refused to use their real names. It was humiliating and degrading, for it removed their individuality and identity, Mrs. Roosevelt observed.

Black porters were denied job promotions. Some wanted to

join newly established labor unions for white porters but were blocked from joining because of their race. In the 1920s, Black porters decided to form their own union.

Mrs. Roosevelt explained that Alfred Jeffers had worked to create the union. As she became more involved in politics, she supported his initiative. They had corresponded. They became friends as she spoke in support of the union to her husband. Mrs. Roosevelt had addressed the Brotherhood of Sleeping Car Porters convention at the Harlem YMCA in September 1940.

Then Kay and Mrs. Roosevelt went downstairs. After seeing Mrs. Roosevelt off in her taxi, Kay took a cab to Union Station.

At the station, Kay hurried down to the platform to meet the *Royal Blue*. She shivered at the sight of it and felt a twist in her heart. People streamed out of the cars, carrying on their normal lives. The world had moved on without Susan Meyer.

Kay climbed up into the lounge car. Her breath came faster. She tried not to think of Susan's body, lying in the washroom, covered in blood. She shut out that horrible black-and-white movie-style imagery that played in her head.

The porter had been bending down behind the bar. As he rose, he grabbed a weapon and whipped around. It was Winston Jackson.

Kay stared at the spoon in his hand. As he realized she wasn't going to murder him, he sheepishly put the spoon down.

"I'm sorry to startle you. My name is Kay Thompson. I wanted to speak to Mr. Jeffers."

"He's not on the train today, miss," Mr. Jackson told her.

"Is he not well?"

"I don't know. I haven't seen him since that day when I found that woman's body."

Kay frowned. She made her way up to the stationmaster's office and explained Mrs. Roosevelt had sent her to speak to Mr. Jeffers.

It never occurred to the stationmaster that Kay had no real

authority to speak to anyone. He stood to attention as he heard Mrs. Roosevelt's name.

The problem, he explained, was that Alfred Jeffers had missed work since the day the body had been discovered. He had telephoned Jeffers at home. Mrs. Jeffers answered and hesitatingly insisted that her husband was sick. She was warned that Alfred would be fired if he didn't show up for work. That was yesterday. As far as the B&O company was concerned, Alfred Jeffers no longer worked for them.

As soon as Kay returned to the suite at the Mayflower, the telephone rang. Pulling off her outdoor gloves, Kay saw it was a call from the front desk. She picked it up.

"Kay, it's Sandy here."

"Yes?"

"Dmitri Petrov has been arrested by Detective O'Malley."

"Arrested?" she cried.

"Yes. Petrov approached the police, declaring he was willing to answer their questions. They found evidence in his room tying him to Susan's murder."

"Evidence?" she exclaimed. "What evidence?"

"I'm working to get Petrov out of their custody. It won't take long—O'Malley knows he is off the case. I'll bring Petrov in here. But Petrov has refused to speak to anyone but Mrs. Roosevelt."

# CHAPTER 14

*To have a friend who knows you by name gives you a
sense that you are not alone in the world.*
    —Eleanor Roosevelt, My Day, April 23, 1962

"I asked for you because you are a champion of justice,
Mrs. Roosevelt. I have learned this about you at United Nations. Especially from my comrades' frustration with you."

"Of course, I wish to make sure that justice is done,
Mr. Petrov."

Eleanor gazed at the weary-looking, young, blond man
seated across from her. They were in a small, windowless gray
room at the police station. Metal cuffs secured Dmitri Petrov's
hands to the table at which they sat. Petrov sat facing the large
mirror behind them. Eleanor suspected it was a two-way mirror, allowing the police to witness everything they did.

This was speculation, for Mrs. Roosevelt had never seen the
inside of a police station. Though she had many political oppo-
nents who claimed they would like to see her in one—prefer-
ably in a holding cell, behind bars.

Dmitri had been brought out of one of those holding cells.
He was being kept in isolation. Protective custody, Sandy called
it. Sandy was working on Petrov's removal from the precinct,
but Eleanor knew it meant incarceration somewhere else. Dmitri
was not going to be allowed to walk free.

"I presume what we say is being overheard and observed," Mrs. Roosevelt said quietly.

"I am innocent man, Mrs. Roosevelt."

At the United Nations, Dmitri Petrov, the cool, quiet blond aide to Lev Valentsky, exuded controlled patience. Valentsky was the great orator, booming out insults to the Americans with passion.

In fact, the only time she saw Mr. Petrov's controlled expression crack was when he had followed her slide across the highly polished marble floor. He whooped and grinned like a happy boy.

Exhaustion showed in his eyes, yet Eleanor knew he had been a sniper in the war, able to remain awake for hours, motionless yet coiled, patient and alert, waiting to kill those who had threatened his homeland.

But that was war. Was he a cold-blooded murderer?

Kay, who had an ability to size up men, believed in him. That made Eleanor think she was not being foolish to believe in Dmitri Petrov.

Eleanor had wished to have Kay here, in the interrogation room. Kay was brave, resourceful, clever and people opened up to her. But Sandy insisted Eleanor speak with Dmitri alone.

Kay was waiting in the police bullpen.

"Has an injustice been carried out here, Mr. Petrov?" Eleanor asked. "Evidence was found in your hotel room—"

"What right had the police to search my room?" he demanded, his voice deep and cold.

That was a shaky point, Eleanor had to agree. Sandy had explained as he drove her and Kay to the police station.

"Valentsky is holed up at Glen Cove, claiming diplomatic immunity. We can't get near him," he complained. "Meanwhile, Petrov presented himself to the police, revealed that he was on the train, that he knew Susan and was willing to answer American officials. While his partner talked to Petrov, Detective O'Malley went to Petrov's hotel. He claims he heard someone shouting for help in Petrov's room and so he had to break in. It's an illegal search, but he knew I was going to come in and get Petrov anyway. Susie Meyer's compact was found under Petrov's bed. And it was Susie's—her fellow waitresses at Martin's Tavern remembered it. It had her initials engraved with a few tiny diamonds. Expensive trinket. Must have been a gift from one of the men she was bedding."

Eleanor had been startled. Not just by the news but by the speed Sandiston raced around the corner. She didn't see the need for such reckless driving. Rather amusing since she had always been considered a fast and somewhat reckless driver herself. Earl Miller, her bodyguard, always warned her to slow down.

"As soon as Petrov saw the compact, he clammed up," Sandy continued. "O'Malley had to let me know he had the Soviet. Hoover wants the FBI to question Petrov. I thought J. Edgar would have gotten his back up when Petrov said he would only speak to you, but he said he'd graciously allow it. He's up to something."

"Who is?" she had inquired.

"Hoover. At least I think he is, since he'd like to brand you a Communist, Mrs. Roosevelt."

"I should think my run-ins with Mr. Valentsky at the U.N. are clear proof I am not a Communist, but if Mr. Hoover wishes to amass more files on me, I wish he would not do so with the public's money," she said. "Do you think Dmitri Petrov is responsible for Susan's death, Sandy?"

Her friend's expression hardened. "I think he is as guilty as sin. The compact is proof."

Eleanor felt unease.

Was Sandy so vehement because he was guilty? In the rearview mirror, she saw Kay's eyebrows rise.

Now, Petrov faced her across the table, his expression frosty yet filled with pride. "Valentsky mocked American prisons. He is right. They are soft. But I do not belong in here. I swear to you, Mrs. Roosevelt, I am innocent."

"Can you tell me how Susan Meyer's compact ended up under your bed?"

"The police ask me about this compact. I have never seen this thing. I do not know what it is." Dmitri's handsome brow furrowed. He had film-star looks. Even now when he looked as if he had not slept all night.

She supposed it was possible he did not know. Eleanor, who never used one, thought of how to explain it. She thought of the one she saw Kay use regularly.

"It is a round metal case with a lid that flips up. There is a mirror on one side and pressed powder in the other. A woman opens the compact, uses a little pad, and powders her nose."

His brow cleared. "I have seen Susan do that. Gazing into a tiny round mirror, she banged a pad against bridge of her nose and made dust."

"Yes, that is a compact. Susan Meyer's compact is distinctive, with her initials engraved on it, decorated with diamonds. Why did you have it, Mr. Petrov?"

"I did not. The police say I dropped it out of Susan's handbag, which I stole when I killed her. This is not true."

"How did it get in your room?"

"The way it is always done." His voice heavy with cynicism, Mr. Petrov leaned back in his chair. "It was put there."

"By whom?"

He hesitated, then shrugged. "American police."

Eleanor shook her head. "I am here to help you, Mr. Petrov. But lying to me will not help."

"I do not lie. Your secretary knows my plans. I want to stay in America. But Mr. Sandiston of your State Department wants to see me convicted. It would be convenient."

"Why do you say that? Who do you believe harmed Susan, Mr. Petrov?"

"I have no ideas. I know only that it was not me."

"Do you think it was Lev Valentsky?"

A long pause. He shifted in his seat. "My comrade would not implicate me. It would stain our Party."

"I believe you told Miss Thompson that Valentsky was instrumental in the death of your father. It seems to me he would then be capable of framing you."

He shrugged again. "But Valentsky could not hurt Susan. He adored Susan. He thought she was in love with him." He said an expression in Russian.

"I'm afraid I do not understand."

"It means, 'Old fool.'"

"What if he learned Susan did not love him and that she loved someone else?"

"I do not think he ever learned that."

"Did you love Susan?" Eleanor asked. She knew he had told Kay he did not, but she wanted to read his expression.

"I did not love Susan. She was my friend. Susan did not love. She planned."

"That is a harsh thing to say."

"It is the truth. Her mother taught her to never love. To love was to be weak. I do not agree, but I was not in love with Susan."

He turned his head to the side. "Your secretary. Kay. She is very beautiful. Her hair is red and soft, like Rita Hayworth. I do not like her to know I am arrested. That I am accused of killing a defenseless girl." He spat out another Russian word. "I would not do that. The act of a weakling."

Eleanor remembered being told by Sandy, when she was first debating with the Soviets, back in 1946, that during the invasion by the Nazis, Petrov lost both his sisters. She could not imagine him hurting Susan.

She also saw he had fallen for Kay.

"You will not be condemned if you are innocent," Eleanor

vowed. But could she make such a promise? Unjust things had happened that she could not prevent or change: segregation, the horror of the Ku Klux Klan, the fear-fueled witch hunts of Communists.

"You believe in human rights. Here, I have no rights. I believed in America, now I see its corruption."

Kay had described Dmitri Petrov as being in love with America. His love had been betrayed. Eleanor knew how harsh and devastating that was.

"You do have rights, Mr. Petrov," she said. "If you are innocent, I will prove it."

"How do you prove innocence?"

"The best way is by discovering who is guilty."

Kay heard two wolf whistles while she sat in the chair at Detective O'Malley's desk. The detective was elsewhere. Kay had taken out her nail file and examined her fingernails.

She crossed her legs. Heard a loud cry of "oof." As she had moved her legs, one of the officers had almost fallen over the wooden gate that defined the bullpen area.

The door to O'Malley's chief-of-command flew open. Detective O'Malley came out. He saw her and stopped in his tracks. Then he paced over to her.

Kay straightened. "Detective, did the police surgeon tell you whether the person who made the wounds was right- or left-handed?"

He looked uncertain, and Kay said, "Detective, I'm not going to tell anyone."

"His conjecture is that the murderer is right-handed."

"Then Dmitri Petrov can't be guilty. He's left-handed."

The detective sat down in his chair. He tossed the folder he was carrying onto his neat desk. "He's missing part of his left pinkie finger from getting his hand shot in the war while he was aiming to fire his rifle," Detective O'Malley said.

"Doesn't that prove he is left-handed?"

"It shows the index finger of his *right* hand was on the trigger. He was using his left hand to stabilize. He was firing as a right-hander."

Kay shook her head. "That doesn't make sense. I *saw* him hold a drink with his left hand."

Detective O'Malley's dark straight brows shot up. "You were having a drink with the Soviet agent?"

"I don't know what you mean by 'Soviet agent.' Mr. Petrov is a delegate to the United Nations. And yes, I had a drink with him."

"Admittedly, a lot of left-handed soldiers learned to shoot with the right hand because the rifles are designed for right-handers. He could have been trained to use his right hand. The question is—as a combat soldier, would he use his left hand or his right if he were attacking with a knife?"

The image flashed before Kay's eyes again. Susan, in the tiny washroom, turning to see Dmitri and realizing she was trapped. . . .

"I'm sorry, Miss Thompson. You've gone deathly pale. Bad choice of words. Let me get you a coffee."

She nodded.

He came back in moments with two cups of coffee, both with cream. "I put a lot of sugar in yours," he said. "I hope it's okay."

There was also enough cream to make it equivalent to a dessert, but she took it and sipped.

"It is possible he used his right hand. On top of that, evidence was found linking him to Susan Meyer. But I can't keep him here. The FBI will be taking him."

"What evidence?" Kay demanded.

"Her compact."

"But did you find Susie's handbag?" Kay asked. When he shook his head, she inquired, "Why would Dmitri get rid of the handbag, but not the compact?"

Detective O'Malley's dark brows went up as she used Petrov's first name. "The compact was under his bed. He must have dropped it when he got rid of the handbag."

Wouldn't Dmitri have looked for something like that if he was the villain? But how did it get there . . . ? "It could have been planted."

"That's what he says. But why are *you* defending him?" Detective O'Malley asked, leaning back so his chair creaked. He lifted his coffee mug to his lips.

"I think he's innocent."

"He's a Soviet."

"That doesn't mean he is automatically guilty. *You* didn't accept that the Soviets must be guilty. You thought it might be a Washington man. Like Sandiston."

"You seem to care a lot about what happens to Petrov."

"I do if he is an innocent man."

The detective moved his chair abruptly. The legs screeched as they moved over the floor. "I have paperwork to do. If you don't mind, I need to concentrate."

"Am I a distraction?"

The detective huffed out a breath. "If you sit in that chair quietly, you can stay, Miss Thompson. Until Mrs. Roosevelt is finished."

Kay leaned back in her chair. She thought of the large bouquet from Mr. Kennedy that now resided in a crystal vase on the dining room table in the hotel suite. She should be thrilled. A rich, well-educated, handsome man who would someday run for president had sent her a bouquet of twelve deep crimson, velvet-soft roses.

This was what she'd dreamed of when Aunt Tommy suggested she work for Mrs. Roosevelt.

But Dmitri Petrov was locked in a cell, accused of murder. Wrongfully.

"I don't believe you would want Mr. Petrov locked up if he is innocent, Detective. Then the real killer gets away with it."

"I don't. But no one is going to listen to me, Miss Thompson. I've got no jurisdiction. And I've been told that if I 'mess around' in the Susan Meyer case anymore, I'll get fired."

"And you're going to let that stop you?" Kay demanded.

"I need the job."

"I always needed my jobs before I got fired from them. Then I discovered I didn't need them as much as I thought."

His green eyes held hers. Kay caught her breath. Then he muttered, "Paperwork," and looked back to the stack of files on his desk.

# CHAPTER 15

*If silence seems to give approval, then remaining silent is
cowardly.*
        —Eleanor Roosevelt, *If You Ask Me*, circa 1946

The twelve-story Hotel Harrington stood at 11th and E Streets.
Kay picked out the backlit letters adorning the Art Deco stain-
less steel canopy. A noticeboard informed her that the famous
Pink Elephant lounge was reopening, with updated décor including red circular booths.

Kay didn't expect to get access to Dmitri's room. It wouldn't
help anyway. The police had been over it. She bet the FBI had
searched too.

Dmitri had told Mrs. Roosevelt the compact was planted.
Kay believed him, but Mrs. Roosevelt had an idea on how to
prove it.

Mrs. Roosevelt had asked Dmitri for his room number. It
impressed Kay how Mrs. Roosevelt juggled so many tasks at
once, kept everything in her head, and made the right decisions.

Kay veered past reception. She'd telephoned and learned the
checkout time. The clock at the reception desk told her it was
fifteen minutes past. The maids had started turning over the
rooms, cleaning them for the next guests.

The elevator slid open on the seventh. Kay got out. The quiet of the carpeted hall was broken by the roar of upright vacuum cleaners.

One vacuum stopped. Over the quieter hum of the others, Kay heard a clear, sultry voice singing "God Bless the Child." She rounded the corner.

An older Black woman with gray hair began to shush the younger singer.

"No, don't stop," Kay implored.

"We didn't mean to bother you, miss," the gray-haired woman said.

The girl who had been singing had straightened black hair held in place with a pink headband. She looked barely eighteen.

"You have a beautiful singing voice," Kay said.

The girl said nothing. The other woman nudged her. "Thank you," she said awkwardly, grinding the toe of her worn flat shoe into the carpet.

"I wondered if you could help me," Kay said brightly.

The gray-haired woman looked apprehensive. "Perhaps, miss."

"My name is Kay. I want to ask you about a room you cleaned." Kay gave the number of Dmitri's room.

"We didn't take anything," the girl said. "If you're missing something."

"No, it isn't that at all. The room was used by a . . . a friend of mine."

"I'm sorry we can't help you, miss." The gray-haired woman began to steer the younger one away, like a hen with a chick. "We have to get back to cleaning."

"If you could help at all . . . it's for Mrs. Eleanor Roosevelt. It's very important."

"*The* Mrs. Roosevelt?"

"Yes." Kay saw a beacon of hope to win their trust, to coax the ladies to talk. "The former First Lady. She would appreciate your help."

"She was a great First Lady," the older woman said. "She tried to do things for Odell Waller. Tried to get the execution stopped. I heard a talk by Miss Pauli Murray, and Miss Murray said that Mrs. Roosevelt tried as hard as she could. When President Roosevelt's appeal to the Governor of Virginia failed, he gave up and said he could do nothing more. Even though he was the president! But Mrs. Roosevelt didn't stop trying."

Another woman had come around the corner, pushing a Hoover vacuum that was not running. "Who are you talking to, Mary? We've got to get this floor finished."

"I am Kay Thompson, Mrs. Roosevelt's secretary."

"This young lady works for the former First Lady."

The new woman gave a beaming smile. "Is Mrs. Roosevelt staying here? I want an autograph for my grandchildren."

The young one said, "Why is this old white lady so important?"

"I went to the Marian Anderson concert," Mary said. "Mrs. Roosevelt was a member of the Daughters of the American Revolution when they refused to let Miss Anderson sing in their hall because of her color. Mrs. Roosevelt denounced their stance. She resigned from DAR because she felt that to remain a member implied that she agreed with them. She and Charles Houston put on a concert outdoors, at the Lincoln Memorial. Seventy-five thousand people stood on an Easter Sunday morning, cheering as Miss Anderson sang. Marian Anderson was called the voice in a million and it was true. I stood, with tears streaming down my face, feeling pride as I had never done before."

Kay explained that Dmitri Petrov had been arrested. "He vehemently insists he is innocent, and that evidence was planted in his hotel room."

"We didn't do anything like that," Mary declared.

"No, I know you didn't," Kay said quickly. "I wondered if you remembered anything unusual when you cleaned."

"I cleaned his room for the first time yesterday," the young girl volunteered. "He smoked a lot. All the ashtrays were full of cigarettes. Some were only half smoked. Some were stubbed out and I don't think he'd taken more than one puff from them. He had money to burn, I thought."

Mary stared at the younger woman. "That's strange. I thought he didn't smoke. I never saw any cigarette butts."

"He sure smoked before I cleaned the room. They smelled awful. I couldn't air out the room enough to get rid of the odor."

Kay hadn't seen Petrov smoke in the diner. "Thank you," she said quickly. She ran to the elevator and tapped her toe impatiently until she was at the lobby; then she bolted to the pay phone. She called Mrs. Roosevelt at the hotel. After the conversation, she took the elevator back up.

Petrov didn't smoke. Lev Valentsky was a chain smoker.

Kay combed the hallways until she found the young maid who had dumped out the cigarette butts. She learned the girl's name was Yvonne. Kay repeated the question Mrs. Roosevelt wanted her to ask. "Do you know what brand the cigarettes were?"

"I don't know. They weren't like any cigarettes I've seen."

"Can you describe them?"

What Yvonne described matched the type of cigarette Mrs. Roosevelt had just described to Kay. The ashtrays had been emptied yesterday morning, just before the detective carried out his search.

Kay telephoned Mrs. Roosevelt. "Yvonne described the cigarettes as a tube that was flattened at the end as if pinched by two fingers. It had a grayish-colored cardboard extension."

"Those are Russian Belomorkanal cigarettes," Mrs. Roosevelt said. "I saw Mr. Valentsky smoke them. He told me they had been created to commemorate the construction of the White Sea–Baltic Canal. The pack showed a map of the canal."

"Valentsky must have been in Dmitri's room."

"Yes."

"He must have planted the compact. And if he did, doesn't it mean Valentsky murdered Susan?"

"It shows that the evidence against Mr. Petrov could have been fabricated. But it is not definitive proof of Mr. Petrov's innocence or Mr. Valentsky's guilt," Mrs. Roosevelt said in measured tones.

"I suppose not." Kay felt rebuked.

As Kay hung up, she wondered why Mrs. Roosevelt wasn't convinced Valentsky was the killer. It made sense. He was involved with Susan, and he had tried to set up his aide. Perhaps he knew Susan was helping Dmitri defect and he wanted to see Dmitri punished.

But she knew, in her heart, Mrs. Roosevelt was correct. It didn't mean for certain that Valentsky planted that compact. He might have been searching for proof Dmitri wanted to defect. Or proof that Dmitri was the killer.

She wanted to believe in Dmitri's innocence. In a Hitchcock movie, she would be rewarded for believing faithfully in the hero. But she didn't know if Dmitri was really the hero, and she feared she was being a fool.

Late the next morning, Mrs. Roosevelt had put together a small smorgasbord of sandwich fixings, including French cheese, sliced Italian sausage, Greek olives, and German rye bread—all the rage after the war. The men who got accustomed to European tastes suddenly wanted them at home, and Mrs. Roosevelt thought two strapping young men would want to be fed. Mrs. Roosevelt was a caring and attentive hostess. Dealing with a murder and international intrigue didn't change that.

Mrs. Roosevelt surveyed the spread on the dining table with satisfaction. She had an available lunch hour and was using it to meet with Jimmy Price and Bobby Kennedy.

"You will sit in, Kay, as you did the work of speaking to the hotel maids. The gentlemen will want the information on the cigarettes firsthand."

Kay nodded, swallowing hard. She was excited to be a part of the investigation, but she was also nervous. She knew her facts, and every detail of her conversations with the maids was in her head.

Jimmy Price arrived first. He exchanged pleasant conversation with Mrs. Roosevelt about his new home in Hollin Hills.

Brand new, it was filled with modern conveniences. Debra, his wife, was awed. She grew up in the Midwest and she'd never seen a fancy refrigerator before.

"She calls it the 'ice box,'" Jimmy admitted, looking embarrassed. "She's happy I'm now mostly at home, as opposed to away on work with the United Nations delegation. But HUAC does demand that I travel around the country. Debbie's sweet. Doesn't care about politics or current events, but she's real attentive to the house and our daughter."

"Why don't you grab a plate of food while we wait for Mr. Kennedy?" Mrs. Roosevelt said. "He warned that he might be late. You have something to eat as well, Kay."

Kay led Jimmy to the dining table in the suite, where the buffet was laid out.

"Debbie always has a cold beer ready for me and a plate of cheese and crackers when I get home. She understands how tired and hungry I am. I'm a lucky man," Jimmy said, grinning boyishly.

"I suppose you are," Kay said, leaning over the table.

Something rubbed across her hip.

Had that been Jimmy's hand?

"Of course, married life makes you both a lot more comfortable. She was as pretty as a picture when we were dating. Now, when I get home, she has her curlers in at night and does the ironing in her favorite robe, which is kinda ratty."

"Why don't you buy her a new one?" Kay said, straightening. Jimmy looked at her in surprise. "We don't have a lot of extra money right now. Debbie is good at making do without very much of an allowance."

Allowance. As if she were a child. Kay looked Jimmy over from head to toe. His suit, shirt, and silk tie looked stylish and expensive.

She would never be like Debra. She would demand a new robe. If she were serving a treat for her husband, she'd do it in a frilly apron and maybe nothing else.

"She sounds like an angel," she said. "I hope you appreciate her."

"I do." But he moved closer to her. His breath was on her cheek. "I could show you a few of the hot night spots in Washington. Places you won't get to with Mrs. Roosevelt."

He smiled at her. Coaxingly. The kind of smile that must work for him all the time.

"Mrs. Roosevelt and I are leaving tomorrow morning," Kay said. She wondered if she should try to go on a "date" with Jimmy. Maybe she could figure out if he was guilty . . . or innocent.

"What if I could maybe fit you in . . . tonight?" she asked, gazing up at him under her false eyelashes. It was so hard not to shout, "And what about Debbie?"

Maybe he sensed something was off because he quickly said, "I can't make it tonight, doll. When are you next in Washington?"

She knew men who gave all women nicknames because they couldn't remember their names. She suspected Jimmy was that type. "I will be back in a few days. Mrs. Roosevelt is bringing Mrs. Meyer. To see her daughter's body."

She watched Jimmy's face. No expression of guilt. He looked more interested in the Italian sausage, but he said, "Poor woman. Must have broken her heart."

Kay wondered what to say next. Clearly if she asked if he was the murderer, he would say no. "You met Susie at Martin's Tavern. Did you ever . . . help her home? Share a coffee with her?"

"I had no idea who she was until Sandy told me, Miss Thompson."

The cute nickname had been dropped. He was wary now. And all business.

"Do you know Robert Kennedy well?" she asked. She sensed it was a good idea to keep him talking. Not that she knew anything about detecting. But talking to the suspects was a large part of detective stories, like Agatha Christie's books.

"He's new at the Department of Justice," Jimmy said. "But I knew of his family."

"Do you like him?"

"I do. A smart man. More down to earth than I expected."

Then Jimmy leaned close. His voice murmured against her ear. "I thought he was in this rich, privileged family and had the perfect life. He told me he was a 'misfit' at school. His father called him a runt. Thought he was too soft and too awkward with girls. He had to work hard at things that didn't come easy: athletics, studies, success with girls, popularity."

"It seems to have paid off," Kay said.

Kay thought: Mr. Kennedy was involved with Susan, bringing in Petrov. Could a romance have sprung up? Kay didn't want to think so—not when he had a new wife.

Jimmy's description did not sound like a man capable of murder, but what if he were placed in a desperate situation? What if he feared Susie would talk and ruin his career?

The same theory could apply to Jimmy.

"Have you ever been to the Harrington Hotel?" she asked.

He grinned. "Propositioning me?"

Oh no. Oh dear. Oh shoot.

She was trying to think of what to say, when she heard

Robert Kennedy's drawling vowels as he greeted Mrs. Roosevelt. Deep in her conversation with Jimmy, she hadn't noticed his arrival.

"It's Bobby Kennedy. I must—" Escape? "Show him where the buffet is."

Of course, she didn't need to. Mrs. Roosevelt had directed him to the food. But her conversation with Jimmy Price had come to a distasteful end.

Bobby Kennedy reached out and shook her hand. "Nice to see you again, Miss Thompson."

Kay studied him. There was no way to know if he had fallen in love with Susie, but Jimmy and Sandiston seemed the better bets.

Soon Bobby had a plate piled high with cold meats, cheeses, rye bread and he followed her into the sitting room of the suite. Jimmy had already settled in an armchair and was biting into a thick sandwich.

"Sandy told us that Dmitri Petrov has been taken into FBI custody," Bobby Kennedy said.

"Then time is of the essence," Mrs. Roosevelt declared. "You have the floor, Kay."

Kay felt a frisson of nerves. As a secretary, she was always in the background. But Mrs. Roosevelt had bucked up her courage earlier. She had explained, "Louis Howe, my husband's advisor, told me I must learn how to make speeches. In unguarded moments, my voice rose in pitch. He made me work to lower the timbre of my voice for speeches. And to remove my nervous giggle."

Astonished, Kay had said, "But you are so good at it. I thought you had been born to make speeches."

"I had to work at it, just as anyone else. I was terribly self-conscious at first. Until I realized that if what I had to say was worthwhile, I needed others to hear it."

Kay cleared her throat. Carefully, she gave them the description of the many cigarettes found in the ashtrays. "That was the one time they found cigarettes in . . . in Mr. Petrov's room." She caught her breath. She had almost called him "Dmitri." That would have been a mistake.

"I recognized those cigarettes," Mrs. Roosevelt stated. "They are Belomorkanal cigarettes." She explained why the cigarettes were distinctive, including the fact that the tobacco was strong and very smelly.

"Could someone buy them here?" Bobby Kennedy asked.

"I sent Kay to inquire at various tobacconists. Belomorkanal cigarettes are not imported. At U.N. meetings, Mr. Valentsky chain-smoked them, beginning one, then starting another without finishing the first. Once I asked him, when we were at an informal gathering, why he did not finish one cigarette before starting another. He shrugged and claimed that his mind was busy with protecting the interests of the Soviet Union and he had not the time for the trivialities of remembering where he put down his cigarette. But his characteristic behavior would explain why so many half-smoked cigarettes were found by the maids in Mr. Petrov's room."

"Then Valentsky is the killer," Jimmy said.

"Valentsky is a high-ranking member of the Soviet delegation. I need more to go on than cigarette butts," Bobby Kennedy said. "I guess we can't even produce those, can we? The maids dumped them out?"

Kay nodded, crestfallen. "The garbage was hauled away to the landfill."

"But," Mrs. Roosevelt said, "we cannot allow Mr. Petrov to be charged with murder based on false evidence."

"No, ma'am."

"Hoover won't be happy to see Petrov released," Jimmy said. "He'll suspect you of having Communist sympathies again for helping Petrov."

Kay watched uncertainty cross over Kennedy's handsome

features. "Mr. Kennedy, you don't seriously believe Eleanor Roosevelt is a Soviet agent?"

He gave his grin. "I don't. But there are men who would like to have you painted as one, ma'am."

"Of that, I am well aware."

"I need to question Valentsky. But how do I get close to him?" Mr. Kennedy mused.

"Perhaps you could contact the embassy and ask him if I can speak with him," Mrs. Roosevelt suggested. "I am sure the message would be relayed to him. Then the decision will be his. Do mention the cigarettes. He will understand that I know."

"I'll try, ma'am."

# CHAPTER 16

*Even in our blackest moment, we have to acknowledge
there is something very fine in human beings.*
—Eleanor Roosevelt, My Day, November 3, 1943

Sandy came to the Mayflower later that evening, their last evening to be spent in Washington, DC. As Kay opened the door to him, he leaned close to her as he shrugged off his overcoat. "I'd like to take you out for a drink sometime. Talk about how the job is going."

"The job is going fine," Kay said coolly. Hoping it was. "Let me get you a coffee. Mrs. Roosevelt is waiting by the telephone."

As she put his coat in the closet, Kay heard his loud tones all the way from the sitting room. "I never thought Valentsky would agree to talk. It was only the promise that he would speak to you that made him agree. Valentsky will call from Glen Cove. He agreed to call the hotel at eight o'clock, and the call will be put through to your room by the operator." Sandy paused. "I'd like to get a confession out of him. Even if I can't prosecute him, I'd like to know. Try to make him see that he owes it to Elsa Meyer. She needs to know whether he did it or not. She needs that to make peace with this."

Kay heard Mrs. Roosevelt answer. "I will do what I can. But

as I know from experience, Mr. Valentsky does not concede easily."

"You got a Declaration of Human Rights accomplished with Lev Valentsky fighting us every step of the way. If anyone can do it, it's you, Mrs. R," Sandy said.

Kay slid his coat onto a hanger. Studied it thoughtfully. Then she searched the pockets. But they were empty. So much for detecting, she thought.

Kay hurried to pour coffee and put out biscuits.

At the appointed hour, Sandy stood by the desk. Mrs. Roosevelt was seated. Dressed in a cardigan, a long skirt, her hair in a bun, Mrs. Roosevelt looked like an ordinary woman, not one about to quiz a Soviet diplomat on his possible guilt in a murder.

The moment the telephone rang, Sandiston grabbed the receiver. Before Kay could reach it.

He greeted someone. Then he held the receiver with his left hand covering the mouthpiece. "They are putting him on the line." He scowled. "They knew the time of the call. Grandstanding to ask you to wait, Mrs. Roosevelt. Valentsky can't hide in that house forever and he knows it. If he doesn't play ball, I'm happy to grab him the minute he is off diplomatic soil. I'd have to release him, but I could make him sweat for a while. . . ." He abruptly moved his hand and lifted the receiver to his ear. "Thank you. She is here."

Kay wished she could hear the voice of Valentsky. But Sandiston handed the receiver to Mrs. Roosevelt, and all Kay could hear was Mrs. Roosevelt's articulate, gentle tones greeting the Soviet delegate.

"You have agreed to speak with me, Mr. Valentsky. It is regarding the horrible murder of Susan Meyer—Mr. Valentsky, you did indeed know Susan Meyer. I saw you out at a restaurant with her." She let out a soft breath. "No, I am not accusing you of murder, Mr. Valentsky . . . Lev. I am about to do the exact opposite."

Mr. Sandiston knocked the plate of remaining biscuits off the edge of the desk.

Kay picked them up, as astonished as he was.

"The truth is that you entered the hotel room of Dmitri Petrov, and you placed Susan's compact in his room. I am appalled that you would plant evidence to condemn your comrade," Mrs. Roosevelt said.

A deep stentorian voice protested over the line—Kay could discern that much.

"The cigarettes, Lev. You filled the ashtrays while you were there. It confused me as to why, but I believe it was because you spent some time in his room."

More protests.

Kay was startled. She hadn't realized the cigarettes meant Valentsky had spent *time* in the room.

"I tried to understand why you lingered in Mr. Petrov's room. It was a simple task to plant Susan's compact and leave. But you remained. The very fact that you had Susan's compact makes you appear guilty."

There was loud talking from Valentsky's end, undecipherable to Kay. Sandiston was pacing, clearly wishing he could hear both ends of the conversation.

Mrs. Roosevelt listened.

"I see. It was a gift from you. But how did you come to have it, Lev? The authorities think you removed it from her handbag. They will presume you had the handbag because you stabbed her."

Once again, Mrs. Roosevelt listened, this time for a long while. Valentsky was clearly explaining something—probably why he had the compact. He ended with a shout so loud, Kay heard it through the receiver. "But I did not do this! I would never hurt her!"

"I believe you," Mrs. Roosevelt said. "I believe you spent that time in Petrov's room seeking evidence that he was responsible for Susan's death. When you found none, I believe you wrestled with your conscience before pushing the compact beneath his bed. During that time, you calmed your nerves with your Belomorkanal cigarettes. Not even aware you were doing it." She paused. "You think Petrov murdered Susan."

Kay heard his bellowed response. "If I did, I would have already ripped out his heart."

Sandiston muttered, "Then why plant the compact?"

Mrs. Roosevelt held up a quelling finger. "Did she spy for you?" she asked Valentsky.

Kay could hear his response. Barely. "That I cannot answer. . . ."

"You tried to see Dmitri Petrov imprisoned for a crime he did not commit," Mrs. R said firmly. "You always declared yourself just. You claimed you have always followed the law. You did not do that with Mr. Petrov."

Valentsky spoke softly. It was a muffled sound.

"I saw the intimacy in the way you caressed her back at the restaurant," Mrs. R said. "It was a loving gesture. You cared very deeply. It does not matter that she was younger or that you feared she would not love you in return. You loved her."

Kay thought of what Aunt Tommy had told Kay about David Gurewitsch.

"Love can be given without any expectation of it being returned," Mrs. Roosevelt said. She motioned Kay to come closer to hear.

Bent close to the receiver, Kay heard Valentsky's deep voice. "Yes, I loved Susan. Petrov called me a fool. I knew she would not love me in return, but I savored her company. I enjoyed looking upon her beautiful face. But she loved another. I do not know who."

"Did Susan tell you anything at all about this other man?"

"Once she told me that she might like to be married with a house in the suburbs and children. I knew Petrov wanted to stay in America. At first, I thought they had made that as a plan. Then I realized it was not Petrov she cared about. But she told me she would not see me again."

"Lev, you should speak to the authorities and tell them that you planted that evidence. Petrov should be released."

"I will not speak to authorities. I will not risk arrest."

"There would be no arrest. You would help with inquiries. You are a diplomat."

"But do I trust officials to respect that, or will I just disappear?"

"Of course, you will not just 'disappear' if you speak to authorities here."

"Tell him this is not the Soviet Union," Sandy said.

"Tell Mr. Sandiston that I do not believe that I, a staunch and loyal member of the Communist Party of the Soviet Union, will be guaranteed rights in America. I am not so trusting, Mrs. Roosevelt."

"What is your plan then, Lev?"

"A return to Moscow. You can take this statement to your authorities. I am innocent of the murder of Susan Meyer, that lovely young woman. As to Dmitri Petrov, I do not believe he murdered Susan. But he was disloyal to the Party, to our country. He might not be a murderer, but he was a defector. I did place that compact in his room. That evidence was false. Goodbye, Mrs. Roosevelt. Perhaps, in Geneva, we will meet again."

Seated beside Mrs. Roosevelt, Kay heard the click and the dial tone.

Sandy exploded, "He hung up?"

"Yes," Mrs. Roosevelt said calmly.

"But why did he take the compact in the first place?" Kay asked.

"He said he stole back his gift because his heart was broken when he realized Susan loved someone else. I think, when Susan told him she would not see him again, it could have meant that Susan no longer wanted to be a spy."

Sandy whistled. "That gives Valentsky a reason to remove Susie Meyer. She was no longer of use to him. And he's going to run."

"If he is innocent, that does not matter. The real culprit must be found."

"I'm sorry, Mrs. Roosevelt, but I believe he is the real culprit."

"Why are you so convinced, Sandy?" Mrs. R asked. "I agree it would be convenient. The question is, convenient for whom?"

"If he runs, he must be guilty," Sandy said. "And it means it is case closed."

Kay exchanged a glance with Mrs. Roosevelt, who looked grave.

# CHAPTER 17

*One's philosophy is not best expressed in words; it is expressed in the choices one makes.*
—Eleanor Roosevelt, *You Learn by Living: Eleven Keys to a More Fulfilling Life*, 1960

"It's delayed!" Kay exclaimed, looking for Elsa Meyer's flight at the notice board at the New York International Airport.

"Only an hour," Mrs. Roosevelt pointed out cheerfully.

Kay was astonished. "*Only* an hour?"

"For flights, that is almost like being early," said Mrs. Roosevelt, who spoke from a great deal of experience. "I was delayed with David Gurewitsch in Ireland for two days due to fog."

"Two *days*?"

"David was traveling to Switzerland for treatment for tuberculosis. He was ill, but I was able to nurse him until he could reach the clinic."

That didn't surprise Kay at all. Mrs. Roosevelt had the capacity to care greatly.

There was nothing to do in the arrivals lounge but wait. And order drinks. A group of air hostesses in trim uniforms passed by, carrying their cute powder-blue bags. But it was the handsome pilots with aviator sunglasses that made Kay's head swivel.

Travel looked glamorous.

Sleek airplanes lined up on the tarmac. Stairs were pushed up to them, and people emerged into the sunlight of a warm autumn day, the wind tossing their hair. She imagined doing that herself, wearing large sunglasses and a sleek dress, a cape draped around her shoulders, arriving somewhere exotic and far away. London. Paris. Los Angeles. Or Miami Beach.

Those pilots were fine specimens of men, but Kay knew a man who was always away, working with pretty women and staying in foreign hotels, would make an awful husband. Not quite rich enough or interesting enough to make the cheating worth it.

Cheating was something Kay could not live with.

For all Sandy said the case was closed, Mrs. Roosevelt's role was not ended. They had traveled by train from Washington, DC, to Grand Central Station. Due to Mrs. R's schedule, they had traveled on the *Marylander*, the other B&O train that serviced the route. A luncheon of buttery broiled Chesapeake Bay fish with cornmeal muffins had been served promptly in the Martha Washington dining car. It was a beautiful space. Arched windows sent light spilling across the tables, covered with a snow-white linen tablecloth. Dresden china, linen napkins, silver cutlery marked each place, and the chairs were Queen Anne with lush cushions.

The meal smelled delicious, but Kay picked at it. She noticed Mrs. Roosevelt barely touched it as well. They had both sat in the lounge car with coffees, and Kay guessed they were both thinking of Susan's murder. Kay had used the washroom, and again she had imagined Susan's murder happening as if it were a movie.

It didn't give her any deeper insight. Or clues. But it had scared her.

"There she is. Elsa!" Mrs. Roosevelt called.

Jolted out of her thoughts, Kay looked up. An older woman had just come through the arrival gate doors.

Elsa Meyer wasn't what Kay had expected.

Mrs. Meyer was tiny, barely over five feet. And thin. She was almost drowned by her gray raincoat. She carried a small pale-blue suitcase.

The first day Kay met Mrs. Roosevelt, Mrs. Roosevelt had come to New York from her home at Hyde Park. She came up the steps to the apartment, carrying a bag and her typewriter case by herself and shooing away the doorman when he tried to take the typewriter.

Kay never carried her own bag. She always got a man to do it. Kay had learned a lot about Mrs. Roosevelt in that moment.

Sensible shoes smacked the floor as Mrs. Meyer strode toward them. Her hair was pulled back into a tight bun. Susan had light blond hair, as platinum as a movie star. Elsa Meyer's was iron gray. Though she was much smaller than her daughter, Susan had inherited the magnificent cheekbones and the large dark eyes from her mother. Mrs. Meyer must have been very pretty when she was young.

But Mrs. Meyer obviously didn't care about her looks. Certainly not now that her daughter was gone. Her hairstyle was harsh, her dress was black and shapeless, and her stockings were gray wool.

Mrs. Roosevelt had said that Mrs. Meyer's mind was truly beautiful to have made amazing discoveries, persevering when her male counterparts didn't give her the recognition she deserved.

Mrs. Roosevelt didn't find it odd that Mrs. Meyer had gone to her laboratory the day after she learned her daughter was dead.

Kay did.

Mrs. Roosevelt approached Mrs. Meyer slowly, her head cocked a little to the side. The way Mrs. Roosevelt did, Aunt

Tommy had told her, when she seemed to want to diminish her height.

"Eleanor," Mrs. Meyer said, her voice cool, as if she was about to begin a scientific lecture.

"I am so sorry," Mrs. Roosevelt began, but Mrs. Meyer stepped forward and embraced her friend, who stood many inches taller. "It was not your fault, Eleanor."

"I know. But I wish . . . I wish I had found Susan before this awful thing happened. Elsa, I thought it would be best to take you to Hyde Park tonight. It's quiet there, cozier than the apartment, and you can recover from the time difference before we go to Washington."

Kay wondered how Mrs. Meyer would react. Would she refuse?

But she nodded. "Yes, I should like to see this house you talk of, at Hyde Park. Your home. I am tired. Very tired. Susan was foolish. She made the wrong choice and now she is gone."

Kay gasped softly in shock. That was not how she expected Susan's mother would feel. Mrs. Meyer seemed to be blaming Susan.

Kay stood by Mrs. Meyer's bag, waiting until one of the airport porters placed it into the trunk of Mrs. Roosevelt's car.

Mrs. Roosevelt took the wheel. Mrs. Meyer settled in the front passenger seat. Kay let the porter open the door, then slid into the back.

Mrs. Roosevelt started the car and glided out into the traffic flowing away from the airport.

Silence filled the car. Elsa Meyer stared resolutely ahead. Kay saw the tight grip of Mrs. Roosevelt's fingers on the steering wheel.

To break the quiet, Kay said, her voice more breathy than usual, "I don't know how to drive. I've always been . . . driven places by men."

Mrs. Meyer made a dismissive sound. "Do not always defer to men."

"You should learn," Mrs. R said. "I drove with my good friend Lorena Hickok all over the country. Just the two of us. We traveled so I could report back to Franklin about what was really happening in the country."

Kay knew a little about Hick, which was the nickname for former AP reporter Lorena Hickok, from her aunt Tommy. But she asked, astonished, "You two went alone? I would have thought the First Lady traveled with all kinds of people."

"I didn't. I refused having the Secret Service men accompany us. Hick and I didn't need them."

"If I could have Secret Service men accompany me, I would take them," Kay said.

"It is more of a bother than you know," Mrs. Roosevelt said. "When they warned we could be kidnapped, I asked where they would hide us. I am almost six feet tall and at the time, Hick—Lorena Hickok—weighed almost two hundred pounds."

Aunt Tommy had told her that when Mrs. R expressed concern for Hick's weight and urged her to cut back, Hick had just laughed and declared, "Lady, I like to eat."

Kay also knew Mrs. Roosevelt had faced assassination attempts on her travels. And she still insisted on her independence. Kay saw how strong and courageous Mrs. Roosevelt truly was.

"Did you enjoy those travels?" Mrs. Meyer asked.

"I did. I got to see what was happening in my country with my own eyes."

"I am always in the laboratory or in my apartment with my books. Susan said she felt as cloistered as a nun. I told her that the truly important things were done in isolation, with hard work and dedication. Susan did not understand. . . ." Mrs. Meyer's voice trailed off. She put her head back. "I would like to rest. I will not be good company."

"Of course, you must rest, Elsa. I will drive."

Kay fell silent too. She looked out the passenger window as they crawled out of New York, passing over the bridge from Manhattan. Before she began her job, she had researched some history of the Roosevelts.

One of Mrs. Roosevelt's ancestors had bought 150 acres in Harlem, owning land from Fifth Avenue to the East River and 110th Street to 125th Street. He sold it to John Jacob Astor and built a house on the Hudson.

Kay couldn't imagine owning such a huge part of Manhattan—one person possessing all the blocks now filled with apartments and skyscrapers. She certainly couldn't picture it as rocky farmland.

Eleanor was a Roosevelt before she had married FDR, who was her fifth cousin once removed. His family lived at Hyde Park, Eleanor's at Oyster Bay. Her uncle Teddy Roosevelt, President of the United States, gave her away at her wedding and commented to the press that it was good to "keep the name in the family."

Kay thought Mrs. Roosevelt had been born into good fortune. She grew up in a mansion; her mother had been a society beauty; she married a handsome, wealthy man; she became First Lady, living a glamorous life.

But Kay found and read Mrs. Roosevelt's autobiography, *This Is My Story*, and learned that things were not always as they appeared.

Mrs. Roosevelt's father had called her his "Golden Hair," but her mother was dismayed by her plain looks and serious expression, calling her "Granny," which hurt Eleanor deeply. She had been sent to her grandmother's mansion when both her parents died. But her grandmother's home was an unhappy place. Her grandmother had been too meek with her own children and was determined to be stern with her young grandchildren. Eleanor's uncles, who lived in the house, drank too

160 Ellen Yardley

much. Aunt Tommy told her that extra locks had to be put on her bedroom door.

With a shudder, Kay had realized what that meant.

Aunt Tommy told her that Eleanor Roosevelt had never wanted to be in the White House, but in the end, she had been the most remarkable First Lady.

Outside the city, the highway followed the river at times, giving glimpses of rippling water. They passed through Sleepy Hollow, Peekskill, Poughkeepsie. Thickly leafed maples hemmed the road, glowing gold and red on the bright late-fall day. The stretches of woods were broken by long drives, fields, and white-painted farmhouses.

Driving north in the daytime, the highway was quiet. On the other side of the road, a stream of traffic headed south toward Manhattan Island.

Once they neared the town of Hyde Park, Kay expected Mrs. Roosevelt would drive to Springwood, the elegant three-story mansion built by FDR's family. But Mrs. Roosevelt turned off the highway in the opposite direction, following a narrow road. She slowed to cross a rickety wooden bridge. It creaked and Kay let out a little cry. But they passed over it safely.

"That is the brook where we picnicked during the first years after Franklin was paralyzed. The brook is called Val-Kill." Mrs. Roosevelt pointed. As she did the car veered in that direction. She righted it.

"A curious name," Mrs. Meyer said. Her voice was empty of emotion.

"It is the Dutch derivation of Fall-Kill. In English, it means 'waterfall stream.'"

They reached a cluster of gray stone buildings at the top of an expansive sweep of lawn.

"The original stone Cottage is used as the guest house," Eleanor explained. "My son John is interested in living there eventually. I converted the old factory into a cottage for myself."

Built of fieldstone, with gables and many windows and chimneys, the cottage was pleasantly large—Kay wouldn't have called it a cottage at all. It certainly didn't look like a factory. But it was much simpler than elegant Springwood.

Standing on the porch, wearing a pale-blue cardigan, with her graying hair neatly styled, was Aunt Tommy. At her side, rising slowly to his feet, was Fala, Mrs. Roosevelt's Scottish terrier. He had lived with FDR and ER at the White House. He was, at one time, the most famous dog in America.

Kay waved nervously to her aunt. She got out of the back seat, her stiletto heels sinking into the gravel of the drive, and waited while Tommy hurried down the steps. Mrs. Roosevelt swept Aunt Tommy into an embrace. "Here we are," Mrs. Roosevelt said. "How are you, Tommy?"

Aunt Tommy had been living at Val-Kill since her health had declined.

"I am much improved. The air here does wonders for the health. I'm so happy you arrived safely, Mrs. Roosevelt."

Mrs. Roosevelt bent over and stroked Fala's head. Despite his advancing age and his poor health, Fala barked happily.

Tommy then shook hands with Mrs. Meyer, stating, "It is an honor to meet you, Mrs. Meyer. I am so very sorry for your loss."

Mrs. Meyer nodded stiffly.

Kay expected her aunt to be angry with her. Perhaps recommend that Mrs. Roosevelt fire her. She had failed to keep Mrs. Roosevelt out of the newspapers. And off the investigation.

But she agreed with ER—finding the guilty person would prove Dmitri Petrov's innocence.

To Kay's surprise, her aunt gave her a kiss on the cheek. "It is lovely to see you."

Confused, Kay went to the trunk of the car and pulled out the suitcases. It didn't prove as hard to lift them as she thought. Maybe she didn't need to wait around on men.

Mrs. Roosevelt directed Aunt Tommy to take Kay to her room. Mrs. Roosevelt would show Mrs. Meyer to hers.

Kay followed her aunt through the ground floor of the cottage. "Oh," she cried. "I thought it would be huge and fancy. I didn't expect it would be all these small rooms."

"Mrs. Roosevelt says it is like a rabbit warren," Tommy said. "She likes it this way. She savors the atmosphere of simplicity and relaxation."

It looked like a cottage for a grandmother. A fire burned in a sitting room. A large basket contained wool and knitting needles. Books were scattered and pictures covered the knotty-pine paneled walls. It was how Kay imagined a cottage in the country—but not the cottage of a former First Lady.

"As Mrs. Roosevelt said, this was once the Val-Kill furniture factory," Aunt Tommy explained. "Mrs. Roosevelt began the venture with her friends Nancy Cook and Marion Dickerman in the twenties to provide job opportunities for farmers in the area by teaching them furniture, metal, and cloth making. That venture did not survive the Great Depression, but the ideals of the Val-Kill program were incorporated into the New Deal work-relief programs. Even though FDR's will allowed her to stay at Springwood for her lifetime, Mrs. Roosevelt turned over the house as a historic site a year after his death. She had the factory converted into a cottage."

"Isn't Springwood a grand house? Why wouldn't she want to live there?"

"That house did not feel like her own home." Tommy led her to the stairs. "Val-Kill cottage was her first home that was completely hers."

Kay had never had a house that was completely hers. She had lived with her mother in apartments—her mother had struggled financially while raising Kay alone. Now she had a room at Mrs. Roosevelt's apartment.

She had imagined she would have a home when she married— one provided by her husband.

But Mrs. Roosevelt loved having a home that was solely her own.

Kay had never thought she could achieve such a thing.

"Many foreign dignitaries have stayed here, at Val-Kill," Aunt Tommy said.

"Really?"

"Mrs. Roosevelt has hosted Madame Chiang Kai-shek, Queen Wilhelmina of the Netherlands, the King and Queen of England, Sir Winston Churchill."

Kay ran her hand along the wood banister as she followed Aunt Tommy upstairs, thinking that the King and Queen of England might have done the same thing.

Someday Prince Rainier might do the same thing.

"This will be your room," Aunt Tommy said.

Kay stepped in, taking in the old-fashioned four-poster bed, the wardrobe, small dressing table, and Queen Anne chair. "It's lovely."

"My apartment is also Mrs. Roosevelt's office and study. If she asks you to do work, that's where it will happen. Mrs. Roosevelt and I accomplish an incredible amount of work there."

Tommy was all Kay had left, and her mother, ashamed to have been abandoned by her husband, had kept to herself, relying on only Tommy.

"Are you really feeling well?" Kay asked tentatively. Kay had the job because Tommy's health was declining. Not that Tommy liked to admit to any weakness. And she never complained about illness. Tommy spoke of Mrs. Roosevelt's inner calm, but Kay saw her aunt possessed a lot of inner strength.

"I am *really* very much improved."

Kay felt relief for Aunt Tommy but also a tug of sadness as she realized her work for Mrs. R could come to an end.

"With Mrs. Meyer here, I think we should discuss funeral arrangements," her aunt continued briskly. "I wondered if a service should be held in Washington. Susan lived there, and I'm sure she had friends there."

Kay hesitated. From what Lucia had said at Martin's Tavern, Susie hadn't been close with any of the other waitresses.

Dmitri Petrov seemed to be her only friend.

Other than her mysterious lover.

Kay shivered. If Petrov was used to firing a gun with his right hand, was it possible that in a moment of fury, he reverted to what he did in combat, and used his right hand with a knife?

The thought made her stop dead in her tracks.

Aunt Tommy stopped. "Is something wrong?"

"No. I . . . I hadn't thought about a funeral service."

"I really wish Mrs. Roosevelt was not involved in this," Tommy said, worriedly. "But she says she must find the guilty party—to protect a Soviet man named Petrov!"

"I guess I failed to keep her out of this," Kay admitted.

"If Mrs. Roosevelt is removed as a U.N. delegate, it could derail her work to expand the Universal Declaration of Human Rights into international Covenants."

"On the what?" Kay asked.

"The declaration set forth general principles of human rights, for everyone in the world," Aunt Tommy explained. "But as ER explained to me, the U.N. General Assembly is not a world parliament, and its resolutions are not legally binding on member states. It was decided that the declaration would be followed by two covenants that would contain binding commitments that governments must follow. Mrs. Roosevelt was hard at work on the first. I feel these are documents that could change the world," her aunt declared.

"I don't think I could have stopped Mrs. Roosevelt from seeking justice. It is what she believes in," Kay said. "My goal before working for Mrs. Roosevelt was just finding a husband. Now I want to help her get justice for Susan. And for Dmitri Petrov. I don't think she should stop investigating. And I want to help her until we solve this!"

Her aunt looked shocked. But Kay wasn't going to back down.

She had lost her jobs for standing up before.

And this was the most valuable thing she had ever stood for.

As if on cue, Mrs. Roosevelt looked around the door. She had removed her hat and coat and put on an oversized cardigan. She looked more rested, as if being at her cottage had calmed her instantly.

"I am so happy you want to help me, Kay. There are times I feel guilty for dragging you into this."

"I don't feel that I was dragged in, Mrs. Roosevelt. I've never done something so important in my life."

Mrs. Roosevelt nodded. "Do you like your room, Kay? I feel it has one of the best views at Val-Kill."

"I love it. Thank you for choosing this room for me."

"Tommy, we should speak of what to propose to Elsa for the funeral," Mrs. Roosevelt said. "You should unpack, Kay."

Mrs. R and Aunt Tommy left to discuss the funeral in the study. Kay placed some clothes quickly in drawers. She felt un-certain—Mrs. R had turned at once to Aunt Tommy for help. Of course, she would. Mrs. R and Aunt Tommy had worked together for many years. Mrs. R did not completely trust her yet, Kay thought. She had to remember her job was only *tem-porary*.

What would she do after this? Kay wondered. She walked along the hallway, glancing in the doors. At the end of the cor-ridor, she spied Mrs. Meyer. The scientist was sitting on the bed, a book in her hand. Handwritten notes filled the pages.

She looked up, spotted Kay, and smacked the book shut. "My laboratory notes," she said.

"You are thinking of work now?"

Kay wished she could have bitten off her tongue. Mrs. Meyer made her nervous, but she didn't know why.

"I wonder if you would be willing to talk about Susan," Kay added. "Something she said to you might give a clue about what happened to her."

Mrs. Meyer got off the bed, a tiny, frail-looking figure. She walked to the door and Kay was prepared to listen to every word, gleaning each one for a clue.

"I do not wish to talk to you," Mrs. Meyer said. She slammed the door in Kay's face with even more vehemence than when she had slammed her book.

# CHAPTER 18

*Sorrow in itself and the loss of someone whom you love is hard to bear, but when sorrow is mixed with regret and a consciousness of waste there is added a touch of bitterness which is even more difficult to carry day in and day out.*

—Eleanor Roosevelt, *This I Remember*, 1949

When Elsa Meyer came out of her bedroom, having rested by reviewing her research notes, Eleanor suggested a walk. Elsa wore her black skirt and blouse, her dark gray coat, along with sensible walking shoes. She tied a black scarf over her gray hair. Eleanor laced up oxfords and wore a light man's style shirt with a black sweater over top and trousers. Fala walked at her heels. How much more slowly he moved now. But then, Eleanor thought, so did she.

A tractor rumbled in the distance, harvesting. The fields had taken on a gilded air, rimmed with golden rod and yellowing leaves.

Pausing to turn back, Eleanor gazed on her cottage—her first true home of her own—nestled amidst the richly colored trees and the rolling lawns.

"It is isolated," Elsa remarked. "This is good."

"True, but it is often filled with guests or family. There are times where I have told the cook to prepare for a small family dinner, but that has meant eighteen at the table. My mother-in-law used to tell me that I keep a hotel. But I enjoy it. There is time for work—it is easy to retire to my office and work with Tommy when necessary. And there is time for fun."

Franklin had built the cottage and the factory at Val-Kill for her. Early in her marriage to him, when she was young and Sara Delano Roosevelt, her mother-in-law, ruled their roost, she had broken down, despairing to Franklin that, "I do not like to live in a house which is not in any way mine, one that I have done nothing about and which does not represent the way I want to live."

She feared he thought her tears foolish, but then he had the Stone Cottage built for her. It was his design and his selection of a spot, but intended entirely as a home where she could get away and relax. The factory was built next, which Eleanor transformed into a cottage in 1936.

Their progress on the walk was slow, as Fala had to sniff on the journey. She and Elsa reached the swimming pool, which was a favorite place for the children and grandchildren, and the place where Eleanor did her daily laps when at Hyde Park in warm weather. Elsa asked, "Is there somewhere we can sit, Eleanor?"

"Yes, the perfect place to sit is very close."

Eleanor led her friend to a clearing surrounded by trees. Wood benches and smooth, sloped rocks were arranged in a circle. Here she had discussions with the many people who visited Val-Kill. Once she had brought a dozen UNESCO representatives. The quiet of nature proved conducive to discourse and agreement.

Eleanor took her seat on one of the rocks, crossing her legs at her ankles.

Elsa sat on the bench across from her. "You feel guilty over my daughter's death, and you should not. The fault was not yours. I gave you a terrible responsibility. I am not angry with you. You understand what I feel. You, who also know loss."

"You mean Franklin—?"

"I speak of the small child you lost. The baby, Franklin Junior. He had your heart, your love, and then he was gone. Whether they are with us much time or little time, they are always our children, their loss is almost unbearable. But our bodies awaken each day, we draw breath, and we are forced to continue to live."

Eleanor had gotten up each day because she had other children. She could not stop being a mother, not even for grief. Even when she saw the tiny casket bearing her baby boy, only eight months old, she had thought of the other children—Anna and James—and how sad and frightened they must be.

As difficult as it was, Eleanor said, "Do you wish to hold the funeral in Washington?"

"No, I will take my daughter home with me."

Eleanor nodded.

Elsa stared out straight ahead. "I must telephone my laboratory. I am at a critical place in my research. I must give instruction."

"There is a telephone in my study. Feel free to use it whenever you need, Elsa."

"Thank you, Eleanor. I will call later. To say I have arrived safely."

"Very good."

For several moments, they sat in silence. Birds cawed overheard. The breeze whispered through the autumn leaves, flinging them to the earth.

Eleanor cleared her throat. "Elsa, I presume the police told you that I saw Susan with Lev Valentsky in New York."

"I told you I feared Susan was involved with Communists, Eleanor. And it was true. I think she did this to impress me, after I was so angry that she wanted to waste her brain as an actress. After the war, so often I told Susan that no one country should be allowed to have sole access to a nuclear arsenal that could destroy humanity. The day will come when that country may use it."

Eleanor remained quiet.

"But they would not invite their own destruction," Elsa said. "As I said to you after the destruction of Hiroshima, peace can only be ensured by creating a stalemate amongst world powers. I believe Susan acted to help create that impasse. I believe she did it to appease me. I . . . I feel responsible."

Eleanor did not wish to ask the next question. But she needed an answer.

"Where would Susan get atomic secrets to pass on to Valentsky?"

"Do you think they came from me?" Elsa cried. She rose to her feet. "Do you think I would endanger my own daughter! How can you say such a thing?"

Fala had jumped to his feet, sensing the strain.

"I don't wish to offend you," Eleanor said, "but I think our sensibilities are less important than the truth."

Elsa slowly sank down. So did Fala, realizing his mistress was not in danger.

"If you believe Susan may have tried to create the stalemate you envision for peace, you must have an idea where she got information," Eleanor said.

Elsa did not meet her gaze. "I do not know. But why else would she meet with Valentsky?"

Eleanor explained what she had learned about the Belomorkanal cigarettes in Petrov's hotel room.

"But you think it is not Petrov who is the killer, it is Valentsky?"

"I don't know if Mr. Valentsky is guilty. He says he is not."

"He is a monster. A liar. But he will escape to Moscow, where he cannot be touched by the law."

"That is his intention," Eleanor said.

"He runs because he is guilty. He is a coward. He *murdered* my daughter and refuses to face justice."

Eleanor looked to her friend. "I do not think Valentsky is the type of man to hurt a defenseless young woman with his bare hands. He is a lawyer who attacks with words."

Elsa made a dismissive sound. "Within every man is a monster who wants to come out."

"When I saw Susan's—" Eleanor broke off. She must be careful in what she said. Words had tremendous power, as she had learned through her life. And her words, uttered while she was thinking of this mystery, could hurt Elsa carelessly.

But Elsa said, "You were going to say, when you saw my daughter's body. I am not afraid to hear the words. I can bear pain."

"I do not wish to cause you pain."

"There are times when you must, Eleanor. But why do you defend Valentsky?"

"There was a strong scent of cologne in the small room where she was found. My secretary recognized it as a scent used by many men in Washington."

"I do not understand."

"The cologne is from Caswell-Massey. The brand has been used by politicians for almost two hundred years."

Elsa's fingers twisted together. "I see. You think it was not Valentsky, but a politician. Some man she met in that ridiculous job she had as a waitress. But who was he?"

"I don't know."

"Or maybe it was one of the movie directors. I feared Susan was being pushed onto those infamous 'catting couches' of the movie directors."

"Casting couch, I believe it is called. And I hope that was not true."

"One of these men harmed my daughter. Valentsky. A politician from Washington. Or a movie director."

"Elsa, did Susan ever mention the names of any men she

knew in Washington to you? Did she mention Mr. Sandiston? Mr. Kennedy? Or Jimmy Price?"

"Susan always told me she was a good girl, but I fear she was not."

"We do not have any reason to think she wasn't," Eleanor said firmly. Sandy had said it about Susan, but that did not make it true.

"Mr. Sandiston believes she knew someone from the atomic laboratory at Brookhaven," Eleanor continued. "Perhaps a scientist she knew through you, Elsa. Perhaps there are men there who you worked with before, in Berlin."

"Again, you accuse me," Elsa cried.

"I thought you might know a scientist who felt the same as you—who felt that it was essential to share all knowledge of atomic science."

"How could I know this? No, I have no idea. But it could not be a scientist who harmed Susan."

It could be, Eleanor thought. If he had something to fear. Or she. But they had spoken of these awful things for long enough.

"We should go back to the house, Elsa. Dinner will be ready soon. And you must be tired. I am sorry if you have found this conversation unpleasant."

"I want justice for my daughter." Elsa got off the bench, smoothed her black skirt. "I can endure any amount of discomfort for that."

Eleanor slid off the smooth rock on which she was perched. Fala jumped up to come to her side. She patted him, her thoughts troubled.

Each time she broached the subject of the scientist who provided Susan with information, Elsa became angry.

It worried her.

# CHAPTER 19

*The present is the only thing we really possess.*
  —Eleanor Roosevelt, My Day, September 22, 1941

Aunt Tommy had told Kay that political discussions always erupted around the dinner table at Val-Kill when Mrs. Roosevelt's sons were visiting. The discussions were filled with good-natured arguing, joking, and at times, serious disagreements. But Mrs. Roosevelt would hardly ever participate. She left the boys to fight it out. And listened.

There were no political discussions tonight, but Mrs. Roosevelt listened quietly while Elsa Meyer spoke.

Not about her daughter, Susan, as Kay thought she would.

Mrs. Meyer spoke only about science.

She spoke of an experimental reactor in Idaho that had been a great breakthrough. "The scientists have produced the first electricity from nuclear energy," she declared. "Enough to power four lightbulbs. Instead of putting all resources to weapons, the government could build nuclear reactors to create electricity."

"Such good work can be done," Mrs. Roosevelt murmured.

Mrs. Meyer drained her glass of wine. "What has happened to Susan cannot be changed. But my life will continue, and that means I must have purpose. Eleanor, you must understand.

You found even greater purpose after your husband's death. You now help people of the world, not just of your own country. My work is more important than my grief, my pain, even my life. It will live on long after I am gone. It will be my legacy. None of us live forever. What we leave behind matters most."

Kay thought of her own mother, who had died four years ago. Her mother had been ill and in terrible pain, but she wanted to keep living. She did not want to leave Kay.

Wasn't Susan more important than work? Kay thought.

Before dinner, Mrs. Meyer had insisted on telephoning her laboratory. Her work was all she thought of.

"What was Susan like when she was young?" Kay asked. She wanted to know more about Susan.

She wondered if Mrs. Meyer would refuse to tell her. At least the woman couldn't slam a door in her face right now.

"I would like to hear, as long as it is not painful," Mrs. Roosevelt said gently.

"No, I should like to tell you. Susan was clever. A quick mind. But she was also beautiful, and she saw that her beauty was valued more than her mind. I told her that she could do great work with her mind. She told me, when she left home, that she could also use her beauty to do great things."

Kay wondered what Susan had meant. Had she thought that her beauty would make her a famous actress? Or had she thought she could use her beauty to spy and achieve her mother's ideal safe world?

"What about Susan's father?" Kay asked.

Mrs. Roosevelt gave a gentle shake of her head.

"He is of no importance," Mrs. Meyer snapped.

"Neither was mine, I guess," Kay said. "He was gone from when I was very young."

Mrs. Meyer looked at her in surprise. Kay supposed the scientist was astonished they had something in common.

A ringing sound came from Aunt Tommy's apartment—the sitting room that was also Mrs. Roosevelt's office.

"I'll answer it," Kay said. She jumped up and raced through the doorway and along the hall, snatching up the receiver before the ringing stopped. "Hello," she gasped.

"Miss Thompson? It's Detective O'Malley."

"Uh—hello," she said again. Why was the detective from Washington calling here? Why did her heart beat so much faster? And why was she patting down her hair when he couldn't see her?

"Mrs. Roosevelt gave me this telephone number. I wanted to tell her that there has been another murder. I think it's connected, but the only reason I've been involved is that the brass think it isn't."

Kay was trying to take in Tim's words. "Another *murder*? Who?"

"Alfred Jeffers, the porter from the *Royal Blue* train, was found dead behind a barber shop on Fourth Street."

"Who is this man?" Mrs. Meyer asked. "Did he know Susan?"

"He was a porter on the train," Mrs. Roosevelt said with calm. But she lifted her napkin to dab at tears in her eyes.

Hearing the news from Detective O'Malley, his voice somber and angry, Kay was too shocked to cry. None of it felt real. She had gone back to Mrs. Roosevelt and whispered in her ear that Mr. Jeffers had been found murdered. Kay had suggested they go into the office so she could explain more, but Mrs. Roosevelt said, "Please tell me what Detective O'Malley said."

Kay repeated it, word for word. "Detective O'Malley's boss doesn't think it is related to Susan. They feel it was a robbery carried out by another Black man."

"There is a great deal of prejudice," Mrs. Roosevelt said sadly. "I do not think that is true. It is too much of a coincidence."

"If this was a Hitchcock movie," Kay said without thinking,

"this would have happened for one reason. Mr. Jeffers must have seen something while he was working in the lounge car."

She stopped, realizing she had likened Susan's death to a movie. But Elsa Meyer did not seem upset. Her gaze darted back and forth between Eleanor and Kay. "You think he was killed by the same person who . . . who harmed Susan?" Mrs. Meyer asked.

"I do," Mrs. Roosevelt said. She shook her head. "I still do not understand why he didn't speak of what he saw. This was the murder of a young woman."

"Blackmail?" Kay whispered. "He realized he could blackmail the killer."

Mrs. Roosevelt shook her head. "I knew Mr. Jeffers. I can't believe that of him. Unless . . ."

Kay waited.

"Unless Mr. Jeffers was protecting someone," Mrs. Roosevelt said.

"Who?" Kay asked.

"I'm afraid I don't know," Mrs. Roosevelt answered.

"Oh," Kay gasped.

When the women stared at her, she said quietly, trying to be respectful of Susan's mother, "If Susan's killer attacked poor Alfred Jeffers, it means Dmitri Petrov *is* innocent. He was in police custody when it happened."

Mrs. Roosevelt nodded. "I did not doubt his innocence. But this is proof."

"They will have to release him," Kay declared.

Softly, Mrs. Roosevelt said, "Not as long as the two tragedies are considered unconnected."

Kay saw she was right.

A flash lit the sky. Thunder boomed almost immediately after, the sound only slighter quieter than Mrs. Meyer's shriek.

Her scream startled Kay.

Mrs. Meyer's hands clenched on the edge of the table. She looked terrified.

"You are afraid of lightning?" Kay asked.

"I am not afraid to split an atom—in a laboratory. But I do not like the power of storms. Random and uncontrolled, they frighten me."

Kay's bedroom lit up as if a thousand lights were turned on. Then the flash was gone, and she was plunged into utter darkness.

She counted. One. Two. The thunderclap set her heart pounding.

Kay didn't like storms either. From when she was very young. She remembered a fierce storm with bursts of lightning, explosions of thunder. Between each burst, two people were shouting. She was too scared to get out of bed. She pulled the bedsheets over her head and trembled.

Years later, she asked her mother if it was her father who was shouting. Her mother insisted it had been a bad dream.

The thunderclap ended, and there was quiet, broken only by the steady patter of rain on the roof.

She heard a rumbling sound. It wasn't thunder, it was steady. There was a brief flash of light, much weaker than lightning. Then the noise stopped, and the light went away.

Something made a bang. Not outside, but inside the cottage.

Kay recognized the rumbling sound.

She sat up and slid her legs over the edge of the bed. Dressed in her nightgown, which was slinky, silky, and trimmed with feathers, she slid her feet into her high-heeled slippers. She went for glamour when she slept. No hair curlers and ratty robe for her—not ever.

She moved to the doorway, opening her door fully.

Another bang.

The rumbling sound had been a car's engine. The lights that flashed across her window had to be headlights.

Who would come here in a storm?

The killer? The killer had murdered Alfred Jeffers because he saw something. Was that man here to kill ER? Or her?

The telephone was downstairs, in Mrs. Roosevelt's study.

Kay felt her way along the hall. From the top of the stairs, she saw the golden glow of light from the doorway to Mrs. Roosevelt's office. Since it was Aunt Tommy's sitting room, she thought her aunt must still be awake.

Having the light made it easier to go downstairs. She went to the sitting room doorway, stepped in.

The room was empty. But a lamp on the desk glowed. Perhaps Mrs. Roosevelt or Aunt Tommy had forgotten to turn it off.

Or someone was in the house and had turned on the light.

*Bang!*

Kay jumped. The sitting room was to the left of the front door. The sound came from the entrance hall. She crept out.

The front door was half open and the screen door unhooked. The wind snatched the screen door, flinging it open until the hinges twanged in protest, then it slammed back against the frame.

Mrs. Meyer's shoes had been on the small rug beside the door. They were gone now. So was her black coat.

Two yellow rain slickers hung from pegs by the door along with large rubber boots. Mrs. Roosevelt kept spares for her guests.

Kay grabbed a rain slicker. She kicked off her slippers and stuck her feet in the oversized boots. She saw Fala coming down the stairs.

"Stay, Fala," she whispered. To her relief, he did.

She went outside. Rain pelted her face immediately. The night sky was impenetrably black.

Lightning flashed, its silver-blue light suddenly reflecting on something in the drive. It was a car. And a figure leaning over the car.

Kay heard the engine start. She couldn't see what was happening, but knew the car was driving away.

Elsa Meyer, who hated storms, had gone outside to meet someone.

Kay ran, her boots squelching in the muddy lane.

The car sped up, leaving her behind. Its headlights suddenly turned on and in the pool of light, Mrs. Roosevelt stepped out.

Kay cried out.

But the driver hit the brakes. The car suddenly turned away from Mrs. Roosevelt and slid. It stopped in front of a tree with inches to spare.

The door flew open and a tall figure jumped out.

ER calmly stepped in front of the tall, thin young man. She wore a nightdress, a long raincoat, and galoshes. A patterned scarf was tied around her hair.

"I presume you have come here from Brookhaven laboratory to see Mrs. Meyer," she said.

# CHAPTER 20

*Everything loses interest if you feel you are alone in the*
*world and nobody cares what you do.*
  —Eleanor Roosevelt, My Day, November 22, 1943

"How did you know?" Mrs. Meyer asked. She was huddled on the sofa, wrapped in a large, fluffy towel. Kay thought she looked as tiny as a child. The mysterious young man sat in an armchair. She and Aunt Tommy watched him like hawks. Fala growled at him.

Mrs. Roosevelt picked up the heavy, iron fireplace poker. At the sight of it, the man flinched, but Mrs. Roosevelt went to the fireplace and rearranged the logs. She threw on another log, leaned the poker against the fireplace, then brushed her hands together.

Kay wondered if she should have done the task. Mrs. Roosevelt threw herself into any task with enthusiasm and never asked for help. One almost had to inflict help on her.

Kay tightened her grip on an umbrella she had grabbed from by the door—the nearest weapon available when she had frantically scanned the room, searching for one. Aunt Tommy had looked at it and rolled her eyes, but Kay was certain that having the point driven into one's chest would be painful. It would slow him down enough for her to get to the poker if necessary.

The young man shifted in the armchair. He looked defiant,

his chin held high, his dark eyes snapping with disrespect. His long arms fell over the armrests, and his gangly legs were splayed apart. He was over six feet tall. His pant legs ended three inches above his black shoes—shoes in need of a polish. His jacket sleeves stopped well above bony wrists. His hair was an unruly mass. Other men tamed their hair with hair cream. His thick, frizzy brown hair looked as if it had never met a comb.

"I was told that Susan traveled to Brookhaven Laboratory. The logical assumption was that the scientist Susan was meeting was known to you, Elsa," Mrs. Roosevelt said.

The young man scowled.

Kay watched him. She sensed that Mrs. Roosevelt expected him to sit still and answer questions in a civilized manner. But Kay knew men.

"You wanted to use the telephone. After you called, I did something invasive. I apologize, but I knew you were not telephoning your laboratory. In Sweden, it was almost the middle of the night. I believed if you had orchestrated a connection between Susan and a scientist from Brookhaven, you would want to tell that scientist you had arrived in New York. To test my theory, I had the operator redial the number and of course, I was connected to Brookhaven."

Mrs. Meyer had been surprised into speechlessness.

Mrs. Roosevelt turned to the young man. "Are you Josef Jakuba?"

He glared at her without answering.

Kay stood, holding the umbrella pointing at him. "Answer the question."

"What will you do if I refuse? Gore me with the umbrella?" He sneered.

"I might."

"Yes, my name is Josef Jakuba," he said. "Foolish American woman," he snapped to Kay.

"You were giving atomic secrets to the Soviets," Kay said.

She was about to accuse him of being a traitor, but Mrs. Roosevelt said calmly, "What is more important is that you cared for Susan, Josef."

His eyes glittered. "It is not your business. Mrs. Roosevelt."

"This will help find justice for Susan."

"How can you say that? Unless you hope to put this crime onto me?"

A dislikable man. But despite his overt anger and snide expression, Kay sensed he was innocent. He was the sort of man who wanted to be disliked. She had met a few in her office jobs.

"Tell me about Susan," Mrs. Roosevelt said firmly. "You cared for her."

He glowered. "Susan was beautiful, but she had a good brain. Not as clever on some scientific ideas, but I was patient, and I could see when an idea bloomed for her. It made me angry that she believed she had to hide her brains. With men— she stared at them with big eyes and spoke in a little girl's voice and acted like she had no wits, so they would take her out."

"It is very good that you respected her mind, Josef."

"She said if she revealed her brain, she would not get acting work. The men must believe she was foolish enough to . . . she said, 'fall for them.' I knew what she meant. They had to think she was brainless enough to let them into her bed." Contempt curled his lip.

Kay had wanted to give this arrogant young man the animosity he craved, but she found she was cheering for him at this moment.

Mrs. Roosevelt said, her voice gentle, "You cared for Susan, but she fell in love with someone else."

"She believed a man's lies."

"Who was this man? You must tell us. It is your responsibility to Susan."

"I have no obligation to answer any more questions to you, Eleanor Roosevelt. You talk to me of responsibility? Your husband began the work that would see the deaths of hundreds of thousands, and did so in secrecy, taking the fates of human life in his own hands. In public, he claimed he condemned indiscriminate bombing. Yet, he created the Manhattan Project and built weapons for his own ends, without scrutiny and without debate."

"He did not use those weapons—"

"Semantics. Because he died and turned over his plan to Truman. But it was clear he intended to."

"I saw Mr. Einstein's letter to my husband," Mrs. Roosevelt said. She turned to Elsa. "In it, he explained that it may become possible to set up a chain reaction and release a large amount of energy from a mass of uranium. Mr. Einstein felt it would almost certainly be achieved. He was proven to be correct. He warned that it would lead to the construction of an extremely powerful bomb of a new type. He also warned that Germany was ceasing the export of ores to build their own bombs. My husband had to respond."

"And did that fear justify the use of unthinkable weapons in Hiroshima, and then, after that horrific devastation, the use of a bomb again, in Nagasaki?" Mrs. Meyer demanded.

"To bring the war to a close—"

"By decimating the civilian population," Elsa Meyer cried. "The careless disregard for life, for culture. The work done in secrecy—kept secret from even the public. A president who made such decisions alone is acting as a dictator, Eleanor."

Mrs. Roosevelt sank down into one of the armchairs. "Let me explain. Our military people were almost ready for the last stage of the war, which was the actual attack on Japan. They counted the costs such an attack would have involved—at least a million lives of American soldiers in addition to complete destruction of as much of Japan as would have been defended. This would have meant cities, towns, villages, men, women, and children, for modern war is no longer a war between soldiers; it is a war between peoples.

"These facts were presented to Harry—to President Truman, for my husband was gone then. He was told that one bomb would not be sufficient. Two, in quick succession, were our only hope of bringing about complete and rapid surrender. The reason for this was that we had people who had seen the defenses in Japan. They reported that these were so strong it was not believed possible for any army to penetrate to the interior.

"The only possible chance was to deal such tremendous blows that the people of Japan would realize that if they wanted to save themselves from complete destruction, they must surrender at once."

Mrs. Roosevelt said gravely, "We should have a horror of the conditions which brought about the need for using the atomic bomb. We should have grief and pity for the people affected and do all in our power to help the innocent who suffer.

"But I do not think any decision could have been made other than the one that was made. Leaflets were dropped over Hiroshima before the attack, warning the people to leave the city, and the same thing was done at Nagasaki. But it is human nature to stay where you are and not believe the worst until it happens. I did wish to do everything possible to aid those who suffered."

Listening to Mrs. Roosevelt, Kay understood. The aftermath of the bombs in Hiroshima and Nagasaki had been horrifying. It had been a terrible decision to have to make. And after, there had been the fear if another country developed the atomic bomb, it would be used on the United States.

Mrs. Meyer snapped, "You say you did this thing to save lives! Nothing justifies unleashing such force on the innocent. If you were to know that you too could suffer in such a manner, it would be different. Susan understood that, as does Josef. There are some things that are worth great sacrifice."

Josef bolted to his feet. "You try to defend what America did, but in reality, it was your husband's chance to dominate the world—"

"My husband did not want world dominance."

"The war is over, but there are more tests carried out in secrecy," Josef snapped. "Mrs. Roosevelt, what would you do if your president said that we must bomb the Soviet Union out of existence? You would not protest. You would accept like a sheep."

Kay's place was to listen like a good secretary, but she couldn't stay silent any longer.

"Mrs. Roosevelt would protest." She walked closer to Josef, staring into his angry dark eyes. "If you were in love with Susan but she did not return your love, that gives you a good motive to . . . to hurt her." She almost said "kill," then thought of Susan's mother, seated on the sofa beside Mrs. Roosevelt.

"I would never hurt her!" Josef growled. "But I know who did. The one from Washington. The one who promised to leave his wife for her. The one who lied to her."

"Who was he, Josef?" Mrs. Roosevelt asked.

"Susan would not tell me. But I saw them together—at your White House—and it made me spit. Susie was dressed for the cameras like a tart—her dress too tight and her hair sprayed with lacquer."

"An event at the White House? What event was this?" Mrs. Roosevelt asked.

"I do not know. I tried to make her see—" He broke off.

"What happened, Josef?"

Mrs. R's gentle, probing question seemed to make Josef furious. "I told her I loved her! She told me I was a good friend but no more. She said she and this man were to run away. I told her that he was lying. She would not believe me. She told me she would not spy anymore."

He rounded on Elsa Meyer. "She tried to tell you, but you refused to let her stop. She planned to force this man to take her away. But he murdered her instead. And you will never let this man be arrested, Mrs. Roosevelt. He is one of your kind!"

Suddenly, Josef launched to his feet, the springs of his chair giving a squeak of dismay. Fearing he would strike Mrs. Roosevelt, Kay moved toward him, gripping her futile weapon, but in a swift move, he pushed her backward, hooking her leg out from under her. She went down on her bottom and the umbrella sprang open. She couldn't see anything for the umbrella, and she had to throw it aside.

Mrs. Roosevelt had jumped to her feet to stop Josef.

But he darted around her. He wasn't willing to hurt Mrs. Roosevelt it seemed.

Seconds later, the screen door banged. Kay pulled up her hems like an old-fashioned heroine and ran after Josef. "I'll stop him."

"No, Kay!" Mrs. Roosevelt cried.

But Kay, who was barefoot after taking off the large rain boots, shoved open the screen door and ran down the porch steps. Her feet hit the cold, wet drive. She almost stumbled as pain shot through her foot.

"Ow, ow, ow," she muttered.

Josef's car started. The headlights came on, throwing a beam down the drive, bouncing off wet trees.

Ignoring the cold that hurt the soles of her feet and the jabs from gravel, Kay ran down the drive as Josef reversed away from the tree. Then he floored his accelerator and took off down the drive with tires spinning.

Knowing she would never catch him, Kay had to stop, puffing. She was wet through again.

"Kay, are you all right?"

Kay spun around. Mrs. Roosevelt stood on the porch.

"Yes, ma'am, but Josef got away."

"It is for the best. I don't know what he might have done if you were between him and escape. Do come in and warm up."

Minutes later, Kay was in an armchair in front of the fire, wrapped in a thick blanket fetched by Aunt Tommy. Fala was curled at her feet, gazing up with curiosity. Mrs. Roosevelt entered, carrying a tea service and a platter of biscuits on a large silver tray. Fala immediately perked up and watched his mistress. "Cook wanted to know what the ruckus was about. I have told her she must wait for the explanation. Thank you, Kay. You managed to coax important information from Josef."

Kay felt a glow at Mrs. Roosevelt's praise.

Elsa Meyer stood by the window, looking out at the rain. She turned. "Are you going to throw me out, Eleanor? Or turn me over to the authorities?"

"No, but I will have to advise the State Department of Josef's actions."

"Why do you not turn me in?"

"You have already paid an impossible price," Mrs. R said. "Josef was wrong to say that you murdered Susan. But, Elsa, do you truly believe your ideas were worth the lives of those two young people?"

Mrs. Meyer tipped her head up. "This is war, Eleanor. A cold war, but it is still one that must be won if we are to survive."

"I do not agree," Mrs. Roosevelt said.

She stalked away. But at the foot of the stairs, Elsa Meyer turned. "I must believe it, Eleanor. Otherwise, I cannot live with what I have done."

The next day, Kay joined Mrs. Roosevelt in the kitchen as she instructed the cook to prepare a large breakfast.

"We will take Elsa to Washington today," Mrs. Roosevelt said. "Tommy has booked us seats on a flight from Idlewild, so we must leave right after breakfast."

A flight? This would be her first trip in an airplane. Kay pictured herself walking across the tarmac, then up the stairs to disappear inside a sleek airplane. She would be one of the women in sunglasses and a flapping scarf.

"I will accompany Elsa to the mortuary," Mrs. Roosevelt said. "That will be very painful. And to Susan's apartment to clean it out. I also wish to pay my respects to Mr. Jeffers's family."

Kay had thought, after last night, Mrs. Meyer might be gone when they woke up.

But Elsa Meyer came down to breakfast. For the first time, her eyes were red rimmed from tears. Perhaps Mrs. Roosevelt's words had gotten through to her.

Mrs. Roosevelt treated her friend kindly and compassionately over breakfast. The argument appeared not to have touched her. She certainly held no grudge over the words Mrs. Meyer had said to her. Mrs. Roosevelt knew how to disagree without being disagreeable. Kay supposed her political life had taught her that.

Kay sat at the breakfast table, across from Mrs. Meyer. Fala stood beside Kay's chair, and she petted him after she finished her meal. Kay had never had a pet, and it was the most soothing thing to stroke his beautiful coat while she thought.

All along, Kay had suspected either Valentsky or one of the Washington men of murdering Susie. She'd been relieved when Josef's story of the "other man"—a Washington man who went to events at the White House—showed that Dmitri could not have been Susan's boyfriend.

Josef was also a suspect. He loved Susan and couldn't have her. He could have traveled from Brookhaven Laboratory and followed Susan onto the train.

But his words revealed there was another possible suspect.

Elsa Meyer knew her daughter no longer wanted to be a spy. And she stated that any sacrifice was worthwhile for her dream of world peace.

What if Elsa knew her daughter had arranged to meet

Mrs. Roosevelt? What if Susan intended to tell Mrs. Roosevelt the truth and reveal that her friend Elsa Meyer was helping the Soviets and had indoctrinated her daughter as a spy?

Elsa Meyer could not have murdered Susan—she was in Sweden.

But could she have instructed someone to do it? Josef? A Soviet agent?

It was an awful thought.

If Mrs. Meyer was responsible and she felt Mrs. Roosevelt was close to discovering the truth . . . Was Mrs. Roosevelt in danger?

After breakfast, Mrs. Roosevelt had to attend to business about the cottage with Aunt Tommy. Wearing an oversized rain slicker, Kay hoisted the luggage into the back of the car. Again, it was surprisingly easy.

Mrs. Meyer walked down to the car. "You think I am a monster," she said.

"I . . . I don't," Kay said.

"You feel I do not care enough for my daughter."

Mrs. Meyer's fierce gaze did nothing to reassure Kay that Mrs. Meyer was innocent.

"I never said any such thing," Kay said.

"You do not need to say it. Your expression spoke for you. I did love my daughter very much."

"Then how could you risk her life?"

Elsa Meyer looked her over from head to toe. Kay wore a full-skirted navy dress with her black pumps, stockings, topped by her fitted black jacket, with wrist-length black gloves. An outfit she found prim, but Susan and Mr. Jeffers were dead, and her somber outfit was for them.

Mrs. Meyer clearly saw the outfit differently. "You are a beautiful woman. Why did Eleanor hire you?"

"Are you saying I must not be competent because I am pretty?"

"I am saying that I am surprised Eleanor puts faith in you."

"Why wouldn't she? I do the best job I can for Mrs. Roosevelt."

Elsa's graying eyebrow rose. "Eleanor revealed to me that even during her engagement to Franklin, she feared losing him to another. 'I shall never be able to hold him. He is so attractive,' she said."

Kay was surprised. "I don't understand what you mean."

"I met Eleanor in 1945, after Hiroshima," Elsa went on. "She was a widow. But it was not losing her husband that was her greatest pain. It was his final betrayal. He was rich, handsome, with women pandering to him. Eleanor told me he once said, 'Nothing is more pleasing to the eye than a good-looking lady; nothing more refreshing to the spirit than the company of one, nothing more flattering to the ego than the affection of one.' How is a woman to feel secure when her husband says such things? It made Eleanor feel rejected. It made her feel less.

"Is it not horrible that Eleanor should feel unworthy, when she has such a remarkable intellect and a good heart?" Mrs. Meyer demanded. "She loved her husband very much, and it was her greatest fear that he did not love her as much in return. That fear was realized."

"Mrs. Meyer, this sounds like a confidence Mrs. Roosevelt shared with you. I don't think you should tell me this."

"I want you to understand. You must understand the betrayal that Eleanor suffered."

Kay knew she should walk away. But curiosity kept her listening.

"During the First World War, when Franklin was Assistant Secretary to the Navy, he sailed to Europe to inspect the American fleet. On his return, Eleanor received a call to meet his ship with a doctor and an ambulance. He was deathly ill with double pneumonia and influenza. As he was being treated, Eleanor found, in his suitcase, dozens of love letters written to him. Love letters from a young and pretty woman named Lucy Mercer.

"This Miss Mercer was Eleanor's own secretary. Eleanor had devoted over a dozen years to her husband's life and his career, no matter how difficult for her. Heartbroken, she was willing to give him a divorce. I believe it was Franklin's mother who refused to allow it since a divorced man would not become president. Eleanor stayed in the marriage because Franklin promised to never see Miss Mercer again. Yet after his death, Eleanor learned he broke that promise. The woman was with him on his deathbed. It must have been a painful betrayal for Eleanor. But then, as before, she found solace in public service. Eleanor has made great achievements."

Kay saw why Mrs. Roosevelt understood Mrs. Meyer throwing herself into her work to cope with her grief.

"You should not have told me this," Kay said. "This was private and personal."

"But you understand now that Eleanor deserves loyalty."

"Mrs. Roosevelt did not deserve to have her heart broken," Kay said. "And she will always have my loyalty. She is seeking justice for your daughter. But last night, you condemned her for dropping the atomic bomb—a decision that had nothing to do with her."

Mrs. Meyer flinched. "That is true. But I fear your government. There are men who want to see Eleanor's voice silenced. Do you think that sort of man should have the sole power to destroy the world?"

"Of course not."

"You think I am responsible for the murder of my daughter. You think that I was so angered by Susan's betrayal—by her choice of a man over the great work I needed her to carry out— that I had her killed. Is that what you have said to Mrs. Roosevelt?"

"I don't think that," Kay lied. And then she said truthfully,

"Mrs. Roosevelt draws her own conclusions. From fact. She is the most open-minded, logical, thoughtful woman I have ever met."

"But you suspect me." Mrs. Meyer stepped closer. Kay had to look down on her, but the woman's eyes were commanding.

"I did," Kay said. "I couldn't understand why you could work after you lost your daughter. I guess I thought you were being heartless. I thought you were capable of removing Susan to protect yourself. I'm sorry if I am wrong."

The porch screen door slammed. Mrs. Roosevelt came out on the porch, drawing on her driving gloves. Aunt Tommy followed her.

Kay realized the two women must have heard her. Mrs. Roosevelt looked concerned as she took Kay aside. "Everyone shows their grief in different ways, but it is no less real and agonizing. I believe Elsa Meyer deeply loved her daughter."

Kay feared the next words would be: "You are fired."

"Mrs. Meyer asked if I suspected her, and I had to be honest," Kay said.

"Thank you for being honest with me. Now we should hurry to catch the flight."

To Kay's surprise, she still had her job.

The air hostess, a trim young woman in a dark blue suit, herded them out toward the tarmac, now slick with rain. Kay held the umbrella she had used as a weapon over herself and Mrs. Roosevelt. Mrs. Meyer had her own. She began to feel there was no glamor in waiting to mount the stairs in the rain. Even with the umbrella, her coat began to sag with damp, her shoes were soaked.

Both ER and Mrs. Meyer appeared unconcerned over the weather. Kay tried to be nonchalant, but asked, "*Can* we fly? In the rain?"

"Oh yes. It is only lightning that is worrying," Mrs. Roosevelt said. Mrs. Meyer nodded.

That didn't make Kay feel any better.

Up close, the airplane looked much smaller than she thought it would be. It was entirely made of metal, the wings looked perilously flimsy, and she had to wonder: How did it fly?

But Mrs. Roosevelt, who had flown across the ocean, mounted the steps. Mrs. Meyer did too. Kay hesitated, her gloved hand resting on the handrail. Then she found her inner calm and made her way up the steps. How could she not be courageous with Mrs. Roosevelt?

In the cabin, she sat behind Mrs. Roosevelt and Mrs. Meyer in a wide, comfortable seat that reclined back. A man took the seat next to her. Balding and overweight, in a tan suit, he looked her over and introduced himself. Kay didn't even take in his name. She sighed. She realized she was trapped for the flight beside this man who wanted to talk to her.

As his conversation flowed over her, she tuned him out.

Chewing gum and mints were handed out. The engines revved. The air hostess explained what they should do in the event of an emergency, so her seatmate had to stay quiet.

If the airplane crashed, Kay had to wonder if it would make any difference to know where the exits were.

The plane began rolling forward.

"Taxiing toward the runway," the man beside her explained.

They stopped, which seemed confusing. Then the plane shot forward, accelerating along the straight stretch of asphalt. Kay let out a squeak of surprise at the speed.

The man beside her patted her hand. She pulled hers abruptly away.

Suddenly Kay felt the wheels leave the ground. Her stomach dropped. Maybe it wouldn't really work. At any second, they would fall to the ground.

Then she looked out the window and awe overwhelmed fear. Under the clouds, the world was a patchwork quilt. They rose higher, passing through cotton-candy wisps of cloud; then she gasped. The sun shone up here, turning the tops of the clouds into golden pillows. It looked as if she could walk onto the clouds, like a magical world.

The man beside her made a comment, ending it with "little lady."

"Please don't speak to me," she said. "I would like to rest."

"What's wrong with a little conversation?"

"A lot, when I want to rest."

Mrs. Roosevelt turned. "Sir, that is my secretary, Miss Thompson. She asked for some quiet."

He looked startled. "Mrs. Roosevelt?"

"Yes."

He wanted to talk to Mrs. Roosevelt, but the air hostess stuck a magazine into his hands. Kay had to smile. All the women around her were trying to help.

When the man fell asleep, Mrs. Roosevelt nodded toward him and said, "It is one of the perils of air travel. I have had gentlemen like him wish to talk to me on transatlantic flights that last nineteen hours."

"The least glamorous part of air travel," Kay sighed.

Kay's heart broke as they stood in the funeral home where Susan's body had been moved. Standing beside Mrs. Roosevelt and Elsa Meyer, Kay looked down on Susan lying in a coffin. No matter how pretty the ivory satin lining was, and how polished it was, it was a box. Susan had been made up to still look beautiful. The delicately shaped nose, the arching brows, full lips. But she also looked like she was made of wax.

Susan was going to be placed in the ground.

It was the end.

The thought terrified Kay.

"Susan—" Mrs. Meyer choked.

Kay saw her sag downward, and grasped her elbow to support her. Mrs. Roosevelt caught her other elbow. Following

Mrs. Roosevelt's lead, Kay helped her take Mrs. Meyer to a chair. Sobs wracked Elsa Meyer's slender frame. She hunched forward, dropping into her open hands to hide her face.

Kay struggled to think of something to say. She was waiting for Mrs. Roosevelt to say something wise, something that would make the sobbing stop. But she didn't say a thing. She simply let her friend cry.

Watching Mrs. Meyer break, Kay thought it had to be evidence Mrs. Meyer could not have been involved in Susan's death.

Weakly, Mrs. Meyer lifted her head. She wiped at her eyes with a plain white handkerchief. "I am ready to make the arrangements now. And then, please take me to Susan's apartment, where I can gather her belongings."

"Kay and I will help you with the arrangements," Mrs. Roosevelt promised, with her customary concern and kindness.

In fact, Mrs. Meyer let Mrs. Roosevelt orchestrate all the details with the funeral home. An hour later, they left and soon reached Susan's apartment. A young woman trying to make a living on her own, Susan shared the Georgetown apartment with another young woman after answering an ad. Kay had lived with a roommate only once. She hadn't enjoyed it.

Susan's apartment consisted of two large bedrooms, a glass-enclosed balcony, a complete bath and shower, a modern refrigerator and stove. The building in Georgetown was a large, brick edifice with Art Deco styling. It was one of the many apartment buildings built because of FDR's New Deal spending.

Kay and Mrs. Roosevelt had come here while they were looking for Susan. Kay had whistled when she entered the lovely apartment. Maybe she should have tried tolerating a roommate, she'd thought. She could never have afforded such a huge, attractive place on her own.

Susan's room had been tidy and as Mrs. R had noted, worryingly free of anything personal. No photographs. No diary or engagement book that might give a clue to her whereabouts. No cards or letters that might identify the man she was seeing.

"Perhaps, though, Elsa will recognize something," Mrs. Roosevelt had said to Kay that morning at their hotel suite. "Perhaps she will see a clue where we do not."

Kay rang the buzzer to apartment 310. Two names were written beside the bell in a lovely, sloping handwriting. Taylor (Susie's stage name) and Smith. Dorothy Smith, Susan's roommate, buzzed them in. Mrs. Roosevelt tried to carry the boxes they had brought for Susan's things, but Kay took half of them away from her. They took the elevator up to the third floor.

Dorothy opened the door. A slender young woman in her early twenties, Dorothy stood eye-to-eye with Mrs. Roosevelt. She wore a clinging black top and cropped black pants with flats. She had a doll-like face with large blue eyes. Her long brunette hair was pulled into a ponytail, and she had a thick, straight fringe, like pin-up model Bettie Page.

Mrs. Meyer was introduced, and Dorothy showed a look of surprise. Mrs. Meyer was so much smaller and thinner than Susan. But she clasped Mrs. Meyer's hand. "I'm so sorry about Susan. I liked her."

Elsa Meyer asked, her voice hoarse, "Can I see Susan's belongings?"

"Of course. I haven't touched anything in her room yet," Dorothy said.

Dorothy had reluctantly let them in Susan's room before, and only because she was worried when Susan hadn't been back to the apartment for three weeks.

In Susan's bedroom, Mrs. Meyer took in the pink bedspread and the vanity table with its lighted mirror that looked suitable for a movie star. "She had frivolous things."

"She has very good quality makeup," Kay said, but Mrs. Meyer looked appalled when she saw the drawer filled with cosmetics.

"She has no photographs," Mrs. Roosevelt said. "I had hoped

for a snapshot of a boyfriend or a date book that might tell us where she went. But there is nothing."

"We know now that she attended an event at the White House with a man," Kay said. "If only she'd kept something that would tell us who he was."

"She didn't deserve this at all," Dorothy said. "She was a good roommate. I've had girls who wouldn't pay the rent and who wore my clothes without even asking. I'm a mannequin and I get to buy sample clothes cheap. Some of my roommates even stole my good silk stockings. Susie wasn't like that at all. In fact, she had a beautiful short jacket. It was white mink. A gift, she said, from an admirer who was Russian. She gave it to me."

"Valentsky," Elsa Meyer muttered, as if speaking a swear word.

"Pardon?" Dorothy looked confused.

"Mrs. Meyer meant Mr. Valentsky must have bought her the jacket," Kay said.

"I don't know. Would you like to see it?"

Dorothy went into her own bedroom, then came out, reverently holding the coat over her arm. Kay gasped. It was beautiful—soft, lush, and pure white. The lining was white silk. An expensive gift.

Would a man who gave a gift like this accept losing the woman he loved?

Kay wasn't certain he would.

"She said she wore it to an event at the White House. I've never been to the White House," Dorothy said. She looked at Mrs. Roosevelt, who was looking through Susan's closet with Mrs. Meyer. "Of course, you lived there for years, ma'am."

"I did," Mrs. Roosevelt said.

"Did Susie tell you about that White House party?" Kay asked.

Wide-eyed, Dorothy shook her head.

To Mrs. Roosevelt, Dorothy had said Susie didn't have a boyfriend. But Kay thought Dorothy looked nervous. And guilt-ridden.

Kay drew Dorothy out of Susan's room while Mrs. Roosevelt and Mrs. Meyer looked through the closet. Last time, Mrs. Roosevelt had checked all of Susan's pockets for any clues. Now she carefully scoured the closet, perhaps looking for a hidden diary or datebook.

"Is there something you know that you didn't tell us last time?" Kay whispered.

Dorothy squirmed.

"Susan was murdered. It's important."

"It was just something Susan talked about, but it never actually happened. I think she was making it all up," Dorothy muttered.

"What?" Kay had to restrain herself from shouting.

"Susan said she was going to Hollywood." Dorothy lowered her voice until Kay could barely hear. "She told me she didn't want her mother to know about it. I thought that meant she was going there with a man. You know, living in sin. I asked if there was a man, and she gave me a fake innocent look and said no."

Dorothy hesitated, then added defensively. "It wasn't as if she went. I knew that she hadn't gone to Hollywood when you and Mrs. Roosevelt came here. She wouldn't have left behind all her clothes and makeup."

"Thank you for telling us what you know now, at least," Kay whispered, noting that Dorothy blushed.

Kay went over to help box Susan's things. Despite searching very carefully, they found no clues to Susan's mystery man. Mrs. Meyer offered Dorothy her choice of Susan's clothes. The rest would be given away to Goodwill.

Kay noticed Mrs. Meyer didn't keep anything. That seemed strange to her.

When they returned to the hotel, Mrs. Meyer said, "I am very tired. I must lie down."

"Of course," Mrs. R said. "And while you are resting, Elsa, I would like to pay my respects to Alfred Jeffers's family. Would you come with me, Kay?"

"Yes, Mrs. Roosevelt."

"That White House event has given me another idea," Mrs. Roosevelt said. "A way we might be able to identify Susan's boyfriend."

"How?"

But Mrs. Roosevelt would say no more. Kay had no idea what she had in mind.

# CHAPTER 21

*Courage belongs to no one race or no one religion.*
—Eleanor Roosevelt, My Day, May 19, 1943

The autumn afternoon seemed to mourn for Alfred Jeffers. A drizzle fell, enough to turn the streets slick and make Kay shiver through her sensible dress and black lambswool coat.

Mrs. Roosevelt wore a black dress, a heavier winter coat, her customary fox fur and carried a black umbrella.

As a taxi took them to Alfred's apartment, Kay commented, without thinking, "I was so surprised that Mr. Jeffers lived in Georgetown." Then she blushed. "There is no reason why he shouldn't."

"In the late eighteen hundreds, many freed people came to Georgetown to live," Mrs. Roosevelt said.

It was hard to remember Mrs. Roosevelt herself had been born in 1884. She had seen the turn of the century at age sixteen. She had seen much change. From horse and carriage to automobiles. Then air travel. She had lived through two world wars. Some changes were slow—especially changes that improved human rights.

Mrs. Roosevelt paid the driver, and Kay slid out first so she could open the umbrella and shield Mrs. Roosevelt from the rain.

She had to hold it high for Mrs. Roosevelt was two inches taller than she was, even though Kay wore heels. At the top of the steps, Kay rang the buzzer. A voice crackled over the intercom. "I'm Kay Thompson. Mrs. Eleanor Roosevelt is here and wishes to pay her respects to your family." Would she be turned away?

"Mrs. Roosevelt? The former First Lady?" It was a female voice.

"Yes. She is here in Washington and wishes to speak with Mrs. Jeffers, if she is available."

Kay heard a conversation in the background.

The woman's voice returned. "Mrs. Jeffers says how could anyone ever think she was not available to Mrs. Roosevelt?"

A buzzer sounded. Soon they were in the elevator, a creaking machine with a wrought iron, accordion-style door that Kay struggled to pull across. A window at the end of Mr. Jeffers's hallway showed the dull skies and rain, but bright bulbs gave a warm glow to the parquet floors and wallpapered walls.

"This was what the Brotherhood of Sleeping Car Porters provided," Mrs. Roosevelt remarked. "A proper life for hard-working men and their families."

Kay rapped on the door—her thin leather gloves hadn't kept the autumn chill from making her fingers freeze. It was opened by a full-figured woman with neatly braided black hair.

The woman smiled, then her expression sobered. "I'm Emily. I'm a friend of Alma Jeffers. It's an honor to meet you, Mrs. Roosevelt. Come in."

She clasped Mrs. Roosevelt's hand and almost pulled her across to the sofa, where a tired-looking Black woman was rising. Her hair was free, in a soft frame around her face. Mrs. Jeffers wore a neat black dress with a Peter Pan collar and a small belt.

Mrs. Roosevelt warmly clasped her hand. "I am so sorry about your husband."

Kay sensed a wariness as Mrs. Jeffers shook Mrs. Roosevelt's hand. Why?

A group of Black women, ranging from their twenties to their fifties, sat on two sofas. An elderly woman with pure white hair sat with a very upright posture in an armchair.

Emily introduced Mrs. Roosevelt around and Kay took in the ladies' names. Their jaws dropped as they realized it was *the* Eleanor Roosevelt, former First Lady, here to give condolences.

The furniture, Kay noted, looked new. Growing up without a father, Kay lived with worn hand-me-down furniture and things discarded by neighbors. Her mother would be envious of the matching upholstered settee and armchairs. Kay had always wanted a place with brand-new things—that had been her plan when she got married and got her house in the country.

Mr. Jeffers had provided a good life for his family, she thought.

"This is my secretary, Miss Thompson," Mrs. Roosevelt said.

Kay turned to Mrs. Jeffers. She touched the woman's hand. "I'm sorry for your loss," she said, though it felt inadequate.

"I think Mrs. Roosevelt should sit down, Alma," Emily murmured. "Why don't you sit there, ma'am?" She pointed to an armchair of blue velvet with white lace coverlets.

As Mrs. Roosevelt took her seat, Kay was ushered to the end of the sofa.

Emily motioned to the oldest lady in the room, who was squinting at Mrs. Roosevelt.

"This is Mrs. Rosina Tucker," Emily said. "She was one of the most important people involved in the formation of the sleeping car porters' union. Why don't you tell her Alfred's story, Alma?" But without stopping, Emily plunged on. "Back in 1925, Alfred was approaching forty. He and Alma had five children and they were struggling. The union changed that.

With the union, Alfred received a dependable wage. A rise in their living situation. A future for their children. Their son has just finished law school. Their daughter is working toward being a doctor."

"I think you've already done all the talking, Emily," Mrs. Jeffers said, but she sounded relieved.

"Alfred used to say he never dreamed he would send one child to college. But all his children plan to attend. Right, Alma? Alfred won't see them succeed, but he is going to know they've done it."

"You must be very proud of them, Mrs. Jeffers," Mrs. Roosevelt said.

"I'm scared for them," Mrs. Jeffers said, her voice soft and heavy. "But they want success so badly, I'd never stand in their way or tell them that the world out there won't let them achieve it. My Alfred said that the union was worth fighting for and he was right. He was a good man. A brave man." She took a shuddering breath. "Mrs. Roosevelt, all my friends have brought all kinds of food. Let me bring some for you."

"It isn't necessary, my dear."

"They'd never forgive me if I didn't give each one the chance to say Mrs. Eleanor Roosevelt sampled their sandwiches, or their cookies, or their cakes."

"Let me help you, Mrs. Jeffers," Mrs. Roosevelt said.

"No, ma'am. You're a guest in this home. You sit right back down. I will make tea."

As Mrs. Jeffers moved with slower, heavy steps to the kitchen, Kay got up and followed her. Kay bustled around in the kitchen, opening two cupboards before she found the cups. She set those out. "Why don't I pour you out a cup of tea, Mrs. Jeffers. Or maybe something a little stronger?"

"We don't have drink in this house."

"I'll make the tea. Or would you like coffee?"

"I'll take tea."

With a swirl of her skirt, Kay set the kettle on the stove and turned on the burner. "Why don't we sit down at your table while the water is boiling? This is such a shock for you. Are you going to be all right? You have those children to put through college."

"My eldest son said he would help put all his siblings through school now that Alfred is gone. I don't want to burden him with that, but I don't know what to do now that I don't have Alfred's wages coming in."

Kay looked around. Alma Jeffers had made a successful marriage. She married a man who had elevated himself, who earned a good wage, who provided for the family he loved. That was what Kay wanted.

Just a week ago, Mrs. Jeffers thought her world was just fine. Now it wasn't. Her dependence on her man left her in trouble now.

"They were frightening times when Alfred was starting the union," Mrs. Jeffers said.

Kay listened sympathetically.

"Rosina would come to our homes, pretend that we were just friends visiting for coffee, and she brought union information. When she was found out, her husband was fired, just like that. I begged Alfred to stop, but he said he couldn't. He wasn't doing it for us, he said. It was for our children. So they could do better than work for four hundred hours a month with barely any sleep and rely on tips to buy food for their families."

"Mr. Jeffers was a brave man," Kay said.

"He was. Rosina is a courageous woman. She confronted her husband's supervisor and said she was not employed by the Pullman company and her husband was not engaged in her activities. She shocked that man. He had never had a Black woman speak to him in that manner. And her husband was reinstated on his run."

"I am impressed." Kay took a deep breath. "Mrs. Jeffers, the day Susan Meyer was murdered on his train, your husband was nervous."

"I knew that's why you came here." Mrs. Jeffers looked down at her hands.

"It isn't. Mrs. Roosevelt wanted to pay her respects. Honest. But I thought I would ask if you could help us. To get justice for Alfred."

"I've already told the police everything. Alfred Junior didn't want me to talk to the police, but I did. Because I want justice. As for the murder on the train, I swear he had nothing to do with that. But I know why he was scared."

"Why, Mrs. Jeffers?"

"He was scared of getting fired because the men that own the railroad would make him a scapegoat."

"For the murder?" Kay was aghast.

"For the bad press. They would say it was Alfred's fault. He could have prevented it."

The kettle whistled.

"It can wait a moment," Kay said softly. "Mr. Jeffers was the porter on the lounge car, wasn't he? He didn't tell Mrs. Roosevelt that."

"He . . . he couldn't tell her. But he regretted it. He didn't sleep a night since that girl was killed. All these years to get to the place where he worked on the *Royal Blue* and got to come home to me most nights. After that girl was found, he was awake all night, pacing in the parlor.

"I got up and I told him he had to put this to rest. If he was afraid of something, he had to face it. He told me then that he could have prevented it. And that he hadn't been honest to Mrs. Roosevelt. She had been so good to him when they were building the Brotherhood. She went to meetings. She praised their efforts in the press. I told Alfred to go to Mrs. Roosevelt and tell her the truth. I said he would never get any peace until he did."

"I don't understand how he thought he could have prevented a murder. What was it that he didn't tell Mrs. Roosevelt?"

"He said he left the bar unattended, and that was when the girl was stabbed. If he had been at his post, he said, it couldn't have happened. He left a knife on the counter, he said. Instead of putting it away."

"That was the murder weapon," Kay breathed. "He must have known who did it."

"I asked him. I thought he should go to the police if he knew."

"What did he say?"

"He said he didn't know." Mrs. Jeffers sighed. "After forty years of marriage, he lied to me. And I knew it. I was angry. I've never kept a secret from him. How could he not have trusted me?"

"Maybe he was protecting you," Kay said, for the idea just came to her. "If he knew who the murderer was, he didn't want you to know it. I think he saw something, and that is why he was murdered."

Tears ran down Mrs. Jeffers's lined cheeks. "The night before . . . before he was killed, he did tell me something. It was only one thing, and it didn't make sense to me."

"Could you tell me?"

"It doesn't mean anything."

"Please, Mrs. Jeffers. If your husband said it to you, I think it must have been important. I sense that Mr. Jeffers was not the sort of man to waste his words."

Mrs. Jeffers gave a small smile. "You have the truth of that. This is what he said. He said: 'The poor girl didn't know what she was doing.'"

"That's all?"

"Yes. It doesn't help at all, does it? I don't know what he meant."

Kay saw two possibilities. Had Mr. Jeffers known Susan was a spy? Was that what he meant—that she hadn't known the danger she had gotten herself involved in? Or that she hadn't known what she was doing when she was with a married man from Washington?

But how could he have known she was a spy?

Kay got up, took off the kettle, which was boiling furiously. Instead of making tea, she bent over, and she hugged Mrs. Jeffers and let her cry. It felt like something Mrs. Roosevelt would do.

"I feel so ashamed meeting Mrs. Roosevelt and knowing Alfred wasn't honest with her," Alma Jeffers admitted.

"You shouldn't feel ashamed about anything," Kay said. "Why don't you tell her that? You'll feel better. I haven't worked for Mrs. Roosevelt for very long, but I know she will understand."

"But if Alfred knew . . . if he could have told the police who did it . . . why didn't he?"

"I don't know," Kay said.

She thought of five children who needed tuition for school. Was it possible that Mr. Jeffers did take a bribe? And then he was in too deep to admit the truth?

"I'll get Mrs. Roosevelt," Kay said. "Then I'll make the tea."

Kay went into the sitting room. Mrs. Roosevelt held a small plate with a seed cake on it. She was talking to the woman beside her about recipes for sweet desserts that didn't cost very much money. It turned out that the cake, and its recipe, was one of the things Mrs. Rosina Tucker took with her when she had visited other union wives. "It just looked like we were getting together for tea and cake, not talking about a union."

"I would like this recipe," Mrs. Roosevelt said. "I will give you my address at Hyde Park."

The woman looked surprised, but happily so.

Kay bent to Mrs. Roosevelt's ear. "Mrs. Jeffers would like to speak to you. About what Alfred said to her . . . about the train."

Mrs. Roosevelt nodded.

The two women went into the kitchen and had been there only a few minutes when the front door opened. A deep, strong voice declared, "Momma, it's A.J."

A moment later, A.J. came into the room, a tall, young Black man wearing a well-cut charcoal-gray suit, with a black overcoat. His hat was trimmed with a deep purple hatband, the only touch of daring to his conservative air.

"Who is this? What do you want?" The handsome man glared at Kay.

"Alfred Junior, be polite. This is Mrs. Eleanor Roosevelt and her secretary . . ."

"Miss Thompson." Kay held out her hand to the glowering man. "Mrs. Roosevelt wished to pay her respects to your mother and your family."

"Does she?"

"A.J., the former First Lady is in our household."

"And my father is dead, and the police aren't going to do anything. They figure he was killed for his money by another Black man."

"I will ensure the police act and carry out a thorough investigation," Mrs. Roosevelt promised.

"No offense, Mrs. Roosevelt, but the police aren't going to listen. What about Odell Waller?"

"I am sorry about that. I tried. I wanted my husband to intervene, but even as the president, he did not have authority to tell the governor what to do."

Alfred Jeffers Junior snorted.

Kay knew how much failing to help Odell Waller had affected Mrs. Roosevelt.

"What really matters is getting justice for your father," Kay said, staunchly. "I'd suggest you be as helpful as you can be. I don't think your father would approve of you glowering at Mrs. Roosevelt."

A.J. leaned forward. He looked up at Kay. "My mother telephoned me because she was worried because Father said he was going out for a drink. He didn't drink. She challenged him about it."

"But he wouldn't tell me the truth," Mrs. Jeffers said. "He went out."

"He must have been meeting someone," Kay said. "Did anyone telephone him?"

Mrs. Jeffers shook her head.

"Perhaps Mr. Jeffers was the one to make contact," Mrs. Roosevelt suggested.

"His body was found off Fourth Street. He was found sprawled in an alley, lying on the wet, stinking ground," his son said.

Kay looked at the young man. His fists were clenched in rage, but tears welled in his dark eyes, and the pain in them ripped at her heart.

"His head was bashed—"

"I understand," Mrs. Roosevelt said. "We understand. The horror of seeing him like that must haunt you, but perhaps your mother should be spared thinking of such a thing."

"I think of it every minute of every day," Mrs. Jeffers whispered.

"She went to see his body. I tried to keep her away, but she had to see him," Alfred Junior said, deep bitterness in his voice.

"Why did he agree to meet with a murderer?" Mrs. Jeffers said. "Why didn't he just go to the police?"

"I can think of a very plausible reason," Mrs. Roosevelt said.

"What do you mean?" A.J. Jeffers demanded.

"Do you think he was bribed?" Kay ventured.

"No!" Mrs. Jeffers exclaimed. "That would be like . . . like blackmail. Alfred would never have done that!"

"You have children in college. Maybe he wanted money to give all your children the chance for success," Kay said.

"It would mean letting the murderer of a young woman go free. I don't believe it. I *can't* believe it of Alfred," Alma Jeffers cried.

Mrs. Roosevelt patted her hand. "I felt on that day, when he took me to the body, that Alfred was warring with his conscience. He wanted to tell me something, but he could not. If he was protecting someone, it was for what Alfred believed was a good reason. I don't think that reason was money."

"Why would he protect the murderer?" A.J. Jeffers asked.

Kay stared. "If it was someone important? Someone powerful?" But who was important enough for Mr. Jeffers to protect? "A . . . a politician? Someone in government?"

Would Mr. Jeffers protect Sandiston? Or Jimmy Price?

"I think it was a person who Mr. Jeffers feared would be destroyed by this coming to light," Mrs. Roosevelt said.

Then she repeated thoughtfully, " 'The poor girl didn't know what she was doing.' "

Kay gave a small sigh of relief that Mrs. Jeffers had been able to explain to Mrs. Roosevelt what her husband had said.

"I believe Susan truly didn't," Mrs. R said gently. "She fell in love and that was all that mattered to her."

# CHAPTER 22

*I don't know of anything I like better than meeting people whom I love, but oh, how I hate to see them off! Perhaps absence makes the heart grow fonder, but I always wish there was some magic wand one could wave, which would transport one whenever one wished to sit and talk with the people one thinks about.*
—Eleanor Roosevelt, My Day, June 13, 1938

Mrs. Meyer left for Sweden with Susan's body in the morning. Kay had handled the final arrangements between the funeral home and the airline. She saw Mrs. Roosevelt's hesitation as Mrs. Meyer told Mrs. Roosevelt not to come with her to the airport to say goodbye.

"I wish to be alone," Mrs. Meyer had said. "I know you do not agree with what I did. You feel I used Susan, and I sacrificed her. I . . ."

Kay thought Mrs. Meyer was going to claim that her goal for peace had been more important.

Instead, Elsa Meyer said softly, her face crumpling in grief, "I fear you are right. I should not have involved my daughter. And now, what will happen to Josef?"

Kay's heart ached. Mrs. Meyer was truly grieving.

"I am afraid he will be tried for espionage, like Klaus Fuchs,"

Mrs. Roosevelt said, her tone gentle but her words blunt. "He will be sentenced to prison for giving information to the Soviets. It would be many years of incarceration. Unless he can be helpful to our officials and then they may reduce his sentence. I am afraid it is not a very pleasant outcome."

"I am sorry," Mrs. Meyer said. "But Josef assured me he was willing to risk any penalty for peace. And this *is* a war, Eleanor. It is a war against the hubris and greed of men in power. If all countries know that another country can respond to an attack with utter destruction, perhaps the men of governments will learn peace. Otherwise . . ." She sighed grimly. "I know Josef did not harm my daughter. I am certain it was Valentsky. Once Susan wanted out, he would not let her go. I also know that he can never be touched by your system of justice."

"I want peace as well," Mrs. Roosevelt said. "I could not break laws or risk lives to achieve it. But I am sorry for what you have endured."

"But you do not think it was Valentsky."

"No, I do not, Elsa."

"This is goodbye," Mrs. Meyer said.

"It is 'farewell.' I do not intend to lose touch with you, Elsa. Not now, when you are going through such grief." Mrs. Roosevelt opened her arms and embraced her friend.

As Kay helped Mrs. Meyer downstairs, through the lobby of the Mayflower Hotel and out to the waiting taxi, Kay saw that despite their different points of view, the two women respected each other. They cared for each other.

Later, Kay waited in the departures lounge with Mrs. Roosevelt for their return flight to New York. Kay asked, "Should we have just let Mrs. Meyer leave? She orchestrated Susan's spying. She might have the key to this mystery. And she did act against our government."

"She is a Swedish national. We have no authority to keep her here. It would be hard to convict her of spying as Josef was the one to turn over information."

Kay nodded. Then she asked, because she kept thinking it over but could not come up with the answer, "When we were at the Jeffers home, what did you mean that Mr. Jeffers was protecting someone who would be destroyed? Do you know who?"

"Do you have any ideas, Kay?" Mrs. Roosevelt asked.

Kay felt a surge of pride to have been asked her opinion. But she had to admit, "No, because I can't imagine Mr. Jeffers willingly protecting anyone—at least anyone who was not a member of his family. If he protected Valentsky, it must have been because Valentsky threatened him. The same for Josef. He could be guilty, despite what Mrs. Meyer says."

"I don't think Mr. Jeffers would be pressured by fear," Mrs. Roosevelt said thoughtfully. "Such tactics did not work when he formed the union."

"I can't imagine he would lie to protect Jimmy Price or Sandy Sandiston," Kay said. "I just can't see who he would protect."

"I have an idea," Mrs. Roosevelt said. "But I may be wrong."

Their flight was called. Mrs. Roosevelt stood, carrying the small bag she took inside the airplane. Kay followed her onto the plane. This time Kay had the window seat beside Mrs. Roosevelt, and she didn't have to worry about unwanted conversations.

Over the sound of the engines revving, Mrs. Roosevelt said, "I'd like to travel to Long Island tomorrow, Kay. There is someone very close to me I would like you to meet. I think you will approve of each other. And there is a theory I would like to test on her."

Curiosity ate at Kay. "What is your idea, Mrs. Roosevelt?"

"Until I know more, I should not say," Mrs. Roosevelt answered.

Kay wished Mrs. Roosevelt would take her into her confidence. She felt she hadn't proven herself yet.

Midmorning the next day, Kay slid into the passenger seat, Mrs. Roosevelt put the car in gear, and they started out from Manhattan. They crossed the Brooklyn Bridge, which Kay still marveled at because it had been built almost seventy years ago.

As they traveled across Long Island, Kay realized to her surprise that if they turned north, they would reach Glen Cove. But they drove on, and again she was startled when a sign appeared, showing a turn toward Brookhaven.

Mrs. Roosevelt turned southward, away from the laboratory. By lunchtime they reached a tiny town called Mastic. The sun shone through the red and gold leaves, and the air was as crisp as a fresh autumn apple.

Mrs. Roosevelt chatted as they drove through the town. "You will meet my old friend Lorena Hickock. I call her Hick, as do most people."

"Aunt Tommy told my mother and I about Hick when she lived in the White House," Kay said.

Mrs. R nodded. "Yes, she lived there at my invitation and had a room adjoining mine."

"I heard she was a great reporter and writer," Kay said.

"Hick is no longer reporting, but she will always be a great writer," Mrs. Roosevelt said with a smile. "She inherited this house from her aunt Ella. It's been a refuge for her since before the war. Hick would take her beloved dog Prinz down to the shore at Narrows Bay and enjoy the wind and tang of salt air. She had lost Prinz in forty-three. But I had an English setter puppy named Mr. Choate delivered to the White House for her."

"That was a lovely thing to do," Kay said.

Aunt Tommy told Mama and her that Mrs. R and Hick had been inseparable during the White House years, and Mrs. Roosevelt was still worried about Hick. Hick's career as a journalist was behind her. Her autobiography was beautifully written, but she couldn't find a publisher for it. Her health wasn't good as she had developed diabetes, though that meant she had to eat more carefully. She'd lost weight and was now a slim 140 pounds.

Mrs. Roosevelt loved people and she loved them forever, Tommy said.

In front of a neat cottage, Mrs. Roosevelt stopped the car, shifting into park. A woman with graying hair reclined in a wicker chair on the porch. She wore a white cable-knit sweater, dark trousers, and tall boots. She got up from her chair and stubbed out her cigarette. No, it was a cigar, Kay saw.

A beaming smile lit up her round face as she saw Mrs. Roosevelt get out of the car.

An equally glowing smile lit up Mrs. Roosevelt's face.

"Eleanor!" the woman exclaimed. She hurried down the steps.

"Hick, you look so trim." Mrs. Roosevelt bent to embrace Lorena Hickok, who was much shorter.

From Aunt Tommy, Kay knew Mrs. Roosevelt and Hick became great friends when FDR was elected in 1932. Lorena Hickok was the top reporter assigned to cover the new First Lady for the Associated Press. She was the only one who recognized Eleanor's reluctance to become First Lady. And, Aunt Tommy said, Mrs. Roosevelt's unhappiness.

Kay had wondered why Mrs. Roosevelt had been unhappy. To be married to the president and live in the White House seemed like a dream. What Mrs. Roosevelt had revealed about her insecurities and what Elsa Meyer had told her about Franklin having a love affair showed that Eleanor Roosevelt's life had been much more complicated.

Aunt Tommy told her that Eleanor proved to be FDR's true partner in the White House. It was the Great Depression, and Eleanor was his social conscience, reminding him of the human

side to the government's actions. She urged him to speak courageously about racism and inequality. But she spent her days
and nights with Hick. They were an unlikely pair. Eleanor had
grown up in a mansion with nannies and maids, while Hick had
grown up with an abusive father, had been thrown out by his
second wife, and worked as a maid. "As a reporter, Hick com-
peted with the men in every way," Aunt Tommy had said. "She
likes her drink, plays a good game of poker, and can swear a
blue streak."

Hick exuded a gruff charm as she left Mrs. Roosevelt's embrace and threw open the door to her home. "Come in and take
a look at it, Eleanor."

"At least you don't need to iron your tea towels," Mrs. Roosevelt teased, stepping inside.

Hick laughed as she shut the door. "I guess that was a trans-
parent excuse when people arrived to visit and I didn't want to
spend time with them. But it got rid of them."

Then Kay felt Hick's gaze look her over, head to toe.
"Who's this? Is she one of your daughters-in-law? Not a new
one, is she?"

"This is my secretary, Kay Thompson. She is filling in for
her aunt Tommy."

"She's your secretary?" Hick looked her up and down. "You're
a good-looking girl, Kay. Playing secretary until you land a
husband?"

Even though it was her plan, Kay smarted at the comment.
She wanted this tough-looking woman to think she was capable of more.

"I'm enjoying my work as Mrs. Roosevelt's secretary," she
said.

"Good answer." Hick grinned. "Let me pour you both some
coffee."

The coffee was strong and welcome after the drive. Hick
grabbed a heavy jacket from a peg. "Let me show you around
outside."

They walked along paths over the two acres surrounding her home, with Mr. Choate running by Hick's heels. As usual, Kay wore her stilettos—she hadn't planned on a walk. She followed, but by now she was used to her heels sinking in the mud when she was with Mrs. Roosevelt.

"I may not write for the papers now, but I read them," Hick said. "I read that you found the body on a train, Eleanor. According to the papers, she was the good-looking daughter of an atomic scientist."

"Yes, the daughter of Elsa Meyer."

"How did you happen to find her body?"

As they walked back to the house, Mrs. Roosevelt told the story.

When they reached the house, Hick whistled through her teeth. "Two murders. And you right in the middle. I don't like it, Eleanor."

"I was supposed to stay out of it. But I can't if innocent people are being killed. And accused."

Hick poured tea for Mrs. Roosevelt, then whiskey for herself. She looked up at Kay.

"I'll have a whiskey," Kay said.

"Good girl." Hick gave her a generous pour. They sat in the parlor. Hick lit a cigarette. "I don't see why you think the Soviets didn't do it, Eleanor. Seems to me you're just accepting Valentsky's word. He admitted to planting evidence on Petrov to frame him. But you think he's innocent?"

"I do. My friend Sandy Sandiston insists the Soviets are involved. I fear prejudice is clouding his judgment."

"Or something else." Hick blew out a smoke ring. "Who did it if it wasn't the handsome young Soviet or the wily old one? What do you think?"

Kay started. Hick directed the question at her. At Mrs. Roosevelt's nod, she spoke her mind.

"I believed Sandiston blamed the Soviets to keep Mrs. Roosevelt off the scent—a diversion. But is that because Sandiston is guilty, or is he trying to keep Mrs. Roosevelt from discovering a Washington politician is a killer?"

Hick leaned back, thinking. In a moment, she straightened up. "It could be the young scientist who told you that he was in love with Susan, but she broke his heart because she was in love with someone else. A broken heart is a good motive."

"True. But Josef just does not feel to me like a murderer," Mrs. Roosevelt said.

"Murderers comes in all shapes and sizes. I wrote about 'em for the newspapers. A killer can be a woman who gets beaten up all her life and shoots her husband because this time he hurt their child. A killer can be a man who got caught stealing at work and needs to cover up his crime. A killer can be an ordinary person who gets scared. Or gets greedy. Sometimes murder is about love. When people get hurt, they want to cause pain."

Hick sipped her drink thoughtfully. "What is the story here?" she mused, her voice husky. "Was Susan Meyer in love with a married man who needed to end their relationship before his wife found out? Was she a Communist spy who paid the ultimate price for trying to escape that life? Or was she a spy who was also the lover of a politician in Washington, and he realized his career would be ruined if their affair was discovered?"

"But it could have been Josef, the atomic scientist from Brookhaven. Or—" Kay hesitated. Then she plunged on. "I wondered if Elsa Meyer might have been behind it. Because Susie wanted to stop spying." She quickly explained Elsa's ambition.

"I think it would take a great deal for a woman to have her own daughter killed," Mrs. Roosevelt said quietly.

Kay knew Mrs. Roosevelt disapproved of this theory, but she could not ignore a possibility. Even if it got her in trouble.

"Not for some folks," Hick said. "You must keep open minds.

Kay is right—we can't just discount someone because we want to."

"I concede that is true," Mrs. Roosevelt said. "I came here because Josef gave us a clue. He said Susie and her mysterious male friend attended an event at the White House. Josef mentioned cameras. I thought you might know who I could contact in the Washington press, Hick."

"I've heard there's a young girl with the *Washington Times-Herald* on the Inquiring Photographer beat. She's a society girl. Her mother's second marriage was to an older man who's heir to an oil fortune. Despite all that, the girl fetches coffee for the men, gets paid a pittance, and doesn't even get a byline."

Hick blew a smoke ring. "You can be like her: pretty, whip smart, Deb of the Year, and have a rich stepfather's friend recommend you for the job . . . or you can be like me, thrown out of the house at fourteen, broke, able to drink and smoke as much as the men, and you write articles with punch, but nothing changes the fact that they see you only as a woman."

Kay realized that was true.

"I know the Inquiring Photographer column," Mrs. Roosevelt said. "I didn't realize it was a young woman."

"I read her column in the mornings at the Mayflower Hotel," Kay said. The reporter asked questions of people around town, wrote up a few of them, and printed them with photos of the respondents.

"She's hoping to write a big story and get a byline on the front page," Hick said. "Her questions are interesting. Things like: Should a young woman live on her own before she gets married? Who is the most interesting man you've ever met? Who should be the next president? Would you rather have men whistle at you than respect you?"

Hick looked at Kay. "I bet I know your answer."

"I want them to respect me. But if all I'm going to get is a whistle, I have to learn how to use that," Kay said.

Hick gave a bark of a laugh. "I like you. The young reporter's name is Jacqueline Bouvier."

Mrs. Roosevelt looked thoughtful. "I will start with Miss Bouvier."

"My friend also says there's a rumor that Congressman Kennedy was set up by friends to meet Miss Bouvier back in May, but he dates a lot of women. Like his father, Joe Kennedy."

Kay felt her cheeks heat. She remembered the roses and his promise of a telephone call. It hadn't come.

This might be why—he was dating a society girl.

So much for her fantasy of being First Lady.

She wondered what Mrs. Roosevelt would advise if she dared ask her boss. She could guess.

Mrs. R would say that Kay needed to do great things without waiting for a husband to open doors for her.

Hick blew a series of smoke rings. She tapped out the cigarette in an ash tray. "You know, there are a lot of scandals that happen in Washington that *don't* get reported. There's an unspoken agreement between the male politicians and the male journalists to keep things quiet."

"If a male politician can keep a scandal quiet, he wouldn't have needed to murder Susan," Kay said. Her whiskey was making her warm inside, but her wits didn't feel as sharp. "But keeping it a secret from the public doesn't mean it's a secret from his wife. Susan thought he was going to run away with her. A lot of men make empty promises."

"Exactly," Hick agreed.

"I hadn't really thought what Susan would do if she found out the man she loved was lying to her," Kay continued. "She must have threatened him. Threatened to tell his wife. Threatened to hurt him, ruin him. She was so beautiful she could have had another boyfriend in a heartbeat." The whiskey was making the words flow. "She must have really loved this man. To her he must have been something special. It's so awful that in her last moments, she saw that he really wasn't."

Hick and Mrs. Roosevelt were quiet for several moments.

Then Mrs. Roosevelt said, "We should start back. We'll stay in New York today, but I want to return to Washington and speak to Miss Bouvier."

Before they left, Mrs. Roosevelt went upstairs to the washroom, and Kay went into the kitchen with Hick to help clean up. Hick turned off the stove, Kay emptied the coffee percolator.

Hick looked her up and down as she rinsed and dried the coffee cups. "Gotta ask: When you look like that, why *aren't* you married?

"I haven't met the right man."

"And you figure you will by working for Mrs. Roosevelt?"

"I might meet the Prince of Monaco," Kay said lightly.

"You don't want to be a housewife with a husband who isn't going anywhere."

"Of course not."

"Maybe you don't want to be a housewife period. Have you thought about that?"

"I do want to get married," Kay said firmly. "I think."

"When you meet the Prince of Monaco." Hick laughed. "You know, Mrs. Roosevelt is a remarkable woman. There was always a difference between the 'Mrs. R' of public pronouncements and Eleanor Roosevelt in person. It was the difference between the 'personage' and the 'person.' Eleanor the 'person' has a unique ability to connect with people one-on-one."

Kay nodded. She had seen that too.

"Eleanor Roosevelt is a lovely woman who deserves to be loved," Hick said. "She's the kind of woman who champions justice and cares about people. But because she cares so much, she is putting herself in danger, chasing a murderer." Hick wagged her finger.

"I was told by Aunt Tommy and Mr. Sandiston to keep her out of this. But Mrs. Roosevelt believes in justice," Kay declared, defending Mrs. R. "I won't let Mrs. Roosevelt get hurt, but I think she *should* be involved. She is the one person who truly cares."

"When you are back in Washington, you better make sure she doesn't get hurt," Hick said.

"I promise," Kay said, loyally.

# CHAPTER 23

*Photographers are not accustomed to being their own victims, and I think it is probably very good for them.*
—Eleanor Roosevelt, My Day, November 29, 1944

Kay looked at Jacqueline Bouvier's desk with a raised eyebrow.

The desk looked like a hurricane had deposited a pile of paper, file folders, and pens on top of it. A camera with flash attachment sat at the end, beside Miss Bouvier's typewriter. A telephone was at the other end.

As a secretary, Kay had to keep her desk tidy. Her desk reflected on her boss. In the men's offices, the less paper on the desk, the more important you must be. The ones at the bottom did the work. Miss Bouvier obviously did a lot of work.

Her desk wasn't the only one that looked like a heap. Many were buried under paper. The staff of the *Washington Times-Herald* was in close quarters, with newspaper pages spread everywhere. Voices shouted into telephones. Typewriters clacked furiously.

A slender young woman—almost a girl, Kay thought—threaded her way through the tightly packed reporters, carrying coffees in a box. She dropped them off as she went, handing them to good-looking, grizzled journalists who tapped at their typewriters with one finger and smoked at their desks.

Kay recognized Jacqueline Bouvier. She was the young reporter who had been on the platform by the *Royal Blue* train. Miss Bouvier was enterprising. She'd been the first on the story.

Watching her hand out coffee, Kay admired her style. Miss Bouvier wore a plain black dress topped with a wine-red belted coat that emphasized her gamine figure. A string of pearls ringed her neck. Her hair was dark and cut short, framing her heart-shaped face, her dark eyes, and high cheekbones. She had a much different look than film-star curvaceous, but she was striking.

"Miss Bouvier?"

The young woman stopped and stared in surprise at Mrs. Roosevelt. She set the coffees on the desk of the man next to her. "Mrs. Roosevelt, this is an honor. Could I snap your picture?"

Mrs. Roosevelt considered. "Why not?"

Jacqueline took two shots, then asked Kay, "Yours too? I love your hairstyling. And the color. It's such a dark red. Really unusual."

Normally Kay knew just how to smile for a camera. Not too much so she didn't look like a braying donkey (as her mother had warned). The right tip of the head to shorten her nose and emphasize the curve of her cheek. But this time she stared flatly at the lens. She just couldn't smile.

Miss Bouvier slowly lowered the camera. "Sorry, I didn't wait for you to approve. Sometimes I'm too eager for the picture. Or the story." She turned to Mrs. Roosevelt. "How can I help you? Or can I interview you? Would you be willing to address rumors that Communists have infiltrated Washington? They've been flying since that terrible murder on the train."

Kay realized Miss Bouvier's effervescent, slightly naïve way of broaching a subject must work to her advantage. From the knowing smile on Mrs. Roosevelt's face, Kay saw her boss guessed it too.

"That is why I am here, Miss Bouvier."

"Do call me Jackie."

"All right, Jackie. My friend Lorena Hickok suggested I talk to you."

"I've heard of Lorena Hickok," Jackie said. "I've read her pieces. She is a great writer."

"This is my secretary, Kay Thompson."

"Delighted to meet you, Miss Thompson." Jackie shook her hand. Kay saw a sparkle on her left hand. An enormous diamond engagement ring adorned her finger.

"Perhaps I can get you a coffee for a change," Mrs. Roosevelt said, "and we can speak about the murder."

When Jackie smiled, she glowed. "I'm the coffee gofer, as you guessed. I would love to have coffee served to me. Do you mind if I take my camera? Convinces the boss that I'm on the job."

"That will be fine. It is a very nice camera."

Jackie dismissed it with a wave of her hand. "It's functional. I don't like the Graflex. It's more unwieldy than my own Leica, which is as precious to me as my unruly car Zelda. But this is the one the paper wants me to use."

The three of them left the crowded newsroom, making for a nearby diner.

As they settled in at a booth, Kay let her gaze slide to the beautiful ring.

Jackie noticed Kay's glance. "I just got engaged to John Husted." She fiddled with the ring. "But I've got my career. I'm angling to get a regular byline and I love Washington. I just don't have time for marriage."

"You know Congressman Kennedy, don't you?" Kay asked. She was aware of Mrs. Roosevelt quietly observing.

"Friends invited me to a dinner party he attended. I enjoyed talking to him. But he never called me again. That was back in May." A wistful look came into the large dark eyes. Kay realized Miss Bouvier wanted to see Mr. Kennedy again, regardless of the engagement ring on her finger.

They were both hoping Jack Kennedy would pick up the telephone and call.

Over coffee, Mrs. Roosevelt explained Hick's idea to Jackie. "A Washington event, held on the grounds of the White House, would have been photographed. Susan Meyer attended one of those events. Given her striking looks, I am certain she was photographed. I hope the photographer also captured the face of the man she was with."

"Not every picture makes the paper. I shoot dozens but use only a few," Jackie explained. "But we keep them all. There are files of pictures in the newspaper's basement. I'd be happy to show you." She looked thoughtful while stirring her coffee. "Since we don't know which event, or who she was with, that is going to make it more difficult."

"Do you think it is impossible?" Mrs. Roosevelt asked.

"No, Mrs. Roosevelt." Jackie's eyes lit up with girlish pleasure. "I'm fascinated. Mysteries intrigue me. I want to help you solve this. I feel like Washington's Nancy Drew."

Kay sipped her coffee. With her red hair, she resembled Nancy Drew. But Jackie, who looked about the same age as Susan, really did strike Kay as a perfect Nancy Drew.

"I still have to write my column," Jackie admitted.

"If you show me where the photographs are," Kay said, "I'll go through them. I know you have to go back to work."

"Thanks. I'll take you down there and leave you to it."

As Mrs. Roosevelt thanked her for her help, Jackie added, "I know you held the first all-female reporter press conferences. That was very daring."

"It was Miss Hickok's idea. It was in 1933, two days after my husband's inauguration." Mrs. Roosevelt smiled, reflecting on the past. "Over thirty women came and there weren't enough chairs to go around. Some had to sit on the floor. I had learned that unless women reporters could find something new to write about, the chances were that some of them would lose their jobs in a very short time."

"I learned from women reporters on my paper that you held hundreds of conferences. It was inspiring. And it did keep them in jobs."

"I am happy to give you an interview whenever you want, Jackie," Mrs. Roosevelt said. "To thank you for your kind help."

After coffee, Mrs. Roosevelt headed off to a meeting by taxi and Kay returned with Jackie to the *Washington Times-Herald* offices. After passing the reception desk, they took the elevator downward.

"The morgue is way down in the basement."

"The morgue? It sounds like a horror movie."

"No." Jackie laughed lightly. "The morgue is the name we use for the filing storage of clippings, photographs, old stories, and . . . well, really all the junk. I guess it is filled with the dead."

The elevator made a small grinding sound as it halted. The doors opened, revealing a corridor painted in dull gray.

"I've heard the *New York Times*'s morgue is so deep you can hear the subway in it. We're not that deep, but there are tens of thousands of pounds of paper in here." Jackie led her to a door, pushed it open, and flicked a switch.

Overhead fluorescent lights made a noise like a sizzle and then came on, several banks of them at a time. Illuminating row upon row of dark metal filing cabinets. They stretched away from the entrance, lost in shadow like a deep, unfathomable maze.

There weren't any grizzled, attractive male reporters down here. The place was dreary, shadowy, and deserted.

But Jackie glowed with excitement. She led Kay to a card catalogue—a series of long, shallow drawers filled with cards arranged in alphabetical order.

"Susan Meyer has a file now, but no one knew who she was when the society event photos were taken, so nothing from that event will be sorted or filed according to her name."

"It will have been an event held over the last few months. Probably the summer," Kay said.

Jackie nodded. "That helps. I'd look through every file on every event, but I must prepare the Inquiring Photographer column. On top of that, I'm working on my own ideas, trying to get my feature articles included. It was nice of Mrs. Roosevelt to offer an interview in return for my help. It could help me get that byline."

Kay remembered the swift discussion at the diner. Jackie had asked at once, "Can I interview you about the mystery of Susan Meyer, Mrs. Roosevelt?"

Despite what Sandiston had said, Mrs. Roosevelt observed, "Keeping Susan's name alive in the press is important until this case is solved. When there is scrutiny, it is much harder to obscure the truth."

Kay was impressed. She had added, impetuously, "The truth is that Dmitri Petrov isn't guilty. He can't be." She was about to say more but stopped. It meant revealing that Alfred Jeffers's death was connected to Susan's. The FBI would swoop in at once. Detective O'Malley would be off the case. Though he was annoyed with her for believing in Dmitri, Kay realized he could be trusted.

He had telephoned the suite before they left for the *Washington Times-Herald*. He revealed that Petrov had been taken into custody by Sandiston. He also had said, "Miss Thompson was right. I'm certain Alfred Jeffers's murder is connected to the murder of Susan Meyers. Petrov could not have murdered Alfred Jeffers. But I'm not putting that out there. Looking into the Jeffers case lets me keep hunting for Susan Meyers's killer."

Detective O'Malley, Kay realized, was like a dog with a bone.

"I cannot talk of any new developments," Mrs. Roosevelt said. "But I can speak of Susan's mother and of Susan's life. I can answer some speculation that you might want to throw at me, but I won't be able to answer all your questions. I will offer you the first interview when the case is solved."

Jackie had stuck out her hand to shake on it. "Deal," she had said.

Now, down in the morgue with Jackie, Kay said, "I'm a secretary. I know filing. If you explain the system you use, I can search and you can return to work."

"I can stay down here for a while. Maybe an hour. I think I'm too curious to leave."

Jackie showed her the system and the two women calculated which cabinets held the photographs of spring and summer White House events. Side by side, they pulled out drawers, lifted out file folders, and leafed through them. Kay was used to standing in heels for hours. Jackie began taking stacks of files to a nearby table.

Jackie paused. "I hope we find what you need. I've always wanted to do something worthwhile. I thought it would be writing the Great American Novel. Catching a killer seems even better."

"I agree," Kay said. It seemed more important than the secretary jobs she'd had before.

"My mother's ambition is for me to marry a rich man. Period," Jackie said with a sigh. "She doesn't expect me to have a career. Just make a 'good' marriage. People think I'm an heiress, but I'm not. My father was a stockbroker who lost a lot of his money. He was considered a rogue, but I love him. My stepfather has his own children. My mother rates every man I meet by his family's net worth. My motto is to 'be distinct.' I don't think I've done that yet. Catching the man who murdered Susan Meyer would be something no one else has done."

"It would be distinct," Kay agreed. She pulled out another

file folder and began flipping through the photos. Thank heaven they were printed. Squinting at negatives was hopeless. The photos in this file were for an evening event. She was about to shove them back when she noticed Congressman Kennedy.

She noticed Jackie's gaze go right to that picture.

"You like him, don't you?" Kay asked. "Whether he called you or not."

"I thought he had a strange, intelligent, inquisitive—rather irreverent face," Jackie said. "I just knew he would have a profound effect on my life. But he didn't look like someone who wanted to get married. I pictured heartbreak. You know, it seemed worth it."

"I don't know if it is," Kay said. Jacqueline Bouvier had been smitten by Jack Kennedy, Kay saw. Regardless of the ring on her finger. She should envy Jackie for having two wealthy suitors.

She didn't.

It surprised her.

Kay pulled open the drawer for July 1951. She found many more photographs of Congressman Kennedy, but then, he was awfully photogenic. Young, rich, dashing. In some he was with his brother Bobby. Kay peered at the photos through a magnifying glass, searching for Susie.

Kay saw a blonde head beside Jack Kennedy's. She peered closely.

"Oh!" she gasped.

This photograph had been taken from a distance, but the lens had been zoomed in. The blonde with Mr. Kennedy wasn't Susan. But another couple had been captured in the background, under the spreading branches of a cherry tree.

The woman was Susan Meyer. Not in the mink, but in a pink summer dress. The man's hand was on her waist. They stared at each other as if no one else existed.

Even though only his profile could be seen and he stood in the shadow of the tree, Kay knew who he was.

Jimmy Price.

*    *    *

After returning to the *Washington Times-Herald* offices to meet Kay and see the picture she had found with Jackie Bouvier, Eleanor gave the interview. She asked Jackie to keep quiet about the photograph. "It's not conclusive of anything. Simply two people together at a party."

Jackie nodded. "I understand. But if it becomes more, please keep me in the loop!"

Eleanor praised Kay for her success in finding the picture. Kay brushed off the compliment. "It was nothing. And Jackie was a huge help."

"It was not nothing. I know we did not agree about Elsa's possible involvement, but I respect your opinions, Kay. And your work."

"Thank you, Mrs. Roosevelt," Kay said. Then she added the phrase that most pleased Eleanor. "I respect you so much."

Kay was thinking for herself more, Eleanor realized. Thinking beyond marriage. This investigation was making her see the possibility of more. Involving her had been a good decision.

In the hotel suite, Eleanor telephoned Hick. It was late. Squinting at so many photographs had given Kay a headache. Eleanor had dispensed hot tea, an aspirin, and insisted she go to bed early.

The phone was answered. "Hick. Who's this?"

Eleanor smiled. "Your idea brought us a valuable clue." She explained what Kay had found.

"Jimmy Price? He was Susie's lover?"

"In the photograph, they are gazing at each other as if they are the only people on earth. Since they were in the background of another photo, standing in the shade of a tree, I don't believe they knew their picture was snapped. They were caught in a clandestine moment."

"Jimmy Price looks guilty, Eleanor," Hick said.

"I am not certain of that yet, Hick."

"I remember how much you cared for younger people, Eleanor. I remember how fond you were of your bodyguard, Earl Miller." Hick's tone sounded wary.

"He taught me to shoot a pistol and encouraged me to ride horses," Eleanor said mildly. "He was a handsome man and a good friend."

Eleanor had enjoyed those times very much. Earl helped her blossom as a First Lady. But there were people who disapproved of her closeness with Earl.

"You may not approve," Hick said, almost mirroring her thoughts, "but I'm having a neat whiskey right now."

Eleanor could picture Hick bolting it back in one swallow. Working in newspapers, Hick learned to drink like the men. Eleanor almost never drank.

"Now you are friends with your doctor, David, a handsome man who has brains, charm, and who benefits from your attention," Hick pointed out.

"Are you going to lecture me, Hick?"

"No, I'm not. You are entitled to have an attractive younger man to squire you to events. The reason I'm worrying is that you trust good-looking, young men, Eleanor. You worked with Jimmy Price for years and you think he is a nice man. Miss Thompson and I—we know to be suspicious of the appealing ones."

"Yes. Kay is wary of 'likable young men,'" Eleanor said. "I promise I don't blindly believe Jimmy is innocent just because I liked him. I also don't have concrete proof he committed a murder. I must speak to him."

"To accuse him? That isn't wise, Eleanor."

"I don't intend to accuse him. I simply want to ask some questions."

"I don't like this."

"I won't talk to him alone. I will bring Kay."

Eleanor rang off and went into the suite's largest bedroom.

She felt all her sixty-six years. She changed into a warm night-dress and curled up in the bed.

Five years ago, she had begun her new job as a United Nations delegate. That was when she met Jimmy Price. . . .

*She arrives alone in a taxi. And carries her own bags up the gangplank of the* Queen Elizabeth.

*She has no Tommy with her for this trip. For the first time in almost two decades, she must meet the challenges of each day without Tommy's help, wisdom, and much-appreciated companionship.*

*The* Queen Elizabeth *is glossy black on the bottom, bright white above, and topped with two huge red funnels. The war is over, and ships no longer have to be painted battleship gray. Music plays from one of the decks, a jaunty and cheerful tune, more attuned for a bright summer's day. They are setting out for England in late December.*

*A pile of State Department papers await her in her spacious cabin. Eleanor hangs up her coat, slips off her shoes, and stretches out her legs. She picks up the first document. She knows her duty when she sees it.*

*The report is marked "SECRET."*

*She reads it. And reads it again. Then two more times, and her frown deepens so much she feels a tug in her forehead.*

*The outbound* Queen Elizabeth *leaves the harbor and the Narrows behind. They creep along for hours through a thick fog. As they reach the open ocean, daylight penetrates the fog and spills in through the porthole of her stateroom. It does not penetrate the fog of the paperwork.*

*A knock sounds on her door.*

*"Enter," Eleanor calls. She is soon pleased she did.*

*A young man comes into the room. He reminds Eleanor of FDR when he was in his twenties—tall, strapping, broad-shouldered, fair hair slicked back so it appeared darker. He*

*looks almost too young for such a job, but she knew better,
having sent four boys off to war.*

*He introduces himself with an engaging smile. "Call me
Jimmy. I'd be honored if you did, Mrs. Roosevelt."*

*There is no point in trying to conceal the truth. "I have
read these documents four times. I still do not know the
United States' position on anything, Jimmy."*

*Jimmy keeps his face expressionless. Then he says, "I've
already read them. If this is what they give the president,
ma'am, then God help the president."*

*Eleanor laughs. In that moment, she recognizes an ally.
Jimmy Price proves to be a great one. And a good friend.*

*Then, two years later, Jimmy approaches her on the day
after the Universal Declaration of Human Rights has been
ratified.*

*"I'm leaving the State Department, ma'am. Watching the
Communists criticize American freedoms has made me
angry. I'm afraid there are Communists at home, hoping to
bring down our democracy," Jimmy says. "Debating men
like Valentsky had made me see that I must protect
America."*

*Admirable motives, Eleanor tells him. But she plainly
states that she does not like the thought of him working with
Senator McCarthy at the House Un-American Activities
Committee. She firmly disapproves of McCarthy's methods.
Her own beloved groups have appeared on his list of suspi-
cious organizations.*

*But Jimmy is adamant. "I'm afraid the Communists could
get a foothold."*

*"What you must fear, Jimmy, is fear, as my late husband
said. Do not let fear cloud your judgment. Never forget that
we all must adhere to human rights. With no exception. It is
the only way we can ensure we do not slide down a slippery
slope and become autocratic and ruthless ourselves."*

*"Agreed, ma'am. I always think of your principles, and
the courage you have to defend them. I will do you proud.
And my country proud."*

Eleanor had told Hick an untruth. Something she'd never
done before. She said she would take Kay with her. But she felt
Jimmy would be less on his guard if he was talking only to
Mrs. Roosevelt, the grandmother who trusted him.

Neither Hick nor Kay would approve of her plan.

But she had to do it, she thought, as she hailed a taxi to Martin's Tavern the next afternoon. Rain pattered down and the
skies were dreary. When the taxi arrived, she gave a generous
tip, then stepped out into the chill of the autumn rain. She made
haste into the welcoming warmth of the tavern.

As she'd hoped, Jimmy was there. He sat at the bar. His head
hung down and he threw back the remainder of his drink like a
man trying to drown his demons.

The mirror behind the bar reflected his face. The charming
smile was gone. His eyes looked bleak and hollow. He looked
like a man in grief.

Grief for Susan Meyer, Eleanor believed.

Kay had told her of Jimmy's hand on her backside. He was
not the decent all-American boy and devoted, loving husband
that Eleanor had thought he was. That she wanted him to be.

In truth, she felt . . . betrayed.

Perhaps Hick was right—she wanted to idolize certain people and see only the best in them. But she did not want to become cynical or jaded. People might think her naïve, but she
had to nurture hope.

Instead of pushing up onto a bar stool, Eleanor invited Jimmy
to join her at a booth.

"I don't think you want my company today, Mrs. Roosevelt," he said.

"Nonsense. Your company is always charming. I will buy you a drink."

"Music to my ears," he said. He picked up his empty glass and carried it with him. She let him settle, and ordered another drink for him and tea for herself. Then she got to the point. "Were you involved with Susan Meyer, Jimmy?"

Jimmy set down his glass, startled. He frowned. "Are you accusing me of murder?"

"I am asking if you were having an affair with Susan."

"Mrs. Roosevelt, I'm hurt. Don't you know me better?"

His affront implied that she was in the wrong. But she was not going to fall for that. "Others will ask these questions of you, Jimmy. I have seen photographs of you with Susan. It was obvious that you were involved with her."

"Photographs? Who in hell took photographs of us?" A flash of panic crossed his features.

When Eleanor did not respond, he said, "This doesn't have to come out. You know me, Mrs. Roosevelt. I'm one of the good guys. We worked together for years. I've loved Debbie since we met in high school. You know I would never hurt anyone."

He gave her a cajoling smile.

Eleanor's heart was sinking. His behavior was that of a manipulative man. His affront before, the pleading smile now. Hick feared she wouldn't see through it, but she did.

Her thoughts flashed back to Franklin, when she had asked him if he cared for anyone else. He had called her a "goosy girl" for having such thoughts. She had felt stupid and awkward for having doubts. Then she found the letters he had kept from Lucy Mercer.

"Do you think I'm a spy, Mrs. Roosevelt? You know I'm loyal to my country, patriotic to the core."

"I only asked if you loved Susan Meyer, Jimmy. Did you plan to leave Debra for Susan?"

He jolted back in his seat. "I'd never leave Debra and our daughter. Debbie knows that. She knows that I stray sometimes, have a little flirtation, but I always come back to her. Men are like that. She's the woman I love with all my heart."

"You looked very heartbroken earlier," Eleanor pointed out softly.

"Not heartbroken. Pissed off—sorry—angry with myself for falling for Susie. Susie seduced me. She kept flirting with me until I gave in. Now she's dead and I've been on a knife's edge these last days, worried that our meaningless affair would be discovered, and I would be suspected of murder. Like you just did."

He leaned close. Eleanor smelled the alcohol on his breath.

"I have an alibi, Mrs. Roosevelt. I was with Debra for the end of the journey and with her when the train arrived at the station. I could not have murdered Susan. Debra will swear to it, I promise."

"I should discuss this with Sandy, Jimmy."

Jimmy grinned. For the first time, Eleanor saw the smugness in that grin she used to think was boyish and charming.

"Sandy knows," he said. "I told him. He also knows that Debbie is my alibi. He doesn't consider me a suspect."

"I'm sure *he* doesn't." For she sensed the two men would protect each other. And it was another blow that Sandy had kept this knowledge from her.

The waitress brought another drink for Jimmy, though Eleanor suggested he should slow down. She received a cup of tea.

"You can't think I did this, Mrs. R," he said, using her nickname. "You know me better. Besides, I don't wear Caswell-Massey Number Six. Never have done." Jimmy sat back in the booth. "You can ask Debra if you want. You can ask her about my alibi. She's coming into town tomorrow afternoon to do some shopping at Woodward and Lothrop."

Debra might swear that she and Jimmy were together, but was it true?

"Your scratch is healing well, Jimmy," Eleanor said.

He finished his drink. "I hope it's going to disappear without leaving a scar."

But this conversation had left a scar on her, Eleanor realized.

# CHAPTER 24

*Both* must *love.*
  —Eleanor Roosevelt, Advice to David Gurewitsch,
                      fall 1951

"What were you thinking, lady?" Hick exclaimed over the telephone.

Mrs. Roosevelt said, "I knew Jimmy would not try to 'silence' me in Martin's Tavern, in front of a dozen witnesses."

"He might have silenced Alfred Jeffers pretty effectively, Eleanor." Hick frowned.

Seated beside Mrs. Roosevelt, Kay could hear Mrs. Roosevelt and Hick bicker. It amazed her that Hick would speak to Eleanor Roosevelt on such equal terms. Mrs. Roosevelt didn't seem to mind.

"I was not afraid to meet with Jimmy," Mrs. Roosevelt protested.

"Maybe you should have been," Hick said. "You've always been fearless, Eleanor. This time, maybe too much."

"That's not true. I was afraid of everything when I was a child. My father told me that I must learn to be brave."

"Well, you did. But there is brave . . . and there is foolhardy. If you are meeting this woman, you should take care. How do you know Jimmy Price isn't setting you up?"

"If you were here, I'd bring you, Hick."

"Go to a large department store? I'd rather wash my tea towels. Then iron them. And fold them into tiny squares. But I'd do it to keep an eye on you."

"I'm happy to go," Kay said. Why hadn't Mrs. Roosevelt taken her when she decided to meet Jimmy? Kay wondered if she wasn't proving useful enough. Or was it because she had suspected Elsa Meyer and had made an accusation that must have been painful for Mrs. Meyer?

"Put Kay on the line, Eleanor," Hick demanded.

Mrs. Roosevelt handed her the receiver and Kay put it against her ear, carefully, so she didn't knock her clip earring off. She liked the way dangling earrings danced as she moved her head, and men noticed them too.

"I'm here, Hick," Kay said. She felt a little awkward using Lorena Hickok's nickname.

"Go with Mrs. R, Kay. And look after her!"

Kay loved big department stores, and Washington's flagship Woodward & Lothrop store, known as Woodie's, stood ten stories tall. It had been the Capitol's first department store, opening in 1887. Mrs. Roosevelt had been two years old, Kay thought. She had no idea then she would someday live in the White House.

Growing up without her father, Kay had quickly learned there was almost never money for new things. Even though her mother had worked at Garfinckel's, also a department store, she couldn't afford to shop there. But Kay remembered coming to Woodie's. Only a handful of times, but those times had been precious. A soda from the fountain and a new hair ribbon. Once, dreamily, a new pair of shoes that weren't someone's hand-me-downs.

Kay walked beside Mrs. Roosevelt, gazing in the large display windows as they passed beneath the many awnings. A large window showed the latest fashions for winter 1951. On a bed of fake snow, a female mannequin posed in a cape-style wool coat with thick fur trim.

She drooled over the next window of new evening dresses. She yearned for the fitted black velvet dress with an angled skirt that revealed layers of pleated rose silk petticoats.

The next window mocked up a wood-paneled living room with brand-new furniture. Beside the front door of Woodie's, two small boys were pressed to a window that had a model train running on a table, surrounded by a menagerie of stuffed toys.

Inside Woodward & Lothrop, people milled around the glass-topped counters and the standing displays. An older lady in a tweed suit sat in the cylindrical information booth. Kay looked around her, as excited as the two small boys. That had been the plan if she married well. Her daily life would be spent deciding on new fashions for their home and purchasing party dresses.

Then she remembered why they were here. This was for Susan and Mr. Jeffers. After her conversation with Hick, Mrs. Roosevelt had told Kay of her meeting with Jimmy.

Kay understood Jimmy in a heartbeat. "He is so attractive he feels he is entitled to whatever he wants," she said to Mrs. R. "Rewarded in his career and in his love affairs, he thinks it proves that he's privileged and special and he deserves it all."

"He was always so self-effacing and modest," Mrs. Roosevelt said.

"That is what he shows on the outside. On the inside, he's arrogant. He is exactly the kind of man who would kill a woman to protect himself."

"You are very cynical about men, Kay," Mrs. Roosevelt said.

"Not all men. But a woman must learn to know when a man is lying to her." She thought of her mother.

"I think Jimmy lied about Susan seducing him, but I don't think he lied about his innocence. And I think you should stay out of sight while I meet Debra Price. She should be at the lunch counter now."

"I think Jimmy is lying. About everything," Kay said stubbornly. "Hick is right—I'm coming with you to talk to Debra. Mr. Jeffers was lured to a meeting where he was killed."

"Kay, I do not believe Jimmy will be lying in wait and hit me over the head in Woodie's."

"He can't do it if I'm there," Kay said stubbornly.

Mrs. Roosevelt's brow rose. "I believe you work for me as *my* secretary."

Maybe she had gone too far. As she always did. "I don't care if you decide to fire me, Mrs. Roosevelt. I'm not going to let you walk into danger. What do you think Hick would say if I revealed that I let you go alone? Or my aunt—she would never speak to me again. And she is all I have. Or your children?"

Mrs. Roosevelt threw up her hands. "You win. Come with me, Kay."

As they made their way to the lunch counter, Kay ignored the perfume counter, the glittering display of jewelry, the lingerie trimmed with lace.

Jimmy had given Mrs. Roosevelt a description of Debra. He thought it might be best if the two women had a bite to eat at the lunch counter. He didn't want Debra to think he was in any trouble. According to Jimmy, Debra always grabbed a sandwich at noon on the dot when she was shopping without their daughter.

Kay remembered her reaction when Mrs. Roosevelt related what Jimmy told her. "Debbie will tell you that we were together on the train. I told Debbie that because I was involved in HUAC, I might need her to confirm where I was."

Jimmy certainly knew how to lie. Apparently, his wife drank it all up.

Mrs. Roosevelt had said she would act as though she had run into Debra by chance, join her for lunch, then speak about the train trip.

As they neared the lunch counter, weaving around the displays of merchandise, Kay felt her heart speed up. In a Hitchcock movie, danger would strike in this happy, normal environment.

A man and his son sat at the counter. Several older ladies with tightly curled hair, shopping alone. And a young woman in a light blue wool coat sat with her back to Kay. She was obviously young. Her dark hair was neatly rolled in a curl at the nape of her neck, and a small pale-blue pillbox hat was perched on her smooth brown hair. A coffee stood in front of her.

Mrs. Roosevelt planted herself on the revolving stool next to the dark-haired woman. For a moment she spun it back and forth. Kay had to smile. At sixty-six, Mrs. R had childlike curiosity and enthusiasm. No wonder people loved her. She was interested in people. She cared about them.

Something fell into place in Kay's brain.

The brown hair. The belted blue coat.

Kay walked with her slow, hip-rolling gait to the counter, where she could see the woman's face. She heard Mrs. Price tell Mrs. Roosevelt, "Yes, I was sitting beside Jimmy as the train came into the station. We were together in the station when we heard the terrible news about that poor young woman."

Then Kay stepped into Debra Price's field of vision. Recognition dawned in Debra Price's large, dark eyes.

And horror.

This was the young woman who had run across the concourse of Union Station, carrying her child.

The woman who had told Kay that she couldn't find her husband.

Debra Price knew she had just been caught in a lie.

*    *    *

To Kay's surprise, Mrs. Roosevelt wasn't angry. She treated Debra kindly. She ordered a piece of lemon meringue pie and more coffee. Kay sat down on the stool on the other side of Debra.

As the pie and coffee were served, Mrs. Roosevelt said, "Something sweet is always good in a time of stress."

Debra took a mouthful, then sobbed into a handkerchief provided by Mrs. Roosevelt.

"Jimmy told me to say that we were together when the train arrived," Debra whispered.

"But that isn't true," Kay said. "I saw you in the concourse, carrying your little girl, looking for your husband. What really happened, Debra?"

She deliberately used Debra's first name. "Mrs. Roosevelt only wants to help you," she added.

"That is true," Mrs. Roosevelt said. "But I also must caution you that I will have to reveal what you tell me to the authorities if necessary."

Kay knew ER would be unwilling to play on Debra's trust or trick her. Even if it meant they wouldn't get the truth.

"I want to tell you everything," Debra gasped. "It's been so awful. I had to tell the same story to Sandy—Mr. Sandiston. Do you know him?"

"Yes, he is an old friend," Mrs. Roosevelt said.

"Sandy told me the FBI would want to talk to me. I was so scared! I don't think Sandy believed me when I said I was with Jimmy. I . . . I tried to look like I was telling the truth, but I didn't know how to do that."

Debra had an unworldly, innocent look about her, Kay thought. She looked like the sort of bystander who would get killed in a thriller.

"Why did Jimmy want you to lie for him, Debra?" Kay asked.

"You keep calling him Jimmy." Debra stared at her. "Do *you* know my husband? How? Mrs. Roosevelt said you're her *secretary.*"

Debra stressed the word as if to say "just" a secretary.

"I met your husband at dinner," Kay said. "A dinner he had with Mrs. Roosevelt. Please say what really happened. Mrs. Roosevelt needs to know the truth."

Debra wiped at tears. "Jimmy said he could get fired from HUAC if he was questioned about that girl's murder. He said it would make it easier if we said we were together. And he was right."

"He asked you to lie because he was having an affair with Susan Meyer," Kay began.

"No, he wasn't." Debra dropped her voice to a whisper and looked around her. "Jimmy told me that HUAC had asked him to flirt with that blond girl because she was a Communist spy. He had to get information from her. Like spies did in the war."

"Oh, Debra," Kay breathed.

"He had to make her think he was in love with her so she would reveal her American contacts to him. But he wasn't allowed to explain that to the police. It's hush-hush. If the police learned he was in an affair with that girl, even though it was fake, he might get arrested. HUAC wouldn't allow him to tell the truth. If he did, he could lose his job. I promised I'd help him."

Kay sighed. It was exactly the kind of convoluted lie that a good-looking man like Jimmy could sell to a naïve woman. "It's not true, Debra."

"Of course, it's true. It's what Jimmy told me."

"Debra, Jimmy doesn't deserve your loyalty," Kay declared softly. "He's been unfaithful to you."

"He is a good provider. We've been sweethearts for . . . forever. He told me that I must understand that he has to . . . do things because of his work. He's protecting the country from Communists."

"Is that what men in Washington call it?" Kay said, unable to keep the cynicism from her tone.

"Debra, what cologne does Jimmy wear?" Mrs. Roosevelt asked gently.

Debra Price stared at Mrs. Roosevelt. Then she licked her lips nervously. "Sandy said you smelled cologne in the washroom."

"I believe it is not the cologne Jimmy wears. You can confirm that."

"Not the cologne?" Kay spun so fast to look at Mrs. Roosevelt, she almost swiveled off the stool.

Mrs. Roosevelt put her finger to her lips while Debra was thinking. Debra ate a big piece of pie. Then looked down guiltily at it. "Jimmy doesn't want me to put on weight," she sighed. She added thoughtfully, "If Jimmy doesn't wear that cologne, then he's innocent, right?"

"Do you remember the name of his cologne?" Mrs. Roosevelt said.

"It's one of those fancy ones that men wear in Washington. It's expensive, but Jimmy says it's important that he wears classy clothes and a classy cologne."

"Is the brand Caswell-Massey?"

Debra thought. "I knew it was two names. That could be right."

"What about the name on the bottle?" Kay said, astonished that Debra had no idea. She would know her husband's cologne. She would probably choose it for him.

Debra frowned. Her dark brows pulled together. She looked so young, but Kay realized Debra must be at least the same age as her.

"Something to do with horses, I think," Debra said.

"Jockey Club?" Kay asked.

Debra smiled with enthusiasm. "That's the one. He wanted me to buy him some, but when I learned the price, I almost fainted."

Kay glanced to Mrs. Roosevelt, who nodded. Obviously, this was the answer she expected. Yet, she also looked unhappy to learn it. Kay suspected Jimmy had lied to Mrs. Roosevelt about his cologne. But why, if he did not wear Number Six?

"Does that mean he is guilty?" Debra asked breathlessly.

"No, it means he was not in the washroom," Mrs. Roosevelt said. "He did not do it."

"I knew it," Debra whispered vehemently. "Jimmy is innocent. It was obviously a Soviet agent. That's what Jimmy said. How could you suspect him, Mrs. Roosevelt?"

"I did not," Mrs. Roosevelt said. "I believed he was innocent." She stood from the stool. "I shall go and pay for the pie; then we should return to the hotel, Kay."

After Mrs. Roosevelt took care of the bill, Kay walked with her through the store. The beautiful displays had become an unimportant blur. "I don't think Jimmy is innocent. Could Debra have lied about the cologne?"

"I don't believe so," Mrs. R answered. "But Jimmy told me he wore Aqua Velva. However, neither are the cologne you detected in the washroom."

Mrs. Roosevelt's tone was surprisingly stubborn. As if she was determined to defend Jimmy Price.

"Are you sure you don't want your friend Jimmy to be innocent so much that you are ignoring the truth, Mrs. Roosevelt?" Kay asked.

Mrs. Roosevelt stopped. "Are you saying I would put my friendship with this young man over justice for Susan? Is that what you truly believe?"

"I'm afraid it's happening," Kay said stubbornly.

"That is not something I would expect my secretary to say. Especially my brand-new, temporary secretary."

Kay knew she was sailing perilously close to the wind. But it was more important that she spoke her mind.

# CHAPTER 25

*What should we try to accomplish at home? What should
we put the greatest emphasis on in other countries? What
will bring us the greatest number of friends and develop
the greatest desire among other peoples to resist communism? How will we persuade vast numbers of people in
Asia that we do not plan to conquer the world; that we
have no intention of building an empire; that all we want
to do is to insure freedom both for ourselves and the rest
of the world?*
—Eleanor Roosevelt, My Day, September 14, 1951

As always, Mrs. Roosevelt's My Day column was practical,
honest, and left Kay thinking deeply.

Working with Mrs. Roosevelt, she thought she would be exposed to rich, important men. What she never expected was
that she would be exposed to ideas.

She sipped a glass of dry white Bordeaux and gazed around
Robert Kennedy's Georgetown townhome. His wife, Ethel
Kennedy, looked so young. She was twenty-three, but with a
bright smile and slightly upturned nose that made her look like
a sweet high school girl. Ethel wore a white and black A-line
dress, and she was discussing babies and pregnancywith Letitia
Sandiston and two other young women.

"Once I gained ten pounds," one of the women complained, "my doctor told me I had to stop right there. I was so hungry, but he told me I mustn't gain any more weight."

Kay felt at a loss. She didn't know anything about pregnancy and babies. She wanted all that, but it wasn't part of her life yet.

She had worn her black velvet cocktail dress with the scooped neckline that flattered her figure. Her hair was pulled back into a chignon, held with a small black velvet bow. She wore her tallest heels. She hoped the fact that Mrs. Roosevelt brought her to this gathering was a sign that Mrs. Roosevelt wasn't annoyed with her after their argument about Jimmy.

But she couldn't understand why Mrs. Roosevelt couldn't accept Jimmy's guilt.

Across the well-appointed living room, Mrs. Roosevelt was speaking with a group of men that included two Kennedy sons—Jack and Bobby. They were discussing her My Day column. Now that the Soviets had "the bomb," would they be crazy enough to use it? Was there talk in Washington about a preemptive strike as a show of force? Were they on the brink of World War Three?

Kay knew there were men fighting in Korea, which the president called a "police action." She didn't know how that differed from war.

Mrs. Meyer thought she could use fear to prevent the end of the world.

Mrs. Roosevelt believed that it took as much determination to work for peace as it did to win a war.

Kay overheard Mrs. Roosevelt tell the two Kennedy brothers, "Peace, like freedom, is not won once and for all. It is fought for daily, in many small acts, and it is the result of many individual efforts."

Achieving peace was a battle, Kay realized. One worth fighting. But not in Mrs. Meyer's way. Through the heart.

The same way that finding justice was a battle worth fighting.

Jack Kennedy caught her gaze across the room. He grinned and lifted his drink in greeting. Her heart made a skip and she raised hers in return.

Jack Kennedy was ambitious. Attractive. Interesting. And he'd sent her a dozen roses. Except after that, he hadn't called. But apparently, he hadn't called Jackie Bouvier either.

"Have you heard the rumors?"

It was Sandy Sandiston, holding out another glass of wine for her. He stood so close to her she could identify his cologne as Old Spice. Just as he'd told Mrs. Roosevelt.

"What rumors?" she asked as she took the wine.

He lifted his old-fashioned glass to his lips. "It's all over Washington. The buzz in the corridors of power. About Jimmy's philandering. He was sleeping with Susie Taylor."

"Yes, and you knew all along. He *told* you. But you said nothing to Mrs. Roosevelt."

"I told Mrs. R not to be involved in all this," Sandy said, pompously, as if that absolved him of keeping information from his friend. "People are saying Jimmy is a traitor. And a killer."

"Has he been arrested?" Kay asked.

"Not yet." Sandy tossed back half of his drink. "I didn't want to believe it. But since yesterday, he won't return my telephone calls. He didn't go to work today. I called Debra about a half-dozen times today, to make sure she's okay, but she didn't pick up. This afternoon, I drove by the house to see her. She said Jimmy told her he had to go away for HUAC. He travels a lot in his job of routing out suspected Communists."

"Why are you worried then?"

"Debra's worried. She feels he lied to her. Of course, HUAC won't tell me anything."

"I'm surprised the FBI hasn't brought Jimmy in for questioning," Kay said. "About Susan's death."

"Despite what the rumors say, Jimmy's not a killer. He's a good man. He's innocent."

"Why do you think so?" Kay asked. "Jimmy lied about his affair with Susan."

"I knew him, and I liked him." Sandiston swayed on his feet as he lifted his glass to his lips. Kay realized he'd had a few drinks.

"So if you like him, that's good enough. What about Dmitri Petrov?" Kay asked. "You know he's innocent now. Will he be released?"

Sandy frowned as he swayed in the other direction. "He was asking to see you. I told him that wasn't allowed. Let me give you some advice . . . Kay. Forget about Dmitri Petrov. The Soviets know he wants to defect. If Petrov leaves our custody, he's a dead man. While he's in our custody, he plays by our rules. And who says he's innocent?"

"The fact that he could not have killed Alfred Jeffers. Unless you let him out of custody to go and do that."

"There is no proof that Jeffers's murder is linked to the murder of Susie Taylor," Sandiston said. "The Washington police consider it to be a robbery. Jeffers was mugged."

"It had to be connected. Mrs. Roosevelt believes it is connected," Kay said impetuously. Then she realized that if she made Sandiston believe that, then Detective O'Malley would be removed from the Jeffers case as well.

"I should go and join my wife. All that talk about babies and she might want another one."

He gave a masculine laugh, and Kay heard the dismissive condescension in it. She wouldn't want a husband like Sandy, leaning too close to other women and making lame jokes at her expense.

Kay wanted to see Dmitri. But she couldn't. And she understood that he was in danger. But she feared Sandiston was trying to pin the crime on him. But was that because Jimmy was guilty? Or because Sandiston was?

"Kay, how are you?

Kay turned around. She almost fell off her heels as Jack Kennedy smiled and clasped her hand. "I've wanted to call you, but campaigning is keeping me busy. I hope to take you to the Shore Club for dancing before Bobby and I leave for our tour of Asia. We'll be there for six weeks. I hoped I wouldn't have to wait that long to see you again."

Congressman Kennedy was asking her on a date, but all she could think of was Dmitri locked up, asking about her. "I only have two more nights in Washington."

"I'm booked up for the next few nights," he said. He leaned closer. "I'd like to see you on a sailboat with the wind tossing your hair. You'd look very sexy."

She should be thrilled that one of Washington's most eligible men had just called her sexy.

"Unfortunately, by the time you're back, it will be November. Too cold for sailing."

What was she doing? She was pushing him away.

But he didn't appear to notice. "Not down south. Why don't you come down at New Year's? You could be my guest at the family's place in Palm Beach."

"I'm afraid I don't make it to Palm Beach in the winter," she said, aware of how different his life was. The only way she would be wintering in Palm Beach was if marriage made that possible for her.

She sighed. "I have to work, Mr. Kennedy."

"Can I steal you away for a couple of days? You must get some time off at Christmas." He gave her the most engaging smile. "It would make my new year special if you were a guest."

"I doubt I can," she said.

"Try." He leaned close and gave her a hug. "I'll call you and you can let me know."

Then he was gone, making his way across the room to shake hands with more people.

She heard Ethel Kennedy say to the women, "Next time, I'm going to invite Jackie Bouvier. She works as the Inquiring Photographer at the *Washington Times-Herald*. Jack met her in May. They haven't seen each other since because they were both traveling. I think he's smitten."

Kay had thought that about Jackie. But Jack Kennedy had just asked her to visit him in Palm Beach.

"Jack says that before the election, it's better if he looks single and available," Ethel was telling the circle of women. "But once he's a senator, he will have to settle down. A senator *should* be a married man."

Kay had planned on making a good marriage so she didn't end up broke like her mother, but now that plan felt calculated. And empty.

She realized she wanted to fall in love. And at the same time, she wanted to achieve something on her own.

"Good evening."

It was Mr. Kennedy's strapping, six-foot-three friend Hal. "I noticed the look on your face when Ethel was talking about Jackie Bouvier. Jack's thirty-four and he's been around a lot in his life. He's known many, many girls. He's never really settled down."

"I'm sure he will. When he meets the right girl. Just as Mrs. Kennedy said," Kay replied. As Hal moved away, she knew what he was warning. And she knew Jack Kennedy wasn't the man she wanted. Astonishingly.

Mrs. Roosevelt waved from across the room, then made her way over, but she had to stop and chat with everyone in the room who had not yet greeted her.

Eventually Mrs. Roosevelt was at her side. "You've heard, haven't you, the rumors about Jimmy, Kay? He hasn't shown up for work."

"Mr. Sandiston told me."

Mrs. Roosevelt nodded. "I'm worried. It's too late to call Debra Price, but I think we must see her tomorrow. I fear something terrible has happened."

"I'll telephone her first thing," Kay said. She shivered. Where was Jimmy?

Jimmy and Debra's home was in the Hollin Hills subdivision of Alexandria. Kay had telephoned Debra Price to arrange a meeting. Now Kay and Mrs. Roosevelt had arrived at their beautiful house. Floor-to-ceiling glass walls let in the light, framed by sections of wood siding and a large brick chimney. These were expensive houses, set on lots filled with natural landscaping and trees.

"These houses are gorgeous!" Kay exclaimed. Jimmy's work with the HUAC paid him well.

"I was in the White House when this development was being built," Mrs. Roosevelt said. "The developers placed the houses to ensure that you don't see your neighbors through the large windows, which make you feel that you are outside."

This had been the life Kay coveted. A beautiful house. A handsome, successful husband.

But she knew the truth behind Debra's perfect life. A husband who cheated. Who was meeting his mistress when he went into the city. Who lied. Who might be a killer.

Suddenly Debra Price's lovely home looked like a prison, despite the lovely views.

As Kay rang the bell by the front door, she saw her reflection in one of the large windows. But for once, she wasn't checking that her clothes and makeup were perfect. She looked through the window.

The slender, dark-haired girl from the train station stood at the other side.

Kay smiled at the girl.

Jimmy's daughter moved forward so her face pressed against the glass. She glared with such a look of hatred that Kay felt it like a slap.

Then the child turned and ran away.

The door slowly opened, and Kay gasped. Despite wearing a neat blue dress with a Peter Pan collar and a peach-colored cardigan, Debra Price looked as if she had been through hell. She was pale as a bleached sheet, her eyes red-rimmed. She led Kay and Mrs. Roosevelt into the living room, apologizing for a mess that didn't exist.

The house was spotless. Not a thing out of place. The living room had new, modern furniture. Instead of being heavy and overstuffed, the sofa sat on wooden spindle legs and had a two-pieced backrest of curved shapes in pastel blue and beige. The armchairs were of sinuously curved wood frames with leather. Even a black and white television stood on a wooden cabinet by the huge fireplace. The house proclaimed success.

Was that why Debra put up with Jimmy's philandering? Her whole life was dependent on her marriage to Jimmy.

"The coffee should be ready." Debra turned to head to the kitchen—it appeared to be in the center of the house. From where Kay sat, she could see a brand-new refrigerator in baby blue and white-painted cupboards.

Debra gave a startled gasp. Her daughter had come up behind her and Debra almost fell over her as she turned.

"I told you to stay in your room and read," Debra snapped. "Go up right now. We must talk about grown-up things."

"I don't want to go!"

Her daughter threw her arms around Debra's legs. Her hands slipped under the full skirt to clutch tight to her mother. Her fingers dug into her mother's legs.

"Ow!" Debra grasped her daughter's hands and pulled them free. She gave the girl a shake.

"There's no reason to do that," Kay said. She looked to the

young girl. "Do you have dolls? I love dolls. Would you show them to me?"

Mrs. Roosevelt gave a nod of approval.

Kay got up and held out her hand to the child. "I'd love to meet your dolls."

Mrs. Roosevelt motioned Kay to come over. As she bent down, Mrs. R whispered, "I think it's very wise of you to keep the child entertained. But do not ask her any questions."

"I hadn't even thought of that. But suppose she did overhear things?"

"You cannot ask a child to give away a parent's secrets."

"But this is murder."

"I know. But it would be wrong. The child is too young to understand."

In her heart, Kay knew Mrs. Roosevelt was right. They would have to get to the truth a different way.

But Debra got up. She turned on the television. "You can sit here, Belinda," she said. "The ladies and I will go into the dining room." She gave Kay a narrow-eyed glare. "What I want to show you is on the dining table anyway."

A small package wrapped in pink tissue paper sat on the sleek, modern dining table. Debra pointed at it with a harsh laugh. "I found this, hidden away in Jimmy's bottom drawer."

She shoved it toward Mrs. Roosevelt and Kay knew what it would be. Carefully, Mrs. Roosevelt unwrapped the tissue, revealing a bottle of Caswell-Massey's Number Six cologne. With about a quarter of it gone.

"I've never seen it before. That fussy pink paper—I bet it was a gift from her. From that blond trollop."

Kay saw Mrs. Roosevelt make an expression of pain. She hated to hear Susie described that way. But Susan had been involved with Jimmy. Susan must have bought Jimmy the cologne. Just as she had done for Dmitri.

"He had this and he lied about it!" Debra stared with wide eyes at Mrs. Roosevelt. "He did it! He killed her!"

She burst into tears.

Kay said, "It will be all right." It would be. They now had the truth.

Debra looked up. Her tears had stopped enough for her to gasp, "It *isn't* all right!"

Mrs. Roosevelt reached for Debra's hand, gently asking, "What has happened, dear?"

"I had a fight with Jimmy! I asked him if he was going to leave me for Susie. He denied it. He said he loved Belinda and me. He told me that Susie got demanding and he got tired of her." Debra added, wistfully, "He said he loved only me."

Kay bit her tongue. She wanted to jump in but didn't dare.

"Then I asked him if he had stabbed her."

"Debra, that was a dangerous thing to do," Mrs. Roosevelt said.

"He laughed at me. He said, 'You really think I stabbed her on the train, with you and Belinda in another car, sitting in your seats?'

"When I didn't say anything, his face got red. I could tell he was angry. He shouted at me. He said, 'What kind of monster do you think I am?'

"I told him I didn't know who he was anymore." She broke off. Her gaze met Kay's uneasily. "So I showed him this."

She pulled another package from a pocket in the full skirt of her dress. It was wrapped in white tissue. "It's a necklace. I've never seen it before. He didn't give it to me. And it's broken. In the newspaper, they said there were links from a broken necklace found on Susie's collar."

"Yes, I saw them," Mrs. Roosevelt said. "Mrs. Price, do you have any brandy?"

Debra shook her head. "We have bourbon."

"Perhaps a little of that."

Kay stood. "I'll pour some."

Debra told her where Jimmy kept the liquor. Kay took a crystal glass from the wooden buffet and poured a finger of the whiskey.

Debra took a sip and made a face. "It tastes awful," she said in a childlike way.

"It will calm you," Mrs. Roosevelt said. Kay realized how worried Mrs. Roosevelt was, since she avoided spirits.

"What happened when you showed Jimmy the necklace?" Mrs. Roosevelt asked.

Debra dropped her face into her hands. "He grabbed me by the neck," she mumbled. "I . . . I thought he was going to kill me. But he threw me to the floor, and he walked out."

"What did you do?"

"I lay curled up on the floor for a long time. I simply couldn't get up. I didn't want to. Then I put Belinda to bed. I drank some wine. And I cried."

"Did Jimmy come back?"

"No. I don't know where he is." Debra took another sip of the bourbon. A larger one. "I know my husband is guilty. The necklace proves it. I know I must give it to the police. But I'm so afraid. The rumors about Jimmy have been awful, but it will be worse when people know he was a murderer! I don't want Jimmy to go to prison."

She looked hopefully at Mrs. Roosevelt. Like a child.

"We can't cover this up, Debra. We must give both the cologne and necklace to the authorities. I also think you should not stay in the house. In case Jimmy returns."

"I don't have anywhere to go," Debra breathed. "And why should I go? Jimmy would never hurt Belinda or me."

"He almost strangled you," Kay pointed out.

"But he didn't. He . . . he didn't mean it."

Kay thought it was obvious he did. And if he knew Debra had gone to Mrs. Roosevelt and handed evidence to the police or the FBI, what might he do? He had murdered two people.

"I could put you up at the Mayflower Hotel," Mrs. Roosevelt said.

"No, ma'am. I can't let you do that. We'll stay here," Debra said, and for the first time she sounded determined.

Mrs. Roosevelt gently cleared her throat. "Would you tell us truthfully what happened?"

Debra Price nodded. "Could I have more bourbon?"

After Kay refilled her glass, she took another big swallow. "This is how I remember it. Jimmy took Belinda and I out to the observation deck. He told me he had to meet someone— someone to do with his work for HUAC. I was supposed to go back to our seats, but I was suspicious. I saw that blond woman as we went through the lounge car. She and Jimmy didn't even look at each other, but they made a big effort to not see each other, if you know what I mean. I took Belinda through the lounge car. That woman—Susie—was sitting there having a drink. Jimmy wasn't there. I felt so relieved. I took Belinda back to our seats.

"Belinda was feeling sick, so I took her to the washroom." Debra shuddered. "I guess I was in the washroom in our car with my daughter when that woman was being murdered in the lounge.

"I expected Jimmy would come back. But he didn't. I was going to wait for him on the platform, but there was a huge crowd, pushing and shoving. And someone said a woman had been murdered. I got Belinda away. That's when you saw me, Miss Thompson. Then Belinda felt sick again, so I took her into a washroom in the station. Then the police came. Jimmy found us after that."

"How did he look?" Kay asked.

"He came running up to us. His face was flushed. He looked excited. I asked if everything was okay."

"What did he say?" Kay glanced at Mrs. Roosevelt, who nodded. She was calmly listening.

"Jimmy grabbed my arm. Hard. He said we needed to leave

right away. See, you can still see the bruises he left because he grabbed me so hard."

She unbuttoned her cuff. Pushed up her sleeve. Faint purple marks spaced like fingerprints could be seen on her pale skin.

"I do not think you should stay here. You should come to the hotel," Mrs. Roosevelt said. "Think of your daughter."

"I am!" Debra's voice shook. "Belinda is all I think about. But I can put the chain on the door. Jimmy can't get in." She let out a sob. "I don't know what I'll do when Jimmy is arrested and everyone knows what he did. Sandy—Mr. Sandiston has been helping me. He came over to the house yesterday."

Sandy came to the house.

Kay stared at the packages. It would have been easy for Sandy Sandiston to have slipped the cologne and the broken necklace in Jimmy's drawers while he was visiting.

"Perhaps you should bring in the coffee, Kay," Mrs. Roosevelt said.

Kay blinked. She'd completely forgotten.

"I think a good strong cup of black coffee will help," Mrs. Roosevelt said.

Kay went into the spotless kitchen to get the coffee. Debra had married Mr. Wrong, but was Jimmy actually a murderer or was he being set up by Sandy?

When Jimmy turned up, he would be able to tell the truth.

She opened the cupboard and pulled out three china cups with saucers. Behind the cups was a bottle of sleeping pills. Kay shook it. It was half empty. A doctor's name was on the label. Kay looked at it nervously. She would tell Mrs. Roosevelt.

When Kay brought back the cups, Debra was talking to Mrs. Roosevelt. "Yes, he came to see me too. He asked me to call him 'Bobby.'"

Later, in the afternoon, Mrs. Roosevelt telephoned the police station from their suite at the Mayflower. She had a long conversation and hung up, looking pale.

Kay jumped to her feet. "Mrs. Roosevelt, are you all right?"

"Detective O'Malley is on his way over," Mrs. Roosevelt said. "I discussed the discovery of the cologne and necklace with him, and expressed my concerns as to where Jimmy might be."

Kay was mystified. "Where do you think Jimmy is?"

But Mrs. Roosevelt told her to wait for the detective. A half hour later, reception called up and Kay waited by the door. She opened it to a sharp knock. Detective O'Malley stood on the other side, his fedora hanging off his finger.

"Miss Thompson."

"Detective O'Malley. Come in."

He looked troubled. Brooding and more handsome than any movie star. Perhaps more handsome than Dmitri's cold blond appeal. But Dmitri was a man in need of rescue. Detective O'Malley was not.

"Can I get you a coffee?" she asked. "I can have room service send some up."

He shook his head.

Kay took him into the sitting room. "You found him," Mrs. Roosevelt said sadly.

"You've got that right. Your fears were correct, Mrs. Roosevelt," the detective answered. "James Price's body was found washed up along the Potomac River about an hour ago. A mile downstream from the Key Bridge. I'm on my way to notify his widow."

"We were just there," Kay gasped. "Poor Debra."

"Was it an accident?" Mrs. Roosevelt asked.

"There were no signs of foul play on the body," he said. "There was 'significant bruising' and two cracked ribs, but the police surgeon thinks that came from impact with the water."

He paused. "I had just reviewed the report when Sandiston came in and had a discussion with my commander. I'm off the case again. It's being taken over by the FBI. But my commander brought me in and told me the scuttlebutt is that it was suicide."

"Do you agree?" Mrs. Roosevelt asked.

"Sandiston's theory is that Jimmy decided to spare his wife and daughter the humiliation of going to trial for the murders of Susan Meyer and Alfred Jeffers. Once he knew his affair with Susan was the talk of Washington, he was facing possible arrest. Sandiston mentioned that his wife found the cologne that matched the scent identified by you, Miss Thompson."

"Yes," Kay said. "And Mrs. Price found a broken necklace with a chain that may match the link found on Susan's body."

"I guess that clinches Price's guilt," the detective said. "If they say he committed suicide, that ties Susan's death, Jeffers's death, and Jimmy's up nicely."

"As far as Sandy and the FBI are concerned, I believe it will," Mrs. Roosevelt said.

"But you aren't satisfied," Detective O'Malley said, astutely.

"Why did Jimmy not dispose of those two incriminating items?" Mrs. Roosevelt mused.

"Given he jumped off a bridge rather than face the music, I guess he figured he was never going to be a suspect. He probably planned to direct us, then the FBI, toward the Soviets. Once he knew those items had been turned over by his wife, he knew he was out of luck."

But Kay could see from Mrs. Roosevelt's frown that she wasn't satisfied.

"The scent of the cologne was strong. I'm surprised his male friends didn't comment on his rather powerful cologne," Mrs. Roosevelt said. "Which implies he put it on in the washroom. Why?"

"Maybe he doused himself in the hopes of covering up the smell of Susan's blood. Or her perfume, which was probably on his clothes," the detective suggested.

Kay saw the uncertainty on Mrs. Roosevelt's face. "What are you thinking, Mrs. Roosevelt?" she said.

"I fear the answer is much more horrible," she said softly. "Detective O'Malley, I would like to see the site where Jimmy is presumed to have jumped."

His straight black brows shot up. But Detective O'Malley agreed.

Tendrils of Kay's red hair whipped around her face, blown free of her chignon. It was windy on the Francis Scott Key Memorial Bridge, known as the Key Bridge. Today the sun was out, but it was already low in the sky, and the cold of a fall evening was setting in.

Holding the handrail carefully, Kay leaned over and peered down. The bridge piers set the black water churning around them, creating deadly undertows. The water looked frigid.

She straightened quickly, her body shivering. "Who would want to jump into that icy, horrid-looking water to die rather than take a bottle of sleeping pills and lie down peacefully?"

"Death by overdose isn't all that peaceful," the detective said. "A victim will throw up first as the stomach tries to expel the poison. Often, they choke on their own vomit."

"Thank you for the details, Detective," Kay said.

She saw him blush.

He leaned over as well. "Even if Price isn't officially accused of the murder since he can't go to trial, it's obvious Petrov isn't guilty. He'll be released. I guess you will be happy to hear that."

"Apparently, it's not that straightforward, Detective," Kay said.

Holding back the fluttering strands of her hair, she surveyed the guardrail. It was below her waist height. "If someone pushed Jimmy Price over the guardrail, that person would have to be strong," she said.

"That's what I'm thinking," Detective O'Malley said. "It is easier to picture him standing on the rail and jumping than to imagine someone throwing him over that rail against his will."

"What if Jimmy had been drinking?" Mrs. Roosevelt asked.

"Even then, it's a question of leverage. The guardrail is low, but enough to prevent him being toppled by just a shove. Maybe if someone lifted him . . ."

"Someone strong, as you said," Kay added.

Someone who could plant evidence at his home, then lure him to the bridge and push him into the river. Someone Jimmy trusted.

"Sandy Sandiston is muscular," Kay said thoughtfully. "You said that yourself, Detective. He could have thrown Jimmy off the bridge."

The detective looked doubtful. "Would Price have met Sandiston here? He knew he was suspected of murder. Wouldn't he have feared Sandiston wanted to bring him in?"

"He had already revealed the affair to Sandy—Sandy told me that," Kay said. "Sandy covered up for him. And if Jimmy was innocent, he would have been desperate to turn to a friend for help. Debra told us that Sandiston came to her house, offering to help her. He could have used that opportunity to plant the cologne and the necklace."

Mrs. R wore such a troubled look, Kay was certain she was right.

The detective's brows lifted, making him look curious and unsure. "If I were Price and I was innocent, I'd suspect Sandiston."

"Maybe that is why Jimmy met him on the bridge. Maybe he hoped to get evidence that Sandy was guilty or a confession. They struggled and Jimmy ended up getting thrown off the bridge."

"What do you think, Mrs. Roosevelt?" the detective asked.

"My thoughts have always been centered on a very different

possibility," Mrs. Roosevelt said. "But I may be wrong. Jimmy's murder . . . it makes me think that I must have been wrong . . ."

"What is your theory?" Kay asked.

But Mrs. Roosevelt shook her head.

"If everyone thinks Jimmy is guilty, but he is innocent, someone will get away with murder," Kay breathed, meaning Sandiston.

"No," Mrs. Roosevelt said. "I won't allow that to happen."

# CHAPTER 26

*A woman is like a tea bag—you can't tell how strong she is until you put her in hot water.*
                                                    —Eleanor Roosevelt

"Do order a generous supply of food, Kay. The gentlemen will be expecting their lunch. I feel it will be easier if the men are well fed."

Kay telephoned down to room service. She added items to the order as ER, standing behind her, looked over the menu and said, "A second cheese plate, I think. And another order of lobster thermidor."

"I think even all these men will have enough to eat," Kay said. But then, she remembered the amount of food whipped up at Hyde Park for four ladies. The room service order included salads of chicken, crab lumps, shrimp, Bartlett pear. Two cheese plates including Bel Paese, Camembert, Swiss Gruyère, and blue. Four orders of lobster thermidor, three club sandwiches. Fruit. Coffee and tea.

After placing the order, Kay returned to work at the typewriter. Mrs. Roosevelt was reviewing her daily correspondence. Mrs. Roosevelt worked with her usual studious calm, engrossed in reading letters from the president, so Kay didn't dare interrupt her. She feared she would burst with curiosity.

But she worked diligently. Unlike the morning after poor Susan's murder, she didn't mangle the president's name, she didn't make errors, and she whipped through the morning's work.

Investigating a murder was becoming part of the daily routine.

Mrs. Roosevelt had asked her to invite all the people involved in Susan's death to a meeting in her hotel room. Through the morning, Kay made the phone calls. Sandiston agreed to come and said he would reschedule a meeting with the *president* to attend. Had he done that because he *needed* to know what Mrs. Roosevelt was thinking?

Mrs. Roosevelt had arranged to bring all the suspects together. Was she putting herself in terrible danger?

In a detective story, a desperate criminal pulled a gun. Just like the villain did to Ingrid Bergman in Spellbound.

The telephone rang as Kay swung the carriage return. Startled, she sent the typewriter skidding a foot across the desk. She snatched up the receiver. "Hello?"

"Miss Thompson, it's Jeffrey from the front desk. Some of the guests have arrived to meet with Mrs. Roosevelt."

"Send them up. Mrs. Roosevelt is ready."

Kay looked to Mrs. Roosevelt. Mrs. Roosevelt nodded, but she wore an expression of grave sadness. Not an ounce of fear, but she looked perturbed by what she was about to reveal.

Kay went to the door, waiting to open it. She smoothed down her snug skirt. She wore a different cocktail dress—a navy satin one. It was a sedate color, but it followed the curves of her hourglass shape.

She had wondered if Mrs. Roosevelt would disapprove since she decided not to cover the dress with a cardigan. Instead, Mrs. Roosevelt had said, "You look very nice. Very confident."

"If you think it's inappropriate, I can change," Kay had said hastily, worried even in the face of her boss's approval.

"In the nineteen twenties, I started wearing trousers and shocked many of my female relatives. But I liked the comfort and the freedom. Trousers were more than just the choice of what I would wear, but of how I would live my life. I would rather you dress to express how you want to live your life."

"Thank you, Mrs. Roosevelt." She realized Mrs. R was encouraging her to be herself. No one had done that before.

Kay didn't know how she wanted to live her life anymore. When she started her job with Mrs. Roosevelt, she had wanted Debra Price's life. Now she wanted more—and she wanted to achieve more on her own.

She didn't know how. But she was going to start trying.

As she waited at the door, she knew her duty was to ensure no harm came to Mrs. Roosevelt.

Opening the door, she greeted Mrs. Roosevelt's guests. Sandiston was the first. He took off his fedora, revealing his carefully styled, slicked-back sandy-blond hair, and he greeted her with a tight hug. Then he dumped his coat into her arms.

Bobby Kennedy followed, looking worried and serious. At his party, Kay discovered he was admired for championing democratic rights and social services.

Bobby went into the sitting room and shook Mrs. Roosevelt's hand. "Mrs. Roosevelt, thank you for inviting me. I believe you have some ideas about Susan Meyer's murder."

"I do, Mr. Kennedy," Mrs. Roosevelt said. And that was all.

Even though authorities were convinced of Jimmy's guilt due to Debra's discovery of the cologne and the necklace, and Jimmy's subsequent death by a presumed suicide, Dmitri's innocence hadn't been proclaimed in newspapers. On the phone, Sandy had told Mrs. Roosevelt that Dmitri was being "held" by authorities to assist in the "investigation," which he explained was a cover for the preparation of Dmitri's new, secure life in America.

This wasn't a Hitchcock thriller. No one was scripting her ending—where she and Dmitri could have a future against all odds.

"Thank you for coming, Bobby," Mrs. Roosevelt said. "And you, Sandy. I appreciate you are both busy men."

Kay almost laughed. Mrs. Roosevelt was probably busier—and got more done—than a whole roomful of men.

As the two men took seats in the suite, the room service cart arrived. Mrs. Roosevelt handed Kay coins for the tip, and Kay took over the cart at the door, wheeling it inside. Two urns of piping-hot coffee and a tray of desserts accompanied the other food.

Kay bent over to Mrs. Roosevelt, who had taken a seat across from the two men. Into her employer's ear, she whispered, "May I serve the coffee and foods, or should we wait?"

"Perhaps you can serve coffee now. Before we tuck into the food, let's wait a few minutes for the other gentlemen. And for Mrs. Price."

"Debra is coming?" Sandy looked up sharply.

Kay watched him from under her lashes as she poured coffee. He was startled. He didn't want to see Debra Price. Was it because he didn't want her to find out that he had planted evidence?

As Mrs. Roosevelt took her coffee, she motioned Kay to lean close. In a low voice by Kay's ear, she said, "I want you to stay and be a part of this."

Kay felt her eyes widen. "Of course."

"But do not take any unnecessary risks."

Kay nodded, but she was thrilled. Secretaries were usually sent to their desks. She was part of the action. It showed that despite the times they had disagreed, Mrs. Roosevelt trusted her.

"I'm glad you invited Mrs. Price," Bobby Kennedy said. "I've visited her a few times to see how she is holding up."

He said it so casually, Kay found it hard to think he had an ulterior motive. She waited for Sandy to say he had also visited, which would be natural. But he stayed quiet.

"She's devastated by Jimmy's death," Bobby Kennedy added.

"I am sure she is," Mrs. Roosevelt said. "A sudden, unexpected death knocks your legs out from underneath you."

"Ethel wanted her to come and stay with us, in hopes of keeping her away from the gossip about her husband."

"It is so easy to spread gossip. It takes no courage."

"You're right, Mrs. Roosevelt," Bobby said. "I wanted to think those rumors about Jimmy Price weren't true. Looks like I was wrong."

"Maybe not," Sandiston said. "The Soviets had the real motive for murder. Susie knew Petrov wants to defect. One word to his Russian masters and he'd disappear into Siberia. I bet he would be ruthless if his dream was threatened."

"I don't think Susan would have betrayed him," Kay argued.

"He's left-handed," Bobby Kennedy said. "My understanding is the wounds were caused by a right-handed person."

"Left-handedness is often corrected," Mrs. Roosevelt said. "Mr. Petrov was a sniper. He is missing part of his left pinkie finger where he was struck by a bullet when he was firing. Detective O'Malley explained that he must have had his right finger on the trigger and was using his left hand to line up the shot."

"You mean it *was* Petrov?" Sandy said. "Is that what you have us here to reveal? I figure Jeffers was mugged. The Washington police consider it a robbery gone wrong. That leaves Dmitri Petrov. Or Vishinsky, since he admitted to planting evidence."

"The murderer was not one of the Soviets. It was also not Jimmy Price."

"Then who was it?" Sandy asked.

"I will explain. Once the other guests arrive."

Sandy and Bobby exchanged glances. "I don't think Mrs. Price needs to listen to speculation about the murder of her husband's mistress," Sandy said. "I hate to admit it, but it looks like Jimmy is guilty. As much as I'd like it to be the Soviets. Debra doesn't need to listen to more proof that she married a murderer."

"I think it is crucial that she hears my theory," Mrs. Roosevelt disagreed with calm poise. She faced down men in politics for years. Sandiston couldn't intimidate her, Kay could see. "I believe Mrs. Price is not too frail to listen. Now, if you gentlemen will excuse Miss Thompson and I for one moment . . ."

Mrs. Roosevelt rose and motioned for Kay to follow. They moved into Mrs. Roosevelt's bedroom, away from the men. "Detective O'Malley will also be here. I felt an impartial observer would be necessary. And one with appropriate training would be a wise idea."

"Mrs. Roosevelt, are you sure it is wise to 'reveal the killer' like in a murder mystery?" Kay whispered. "What if he does something violent?"

"It is the only way I can have the proof needed. I think Detective O'Malley will keep the situation under control."

The peal of the telephone interrupted them. Mrs. Roosevelt said gently, "That will be our next guest. Have him sent up, Kay."

Over the telephone, the front desk concierge told Kay that Mr. O'Malley had arrived.

"*Mr.* O'Malley? Okay, send him up," Kay said.

The detective wore an elegant dark gray pin-striped suit that made his shoulders look a mile wide. His tie was silk instead of rayon. His shoes bore a fresh shine. He looked more at home in his suit than John Kennedy had looked in his.

"Detective—" she began.

"Tim is fine," he said, his voice soft. "I'm not a detective anymore."

"What?"

He leaned close to her. She smelled his aftershave. It wasn't expensive but on him, it smelled good. "Yesterday, I talked to my commander about Sandiston, insisting they were taking orders from a man who might be guilty of murder. I was suspended without pay. I'm out of a job."

"It looks like Sandiston *is* guilty," Kay whispered. "He knows you suspect him, so he got you fired."

"He didn't get me fired. My commander has been looking to get rid of me for a long time. I've been too outspoken about corruption I've seen there. I've rocked the boat. I spent the afternoon at Martin's, drinking whiskey. Then I started thinking about Mrs. Roosevelt. I called her up and told her I wanted to help her pursue justice. After all, I've got nothing else to do with my time and no boss to answer to. She invited me to this shindig. So, I put on my best suit to come over. I also remembered you said that after you lost a job, you discovered you didn't need it as much as you thought."

He grinned at Kay, and she couldn't resist falling a little into that smile. It meant a lot that he took her words to heart.

"Mrs. Roosevelt has gathered everyone together. I feel like Hastings to her Poirot." Tim looked blank, so Kay added, "Agatha Christie, Tim."

"Christie? Never read her," he said.

"And you were a detective?" she teased.

"Maybe I should have read her. I might still have a job."

Kay led Tim O'Malley into the sitting room of the suite. Sandiston knew him, of course, so he introduced O'Malley to Bobby Kennedy. "This is Detective O'Malley of the Washington PD."

"Formerly of the Washington PD," the detective said. "I gave in my letter of resignation this morning."

Sandy frowned. "I don't understand."

"I decided I didn't like the way things were being run," Tim said. He took the seat by Mrs. Roosevelt, who politely asked Kay to bring him a coffee.

Kay almost walked into the room service cart, she was trying so hard not to be aware of Tim in his best suit with his long legs stretched out. She poured him a coffee with cream, no sugar. He looked surprised as she handed it to him.

"I remembered," she said. "From the police station."

Mrs. Roosevelt must have invited Tim to arrest Sandy when she revealed him as the killer. But Tim couldn't do that now. And Sandy knew it.

The telephone rang again. This time the concierge advised it was a man named Josef. "I don't believe I should send him up. He's oddly dressed and angry about something."

"Mrs. Roosevelt knows him. You can send him up. He always appears to be angry about something."

Within minutes, Kay opened the door to Josef.

He wore the same blue suit, his socks visible beneath his too-short pant legs, his white sleeves showing where his lanky arms were too long for his sleeves. His hair was even more wild, sticking straight up.

He walked in and stared at Mrs. Roosevelt. "You are going to reveal the name of Susan's killer?"

"Yeah," Sandy said. "That's why we're all here, along with a police detective."

"Former detective," Tim corrected affably.

"I know you," Sandy continued. "You are Josef Jakuba. Of Brookhaven nuclear laboratory."

"I am. I came because Mrs. Roosevelt says she knows the truth of what happened to Susan."

Sandy leaned forward. "I could arrest you for espionage."

Josef sneered. "You have no proof."

"You met with Susan in New York City, after she made visits to Brookhaven."

Josef shrugged. "I was friends with her mother. I met her to talk about Mrs. Meyer. We spoke about her mother's health. That was all."

"I'm going to be watching you," Sandy said, glowering.

"Waste all the time you want," Josef threw back, as he dropped into an armchair.

"Gentlemen, this is not the most important issue right now," Mrs. Roosevelt said. "We are here to discuss what happened to Susan."

Kay realized Josef had come because he felt confident that Sandiston had no grounds to arrest him. As Josef said, he had no proof.

"We know what happened to Susie," Josef said. He snarled as he said, "A married man killed her in cold blood."

"Jimmy Price, the man Susan fell in love with, did not kill her," Mrs. Roosevelt said.

"You are lying to protect your friend," Josef said. Then he jumped to his feet. "Am I here because you are going to accuse me?"

"I would not make an accusation without proof, Mr. Jakuba. Please return to your seat."

Sandy was about to speak, but the telephone rang again as Josef obeyed.

"That will be Mrs. Price," Mrs. Roosevelt said.

Kay went to the door and waited for the soft sound of the elevator bell. She opened the door to Debra Price, who wore the prettiest dress Kay had seen her in. Black satin with a full skirt. Her hair was neatly smoothed back into a chignon. Her face was pale. She carried a black leather handbag. "I left Belinda with a sitter," she said softly.

Kay led her to one of the armchairs, but Mrs. Roosevelt patted the empty place on the sofa beside her, on the opposite side to Tim O'Malley. "I believe you will be comfortable here. Kay, would you please bring Mrs. Price some lunch? An assortment of everything, does that sound pleasing?"

"I don't think I'm hungry," Debra said.

"You should try to eat," Mrs. Roosevelt urged. "Even if you only pick at it."

Debra sat on the edge of the sofa, looking like a nervous girl in a job interview. "I've accepted that my husband was guilty, Mrs. Roosevelt. He was having an affair with Susan, and he killed her to cover it up. He hid that cologne and the broken necklace. I don't know why you want me here."

"Mrs. Price is right," Sandiston said. "We've said Jimmy is innocent, but I know we have to accept his guilt. The evidence is conclusive. For your sake, Debra, I promise to keep it out of the press as much as possible."

"It is not conclusive at all, Sandy," Mrs. Roosevelt said. "It is also not the truth."

Mrs. Roosevelt insisted the men fill their plates and Kay bring a full plate for Mrs. Price. Then Mrs. Roosevelt stood in front of the small group. "Let me explain the truth of what happened."

Debra Price shot an uneasy glance to Tim. He had been introduced to her as the former police detective on Susan's case and on the death of Alfred Jeffers.

Kay saw Debra's fingers tremble as she tried to eat.

Suddenly it fell into place. She knew what Mrs. Roosevelt knew.

Debra had no motive to murder Susan if Jimmy wasn't going to leave her. But what if he was? Jimmy told Mrs. Roosevelt he wouldn't leave Debra, but that was after Susan's murder. Of course he would say that *now*.

Debra might have followed Jimmy to the lounge car. She saw Jimmy with Susie. Perhaps she saw them both go into the washroom. Maybe he heard Jimmy promise that he would leave her for Susie.

Debra waited for Jimmy to come out. She snatched up the knife that Mr. Jeffers left on the bar counter, and she attacked her rival.

The thing that gave her away, Kay thought, was her insistence on Jimmy's guilt. Wouldn't a wife want to swear to her husband's innocence? Even if that was a lie?

But could Debra Price have pushed Jimmy off the Key Bridge? She was much smaller than her late husband.

"Susan Meyer was murdered on the *Royal Blue* train," Mrs. Roosevelt began. "I thought that was a curious thing. If the Soviets were involved, surely they would not pick so public and risky a place."

"It seemed to work," Sandiston murmured. "The killer walked away undetected."

"Not undetected, as we will see. Also, if this act was planned, it would have been simple to make it appear Susan ran away. I felt the train was used because the murder was not premeditated."

"Makes sense," Sandy assented. Then he glowered. "Are you going to tell us that it was a chance robbery after all?"

"I will explain, Sandy," Mrs. R said politely, but with the kind of quiet power that took control at the U.N.'s Committee Three meetings, Kay guessed.

Sandy fell silent.

"I learned that the murder weapon was taken when Mr. Jeffers left the bar, which was another clue the crime was not planned. In fact, there were many clues as to what happened. I have typed up a list," Mrs. Roosevelt said.

Kay looked startled. She should have done that.

Mrs. Roosevelt picked up a small sheath of papers from the coffee table. There was a copy for each person.

"I did not ask you to type this, Kay, because I needed to assure myself that this was all I needed on my list." Mrs. Roosevelt handed Kay a copy too.

The list included the following:

No handbag
Missing necklace
Torn stocking
Splashed water
Strong scent of cologne

"I'm none the wiser," Sandy said.

"We assumed the handbag was taken to remove Susan's identification," Mrs. Roosevelt explained. "But I believe there was another reason. It was done in case it contained any connection to Jimmy Price. Letters, for example."

Kay could imagine Debra searching her rival's purse. Then taking it.

"If Price took the handbag, he had to be the killer," Bobby Kennedy said.

Bobby Kennedy looked at the list with deep curiosity. Josef had crumpled his.

Sandiston looked up from his copy. "Jimmy took the necklace because he gave it to her. He tore the stocking when he grabbed her. Or maybe—maybe she thought they would be amorous in the washroom, and he tore her stocking when he parted her legs. I beg your pardon, Mrs. Price."

Mrs. Price didn't look up from the list. She stared at it as if it might attack her.

"After it happened, Jimmy must have turned on the water to clean up," Sandiston said. "He must have been wearing that cologne. He obviously owned a bottle. Maybe he added more before meeting Susan."

"There is another very distinct possibility," Mrs. Roosevelt said. "The handbag contained the cologne intended as a gift for a man. It was used to literally throw the police off the scent."

"What do you mean, Mrs. Roosevelt?" Bobby Kennedy asked.

"Miss Thompson noticed that Dmitri Petrov smelled of Caswell-Massey Number Six. He told us that Susie had bought some for him. It was one she liked. And it was fitting: an American cologne because he wanted to live in America."

"That brings us back to Petrov," Sandy said.

"Not necessarily. I believe Susan had bought the cologne to give to Jimmy as a gift. I think she hoped to see him in New York; then she discovered he brought his wife and child instead. She thought Jimmy intended to leave Debra for her. She wanted to escape her life as a spy and Jimmy was her way out. Then she thought he was going to renege."

"How do you know this?"

"From what she told me on the telephone, when she asked me to meet her on the *Royal Blue*."

"She told you all that?"

"She wanted me to tell her mother she was safe and sound, but she said that she'd been a fool."

Kay sighed. "A woman always calls herself a fool when she has been duped by a man."

"This is speculation, of course, since Susan can no longer confirm any of this," Mrs. Roosevelt said. "But I am quite certain the necklace was removed because it was a gift from Mr. Price. The most telling thing was the splashed water. Susan's hands were damp. I noticed that when I felt for her pulse. The water in the sink was run by Susan, not by the killer."

"Why would Susan run the water?" Sandy asked.

"Because she wanted to remove blood. While she did that, she saw the murderer in the mirror, turned, and was fatally stabbed." Mrs. Roosevelt paused. "It was the height of the tear in the stocking that made me wonder."

"The tear in the stocking," Kay let out a gasp. She understood now. The tear in the stocking. The scratch on Jimmy Price's cheek.

She thought she'd cleverly deduced Mrs. Roosevelt's thinking. She thought it was Debra. . . .

"Oh no!" Kay gasped.

The men stared at her in confusion.

Debra looked wildly from Kay to Mrs. Roosevelt. "It was *Jimmy*. It was my husband. He admitted it to me! I will testify to that."

"It wasn't Jimmy, Debra."

"I will swear to it. You can't *prove* that it wasn't my husband."

"Are you accusing Debra?" Sandy demanded. "That's ridiculous."

Debra Price looked at the men with exasperation. "It *is* ridiculous. Jimmy was responsible. I didn't do it."

"It was done by someone you love. Someone you would do anything to protect. Including murder Alfred Jeffers, a man who wrestled with his conscience after he chose to protect you and your daughter."

The men looked confused.

"It was Belinda Price who stabbed Susie Meyer. That is what you mean, Mrs. Roosevelt," Kay said. "Jimmy's daughter."

"No!" Debra cried. "It was *Jimmy*. He was responsible for *all* of this! He murdered that porter. The porter saw him but agreed to keep silent because of my husband's position. He told Mr. Jeffers he was hunting Communists and that his work was too important. He said Susan tried to kill him because he recognized her as a spy."

Kay had to admit Debra had a quick wit. She could almost believe that story.

"I realized Mr. Jeffers was not telling me the entire truth," Mrs. Roosevelt said. "He did not lie, but he omitted facts. He did not reveal he was working in the lounge and let me think another young porter was attending the lounge car. I believed that Alfred Jeffers must have been protecting someone. I don't think he would have agreed to keep silent to help Jimmy. But I do think he would have done so to protect a child—a child he saw as innocent."

Mrs. Roosevelt paused. "He talked to his family before he was killed. He said that Belinda did not know what she was doing."

Kay caught her breath. Mrs. Roosevelt was bluffing.

Wild panic lit up Debra's dark eyes.

"It wasn't her fault," Debra cried. "She thought that awful woman was going to destroy our family. I took Belinda for a walk on the train and followed Jimmy to the lounge car. I overheard him beg that blond hussy to give him more time. He said he was going to take her to Hollywood, like she wanted. I didn't realize Belinda even understood what was happening.

"When Jimmy left the lounge, I confronted the witch. The train had reached the station, so I told her to wait until everyone got off. I didn't want to fight in front of everyone. Once the car was empty, I told her that I would never give up my husband. She laughed at me! She said Jimmy loved her. She said he couldn't wait to leave me and Belinda."

Susan had been cruel, Kay saw.

"Then it happened. Belinda must have picked up the knife from the bar. She grabbed Susie by the leg and stuck the knife into her stomach. She said, 'You aren't going to take my daddy.'

"It wasn't a deep wound. Belinda didn't really hurt her, but

Susie was furious. She rushed into the washroom. She ran the water to clean up the blood. She said she would call the police. She would make sure Belinda was taken away to a reform school.

"I couldn't let her do that. I had to protect Belinda. You understand, don't you?"

Debra gazed around at the circle of people. She looked so frightened that Kay wanted to comfort her.

But Debra jumped to her feet. From her handbag, she pulled out a gun. "It was Jimmy's, but I know how to fire it," Debra said. Her hand shook.

Kay watched her trembling hand, afraid she might pull the trigger by accident. Debra held the gun on Mrs. Roosevelt. Kay jumped up from her chair and stood in front of her boss. Her heart pounded so hard that it was all she could hear. But she wasn't going to let Mrs. Roosevelt be harmed.

"Kay, dear, you should step out of the way. I don't want you in danger."

"No, Mrs. Roosevelt. I'm not going anywhere."

"What are you going to do, Debra?" Mrs. Roosevelt asked in gentle tones.

"I need to go to Belinda," she whispered. She waved the gun. "I don't want to hurt you, but I will if I have to. Let me go."

"Debbie—" Sandy was slowly rising to his feet.

"Sit down, Sandy. Don't try to stop me."

Debra wasn't looking at her. Kay knew she could grab Debra's arm. But if she tried to wrestle the gun away, it would go off. It would in a Hitchcock movie. And there would be that flash of a black screen so you wouldn't know who was killed by the gunshot. It could be Mrs. Roosevelt.

But Kay had to try.

She took a step forward, heels sinking in the carpet, which made her step soundless. But Debra had a woman's intuition. She turned the gun on Kay.

"You aren't going to stop me. I'm not going to lose my daughter!"

Spittle flew from Debra's lips. Her eyes were large, wild, like a trapped animal.

"No!" Sandy cried out.

Debra let out a scream. Something dark moved in front of Kay as the explosion of the shot burst in her ears. Then there was blackness.

There was no pain. Was that shock?

It went black because she had closed her eyes. She was terrified she would open them to see blood on her dress. Or worse, to see Mrs. Roosevelt had been shot.

But Mrs. Roosevelt would open her eyes and find out. Mrs. R would do the thing she feared.

Kay's eyes snapped open. The first thing she saw was Tim O'Malley's broad shoulders in front of her. He had stepped between her and Debra. He had Debra clamped against his body. His hand gripped her slender wrist, pointing her hand and the gun at the floor. Debra was struggling to break free, but he deftly removed the gun from her grasp.

The other men were on their chairs, stunned.

"Were you shot?" Kay gasped.

"The carpet took the bullet," Tim said.

"Mr. O'Malley put himself between you and the gun, Kay, and he was able to redirect Mrs. Price's hand. Thank goodness you are both unhurt." With her remarkable inner calm, Mrs. Roosevelt approached Debra, who was sobbing and shaking. Kay wanted to stop her, protect her, but she knew Mrs. Roosevelt was not afraid.

Mrs. Roosevelt put her arm around Debra. "My poor dear girl. You wished to protect your daughter, but that does not make this right."

"What will happen to Belinda?" Debra sobbed. "What will happen to her when I'm in prison? You won't let her be taken away. She can't go to prison. She didn't do anything. I did it all. I stabbed Susan Meyer. It was all me!"

"She is a child. She did not understand what she did, Debra. She won't be punished. She will be helped," Mrs. Roosevelt said.

"I was so afraid. So afraid," Debra sobbed.

"I know. But it is over now," Mrs. R said.

"Jimmy found the broken necklace. I thought he'd understand what I did for our family. But he was angry that I'd killed his awful mistress. He grabbed my wrists and shook me! He said people suspected him of murder. He was going to turn me in to the police to protect himself!" Tears flowed down Debra's cheeks.

Jimmy had been lying all along to protect himself, Kay realized, even before he knew his wife had murdered his mistress. He had coerced Debra to lie for him with no idea that he was giving her an alibi. The bruises she had shown had truly been made by Jimmy. But Kay didn't know if he had grabbed Debra by the neck as she had claimed.

"She wasn't of sound mind," Sandy said. "Let me take her," he added. "I'll bring her in to the authorities."

"Call the FBI," Tim said. "Have them send agents to get her. I will give her over to them."

"It isn't necessary," Sandy said. "I'll take her."

"To be honest, Sandiston, I don't trust you," Tim said.

The two men glared at each other.

Kay looked up at Tim, the man who had saved her life. For the first time in her life, she had met a man who really was a Hitchcock hero.

Her knees felt wobbly as she thought of what would have happened if Tim hadn't been that hero. But she would never have acted any differently. She would have stood up to protect Mrs. Roosevelt no matter what.

Now she knew she had courage.

Cooly, Kay said, "I will call the FBI right now, Mr. Sandiston. Tell me the telephone number." She paused. "I know Debra wanted to protect her daughter, but she also murdered Alfred Jeffers to silence him."

Sandiston looked to Mrs. Roosevelt, his face a portrait of despair.

"I'm sorry, Sandy," Mrs. Roosevelt said. "I know you care for Debra, but Kay is quite correct."

"I'll make the call," Sandy said gruffly. And he marched over to the telephone.

# CHAPTER 27

*When people's hearts are freed by sympathy and sorrow, it makes them wonderfully kind.*
—Eleanor Roosevelt, My Day, April 18, 1945, following the death of FDR

Sandiston led Debra Price to the elevator, along with two FBI agents. Kay followed them out of the hotel room door. Noticing her hurry toward them in her heels, Sandy told the agents to wait at the elevator with Mrs. Price.

He drew her back against the corridor wall, but this time he did not press in too close. He kept a respectful distance. "You are a brave woman, Kay," he said. "You could have been shot."

"Tim O'Malley is the true hero," she said.

"Yeah. He stepped between you and the gun without even blinking."

"Now you know that Dmitri Petrov is innocent, without a doubt, what are you going to do? You can't hold him in custody anymore. Where is he?"

Sandy was silent.

"Is he safe?" she demanded.

"All Petrov could talk about was you," he said finally. "When could he see you? Could we make this happen for him? I told him he would get a new name, money, and he would be settled. Somewhere small, out of the way. I told him there was no way we would help him if he planned to be in contact with Mrs. Roosevelt's secretary."

"Why?"

"For Mrs. Roosevelt's safety."

Kay swallowed hard. She saw that he was right, but there was one thing he had gotten wrong. "I'm her temporary secretary. I may be out of a job."

"Doesn't matter. For your own well-being, Miss Thompson, stay away from Petrov."

"Since America is a free country, I don't believe you can tell me that, Mr. Sandiston."

"How do you think the Soviets could get Petrov to willingly go back? They send a few KGB agents to hurt you. I told him to keep away from you to protect you as well."

"I'm not afraid, Mr. Sandiston."

He pressed his hat onto his sandy hair. "Petrov is. He agreed to those terms. He agreed to drop contact with Mrs. Roosevelt. And with you."

She watched Sandiston walk away. He put his hand on Debra's shoulder to guide her into the elevator after the doors opened. But he did it gently.

Kay turned. Tim stood in the doorway. "Sorry," he said. "I wanted to ensure Sandiston handed Mrs. Price over to the agents. I didn't mean to overhear."

For once, Kay was at a loss for words. Tim O'Malley had stepped in front of a gun for her. He had risked his life for her.

Because he was a good cop, she thought. "Thank you for saving my life. I don't believe I've said that yet."

With a soft smile, he turned and walked back into the suite.

Kay returned to find Mrs. Roosevelt encouraging all the men to eat more. Josef Jakuba was polishing off the remainder of an entire cheese plate. "There is no justice in taking that woman away," he complained. "Even though her husband was not guilty, he was responsible. He should have left Susan alone. And now I will be brought before McCarthy and his committee because you bring me here. I trusted you, Mrs. Roosevelt."

"Mr. Jakuba, did you give the Soviets real information?" Mrs. Roosevelt asked.

"I was expected to do so. Mrs. Meyer and I believed the Americans would not launch a nuclear weapon if they believed the Soviets would launch one in return. But as much as I do not trust your government, I do not trust the Soviet government."

"So, you did not give away our secrets?" Mrs. Roosevelt said.

"No, I did not."

"I think arrangements can be made to avoid hauling you in front of HUAC, Mr. Jakuba. Or prosecuting you," Bobby Kennedy said, loading his plate at the room service cart.

"You wish me to make what is called a 'deal.'"

"We can talk." Bobby sat down with his plate filled again.

Kay poured another coffee for Tim, who was calmly eating lobster thermidor. But he looked up as she gave him the coffee and she saw something in his eyes that took her breath away. Hope.

Then he flashed her a grin. "Thank you for the coffee."

"Anytime," she said, and her voice was husky.

"How did you figure it out, Mrs. Roosevelt?" Bobby Kennedy asked.

"The torn stocking, the scratch on Jimmy Price's cheek, which he said truthfully was caused by his daughter. And the words spoken by Alfred Jeffers to his wife."

"The poor girl didn't know what she was doing," Kay remembered. "He meant Belinda, but he didn't use her name."

"I did bluff when I told Mrs. Price what he had done. Sometimes such tactics need to be used."

Kay thought the Soviets had been up against a formidable

289 ELEANOR AND THE COLD WAR

woman over the human rights declaration. No wonder she pre-vailed.

"Jimmy Price was the mysterious tall and blond boyfriend," Kay said. "Debra acted as if she was not very bright, but she was obviously very brainy. She almost got away with it."

"She might have if you had not seen her in the concourse. That destroyed the alibi that she gave to Jimmy."

"I realized today that it also meant Debra had no alibi," Kay said.

"Exactly. I realized from the beginning that if Susan was having an affair with a married man, his wife had motive. But then, I began to realize the truth was more tragic," Mrs. Roo-sevelt said. "I can only speculate, but the poor child probably heard her parents fight about Jimmy's affairs. She feared her fa-ther would leave her mother for Susan, which meant he would leave her. It must have been traumatic—she obviously loved her father very much."

Aunt Tommy had told Kay how much Mrs. Roosevelt adored her father, though he died when she was almost ten years old. Mrs. Roosevelt had been rejected by her mother for being plain, but she had her father's special "golden hair."

Mrs. Roosevelt understood Belinda's fear of losing her fa-ther.

"Belinda saw the knife and decided to save her family by re-moving Susie," Kay conjectured.

"Yes. I think she wanted to hurt Susan because she felt that would make Susan go away. Once Susan threatened to ensure Belinda was taken away, Debra believed the only way to keep her family intact was to remove Susan. She took the knife and . . . well, finished it." Mrs. Roosevelt paused and sipped her coffee. "I suspect Susan screamed, but Debra had locked the door. Mr. Jeffers heard the cry, knocked on the door, and Debra opened it. The answer to the puzzle was that Susan did scream and Al-fred Jeffers heard her scream, but he was willing to cover it up."

"Why did Mr. Jeffers protect her?" Kay asked.

"Debra was clever. She knew Alfred Jeffers saw her husband and Susan together. She could have told Mr. Jeffers that her husband knew Susie was a spy and Susie threatened her and her daughter. I'm sure she told him that Belinda stabbed Susie in self-defense," Mrs. Roosevelt said. "I know this is conjecture, but Debra revealed she could invent a plausible story quickly. She begged Mr. Jeffers to stay quiet because exposure would destroy Belinda's life.

"The poor child would have been in shock, I am sure, having stabbed Susie and then witnessing her mother's attack on Susan. Mr. Jeffers recognized Belinda's distress and agreed. We learned that family was very important to Mr. Jeffers. He may have felt responsibility for leaving the knife on the bar counter, where the child could grab it.

"Debra picked up Belinda, wrapping the child in her cardigan to hide the blood, and quickly took her into a washroom in the station. She kept the child in her cardigan and fastened and belted her own coat to hide the damp spots where she must have sponged out blood. She was running out to find Jimmy when you spotted her, Kay."

"Why kill Alfred Jeffers if he agreed to stay silent?" Bobby asked.

"Alfred Jeffers was an honest man," Mrs. Roosevelt said. "An honorable one. Lying did not rest easily on his conscience. Debra would have been afraid—this man knew the truth. I think she went to Union Station to ensure he would keep her secret and quickly realized that his conscience was getting the better of him. I am sure he tried to assure Debra that the child was not responsible, that she would not go to prison. Debra realized Alfred Jeffers was a threat. Unfortunately, he did not recognize how desperate she was. He went alone to meet her."

Kay shuddered. "And she hit him over the head." She added,

"I guess she took the necklace because she thought it was a gift to Susie from Jimmy. I bet she ripped it right off Susie's neck. But why didn't she throw it away? And the cologne?"

"Just as she used the cologne to make us believe a man was in the washroom with Susie, she saw the necklace as a safeguard if anyone suspected her. That was why she kept both items, I think," Mrs. Roosevelt said.

"To plant them on someone. In the end, she used them to incriminate Jimmy," Kay said.

"She killed Jimmy because he was going to turn her over to the police?" Bobby Kennedy asked. "But how did she do it? She couldn't have pushed him."

"When we went to her home, Kay noticed that Debra had a bottle of sleeping pills in her medicine cabinet. The bottle was half empty. I suspect she drugged him. She could have dissolved several in Jimmy's evening drinks. If he were very sleepy after consuming the alcohol, she would have been able to manipulate him into going in the car with her. I think she drove him to the river, convinced him to get out on the bridge. In his unbalanced state, he was easy to push, and he fell over the railing."

"It would have been hard to prove any of this," Bobby observed, "if Debra Price hadn't panicked and pulled the gun."

"I required some proof before I knew my theory was correct."

Mrs. Roosevelt turned to Tim O'Malley.

To Kay's surprise, he picked up the story. "Mrs. Roosevelt outlined her theory to me. I hadn't been able to find witnesses who saw Alfred Jeffers's attacker, but I was asking people whether they saw a strange *man*. I found a barber who had been cleaning up his shop and saw a dark-haired woman get in a car parked by the curb and drive away. She matched the description of Debra Price. There was no other reason for Debra Price to be there at night. I told Barlow to get a warrant to search the home. He's carrying that out right now. I think we'll find the murder weapon that killed Alfred Jeffers in Mrs. Price's garage."

Bobby Kennedy gave a sorrowful groan. "I can't believe it of that nice young lady."

"It was fear, as Mrs. Roosevelt said," Kay said. "She had to protect her daughter. Then herself."

Kay thought of handsome Jimmy Price, the rising star in Washington circles, supposedly a devoted husband and father. On the brink of success, he had given Debra a beautiful house and a seemingly perfect life.

It had been a house of cards.

Bobby Kennedy looked concerned. "Debra did this to protect her daughter and now she will go to prison. What will happen to the child?"

"I hope a family member will take her in," Mrs. Roosevelt said. "After my parents died, I was raised by my grandmother. It was a very different life. My grandmother had been too permissive with her children, and she tried to be the opposite with my brothers and me. But we had a good home, and I was well educated.

"We must ensure Belinda finds a happy and stable home," Mrs. Roosevelt continued. "To recover from this, that child will need love and understanding. When Debra stands trial, she will probably claim her husband was guilty. There is a chance that a jury will believe her. The witness who saw her near Fourth Street may not be enough to convince them. I suspect she will say she followed her husband out of concern of what he might do. Debra Price has more wits than anyone gave her credit for."

"Will you have to go to court?" Kay sighed heavily. "I guess I've failed at keeping you out of the spotlight until the Senate votes for the U.N. delegates."

"I am willing to do my part for justice," Mrs. Roosevelt said.

"You found justice for Susan. You got to the truth. That is not failure," Josef said. "I believe it is time I go."

"I should go too," Bobby Kennedy said.

As the two men left, they were in close conversation. After the elevator took Josef and Bobby Kennedy down to the lobby, Kay walked with Tim O'Malley to the elevator.

"I'm sorry about Dmitri Petrov," he said. "I'm sorry you can't see him. I realize you care about him."

"I'm happy that he will be living in America, which is what he wanted."

"I'd like to ask you to dinner again," Tim said. "If it's not too forward."

"You almost were shot for me. I would like very much to go to dinner with you. But we're leaving for New York tomorrow. Mrs. Roosevelt must prepare to go to Paris—if she is voted in as a delegate again. The Senate hasn't voted yet."

"Are you going with her?" Tim asked.

"I don't know. Maybe I'm going to be out of a job."

Kay had no idea what her future would bring. Except for one thing. "I'd like to go for dinner tonight. If Mrs. Roosevelt can spare me."

"She can," Tim said. "I already asked her."

# CHAPTER 28

*I solemnly answered "yes" and yet I know now that it was years before I understood what being in love or what loving really meant.*
—Eleanor Roosevelt, *This Is My Story*, circa 1937

That evening, in the lobby, Kay caught sight of Tim O'Malley, still wearing his best dark gray suit, sitting in an armchair, twirling a gray fedora on his index finger.

She had that whoosh in her heart as his face lit up with a smile and a dimple winked in his cheek. With the black hair, straight black brows, long black lashes framing his green eyes, he was truly a handsome man.

A handsome man who had saved her life without hesitation.

He smiled like she was the best sight he had ever seen. "You look gorgeous, Miss Thompson."

He said it so earnestly, it held charm.

"So do you, Detective," she threw back.

Hershel opened the door for them. "Have a good night, Miss Thompson. Detective O'Malley."

"Not a detective anymore, Hershel. I spoke out and lost my job."

"I'm sorry to hear that, sir."

"Just means I'm making plans for the future."

Kay wondered what kind of plans as Tim opened his car door for her. He drove a 1949 dark blue Ford Shoebox. She had expected a larger car, something big with a large, growling engine. Opening her door, he waited until she slid onto the seat and arranged her skirts around her before closing her door. He had some experience—a lot of men didn't know it took a woman a while to arrange her skirts in a vehicle.

As he got in, she said, "Hershel knows you?"

"He was accused of stealing a package delivered for one of the guests. I found the real thief."

"Wasn't investigating a missing box a little unimportant for a detective?"

"I was new. You get the low-end assignments."

He cast a sidelong glance to her as he drove, and she discovered she liked that expression on his face. "When I discovered the package wasn't claimed because the recipient had been murdered, my simple case got more interesting."

"You caught the killer?"

Matter-of-factly, he said, "I did. A husband who brought his wife to Washington and murdered her."

Kay settled back as he made a turn. What would it be like to investigate things every day for your living? Exciting. She had thought it would be too risky. But she had taken a huge risk to protect Mrs. Roosevelt, and she knew she had done the right thing.

"Did you solve every case?" she asked.

"I wish I could say I did. Maybe I should. People might not commit crimes if they thought they were destined to get caught."

"Very wise." She noted the streets as they passed them. "Where are we headed?"

"I was thinking of Chinese food. Unless you'd like something else."

She sensed his awkwardness. "I love Chinese food. I love vegetables."

A slow grin lifted his full lips. "I do too. I keep it a secret from my meat-and-potatoes father. He would think he'd failed if he raised a son who ate bean sprouts."

"Did your former partner approve of bean sprouts?"

"Barlow? He would have had me arrested if he knew I ate vegetables. Strangely, though, I'm going to miss working with him."

Tim drew up to the curb and turned off the engine. Above, through the window, a blinking neon sign advertised CHOP SUEY. Below it, stretched above the picture window, a lit-up sign read TAO'S.

Tim got the door. The proprietress, a slender, small lady with gray hair held in a chignon with cloisonné hair combs, greeted the detective warmly. "Happy to see you, Detective. With a lovely lady."

"Good evening, Mrs. Tao. But it's just Tim now. I'm not with the force anymore," Tim said, and Kay was certain he was blushing—though it was hard to tell in the warm red glow of the red lamps.

"I am sorry to hear that," Mrs. Tao said. "This way." With menus tucked under her arm, she led them to a table in front of the large plate glass window.

As they followed Mrs. Tao, Kay murmured, "Another satisfied customer?"

"I guess so," was all he said.

He held out her seat, slid her chair in, then took his own.

Mrs. Tao returned with jasmine tea in a delicate pot and two tiny, handle-less cups. She poured two cups, then faced Tim, her hands on her hips.

"Mr. O'Malley, my husband has promised to cook special dishes tonight. Not on the menu. For two."

"I would be honored to enjoy your husband's specials," Tim said.

"I would too," Kay added.

The task of combing the many pages of the menu had been lifted from her hands. Not by her date, which happened too often, but by the restaurant's female half owner. Kay could not object to that.

She looked out through the window. Outside, the yellow neon CHOP SUEY sign blinked, casting yellow light across the sidewalk and onto the street.

"Do you enjoy working for Mrs. Roosevelt?" Tim asked.

"I do." She considered. "I've never worked for a female boss before. I'm honored to work for a woman who created the Universal Declaration of Human Rights."

Tim nodded. "I was impressed to meet her."

"What amazes me the most is that she is so . . . human. Since she is so busy, I thought she'd have lots of maids and would be waited on hand and foot. She isn't like that at all. She is so practical."

Tim nodded. "My mother died when I was little, but my aunt would bring food sometimes. She used to copy those simple nourishing meals Mrs. Roosevelt made in the Depression."

"My mother did that too. My father was . . . uh, gone when I was little. My mother is gone now too."

He gave his condolences, and she returned them about his mother.

"Why did you become a police officer?" she asked.

"Why did you become a secretary?"

She laughed and he grinned. "I didn't plan to be one," she said. "I knew girls who wanted to go to secretarial school—that was their dream. I wanted to be a scientist. Or a teacher. My mother refused."

"Why?"

"Men don't make passes at girls who wear glasses," Kay said. "Being Mrs. Roosevelt's secretary is completely different. Helping her solve a murder was amazing. Though she was many steps ahead of me."

He nodded.

In that moment, Kay knew she didn't want to lose her job.

Mrs. Tao bore a platter with bowls of soup to their table, placing the bowls in front of Kay and then Tim. She refilled their tiny teacups, then glided away. She was so tiny and graceful, she appeared to float.

Kay tried to pick up a dumpling with chopsticks. She lifted it and squeezed it. With a squishy sound, the dumpling flew across the table, bouncing off onto Tim's lap. She gasped in horror.

He plucked it up and put it beside his bowl. "Would you mind if I give you a few pointers?"

She appreciated that he didn't muscle in and start showing her. He asked. As he demonstrated, he admitted, "Mrs. Tao worked hard to teach me. I think I was her most confused student."

Following his directions, Kay adjusted her chopsticks and gently took hold of a dumpling. She lifted it to her lips. Delicious.

"I became a cop after I got back from the war," Tim said.

"You enlisted?"

"In forty-two, when I turned eighteen. After Pearl Harbor, I was counting the days until my birthday. When I was on Omaha Beach on D-Day, I wondered what the hell I was thinking. But I had to be there. I was no different than any of the thousands of other young men wading out of the water onto that beach."

Her breath caught. "You survived it," she said softly.

He looked down at his plate. The neon light cast his face in light and shadow and Kay was sure his soul was in the shadows right then.

"When the war ended, I thought I'd be blessed to go back to a normal life, but all I felt was restless. I guess I didn't know how to live a normal life anymore. My father was a cop and he got shot in the line of duty. I thought—why is my father risking his life and I'm working in a factory? I joined the force. They were happy to get guys like me."

"For your combat training?"

"Because we were used to blindly following orders." He grinned again and Kay smiled too. "Now we're at war again, though the president is calling it a police action. I wonder where it's all going. It's why we need people like Mrs. Roosevelt at the United Nations."

"Exactly," Kay said.

A sizzling sound drew their attention. Despite her tiny stature and slenderness, Mrs. Tao used one hand to balance a large platter filled with blue willow patterned plates of food. She transferred each plate to the wooden lazy Susan in the middle of the table, describing the dishes: steaming Cantonese fried rice, sizzling Szechuan beef, rich beef curry, stir-fried vegetables.

"Thank you for teaching me how to use chopsticks," Kay said.

"Anytime," he said.

Kay wished that she wasn't returning to New York the next day. But she was. As if he could read her mind, Tim said, "I can take the train up to New York. I'd like to take you out again."

"I'd like that," she said.

"How about the Shore Club for some dancing," Tim suggested.

She thought of Congressman Kennedy and realized she would prefer to go with Tim O'Malley. "I'd love to."

Several days after returning by air to the New York apartment, Mrs. Roosevelt drove them to Hyde Park. The red and orange leaves were falling, leaving the trees swathed in yellow. It gave the sense of ending. Just as before, Aunt Tommy stood in the doorway of the cottage, wearing a dress but wrapped up in a thick cardigan. Fala stood beside her. Kay ran up the steps and Aunt Tommy held out her arms.

"I'm so happy you are both safe," Tommy exclaimed. "Mrs. R

told me what you did. You were almost shot! To protect her. I'm very proud of you. But don't ever risk your life again."

"I don't think I ever will have to," Kay promised.

Fires crackled in the fireplaces, filling the cottage with warmth. First, Mrs. Roosevelt telephoned Hick and told her of the events in the hotel suite. Kay heard Hick exclaim, "A gun! Lady, you better get out of the detecting business!" Hick quieted when Mrs. Roosevelt assured her that she and Kay were safe and sound.

Then, Mrs. Roosevelt telephoned Elsa Meyer, while Tommy brought in tea and Kay opened the correspondence they had brought from the New York apartment.

Mrs. Roosevelt hung up. "Nothing will bring Susan back, but at least Elsa knows the truth," she said sadly. "And Sandy telephoned to let me know that Debra's parents have taken in Belinda."

Kay handed Mrs. Roosevelt the first letter she had opened.

"The Senate has confirmed the nine members of our delegation to the U.N. General Assembly," Mrs. Roosevelt announced.

"No one is preventing you from continuing your work at the U.N.," Tommy said. "I am very relieved."

"Do you think the U.N. will help find peace for the world?" Kay asked.

Eleanor considered, unfolding the next letter. "A peace based on possessing the most powerful weapon is no peace. We must find deeper reasons to put down weapons. And I believe we will. I also think it will be up to your generation, Kay. And future ones."

Kay nodded, but she said, "Mrs. Roosevelt, I think it will also be up to you."

A horn sounded outside. They heard the slamming of car doors. "The children are here. I shall have to do my correspondence later," Mrs. Roosevelt said, setting down the letter. "But before I go outdoors, there is something I must ask you, Kay. Would you accompany me to the U.N. Assembly in Paris? It is very helpful to have you as my secretary."

"Paris?" Kay's heart gave a pang when she thought about Tim O'Malley. But this was her chance to see the world. She had once thought she was a secretary who wanted to be a pampered wife. Now she was a secretary who wanted to be a part of change. Change for the better. "Yes, Mrs. Roosevelt, I would be honored."

"Good."

Wearing a beaming smile, Mrs. Roosevelt went out to the front steps, as three of her thirteen grandchildren raced up to the porch. They cried delightedly, "Hello, *Grandmère*!"

And ran into Mrs. Roosevelt's warm, loving embrace.

# AUTHOR'S NOTE

The events of *Eleanor and the Cold War* come entirely from my imagination, though I endeavored to interweave them with true history. I humbly hope that the dialogue I have invented for Eleanor Roosevelt does justice to her remarkable character and personality.

Eleanor Roosevelt published a newspaper column called *My Day* for many decades. In this, she journaled the daily events of her life, including warm details of her family life, anecdotes of people she met, fascinating behind-the-scenes facts of her work with the United Nations, and her own viewpoints on politics and social change. This proved a wealth of information, but also a challenge, for Eleanor had documented daily where she was and what she was doing. While my story is completely fictional, I hoped to make it plausible.

Kay Thompson is a fictional character, though Malvina Thompson was a real person and served as Mrs. Roosevelt's secretary for many years.

Lorena Hickok, Jacqueline Bouvier, John F. Kennedy, Robert and Ethel Kennedy are, of course, real people. As part of the landscape of the 1950s and known to Eleanor Roosevelt, I knew they were important characters for this story. I strove to be respectful when depicting them, trying to capture their fascinating and colorful characters. Detective Tim O'Malley, Sandy Sandiston, Josef Jakuba, Elsa and Susan Meyer, and the Price family are fictional.

My Soviet delegates to the U.N. are fictional. Lev Valentsky was inspired by the actual delegates Eleanor met and wrote about in her autobiography. Valentsky's words as a prosecuting attorney were inspired by those attributed to Andrey Vyshinsky.

In the story, I bring in actual writing or dialogue and I would like to credit those sources here.

Mrs. Roosevelt's *My Day* quote about Elsa Meyer is in fact her quote for scientist Lise Meitner, from the *My Day* column of August 10, 1945. Her quote from her *My Day* column in Chapter 5 is from the column of October 6, 1951. Mrs. Roosevelt's words in Chapter 20 on the use of the atomic weapons were based on her words in her *My Day* column of May 31, 1956, as I wished to be accurate to her point of view.

Jackie Bouvier's statement about Jack Kennedy (in Chapter 23) was paraphrased from her written account and the source is *Camera Girl* by Carl Sferrazza Anthony, published by Gallery Books, an imprint of Simon and Schuster, Inc. 2023, page 126.

Writing *Eleanor and the Cold War* was an educational and enthralling project for me. I found kinship in the fact she was widowed, as I am. Eleanor Roosevelt's dedication to public service, to helping people, and to championing human rights is an inspiration.

# CHAPTER OPENING NOTES

1. Eleanor Roosevelt, My Day, September 25, 1945, *The Eleanor Roosevelt Papers Digital Edition* (2017), accessed 6 March 2024, https://www2.gwu.edu/~erpapers/myday/displaydoc.cfm?_y=1945&_f=md000139.
2. Eleanor Roosevelt, If You Ask Me, *Ladies' Home Journal*, October 1941, Philadelphia: The Curtis Publishing Company.
3. Eleanor Roosevelt, My Day, January 5, 1939, The Eleanor Roosevelt Papers Digital Edition (2017), accessed 6 March 2024, https://www2.gwu.edu/~erpapers/myday/displaydoc.cfm?_y=1939&_f=md055155.
4. Eleanor Roosevelt, My Day, September 28, 1945, The Eleanor Roosevelt Papers Digital Edition (2017), accessed 6 March 2024, https://www2.gwu.edu/~erpapers/myday/displaydoc.cfm?_y=1945&_f=md000142.
5. Eleanor Roosevelt, *You Learn by Living: Eleven Keys to a More Fulfilling Life*, 1960, 187.
6. Eleanor Roosevelt, My Day, September 11, 1941, The Eleanor Roosevelt Papers Digital Edition (2017), accessed 6 March 2024, https://www2.gwu.edu/~erpapers/myday/displaydoc.cfm?_y=1941&_f=md055986b.
7. "Mrs. Roosevelt Says . . ." *Western Mail* (Perth, Australia), 21 October 1943.
8. Eleanor Roosevelt, *This Is My Story*, New York: Garden City Publishing, 1937, 361.

9. Eleanor Roosevelt, My Day, August 9, 1943, The Eleanor Roosevelt Papers Digital Edition (2017), accessed 6 March 2024, https://www2.gwu.edu/~erpapers/myday/displaydoc.cfm?_y=1943&_f=md056565.

10. Eleanor Roosevelt, My Day, May 17, 1948, The Eleanor Roosevelt Papers Digital Edition (2017), accessed 6 March 2024, https://www2.gwu.edu/~erpapers/myday/displaydoc.cfm?_y=1948&_f=md000968.

11. Eleanor Roosevelt, My Day, October 29, 1947, The Eleanor Roosevelt Papers Digital Edition (2017), accessed 6 March 2024, https://www2.gwu.edu/~erpapers/myday/displaydoc.cfm?_y=1947&_f=md000796.

12. Eleanor Roosevelt, *The Autobiography of Eleanor Roosevelt*, New York: Harper and Brothers, 1961, 436.

13. Eleanor Roosevelt, My Day, February 23, 1943, The Eleanor Roosevelt Papers Digital Edition (2017), accessed 6 March 2024, https://www2.gwu.edu/~erpapers/myday/displaydoc.cfm?_y=1943&_f=md056429.

14. Eleanor Roosevelt, My Day, April 23, 1962, The Eleanor Roosevelt Papers Digital Edition (2017), accessed 6 March 2024, https://www2.gwu.edu/~erpapers/myday/displaydoc.cfm?_y=1962&_f=md005098.

15. Eleanor Roosevelt, *If You Ask Me*, New York: D. Appleton Century, 1946, 75.

16. Eleanor Roosevelt, My Day, November 3, 1943, The Eleanor Roosevelt Papers Digital Edition (2017), accessed 6 March 2024, https://www2.gwu.edu/~erpapers/myday/displaydoc.cfm?_y=1943&_f=md056636.

17. Eleanor Roosevelt, *You Learn by Living: Eleven Keys to a More Fulfilling Life*, New York, Harper, 1961.

18. Eleanor Roosevelt, *This I Remember*, New York: Harper and Brothers, 1949, 230.

19. Eleanor Roosevelt, My Day, September 22, 1941, The Eleanor Roosevelt Papers Digital Edition (2017), accessed 6 March

2024, https://www2.gwu.edu/~erpapers/myday/displaydoc.cfm?_y=1941&_f=md055993.

20. Eleanor Roosevelt, My Day, November 22, 1943, The Eleanor Roosevelt Papers Digital Edition (2017), accessed 6 March 2024, https://www2.gwu.edu/~erpapers/myday/displaydoc.cfm?_y=1943&_f=md056650.

21. Eleanor Roosevelt, My Day, May 19, 1943, The Eleanor Roosevelt Papers Digital Edition (2017), accessed 6 March 2024, https://www2.gwu.edu/~erpapers/myday/displaydoc.cfm?_y=1943&_f=md056499.

22. Eleanor Roosevelt, My Day, June 13, 1938, The Eleanor Roosevelt Papers Digital Edition (2017), accessed 6 March 2024, https://www2.gwu.edu/~erpapers/myday/displaydoc.cfm?_y=1938&_f=md054978.

23. Eleanor Roosevelt, My Day, November 29, 1944, The Eleanor Roosevelt Papers Digital Edition (2017), accessed 6 March 2024, https://www2.gwu.edu/~erpapers/myday/displaydoc.cfm?_y=1944&_f=md056961.

24. Eleanor Roosevelt, "circa fall 1951, Advice to David Gurewitsch," Michelle Wehrwein Albion, *The Quotable Eleanor Roosevelt*, Gainesville, FL: University Press of Florida, 2013, 156.

25. Eleanor Roosevelt, My Day, September 14, 1951, The Eleanor Roosevelt Papers Digital Edition (2017), accessed 6 March 2024, https://www2.gwu.edu/~erpapers/myday/displaydoc.cfm?_y=1951&_f=md002013.

26. Eleanor Roosevelt.

27. Eleanor Roosevelt, My Day, April 18, 1945, The Eleanor Roosevelt Papers Digital Edition (2017), accessed 6 March 2024, https://www2.gwu.edu/~erpapers/myday/displaydoc.cfm?_y=1945&_f=md000002.

28. Eleanor Roosevelt, *This Is My Story*, New York: Garden City Publishing, 1937, 41.

# BIBLIOGRAPHY

Binker, Mary Jo. *What Are We For? The Words and Ideals of Eleanor Roosevelt*. New York: Harper Perennial, 2019.

Eleanor Roosevelt Papers Project, The George Washington University, 312 Academic Building 2100 Foxhall Road, NW Washington, DC 20007, Digital edition published 2008, 2017 by the Eleanor Roosevelt Papers Project.

Michaelis, David. *Eleanor*. New York: Simon & Schuster, 2020.

Pottker, Jan. *Sara and Eleanor*. New York: St. Martin's Press, 2004.

Quinn, Susan. *Eleanor and Hick: The Love Affair That Shaped a First Lady*. New York: Penguin Press, 2016.

Rappaport, Doreen. *Eleanor, Quiet No More: The Life of Eleanor Roosevelt*. New York: Disney/Hyperion Books, 2009.

Roosevelt, David B. *Grandmère: A Personal History of Eleanor Roosevelt*. New York: Warner Books, 2002.

Roosevelt, Eleanor. *The Autobiography of Eleanor Roosevelt*. New York: Harper and Brothers, 1961.

Roosevelt, Eleanor. *If You Ask Me*. New York: D. Appleton Century, 1946.

Roosevelt, Eleanor. *You Learn by Living: Eleven Keys to a More Fulfilling Life*. New York, Harper, 1961.

Russell, Jan Jarboe. *Eleanor in the Village*. New York: Scribner, 2021.

Sferrazza Anthony, Carl. *Camera Girl*. New York: Gallery Books, an Imprint of Simon & Schuster, Inc., 2023.

Wehrwein Albion, Michele. *The Quotable Eleanor Roosevelt*. Gainesville, FL: University Press of Florida, 2013.